This story is dedicated to my darling parents who gave me the courage to rise out of the risks of subservience and stifled compliance and find the strength to dare to be different; and to the love of my life who taught me steadfastness, true love and the power of identity, no matter what the world tried to make us. In this story, is the story of many who have inspired me, saved my life and those whose name I share because of who they are and their unyielding friendship. This book is testament also to the people who challenged me and also the story of my past as I stride forwards to the future.

Rosalynde Marsh

IN TIGER COUNTRY

AUSTIN MACAULEY PUBLISHERS™

LONDON * CAMBRIDGE * NEW YORK * SHARJAH

Copyright © Rosalynde Marsh 2024

The right of Rosalynde Marsh to be identified as author of this work has been asserted by the author in accordance with sections 77 and 78 of the Copyright, Designs and Patents Act 1988.

All rights reserved. No part of this publication may be reproduced, stored in a retrieval system, or transmitted in any form or by any means, electronic, mechanical, photocopying, recording, or otherwise, without the prior permission of the publishers.

Any person who commits any unauthorised act in relation to this publication may be liable to criminal prosecution and civil claims for damages.

This is a work of fiction. Names, characters, businesses, places, events, locales, and incidents are either the products of the author's imagination or used in a fictitious manner. Any resemblance to actual persons, living or dead, or actual events is purely coincidental.

A CIP catalogue record for this title is available from the British Library.

ISBN 9781035862061 (Paperback)
ISBN 9781035862078 (Hardback)
ISBN 9781035862085 (ePub e-book)

www.austinmacauley.com

First Published 2024
Austin Macauley Publishers Ltd®
1 Canada Square
Canary Wharf
London
E14 5AA

Acknowledgements for the NHS and the surgeons whose paths crossed mine and the Austin Macaulay Production and Marketing teams.

Although a story lives within each of us, no story really belongs to one person. Thanks must go to those whose eyes saw what mine could not, whose lives have lived more than mine and those whose paths have inspired the story.

Chapter 1
That Happy Place

Miss Jemimah Withenshawe (FRCS)

There is little more wonderful than sitting out beside the shining water of the quay on a rare sunny winter's day, with an unblemished blue sky and a crisp, clean winter breeze. Jemimah breathed in deeply and held that wonderful, reviving breath for a few moments. She smiled, and a few passersby glanced at her admiringly as they walked briskly past. She had an alluring face with striking grey-green eyes, golden-brown skin, rolling locks of dark silken hair, and gazelle-like long legs. In every way, she was a serendipitous fusion of mixed cultures that few could place, least of all Jemimah.

She carried with her the unsolvable insecurity that resulted from being abandoned at a hospital entrance as a baby in a Moses basket. She was subsequently adopted into a loving English family before conscious life started to record. Her oriental, perhaps Arabic, features were a lifelong mystery to her. Where were they from? In character, she exhibited a curiously diverse mixture of inherited instincts and personality that bestowed something both intriguing and yet alien to many. She had long wondered where "home" was for her; she could see in the mirror that she 'belonged' to many places and to many people. Not just to the people that she had grown up with and loved, but to others far away. Who were they? Where were they? Why had they left her behind?

In England, her adopted country, where she had grown up, she was expected to just fit in. Even her name had been 'normalised'. She was known familiarly by old school friends as Jemmy. That strange thing that happens to everyone here. In her case, they took her ancient name, meaning little dove, and turned it into a nickname, meaning crowbar. Nice. She pondered. Jemimah was a perfectly easy name to say, wasn't it? Alright, there was a sneaky letter H at the end, and forgetting that was alright, but the rest was easy. Or maybe not; after all, Charlotte is Charlie and Elizabeth is Liz. Perhaps Jemmy was just her English name.

Glancing at her wristwatch, she found herself counting down the hours. 18…16…12 more hours to go, and then back to work as a surgeon in the NHS. The modern NHS was at times relentless and, despite being full of passionate and talented people, was at the same time an immense target-led machine that seemed to have the ability to grind down ambition, enthusiasm and autonomy to a point where each doctor was trained to walk the same walk and talk the same talk as the others. Those who did not adapted themselves to stay out of the firing line.

Jemimah had ambition, craved autonomy, and was young; she always felt like a misfit, but thankfully she was intelligent and a talented surgeon. She made it to consultant and yet, despite this, she was filled with questions for which answers were not always forthcoming. A sense of unrest niggled inside her. She ached to know what a different life would feel like one where she knew herself. Be self-assured inside. A Henry. A confident surgeon with a gigantic…no she was not going to go there. Craving the life, of others was not a good thing. She was who she was, and she had to accept that. She needed serenity and patience that the Henrys of this world would never have to find. That was her lot. What mattered was the surgeon's professional façade that she wore every day. That mask that left people in no doubt at all that she was confident and therefore competent, and one of the 'team'. Everything else was hidden.

Jemimah worked at Saint's Bay NHS Trust. A large, white-wall-encased district general hospital set in an idyllic part of the United Kingdom. A somewhat stereotypical, monochromatically led institution whose definition of diversity was just that, a slogan. 'Caring, Diverse, Excelling' written in bold and conspicuous words on every wall. What was it about the painfully ironic tripartite slogans that organisations and governments devise these days to try to deceive the glancing masses with? She wondered. Jemimah recalled well how she had memorised it for her interview, using it like a carefully spun politician in every response that she gave, whilst responding to the uniform nods of approval before her on the interview panel.

"Ah, she will fit in just fine. That is good."

Now, she sat pondering those words and tried to apply them to her every day. Yes, it could be said that they fit her aspirations, but were the aspirations of her trust the same? Maybe not always politically. Well, it was her chosen workplace, in a lovely location, and she had to at least believe that she would succeed there and be as good a surgeon as she could be. She was lucky to be doing the job she had always wanted to do. When she was in that special zone in the operating theatre, scalpel in gloved hand and mind focused on the unfolding anatomy before her, she was at her best. Nothing else gave her so much satisfaction, so much autonomy, and so much freedom to be creative. Being a surgeon was her first love and the identity she knew best.

Returning to her surroundings, one way of appeasing her recurrent feelings of being out of place, was distraction, and what better, at that precise moment, than to look at the dessert menu and order something unashamedly engaging? What could be more restorative than a hot, sticky toffee pudding? And that is what she did today. Jemimah loved two things almost as much as being a surgeon. The first was running, and the second was great food (a healthy combination, she always thought). The niggles in her mind soon dissolved away as she delved into the indescribable bliss of a mouthful of runny hot toffee sauce enveloping a perfect date and toffee sponge. She smiled and sighed happily. "This definitely warrants an evening run," she thought as she sat back, relishing a blissful sense of postprandial satisfaction.

She closed her eyes for a second, allowing the pale sun to lie on her eyes, and was suddenly alerted to a sound approaching her. There was someone shouting her name from the car parking lot.

"Hello, Miss Withenshawe!" It was Eliza, her somewhat gregarious junior doctor colleague, who was rushing towards her with a bulging rucksack on her shoulder and the flushed cheeks of youth.

"What an amazing day! I thought I would catch some fresh air with my books and revise outside for the written paper. Only five weeks to go, and I'm so behind, it's a complete nightmare!"

Jemimah smiled sympathetically.

"Yes, those exams never do get easier, Eliza. It sounds like you are working hard, which is good. You'll hate it right now, but once it is done, you will be so relieved. Just keep at it."

Eliza was nodding enthusiastically. "Yes, absolutely. I feel like a complete hermit, working and studying day after day. No matter how hard I work, I still seem to fall short on the practice papers. It's driving me mad! I need to pass this exam. Oh, do you know what? Mr Blythe-Soames is meeting with me tomorrow to help me out. What a lovely thing to do. How kind he is! I'm so lucky. Such a nice man. You are all wonderful," Eliza slipped into a moment of deep contemplation at that point, and Jemimah nodded gently.

"Yes, Eliza. That is very kind of him. He will give you some great top tips. Did you link up with the study group at the hospital that I told you about? They are doing web sessions in the evening, and it might help."

"oh…er…not yet, but you are right. I think I will do that. I just don't feel ready yet to face the other trainees. I don't want to look like an idiot. I do need to get over that, though. You are quite right. Thank you, Miss Withenshawe."

Jemimah remembered those days of exams and striving to absorb the mountains of facts and smiled kindly at Eliza. "You'll do just fine, Eliza. Just keep focused on the end goal, and you'll get there."

A pause followed as they glanced around, watching people walk about the busy quayside. Sunshine in the winter always had a way of lifting spirits and enticing people to come outside. It was a lovely day to be out, and Jemimah wanted to head off on her run.

"So, Eliza, are you working tomorrow?"

Eliza nodded with a slight grimace.

"Yes, I am. Long days for the next three days, which can be a bit draining. I hope I will get to theatre between on-call patients. What have you got on your list on Tuesday?"

Jemimah paused before answering. She remembered the days when a junior doctor would never dare ask a consultant for that but would instead have read up on the lists beforehand and been prepared and well-read for the week ahead. But with Eliza, it was always an afterthought. Despite this, she had such endearing qualities that any momentary disbelief was soon gone. She was a trainee who might bloom late. That Jemimah could see.

"Why don't you have a look at the list in my office tomorrow and see if it has the sort of things that you are interested in? It would be lovely to see you there but do try to read up if you get a chance. Always makes the list more educational," she stood up as she said this. Keen to get home.

"Well, Eliza, it was lovely to see you. I shall hopefully see you next week. Good luck with the on-call. I hope it is Q… sorry, I mean kind to you," Jemimah stood up as she said this. The on-call law has been corrected. Never use the Q (quiet) word for fear of jinxing the on-call. Jemimah walked away and wondered where the Q-word rule started. Superstition was part of the world she worked in.

Walking towards her car, her trusted 1982 yellow Morris Minor, Jemimah smiled as the setting sun warmed her cheeks. 'Onwards to a lovely run.' The simple things in life have a way of making the noise disappear. Her feet seemed eager to get out of the now pinching pointed heels that she had been wearing and into her trusted running shoes. Home was only ten minutes away. The radio in the car sprung to life with Long Cool woman (in a black dress) as the road rolled by towards her Georgian semi-detached house. She loved her home. It was her other happy place, and she kept the gardens full of flowers and colour to contrast the monochrome white walls of the hospital where she spent so many of her waking hours.

"Home," she said contentedly as she drove into the gravel driveway. She jumped out, ran up the steps, and raced upstairs to the dressing room. Mutty, her cat, greeted her, purring loudly as he rubbed himself against her leg.

"Hello, my beautiful boy. How are you?" she picked him up into her arms and kissed his thick fur. Mutty was another great love of hers. Minutes later, with running gear on and earbuds in her ears playing the latest downloaded audiobook thriller, she headed off on her run. The rhythmic thud of her feet had a way of unravelling all her thoughts into a simple line of tasks for the days ahead. She spotted the first timid colours of early spring breaking through and smiled at the birds teasing her from the branches. In the hours that she spent running, Jemimah was at peace. There, she could decide where she wanted to go, how fast she wanted to run, and what book would play in her headphones, and an innate sense of autonomy and self-confidence filled her. Run, Jemimah, run!

<u>Mr Ibrahim Baba (FRCS (Vasc.Surg.))</u>

Splash! The crisp, cold water cut into Ibrahim's warm brown skin as he cleansed his body in the darkness of the early morning before his Fajr prayers. His favourite time of day is just before dawn. Despite being "British" and spending all his conscious life in the UK, Ibrahim never felt completely at ease, and yet he had known nothing else. He and his mother had fled to the UK as refugees in 1966 after his father was murdered in the coup d'état in Ibadan. There was always a sense of irony in fleeing to the country that had created the political instability that fuelled the war that shattered their lives and the country of many ancient tribes, but when it was a question of live or die, it was the only place they could turn to and live. He was just a few months old when that all happened, and his mother had told him stories of how terrifying things were.

She watched his father die in front of her and fall onto her heavily pregnant belly, protecting them both from a shower of bullets. A single photo survived that world, their Nigeria, and it looked alien to him as it sat alone on the white wall of the cottage hallway next to a vase of fragrant freesias. It was a photo that was a faded black and white, yet so intense in its detail that one could imagine the colours of the fabrics and flowers on that day. The old colonial-style house that his family had lived in stood proud, in recognition of the once-illustrious status of his family and its achievements. His father, Muhammad, stood in front of it, serious, proud, and fiercely handsome; next to him was his young and beautiful wife, Khadija, covering her pregnant bulge with a beautifully embroidered dress, her thick hair crowned with a wide-brimmed hat.

What a contrast to the life that his mother had carved in her new world as a penniless, frightened widow and refugee. Her tired body was eventually hunched from years of physical work as an auxiliary nurse in the local NHS hospital. How she must have cried silently for the wealthy, glittering life that she was born into—a sort of heaven—which in seconds was replaced by the struggle to simply survive and raise her precious son in a world where he could live. A new world that would never see them as equals.

She had cried in her last years, remembering the fear that she had encountered after the words of Enoch Powell filled the hearts of the nation with misplaced hatred for immigrants. Immigrants from countries like Nigeria that had been a source of "common" wealth to this nation. It seemed to her that prejudice was the common stem of all mankind. It had the same expressions on its face, whatever the hue of the skin; the same anger, and the same fear, no matter where it arose. Skin colour was not the fuel; power, greed, and ignorance were. The untamed wild animal smouldering within all humans that 'civilised' society tried and often sadly failed to suppress.

It was everywhere, even in this country where they had sought refuge. Even in the NHS. She had somehow managed to shut her ears to the back stabs and slights, the endless demeaning bullying on the wards from other nurses and even from patients. To survive it all, she filled her heart with the love she had for her son, her family, and her God. She worked hard and made memories. In the end, she found peace and died with hope in her heart.

Ibrahim knelt on his prayer mat with his hands held in the open cup of prayer, thanked Allah for the blessings of his mother and father, and prayed for them in the afterlife. He then gave thanks for the gift of his beautiful wife and two children. This he never failed to say, and every time he did so, a smile appeared on his face. A smile of pure and absolute love and gratitude. A reminder of why every new day is a blessing and one to cherish. He found happiness and peace in prayer, and it was a time to let go of the sense of injustice that gnawed at his soul from one day to the next.

In some ways, the moments of prayer were his time to realign his mind; to reassess his purpose, and to avoid falling into the wrongs of the world around him. He did not need accolades. His wealth was his family. He was grateful for being Muslim and had never faltered in his beliefs, despite the anti-Islamic propaganda that had corrupted the public arena. In many ways, he looked at the horrific stories of cruelty and injustices committed by humans of all kinds and was grateful that he was insightful enough to see that it was not about any religion. It was about prejudice and inequity. At the heart of most stories was the same human toxicity that had also destroyed his own home: misdirected power, politics, and money. Perhaps his history had opened his eyes even when he was in the womb. He was placed, at his precarious birth, on the proverbial fence of life.

He could see and hear the voices of many because he was a child of the world and not of one country. This was the life they had been given, and despite the resurgence of racism that had filled the country with the endless sparks of right-wing politics, this was his land too and his place to do good; at that moment, he was still safe, and he was blessed with the skills of a doctor to help others.

Every day began with reassuring words of prayer for Ibrahim. He had grown accustomed to life not being a straight path. He was externally strong but internally tired of the endless courage needed to endure the cruelty and humiliation of some of his colleagues. There was an unremitting sense of injustice lingering for years after he could not get a training number, enabling him to rise to the ranks of consultants. Always hoping for an opportunity to appear, but realising with time that it might not. He toiled with the frustration of having to accept that if he had been born with a different skin, his life could have been so different. The booming 1980s had been a time of abundance for many, but if you were an African 'immigrant' surgical trainee, there were doors of possibility that were simply not for you.

Watching his white peers obliviously stride through them and leave him behind, whilst he reluctantly conceded to accept the life of a staff grade surgeon was something Ibrahim struggled to accept. He had grown used to being the dogbody of the team, doing the surgery that the 'high-fliers' thought was beneath them. What Ibrahim told himself in consolation was that he had been given the chance to do work that was still very much needed, but too often simply added to the waiting lists where patients became numbers. He loved the opportunity to help others, and where there was little gratitude from the team, he found kindness from many of his patients. They were grateful he was there, even the ones who asked him where he was from, as though he was not from this planet.

The managers were also grateful to him for diligently doing the 'bread and butter' workload and meeting the mounting political targets, keeping RTT (referral to treatment targets), pending list numbers (where patients were held waiting for a place on a list) and COD (cancelled on the day of surgery) numbers low. Despite this, at times, he missed the camaraderie of the wider team, as he was so often sent to peripheral hospitals to do clinics and lists alone. He felt, as he had always felt in this country, like an accessory, an outsider, but only so long as people needed him. Right now, they did. In some ways, those times working alone were his safe places, when he didn't have to stand on the opposite side of the operating table to Henry (Mr Blythe-Soames as people deferentially called him) when he knew a barrage of snide jokes at his expense would leave him feeling small and embarrassed. He wondered why Henry needed to do that. Was he insecure behind all his bravado? Was it a masculine ego thing, as Henry stood 5 inches shorter? Or did Henry just see himself as superior? Perhaps a mixture of both. It is a public school—comprehensive school thing. A white man, black man thing.

Getting dressed for work, Ibrahim looked at himself in the mirror. In honour of his elegant and proud father, he made sure that every day he dressed well. His shoes were polished, and his shirts and clean trousers were perfectly pressed. His beard was kept tidy and, at least for now, was in tune with current fashion and style. Having passed the dreaded 5-0, he was conscious of the loss of his youthful frame, but despite that, he stood tall at 6 ft 2 and was, at least in his mind, the image of how a surgeon should be. Today was Monday, and today was Henry's list. Insha'Allah, today would be a better day. Operating days were always something he looked forward to because, at his core, he loved surgery.

Mr Blythe-Soames (AKA Henry)

Rolling over in his super-king bed, Mr Henry Blythe-Soames (FRCS.) felt the usual morning gush of blood in his groin. He was hard. Very hard. The light was dim, so he rolled on top of Vanessa, his wife, and perfunctorily started to make love to her. Her quiet, rhythmic moans stimulated his manly urges as he lunged back and forth. He loved sex. He loved women. He did not love his wife so much these days, but that was by the by. She was there and willing. In this light, he could even convince himself that she was still the sexy minx he had married a decade earlier. Pregnancy and motherhood had rather taken the shine from her, sadly, but divorce was out of the question. For one thing, she wasn't going to take his hard-earned money. Oh no. He was quite happy to make her think he still loved her, and after all, she needed him.

He was doing his part. Fifteen minutes later, he sprang out of bed. He strode in front of the mirror and was pleased with what he saw. A real man. Rich, virile, attractive, and successful. 'God, life is great, and today is operating day.' He smiled that smile at himself. Thirty press-ups, morning ablutions, and a toast and coffee later, he was outside. It was 6.55 am and his shiny new black Aston Martin DB11 was ready and poised to purr on his command. "This is why I became a surgeon," he muttered with a sense of resounding pride and satisfaction, exuding as he drove towards the hospital. This was the product of years of training, hundreds of exams, and too many hours of learning from the masters. At last, he was there. The consultant. The master, and it was so worth it. Now was his time to lead the game.

He liked to drive in early and park his beloved car as close to the entrance as possible. Two spaces away from the railing, he could get a perfect view of her from the window of his operating theatre. That space was his space in the consultants' car park. There, his Aston Martin would wait for him until the end of the day, and he could check on her. He walked into the foyer. All was quiet except for the cleaning staff.

"Good morning, Mr Blythe-Soames. A busy day ahead for you?" Bernie Sanders was the longest-standing cleaner in the trust. At 64, he had seen it all. He knew everyone who mattered by name, and he seemed to be everywhere. There was no corner, room, staircase, or corridor of the hospital that had not met Bernie, and yet, so many people did not notice him.

He was the invisible constant in a machine that never stopped, 24 hours a day, 365 days a year. Year after year. Henry looked at Bernie and raised his eyebrows and head in presidential acknowledgement. The question, of course, had been presumed to be rhetorical. No, time for needless chit-chat. Work had to be done, and the team was waiting for his arrival. He swept past Bernie, and his musk-laden aftershave lingered around Bernie's nose for a few seconds. Bernie sneezed and muttered into his handkerchief, "Hmmmmm, one day, that door will be too small for that giant head of yours," he shook his head and carried on sweeping the corridor.

Henry charged into his office and sat at his desk. 7.10am. Time for a glance at the emails, and then off to theatre. Maggie, his secretary and living diary, had left him a pile of letters to sign, a pile of correspondence to look at, a copy of his list that day, and a thank you card from one of his patients. Letters were autographed (tick), other letters were glanced at and squiggled on (tick), cards were opened and tossed into an appraisal tray (tick), and a list was collected. 'Let's get started' he thought as he picked up his clogs with HB-S written on the top in black and walked to theatre. Everything was fine until he saw Ibrahim. That moron. "I hope he has done the bloody consents this time," he mumbled as he approached the admissions bay.

"Good morning, Henry, how are you today?" Ibrahim politely stood up to welcome his consultant colleague, the illustrious Henry Blythe-Soames. His polite and gently smiling face belied his sense of disappointment that Henry had not miraculously been swallowed by an alien ship on the way to the hospital. He humoured himself with the image as he then imagined the spaceship spitting Henry out in disgust somewhere around the North Sea…or anywhere except here. No, today the spaceship had not arrived sadly, so another 'joyous' day was to be spent toiling amidst the relentless condescension of his younger and shorter but hierarchically senior colleague in theatre. Today was Monday with Henry. Sigh.

"Morning Ibrahim. Are we all ship-shape? Consents done? Marks drawn? Patients dressed and ready for me?"

"Yes, all is ready, Henry. I just want…"

"What? What? Is there something wrong? Say it man, it is getting late…"

Ibrahim seemed to shrink a few inches, and he recoiled into submission.

"Sorry, Erm…. I was just saying that Mrs Briggs (number three on the list) is very nervous and wondered if we could do her first."

Henry looked sharply at him and replied in a sly undertone, just outside the earshot of the nurses, "Are you joking? Where does she think this is? A bloody hairdresser? Of course, we can't change the list. I sorted out the list last week! Give her a sedative or something as a pre-med to calm her, and I'll see her later. I'm not in the mood for emotions this early on, Ibrahim. Manage it."

He picked up a copy of the list and walked up to Sue, the admissions nurse. His arm slid onto her shoulder, his fingers resting a few centimetres above her breast, and he produced the most heroic of smiles.

"Good morning, dear Sue, is that a new haircut I see? Looking lovely. I hear that the patients are ready for me. Shall we go and see them together?"

Sue blushed and smiled nervously at him. Henry loved to flirt.

"Oh, good morning, Mr Blythe-Soames. Yes, everyone is ready. Let's go and meet the patients. Just give me one second, though, please."

She looked around and spotted Claire, the new HCA on the ward.

"Claire, could you pop some TED stockings onto Bed 3, please, whilst I go round with Mr Blythe-Soames?"

It was a question that had only one answer, and she pointed to the compression stocking packet whilst turning away. Claire was unable to question and so she nodded. Henry swung the curtains of each of his patients aside as he walked from bay to bay. For each, he picked up the consent forms that were already signed, made an approving 'uh-huh' and countersigned them. To each patient, he directed a reassuring and confident smile and good morning.

"Ready to go, are we? I can see that you have signed your consent. Good, good. All will be great. See you in theatre."

Each patient nodded nervously, and in a second, their esteemed consultant was gone. It was Monday, his day in theatre, and all was going to go just fine. Theatre 1 awaited his arrival. Henry loved theatre days.

Chapter 2
The Routine

There is one thing that is certain about the life of a surgeon. Elective (non-emergency) operating days are intended to start in a predictable way. Each operating list begins with ward admission and confirmation of consent, followed by WHO safety checklists, preparing the patients for theatre, and then team huddles in the anaesthetic room around the trolley expectant for its cargo. That the team is always a little different is a given, and in many ways, the huddle is the moment when a surgeon and their team look into the whites of each other's eyes and commit to a day living a life less ordinary. Their job was a 'job' saving lives and often changing them forever. What is curious about the surgical world, however, is that, like a formula one driver acclimates himself to the adrenaline of the race in a potentially lethal vehicle, so does the surgical team.

Preparations have taken years of training and brainwashing; the best are selected through exams, interviews, and sometimes a dash of nepotism; the theatre has been stocked with equipment for every eventuality; and the day begins with the intention of completing the list and reaching the finishing line of a winning team. It is normal for them to render a fellow human being unconscious and then, with sharp tools and devices, cut into that patient's body and explore the often previously untouched depths of the body, where pathology lies. It's a sort of complex archaeological dig or engineering project bathed in warm, fresh blood and other bodily fluids. Goals: Remove what is unwanted; repair what is damaged; replumb what is blocked; and reconstruct as best as you can whilst leaving everything else unscathed. At the end, the surgeon stands before the patient and assesses the day's work, always hoping for a good outcome.

For some, it is about the quality of work done, and for others, it is about the person and life restored. For others, another number on the list of those who do more. It is not only a privilege but also a way of life. A life known to attract a certain type of person. A person who can stand for long hours beneath glaring hot lights in long gowns, gloves, and masks whilst remaining focused and machine-like committed to the task at hand. That person is surrounded by a team that converses in the surgical idiolect of words and body language unique to the demands of each moment and responds to every challenge like the beating of a heart. At the head of the table is the anaesthetist, the cerebral coordinator of the pulse and breath, fine-tuning every changing parameter of life as the body responds to the insult of surgery. This is not a normal world for many, but it is for them.

"Good morning, team!" Henry stood at the head of the empty trolley in the now somewhat cosy anaesthetic room. All heads turned to acknowledge his introduction with nods and smiles.

"Are we all here? Everyone on form today?" Everyone nods and smiles in his direction.

"Let's start with the introductions." They each took turns introducing themselves in clockwise order around the trolley.

Henry Blythe-Soames, Surgeon, Claire Roberts Anaesthetist, Mike Jenkins Anaesthetic Registrar, Dave Jackson ODP, Sue Parkins Scrub, Mark Fowler Second Scrub, Fiona Marsh Runner,

Steve Perks Second Runner, Amy Marsh Med student, Lawrence Pervis Med student, Ibrahim Baba Staff Grade Surgeon.

"So, let's go through the list. First up is Dominic Simms, – left Fem-Pop bypass. Dodgy chest last time, wasn't he Claire?"

Claire was a very senior anaesthetist and had worked with Henry for the last eight years.

"Yes, although I am glad to see that he has lost a few pounds since, cut down, his cigarettes and drinks, and looks a few years younger. Hopefully, he will fare better this time. We are ready for everything, though."

The remaining patients were discussed in list order, and everything was agreed. Henry next turned to the medical students.

"So, students, what year are you?" The two medical students both blushed simultaneously. They were not expecting any questions and timidly said, "Erm, we are fourth years."

"Excellent! You should know your stuff then. I hope you have seen the first patient and examined him. I'll be checking in a bit," Amy and Lawrence had gone a pale shade of unwell and were suddenly wishing that someone had warned them beforehand. Amy had her note pad in her hand and had written down some tips for vascular examinations. She decided to be honest and tell Mr Blythe-Soames the truth.

"Er, Mr Blythe-Soames I am sorry, but I did not get a chance to examine the first patient as he was getting dressed when I arrived. Should we go and do that now?" Henry had a sly smirk on his face and nodded slowly.

"Well, it would be a darn sight better than trying to make up your findings in theatre, wouldn't it?" he laughed mockingly at her, and the rest of the team smiled awkwardly at him.

"Yes, go and do it whilst we finish up here and make sure you know your facts," Amy and Lawrence quietly escaped from the door behind them and sighed.

"He is seriously scary. Do you remember the name of the first patient, Loz?" Lawrence had just recovered from the terror of the last few minutes.

"I hear he made hell for one student last year who complained about him. She had the worst placement report ever. Probably best to say nothing. Let's go and find someone who knows the patient's name. I think it was something like Simms." They found nurse Sue on the ward, and she pointed to the cubicle for Mr Simms.

"Did he just send you both out of theatre? You poor things. Do it to a lot of students so you are not alone. That's Mr Blythe-Soames. Lovely and scary, but he wants you to learn. A very good surgeon too. Just a perfectionist, that's all. A good idea for you two is to check the notes. His registrar usually does everything before the morning round, and his notes will give you what you need to know," she smiled sympathetically at them and showed them the notes cupboard. "C4521 to get into the cupboard and make sure you put everything back in after you're done."

"Thank you very much; we are very grateful," Amy said as she rushed to the note cupboard. The notes were heavy and thick, and they were so glad to see the note from Mr Baba on the front of the file.

Admitted to left FEM-POP bypass with ipsi. SV donor.

Below this, he had written down the history of the patient and all the examination and test results in summary.

"This is great!" Amy said with a face that looked like a child at Christmas.

They brought out their note pad, copied the notes, and carefully put the big folder back into the cupboard. They then timidly peered into the cubicle to introduce themselves to Mr Simms and ask him whether he was happy for them to examine him and to be in theatre to watch his operation. He was delighted with the friendly faces and told them he would be happy to help with their training.

Rushing back to the theatre, both braced themselves for what would follow.

"You go first," Amy said to Loz.

"Thanks a lot!" Loz said sarcastically with a nervous smile as they crept into the theatre. They could hear a raised voice.

"What do you mean that she is going to complain? About what? Ibrahim, I bloody told you to sort it out. Do I have to do everything?" Henry was shouting at Ibrahim as they walked in. He stormed past them, seemingly looking through them as they walked in quietly. Ibrahim smiled with an embarrassed look and ushered them his way. "Sorry about that. How did you get along with Mr Simms?"

"Oh, we had a look at your notes, and they were so helpful. He let us examine him, too. Thank you, Mr Baba." Loz said.

"Ah, I can see you met Sue on the ward. She knows how to look after you. Should we chat about the case so that you are all clued up before Mr Blythe-

Soames comes back? You'll be fine." The two medical students relaxed a little and followed him to the computer, where he had the scans up.

"Have you seen scans like this before?"

"Yes, that is a CT Angiogram, I think," Amy said.

"Hey, why the 'I think?' You are correct, Amy. Well done. Try to reply with confidence. Can you see anything on it?"

Amy moved closer to the scan and tilted her head slightly as she looked at the leg that was on the list.

"Is this artery narrower than the other side?"

"Very good. Well spotted. Now the next question you will not answer with a question," he smiled kindly at her, and she giggled.

"Bad habit," she said with a hand in front of her mouth.

"Now, Lawrence, can you name some of the arteries on the angio?"

Lawrence straightened his back and cleared his throat.

"Is this the femoral artery?" he pointed to the right vessel.

"You are both doing so well!" Ibrahim had also relaxed and was happy to have the medical students there to distract him from the lump in his chest following the earlier insult. 'Henry is such an arrogant idiot!' he thought. He turned with a gentle smile towards Amy.

"Now are you going to get the gold star and name the other vessels with the confidence of a surgeon?"

Amy stood straight and said, "Well, I know that one is the tibial artery…but I cannot remember the others. I'm sorry."

Ibrahim smiled kindly. "That is OK Amy. The first part is spot-on and well done. Lawrence, can you help her?"

Lawrence looked at him then, with his hands behind his back, and leant closer to the screen, saying, "The popliteal artery?"

"Very good. Can you point to it?"

Lawrence pointed to a narrowed vessel, "This one."

"Excellent! Let me just run you through the rest. It is worth doing a sketch in your notebooks of these; the image might help you relate them to what you see in the patient. I always find that you remember anatomy better when you can relate it to a case you have seen," he went on to discuss the various arteries, and the medical students wanted to hug him. Suddenly the lovely teaching session was over, and the prep room door swung open. Henry returned, looking flushed.

"Team, we need to regroup. The order on the list has changed. I'm livid. Before the next patient comes through, can you get a new list printed with Mrs Briggs second, please? It seems she is related to the bloody Chief Executive, and so the list has changed. So much for being in control of my list and putting high-risk patients first. Mrs Briggs' varicose veins are clearly more important than the carotid endarterectomy!" He stopped and looked towards Ibrahim with a scowl.

"Ibrahim, what is going on? Why is the first patient still in the anaesthetic room? Have you not checked?"

"Sorry, no, I have not. I was just doing some teaching…"

The expression with which Henry glared at Ibrahim was somewhere between hate and disgust. Ibrahim stood up and started to walk towards the anaesthetic room.

"No way! Sit down, man. You are too late. I'll do it."

Henry charged past Ibrahim, and the lump in Ibrahim's chest returned. The medical students wanted to run away but instead found themselves stepping back towards the wall at the edge of the theatre. Somehow, they imagined they would be invisible there. They both felt terrible for Mr Baba.

"How's it going, Claire?"

Henry stuck his head around the anaesthetic door.

"Not well. He still has a terrible chest, as feared, and he has been unstable since we tubed him. I am just trying to get lines into him. Going to be another ten minutes, I am afraid," she said all this whilst looking at the ultrasound scan that was hovering over the carotid artery on the patient's neck. The trainee, Mike, was standing next to her, poised and ready to put in the central line and the ODP. Dave was holding the tray and watching the erratic monitor trace. The room was silent apart from the heartbeats from the monitor and quiet words from Claire as she talked to Mike. "Ready?"

"Yes," he said.

"Go for it."

Mike picked up the arterial line Seldinger kit and slid the line into the neck of the patient. A few seconds later, there was a change in the rhythm of the heart tracing, and he pulled the line back slightly.

"All in."

"All looking good," Dave said.

"Well done, Mike," Claire said, and they connected the monitor, cleaned up the neck, and moved to catheterise the patient. A few minutes later, the operating theatre door banged open with a thump at the end of the trolley, and the patient was wheeled into the centre of the room. The tubes were connected to the anaesthetic machine, and like clockwork, Henry and Ibrahim moved to the patient to position him for surgery. They then walked in silence to the scrub room, where the handwashing ritual followed. Brown Betadine liquid splashes onto the floor, and the theatre assistants are poised just outside the scrub room, ready to tie the backs of the gowns and take the headtorch wires to connect to the light sources. Both surgeons twirled round in sequence to tie the front ties, and they were dressed.

"Can the medical students scrub, Henry? They have read up well for the case," Ibrahim glanced at the two silent medical students, who were still standing against the wall, and smiled kindly. "Huh? What? Yes, yes, no problem; just make sure they don't get in my way today, Ibrahim. I'm not in the mood!"

Ibrahim waved to the medical students to go to the scrub room whilst turning to Jane the scrub nurse.

"Jane is there someone who can go through scrubbing up with Amy and Lawrence, please?" Jane nodded and asked Mark, the second scrub nurse, if he would mind teaching the medical students to scrub. Amy and Lawrence looked delighted.

"Have you ever scrubbed before you two?"

Both students shook their heads in synchrony.

"OK, do you know what size gloves you wear?"

"6 and a half, please," Amy said.

"8, Please" Lawrence said.

Any allergies? Both shook their heads.

"Ok, you need to get your gowns from the packs in the cupboard below you, and gloves are in the green boxes above you. Grab a pair, but don't open them yet."

They both reached for their respective gowns and glove packs.

"Right, when you peel open the gown pack, drop them onto the top and carefully open the white packet using the corners only. Do not touch the blue with your hands. Peel open your gloves on top of the blue gowns, and then we can turn to the sink for the scrub. Great. OK, now wash your hands. This is a three-minute scrub. Can you both see the pictures on the wall in front of you?"

They nodded, looking at the handwashing pictures.

"OK, use your forearms to dispense the cleaning liquid. Great. Now, follow the pictures and make sure you keep those hands up and get to the elbows. Don't forget the thumbs and palms. Brilliant, you are doing well."

Both medical students were focused and serious, but also visibly nervous. When they had completed the scrub, they turned to the gown pack to dry their hands.

"Now, do not touch the finger parts of the gloves…no! Lawrence, that is not exactly what you want to do. Hang on, let me get a new pair," Lawrence looked embarrassed and stepped back to allow Mark to peel open another pack. He put the second pair on, and they were both ready to step out of the scrub room for the final step of the prep ritual. The tie up.

"Now this bit is always a little tricky when you start. Hold the paper tab and the free end in your two hands. Do not drop the free end." They both looked down to find the paper tie at their waist level.

"Hmm, this is tricky," Amy mumbled. Mark started with Amy, tied the inner tie, and then walked in front of her.

"OK, now hold onto both ends, give me the paper card, and turn anticlockwise." She followed his instructions and came back to face Mark, where the final front tie was done by her. Lawrence did the same, and they quietly approached the table where the patient had been draped with blue drapes, leaving only the exposed leg and groin. They could see that the operative sites on the groin and lower leg had been marked with pen marks.

The first person to speak or rather shout, was Henry.

"Now, students, one of you will assist me, and the other can assist Mr Baba." He looked at Amy and said, "You, come here. What was your name again?" Amy's heart sank. She whispered behind her mask, "Amy."

"Alright, Amy, when I speak to you, you will need to reply at an audible volume."

"Sorry, Mr Blythe-Soames," her body recoiled defensively to match her eyes.

"That is better. Ibrahim, you work with this young man. Lawrence, was it?"

"Yes, that is right," Lawrence spoke louder and felt so relieved that he was with Ibrahim.

"Are we all ok at the head end, Claire?"

"So so. He's still pink, so that is one good thing. You can start." The gallows humour breaks the slightly awkward atmosphere around the table.

"So, Amy, how many of these have you seen before?"

"This is my first time, but I did watch one on YouTube yesterday to prepare."

"Ha! The wonder of social media!" Henry laughed. "Should I give you the scalpel then, as you know what to do? I can have a day off. How excellent."

Amy looked horrified. "Oh, sorry. No, I did not mean that. I do not want to do the operation. Can I just assist you, please?"

By this point, Henry was positively laughing and holding his arm out towards the scrub nurse.

"Blade and forceps, please, Jane."

Jane handed him the scalpel, forceps, and a clean swab, and the operation began. "Now, Amy, today you will learn the greatest lesson of all in surgery. How to stand properly. There is one thing that every surgeon forgets, and that is your back," Amy realised she had hunched over the operating area in an intense panic-stricken posture. She straightened her back, and her eyes showed that she was smiling.

"That's better. Next, you are going to learn the names of the different instruments and ask for them from Jane. OK?"

"Yes, Mr Blythe-Soames."

"Now, what do you think I might need next?"

He asked her without looking up. His eyes were focused on the operation site. Amy looked at the incision line in absolute panic. 'Think, think Amy!'….

"Erm, maybe a retractor?"

"Yes, yes, but which retractor? Do you know any names? Did you not learn anything from YouTube? Not heard the names Cat's Paw, Langenbeck, or Skin Hook, before?"

Amy suddenly felt very hot in her mask and gown and looked up to Henry. "No, I am sorry; I do not know any of those names, Mr Blythe-Soames. Which one should I ask Jane to give to you, please?"

"Well, it is clear there is no surgeon of the future here! Probably heading for less than full-time working or GP land, eh?"

Amy suddenly felt annoyed and stood up as straight as she could. She was going to say her part, even if she got thrown out of the theatre.

"Mr Blythe-Soames, today is my first day of scrubbing. I have never been in an operating theatre where I learned the names of instruments used in vascular surgery. I am here, however, to learn and would be very grateful if you would teach me, please, as I very much want to be a surgeon." OMG, she had said it.

Henry was aghast. He was used to women being deferential towards him. Even his wife would not dare speak to him like that. He looked straight at Amy.

"Well, now Amy, it seems you do have a voice after all. Understand this, I am here to operate on my patients; I am here as a consultant and not here to pander to the fantasies of medical students who expect me to fill them in on learning they forgot to do before they came to my theatre. If you want to learn, then at least have the decency to read up before the list. I gave you one chance when you screwed up in the anaesthetic room this morning. That was your freebie. De-scrub and go to the library. I don't need you here!" His eyes bore into her, but she was determined to face him.

Amy was shocked. The rest of the team was horrified. Henry was normally brusque, but he had overstepped the line today. The only problem was that there was not one member of the team with the desire to speak up at that point when there was a patient on the table and a list to complete. Amy ungowned and rushed out of the theatre with tears in her eyes. Fiona, the runner, followed her and put her arms on her shoulder in the corridor.

"I am so sorry, Amy. You did not deserve that at all. I think he is just in a bad mood about the list change. Shall we go and sit down and talk about it? A cup of tea will probably do quite nicely, won't it?"

Amy was still tense. She hated herself for crying. He was probably going to label her a snowflake, and she hated that. Being a medical student made her quite powerless, but in her heart was fire. When she was more senior, she promised herself that she would make sure that consultants like Mr Henry Blythe-Soames were corrected, but right now she needed to focus on getting through her surgery block.

Fiona brought a warm cup of tea to her and sat down with her.

"How are you feeling?"

"I am so annoyed with myself for getting upset. I wish I had the right words to say. Is he always like this?"

"Well, he is a bit of a perfectionist and very old-school. That's the way he's trained, and I guess that's what he thinks everyone should go through. I guess it's some sort of initiation. It's all a bit outdated, if you ask me."

She was shaking her head, and her eyes were wide and troubled.

"Will anyone say anything to him? Do you think?"

"No point, my dear. He is fixed in how he does things. There is no magic formula that will change him. Thankfully, he is a good surgeon, so the patients are safe with him. He is the surgeon I would get my veins done by any day. I do feel for his poor registrar, though. He takes this every week and seems to always stay lovely. Now, he is a good surgeon too. Try to spend some time with Mr Baba. You'll learn lots there," Her kind, knowing smile wore a deep understanding of the world of theatre, which to many would seem more like a theatre on stage than in a hospital. A centre for ego, performance, and results.

"Yes, my heart sank when Mr Blythe-Soames asked me to stand with him. I can see that Lawrence was doing some surgery with Mr Baba. Oh well, I guess I just pulled the short straw. Thank you for the tea and chat, Fiona. I really needed that. I think I am going to go and get some reading done now. Are you going back in?"

"Yes, two more cases to get done after this one," she stood up and went back to the theatre. Upon entering, she noticed that the junior doctor, Eliza, had come in and was scrubbed with Mr Blythe-Soames. Everything seemed calm again, and there was some music in the background. It was as if nothing had happened, and Mr Blythe-Soames seemed even more cheerful. That was a surprise. She wondered what had happened to change his mood so much.

The rest of the list progressed without further noise. Even the order change was accomplished without drama, and everyone seemed relaxed, except for Ibrahim. He was watching Henry from the corner of his eye. He resented him so much for what he had said to Amy, and now something else was troubling him. Something that was too horrible to think about. He had to focus. 'Concentrate on the operating Ibrahim; deal with it later.' As the first case finished and the patient was wheeled to recovery, Henry announced that he had to go to a meeting and that Ibrahim was finishing the last two cases. All calm was restored, and the list proceeded without further drama. At the end of list debrief was with the usual surgeon-led summary, no one spoke out about what had happened, and the list was closed on the computer system as though all was well.

Chapter 3
The Clinic

Jemimah's week always began with two half days of clinic back-to-back, colloquially known by some as double maths, in the medical world. In one way, she loved clinic because she knew that interesting and challenging cases would come to see her, but on the other hand, she always dreaded the almost process-line-like flow of patients. She calculated it in her head, 'Twenty patients to see in four hours, so that makes twelve minutes per patient. One patient with a difficult case, and the clinic starts to run late. Two and the nurses start getting twitchy; three and you're in deep shit. Managers come down, and datixes start flying. So how does one make the clinic work perfectly when every patient needs the time they need?' This had long been the question that rolled around Jemimah's head the night before clinic day.

She had long resigned herself to the lunacy of a system that compartmentalises human beings into bite-sized quotas. She was tired of being challenged by target-pressured managers about her time management, being told to see fewer patients by changing her job plan, and then the next day being asked why her RTT targets were falling short of the other surgeons. Apparently, she was not as good as Henry, and they wanted to know why. She knew well why he was brusque and rude to the patients, and they rarely dared to challenge him or ask too many questions.

That was not the sort of surgeon she would ever wish to be, and besides, Henry runs late too. It was just that the nurses rather doted on their beloved Henry, and he could do no wrong. Instead, she knew well that they wanted Henry's overtime back from her clinics.

This Monday was a typical clinic day. For reasons that Jemimah had never understood, she had a gift for attracting patients with rare pathologies and complex presentations. In some ways, she loved it. A chance to push her knowledge and test her skills. An innate quality of many surgeons who secretly harbour a desire for adrenaline and pressure. A bit like surgery itself, the life of a consultant surgeon is a mixture of the mundane "bread and butter" of routine pathology and then the truly obscure—those memorable cases that stretch a doctor's understanding of how the human body works when challenged and allows them to delve into pharmacological and technological innovation, ignore the books, and instead tap into shared discussion with colleagues and the knowledge extrapolated from research and conferences.

If there is one thing truly brilliant about medicine, it is that despite so much being known and methodically rammed into the heads of specialist doctors, there remains far more that is poorly understood and even unknown. It is why the life of a doctor is never dull and why there are so many different specialties.

This is one of the things that gave Jemimah the real love of a career, which often pushed her hard and relentlessly. Her choice of vascular surgery was a gutsy one. A male-dominated specialty where she really played with life in her hands whenever she did an operating list. So often in her training, she faced male trainers who asked her why she wanted to do this for a career instead of having babies. 'It was a physical specialty, and women were not suited to it' several peers had told her. The more they said that to her, the more she became determined to do it. Perhaps a little sadomasochistic, one might think, but the challenge pushed her to work hard and get there. It was all that mattered—to make it to the consultant despite every barrier placed in front of her.

Jemimah was so focused on her career that there never seemed to be the right time to settle down and have children. It's a sadly common story for many of her female peers in surgery. Was it just about the job, or was it something else? Come to think of it, her tally of previous men was also pathetically poor. She had observed, with some sadness, that if there was one thing that turned relatively normal men into complete morons, it was the knowledge that their girlfriend was a surgeon. As soon as they heard the word S-U-R-G-E-O-N, a strange peacock-like transition seemed to happen in each of them, and a spontaneous performance of male feather-fluttering followed.

"Look at me! Look how great I am. I am the best in the world at this. I drive an X, which goes so fast. What do you drive?" And then came the public humiliation of the girlfriend. Repeated slights to undermine her in front of friends. It was as though she was a threat to their masculinity, which was ridiculous. So here she was, a consultant and surgeon, still thankfully fertile, she thought, but also chronically single at 37. Her friends had 'reassured' her that it seemed tough because she only needed one man and there were a lot of rubbish ones to sift through to find THE one, or alternatively, go for the test tube and ignore the man factor completely. No, Jemimah was traditional. For her, it was a full package of men, homes, kids, or nothing. Right now, nothing was just fine.

At patient number fifteen, Jemimah felt thirsty and a little hungry. She went up to Jackie, the clinic nurse, and asked her if there was any chance of a cup of coffee and maybe a biscuit. Jackie was an old-school nurse and brilliant at her job. There was not much that she had not seen in her career; sadly, she was also a stickler for ever-evolving trust policies and regulations.

"Now, Jemimah, you know the rules well enough. Infection control has banned drinks from clinic rooms, and eating is forbidden. You can pop into the staff room if you'd like for a quick glass of water, but you know we are running late again. Can't you hang in there for a bit longer and try to finish the last few patients? The lovely Mr Martin is waiting to see you, which I know will cheer you up."

Jemimah sighed and pondered whether the people who had made the no-drinking-on-clinic rule were also sitting at work feeling like Lawrence of bloody Arabia with an oasis nowhere in sight. She suspected not.

"Jackie, I know we are running late, and there is nothing I can do about it. I need to drink, however, and if you cannot bring a drink to me, I will have to go to the coffee room and get one. I have been talking non-stop for three and a half hours in a dry clinic room and expecting someone to work without any fluid or rest for four hours, beggars belief."

Jackie looked annoyed, "Well, we will have to Datix your late finish again."

"Do whatever you wish, Jackie. I just hope that the nurses are doing the same for all of Henry's late clinics too, as I will be checking."

"W-w-well hurry up then, and I will go and apologise to the patients."

Jackie moved awkwardly, and Jemimah knew that she had hit a nerve. Today, however, she did not care. Today, she would drink some water, because she was thirsty, and the clinic would run late, because that is what happens. As she gulped down a wonderfully cool glass of water in the nurses' coffee room, she thought to herself triumphantly, 'Sod protocol; well, at least those protocols that have the sum total of ZERO concrete evidence backing them.' She quickly walked back to the clinic, rehydrated, and completed the last five patients in record time, which meant only a slightly late finish. The Datix went in still, and Jemimah sighed. Oh, to be Henry.

Chapter 4
The Hunt

There is something almost paradoxical about a doctor who loves to hunt. At one end of life is the pledge to do no harm, and yet as soon as the reins are released, there is a primitive hunger in some to kill. Henry Blythe-Soames was such a person—a skilled stalker. He had learned it from his childhood, when stalking was a source of income and land management on the family estate. To him, they were just killing what needed to be controlled. Something akin to squashing a slug in the garden, except this produced income, a tasty meal, and camaraderie as well, not forgetting the opportunity to prove his skill as a stalker. He chose to stalk by stealth and rifle, and he loved the chase and the thrill of a clean kill. His friend network was largely around stalking, and it was his way of escaping from everything. The epitome of exercise of mind, body, and soul.

He enjoyed hunting with Gus, the estate manager, who had known him for over twenty years and had taught him all that he knew. Today was even better, a stalk with some old school friends, and it was all about the reassertion of hierarchy amongst his pack. Henry was, and intended to remain, the best, and where better than on a hunt in his own family land on a day when the weather was the added definer? The ultimate test of skill, stealth, patience, and control under pressure. This was what Henry was born and trained to do. One day he might apply these honed skills to dissect and conquer disease and save life or limb in the operating theatre; on the other day, they are used to stalk and master the mind of an animal and kill it. In both, life is seemingly his gift, and the thought of that aroused him.

"Looking quite the part, old boy. New clothes, I see?" Magnus strode towards his old classmate and patted him on the shoulder. His Barbour outfit looked weathered but still damn stylish.

"Ah yes, Morning, Magnus. I decided to splash out on the latest Harkila, and I must say it suits this fog and cold rather well. Today is going to be a challenging hunt. We have a few good Roebucks on the chase. The challenge is the first with a clean shot at no nearer than hmmm let's say 400m, and the winner gets the antlers. If two get shots, the one with the furthest distance and cleanest shot wins. Each of us will go in different directions, and you'll each have a man with you as a witness to the shot. I'm with Gus, Eddie; you are with David and Magnus; you go with Simon. Are you up to it?" Merely talking about it brought excitement to Henry's voice and face. Magnus and Eddie were drawn into the moment.

"You really are on form today, Henry. If that is the challenge, then I accept. I do hope this wind settles a bit, though, as the distance is the game."

"Hmmm, me too. Rounds will be turning back on us if it gets much worse," laughed Eddie (Edmund) Tate. "Is that a new rifle you have? Wow, is that the latest Sig Sauer? Impressive."

"Yep, and a lovely beast she is too. 270 Winchester calibre, fluted barrel, bolt action like a knife through butter, Schmidt Bender scope and Sauer Pro moderator; home-developed rounds made for purpose and loaded. Just look at the walnut stock. I haven't missed a shot with her yet. Yes, this rifle is a fine thing indeed."

Henry beamed. Eddie looked on with envy. Henry was always the trend-setter amongst them, and what a role model he was. Costly to keep up with, but very much worth it.

"You really are something, Henry. I intend to have the antlers in my hand, despite our rifles. Mark my words. Today is my day," Eddie gloated.

The adrenaline and bravado were flowing, and the three hunting teams each picked a direction to walk by pulling a piece of paper from a hat to keep things fair. All looked focused.

The banter went on as they zeroed in on their rifles using the preset targets Gus had assembled for them. They acquainted themselves with their hunting partners, and the atmosphere was convivial. The cold air rested on their knuckles, and the barrels of their guns felt like ice. The challenge was set, and the stalk began. The woods looked magical with the cold mist lacing all the branches. The ground was crisp below their feet, making stalking more difficult, but this was no ordinary stalk. This stalk was about pride. It was about control. It was about expertise and skill. The breath of the men formed spiralling plumes in front of their mouths. The terrain was challenging, with slippery paths and sticky mud. The decaying leaves were dried on top, and the sound of the feet crunching was difficult to muffle. Few words were exchanged between the men, who occasionally whispered almost inaudibly.

They looked around them for signs of deer activity on the ground and then scanned the distance with their binoculars. Every now and then, a pheasant would jump out of the bracken or bushes and startle them with a loud cawking cry. They felt as though they were a part of the forest, and the early spring was literally bursting around them. Suddenly, nothing else mattered. The focus was on the objective, and there was a simmering excitement that made the pain of the cold disappear from their hands and feet. Two hours passed, and apart from a few does and their fawns, there was no sign of a buck. Where was he hiding? Henry made a calling sound and then stopped to look if there were any virile bucks hunting for a bit of luck after the rut. It was a game of stealth. It was a task of pure perseverance, and he was determined. He heard a distant crack of gunshots from one of the others. That spurred him on more.

Eventually, they reached a position a few hundred metres from a clearing. The pale early-spring sunshine dressed the frosty blades of grass. Here, Henry chose to wait. He hid between two trees with a clear view of the clearing and fixed his vanguard sticks in place. His heart was palpably beating, and he swallowed. Gus was close to him, and they were absolutely still. Feet positioned in a stable stance, eyes looking through his Swarovski binoculars. Time did not matter. It was about that one perfect moment. He held his hand out to Gus, who passed him the rifle, and he positioned it, ready. They waited. He could feel muscles in his body tense slightly, as though his body knew what was coming.

Suddenly, the Roebuck appeared. It was at least 5 years old and had an impressive pair of antlers. At almost 500m away, Henry used the telescope on his rifle to evaluate the backdrop for safety; the inbuilt laser technology gave him an idea of range far more accurately than his eyes alone, although he had a great eye, even if he did say so. There was a cold, musty smell of the forest that coated their flared nostrils. They waited. Neither moved. The Roebuck was not yet in the right position for a clean shot, but he was close. So very close. Henry held a talc puffer and assessed the wind's strength and direction. Yes, this would be his moment. Aim for the chest. Look him in the eye. With the vanguard prop positioned and the rifle nested onto it, he was in position. The wind was 10mph from the east, and his ballistic chart measurements were running through his head.

Adjusting for drop and side-shift, Henry took the shot as the buck came into the clearing. The bolt was pushed tight and ready, and he squeezed the trigger. He was too far away to hear the thump of the round hitting his chest. The buck jumped back, startled, before the sound of the shot was heard. Before it knew what had happened, he dropped to the ground. A clean shot to the chest. Henry was pleased, as was Gus, as they looked at each other and nodded in approval. It was as though words were not needed at that moment, just looks, and they understood each other. The stalkers' idiolect. They walked out to the dead buck and prepared the body for transport. A fine dinner had been secured. Henry slung the field-dressed body over his shoulders, and they walked back towards the farm where they met the others. Eddie had another buck, and Magnus was empty-handed and looking frustrated.

"The bloody wind was a beast! Every time I wanted to shoot; something was not quite right. Better not to shoot eh, than get a bad kill? It looks like you both had a better day out there. The conditions were tough, though, and it made for a pleasant if challenging outing."

"Ah, Magnus, you are always a decent man. No shame in not taking a bad shot. Hard luck. So, Eddie, which of us won the antlers today? Gentlemen let's see what our colleagues say. Gus and David, what were the parameters? Are we close?"

Marcus produced a sheet of paper, and so did David, who handed it to Henry. The three hunters huddled and read the summary: David: Roebuck, wind 10 mph south-easterly. Chest shot, Clean Kill, distance 473m. Henry: Roebuck, wind 10 mph easterly. Chest shot, clean kill, Distance 489m. The winner was Henry, but by a hair's breadth, and the men laughed.

"Wow, respect where respect is due. Now that was close, gentlemen!" Magnus said as he patted both men on the shoulders. They all laughed.

"A satisfying day out indeed. Shall we head to the lodge and have a drink? I have some warming 20-year-old single malt that I think your palates will appreciate by the fire." Henry said.

"Sounds absolutely perfect, Henry," Eddie said as they stood over their kill.

They walked to the lodge, chatting away about the hunt. There was a relaxed camaraderie between the friends, and there was no need for pretence as they knew each other so well. Henry always thought that these friends knew him better than Vanessa. They got him. Their wives spent the day together with their children, and a meal that evening, eating well-hung venison from a previous stalk, promised to be a hearty one. Henry loved being in control and loved people to admire him. He was used to getting what he wanted.

Chapter 5
Targets

Eliza looked at herself in the mirror. It was 5.30 am and time for an hour of revision before heading out to work. She looked tired, but she was pleased that she had kept herself in good shape despite the gruelling hours. She sat at her desk with a coffee and toast and started the practice EMQ questions online. 'Read the questions, Eliza, and don't overthink. Watch the clock and focus.' She sat up straight, took a deep breath, and positioned herself in front of her laptop. It was a bit like training for a sports event, she thought, but what she was building up was not her body; it was her brain. Practice, practice, practice until doing an exam paper is like breathing itself. The trick to passing the exam was storing an immense volume of facts and applying them under pressure, like operating in a theatre. She felt like she had ingested an entire library of books and downloads. Her multicoloured notes were meticulous and comprehensive. She was so close to passing last time. This time she had to pass and get onto the clinical exam. That would be easier. She knew it.

Mr Blythe-Soames, as training programme director had been so supportive. What a stroke of luck it was to be his trainee at this time! She thought he was the best, and that he also happened to be rather handsome and made the extra MRCS revision sessions he was giving her very pleasant indeed. The MRCS examination was like an Oscar for Eliza. She had imagined the letters M.R.C.S. after her name for so long. How she longed at last to become an actual member of the Royal College of Surgeons and finally apply for a training number—that magical ticket to the last five years of training to become a consultant general surgeon. Her dream. She was ok at exams but always seemed to flounder at the MCQ and EMQ paper stages.

She had wondered whether she had a problem reading. Perhaps she was dyslexic? She even went to an optician to have her eyes looked at, and she bought glasses to correct her miniscule visual discrepancy. Still, it didn't work. She tried blinking more and drinking more water, and then, when that didn't work, she resorted to coffee, which made her pee more. Coffee also did not help with her next plan of sleeping better, so she limited it to before lunch. It was no good. She was a book person, and that was that. She was out of sync with the times. Screens were her weakness, and she needed to conquer them to pass this stupid exam. How she longed for paper. Her revision was, of course, balanced with long working hours and occasionally some food. Social life was a thing of the past, let alone romance. The idea of a relationship at that point was out of the question. She did miss her ex-boyfriend Simon, though, sometimes.

They had split up rather painfully following an argument the week before the last exam attempt. Simon had said he couldn't cope with the distance after she moved to Saint's Bay, as both were working as junior doctors. Oh, the joys of being posted miles away from where she wanted to be. In all fairness, though, there were many more unpleasant places to end up than Saint's Bay. When she arrived, she loved it for its gorgeous countryside, its old, quaint harbour, and its location, being only forty minutes from her favourite city. It was not bad at all if she had the time to get out and enjoy it.

76% FAIL. "Damn! Two percent out again," Eliza let out a big sigh, and she dressed for work.

As she left the quaint cottage that she was renting, Eliza smiled at the sunshine. 'Today is going to get better. Theatre with Mr Blythe-Soames, and then after the ward jobs are done, time for a revision session with him.' She was looking forward to it. She drove to the hospital with a happy feeling and felt positive about things.

"Good morning, Bernie. How are you today?"

Bernie looked up from his gaze on the mop he was using and beamed his pleasant smile at her.

"Well, good morning, Doctor. You all seem cheerful today. I'm guessing it's a good day ahead, right?"

"Yes, it will be Bernie. Busy, but good. There's always lots to learn."

"That sounds great. Have a great day."

"Thank you, Bernie. You too."

A smile lingered on his face. He was pleased that at least the young doctors were turning out OK, even though the papers were talking about pay issues and strikes. Thank God they weren't all like Mr Big Head, whom he had seen first.

He shook his head and carried on cleaning as people walked over to his work in careless oblivion. Over and over again, he went. Without him and his colleagues, imagine what the hospital would look like.

Eliza rushed to the admissions lounge and greeted Ibrahim, who arrived at the theatre doors at the same time as her.

"Hello Ibrahim. How are you today?"

"Good morning, Eliza. I am doing very well, thank you. Are you in theatre with us today?"

"Yes, I am. Mr Blythe-Soames told me there were some interesting cases today that I should see."

"Oh? Really? Which case in particular did he mean? It looks like a rather routine list today to me."

Eliza laughed. "Ibrahim, what is routine to you is all interesting to me. Remember, I am just learning, and I love theatre days. I get really good teaching in theatre too."

Ibrahim felt slightly uneasy. 'What was Henry up to?' He had noticed the rather close attention being given to Eliza a few lists ago and had hoped he was mistaken. Today would be a chance to see if his concerns had some merit.

He walked to the admissions bay, deep in thought. "Good morning, Sue. How are you today?"

"Ah Ibrahim, Good morning to you. I am very grateful to you," Sue replied as she smiled warmly at Ibrahim. "Another day with Mr Blythe-Soames?" She had a sympathetic look in her eyes. "Let's hope the list goes fine."

Ibrahim gave a slightly beleaguered smile, acknowledging gratefully that she understood his struggles with Henry.

"Yes, it is, and I am sure all will go fine. Nothing too alarming on the list today, which I am pleased to see. I imagine he may leave early and let me finish, as he has a meeting this afternoon. Are all the patients here, Sue?"

"Yes, they are, and the first two are all dressed and ready for you. Number 3 is still in the toilet, getting a urine sample for me. Notes are by the trolleys, as I knew you would be here early."

"Thank you, Sue. You are brilliant."

Sue smiled and walked off to tend to the many tasks of the morning admission lounge and its many patients.

After completing all the consent forms, with Eliza helping with checklists and drug charts, they walked to the coffee room to grab a quick refreshment before the arrival of Henry. Why on earth did anyone drink the coffee supplied in the hospital for staff, was one of the great mysteries of the world. The blue metal box said it was coffee, but the powder looked like finely ground soil, and the taste was equally repugnant. Nonetheless, it contained caffeine, and that was what they needed. The key was to add plenty of milk and some sugar whilst stirring fast to make it look like a latte. Why it frothed like that was something Ibrahim neither understood nor wished for. The key was to drink it quickly and not think too much about it, regardless of the bitter aftertaste it left.

Henry charged into the coffee room. "Ah, Ibrahim, you're in. Good. Do you remember now that I have a meeting at 11? I trust you can manage the last couple of cases for me."

"Good morning, Henry. Yes, that'll be fine. All the patients are here, marked, and consented, and I have Eliza here to assist."

"Ah. Yes. Eliza is here today, is she? Excellent."

Ibrahim looked closely at Henry's face and noticed a strange glint in his eyes as he spoke about Eliza. His previous observations appear to have been possibly true. Henry was in the mood for a hunt, and this time the prey was no deer. It was a woman. The problem was that Ibrahim could not say anything without concrete evidence. A hunch was not enough. Even if it was true, what could he really do about it? Henry was the clinical lead and training programme director for junior doctors. He was well-connected hierarchically; white and escalating concerns could result in disaster for Ibrahim. He was very distracted by the thought of it, gazing beyond Henry at the wall. His face was serious, and his eyes were a little narrowed. He was so focused on his thoughts that he did not notice Henry talking to him.

"Hey! Are you on the planet today, Ibrahim? I am speaking to you!"

"Oh, yes, sorry. I was just thinking about something. You were saying?"

"Oh, never mind. Let's round the team up and get started. It is already 8.30. It is late, Ibrahim!"

Ibrahim took a gentle breath and went to find Sister Jane to ask about the rest of the team. He had to find a way to find out the truth. A discrete way, of course, but somehow he had to protect Eliza without her knowing his concerns. He could see that she admired Henry. What was not to admire? He was a good-looking man, confident and attentive towards her. His surgery was of a very high standard. People around him appeared on the outside to like him. There was nothing there for a junior doctor or manager to be concerned about. Ibrahim was internally incensed. He would find a way. This was one conquest that Henry would not win.

Chapter 6
Knowledge and Wisdom

The day seemed to pass like a train, and Eliza's day had gone very well indeed. Ibrahim had let her do a part of the last operation, and that was such a buzz; it was awesome. The ward work in the afternoon passed by effortlessly to handover, and now it was revision time with nothing else lingering over her. She concentrated on time with Mr Blythe-Soames, and she was prepared. She popped to the toilet to freshen up and headed to his office.

Henry's office was in the admin wing, which was typically deserted after 4 pm. This made it a quiet place for a study session after 6 pm which it was. Eliza knocked gently on the door; "Come in," he was on the phone to someone, so he ushered her to the chair next to him and carried on talking, "Yeah. Absolutely. It looks like we are going to have to play this one a bit cleverly and get them to free up the funds and turn a blind eye. I'll meet with Stacey tomorrow and work some magic. This is all going to work out fine. Trust me, mate," Henry had a sly smile on his face and was sitting in a confident posture. A man in control of his game. Although he could see Eliza from the corner of his eye, he was slightly turned away from her. She sat silently and pretended to be searching for something very important in her bag; embarrassed to have intruded on a phone call. A few seconds later, Henry tossed his phone onto his desk and swung round to face Eliza. He had hung his jacket onto the back of his chair, and his red-striped shirt gave hints about his strong torso beneath. Eliza was distracted and needed to pull herself together. She looked at his wedding ring, and sanity returned.

"Hello Eliza. How was today for you?"

"Well, today was excellent. I had such a great morning in theatre. Ibrahim, let me…"

"Yes, that's good," Henry cut her short on hearing Ibrahim's name. "Are you all handed over and free for your revision session?"

"Oh, erm yes, absolutely. Ready and raring to go!" She smiled and blushed simultaneously at him. There was something inexplicably thrilling about having the undivided attention of a senior surgeon.

"So, last time we revisited your issues with the EMQ paper. Any progress there?"

"Well, my scores are getting better, but I'm still not there. I struggle to read longer questions on a screen. I have always been a bit of a bookworm and find screens difficult. I'm still not passing every time, and yet I feel like I know my stuff. What can I do?" Eliza's big eyes looked pleadingly into Henry's. He found her vulnerability very alluring, and he rolled his chair next to her and took her hand into his. For a few seconds, Eliza felt relieved that someone understood her troubles.

"We will get you through this, Eliza. You have worked hard, I can see that, and with the right support, you will smash this exam and get closer to your dreams of being a surgeon. Let's get to work and see how your preparation is going."

"Oh, thank you, Mr Blythe-Soames. I cannot tell you how grateful I am to you."

"Eliza, we are both adults. Fine, call me Mr Blythe-Soames in front of patients and the team, but when we are alone, please call me Henry. The full name thing is rather excessive. Let's make these sessions as comfortable for you as possible. OK?"

Eliza looked surprised, and she felt like no one on the planet was as nice to her as Mr B…Henry.

"Oh, gosh. If you're sure, yes, I will try to call you Henry…even if it feels very strange," she beamed her beautiful smile at him, and Henry felt unexpected feelings inside that he had long forgotten. Was this how it felt when he was chasing Vanessa? Come to think of it, no, Vanessa chased him. This was something new and very interesting, indeed. He was interested to see where it might go. Henry the Stalker flickered in his eyes, accentuating his aura of strength and confidence.

The session was productive, with the body language between the trainer and trainee being much more than simply receptive. Was it a Freudian sort of professional attraction? Compatibility based on biology? Or was it the simplest part of the brain doing what it does best? Relying on instinct alone? Eliza pondered about it on her way home. It's not a good thing at all to fancy your married supervisor, but something just clicked between them. Perhaps her hormones were just tricking her mind. Yes, that was it. Nothing was going to happen, but right now it felt rather nice to be in the presence of an impressive man who seemed to enjoy being around her. Yes, this was perfectly natural, and for God's sake, he was married! What would happen? Nothing. Absolutely nothing. Eliza drove home with a smile on her face. Today had been an excellent day. A great morning in theatre, a trouble-free afternoon on the wards, and a perfect revision session where she shone and reaped the benefits of her hard work. Tonight was a red wine night, and she was on top of the world.

Henry was still in his office after Eliza left. He was flushed and feeling unusually troubled. He grumbled to himself, "OK, mate, you need to get a grip! She is a junior doctor and your trainee, and I'm the bloody TPD! Never cross the sacred line. You're going to get burned. GET A GRIP, HENRY!". He was trying to finish his emails when he suddenly focused on the one he was writing. Complete rubbish! What on earth was he doing? He decided not to send any emails that evening. In the draft box, they went one after the other. He needed to get home, have a triple whisky, and reset with Vanessa. He must be spending too much time at work.

He grabbed his jacket and leather laptop bag and strode out of his office. He swept past Bernie without even a nod, and Bernie stared at him. 'Now I smell some trouble or something else unfolding. That face is one I've seen before.'

Henry jumped into his car and roared off towards home. He could see Jemimah's car a few cars ahead, and for reasons that eluded him, he overtook her fast and with a misplaced air of guilt, as though he were overtaking a police car. Why was he feeling guilty? "For fuck's sake, what is wrong with you, Henry?" He had both hands gripped tightly to the steering wheel, and his eyes were wide.

Jemimah shook her head with a knowing laugh as Henry sped past her towards the red traffic light. 'Going fast, nowhere are we, Henry?' There was something so brazen about her alpha male colleague. If that is what she needed to resemble to make progress in her career, there was an impossible task ahead!

They drove ahead in their contradictory vehicles, an image itself that spoke a thousand words, and turned left towards Hampton-Astley, the quaint village five miles from the hospital that was far enough from the hospital to feel like you were not there but close enough to make on calls at night, not too onerous. As a village, it had a mixture of scenic old cottages and elegant Georgian properties that harked back to a bygone time when industrial and agricultural wealth had settled there. Jemimah's Georgian house was on a hill and looked out over the valley. It was in every way a welcoming and yet not ostentatious home—a place that resembled its owner.

Henry's house was approached through two tall stone pillars capped with spherical stone finials—a great pair of them, which seemed in many ways befitting. The sweeping tree-lined driveway to the Grange was impressive. At the end was a farmhouse that had been extended tastefully over the years. The old barn had been converted into a swimming pool and sauna area, and there was a stable at the rear. The gardens were well stocked, but in many ways functional. The final extension had allowed for a large entrance hall to be added with an oak staircase at its heart. There was a fireplace in the hallway that also displayed a few of Henry's family portraits that he had taken from the estate vaults. Yes, the Grange was smaller than the extensive house that Henry had grown up in, but it carried the elegance of his ancestry in its décor.

"Hello. I'm home. Anyone in?" Henry called out. He was strangely eager to see his children and even wanted to look at Vanessa. Check if he is still sane.

"Daddy!" Amelia rushed down the stairs as fast as her five-year-old legs could carry her and jumped into Henry's arms.

"Woah! Hello there, Amelia, darling," Henry felt the tight squeeze of Amelia's arms around his neck, and he felt complete again. "So, my angel, how was your day at school?"

"Very good, thank you, daddy. We did a play, and I was the princess! It was such fun!"

"The princess, you say? Gosh, that sounds like a very important role. You will have to tell me all about it after daddy has had a swim and changed into something comfy. Fancy a swim?"

"Mummy says I need to get ready for bed, daddy," she looked pleadingly at him whilst the grandfather clock struck 7.30 pm.

"Ah yes, I am afraid your mummy is right. Bedtime, it is. Look, we can talk about it tomorrow, perhaps if I get home earlier. Don't go forgetting it before then!"

Amelia laughed and said, "I won't forget it, daddy. It was too much fun!"

As he lowered Amelia to the ground, Thomas peeped his head around the banister.

"Ah, there you are, Tom. All OK?" Tom nodded silently and ran back upstairs. If there was one thing that Tom was not, it was anything like his father. Tom was a sensitive and shy boy who struggled with anything macho. Having an impressive and exacting father figure seemed to magnify his deficiencies, and despite being good at his studies, Thomas never quite seemed to please his father. He had learned at an early age that saying less and hiding from him was the best thing as far as his relationship with his father was concerned. Henry repeatedly spoke of how he despaired at how his son was. How could he give his share of the estate to him? It was a darn good job that his elder brother had had sons, and maybe genetics had the right idea as far as the estate was concerned.

The last person to enter the hallway was Vanessa. She had been cooking in the kitchen and was wearing her personalised apron that he had bought for her last Christmas. Her hair was roughly tied back, and she had some chocolate on her cheek. She smiled gently at him as Amelia stood between them.

"Hello darling. You must be tired. It is late. Why not go and wind down whilst I finish dinner and get this young lady to bed?"

Henry strode up to her and gave her a short peck on the lips. He could see some of the old Vanessa in her eyes, but she was older and more like an old friend than a sexy wife in his mind. The feelings he had felt as he held Eliza's hand were starkly absent as he stood close to Vanessa.

"Good plan. I am going to have a quick swim and shower. What time shall we meet in the kitchen?"

"Oh, erm, let's say 8.30? Is that enough time for you?"

He looked at the clock. "Perfect." He said.

He turned around, raced up to get his work clothes off. A swim was what he needed. Yes, a few lengths and something would make sense to him.

Five minutes later and he dived into the pool. The water brought his stiff body to life, and as he powered his way up and down the length of the pool, images of Eliza kept filling his mind. He imagined touching her soft neck. He longed to kiss her pink, full lips. He wanted her. He wanted her badly. It was a deliciously dangerous game, and the thrill of it was almost too much for him. The ultimate test of wit and skill. Could he capture his prey without getting caught himself? Now this was just what he needed. One flip later, and his mind woke up again. 'NO! Henry, stop being such a prick! What on earth are you thinking? This is not good at all.' He shut his eyes. His heart was racing faster than normal.

His thoughts and his feelings were at loggerheads. He had to keep control of himself. This was a route that could be a disaster for all that he had achieved. He had to conquer this. Maybe he needed more exercise. Yes, that was it. He would start running. That should cool off the embers a bit. He had a cold shower after his swim and went in for dinner. Yes, dinner smelled lovely. Vanessa wasn't a bad wife at all. 'Focus Henry!'

Chapter 7
Escalating Danger

Ibrahim sat at the table with his family. He was distracted and contemplating what approach he needed to take. He was not going to let Henry get his way this time. He had to find allies. People who could help him expose Henry and, at the same time, not compromise Eliza's reputation. He knew well that Henry worked fast, so time was not on his side. The key was not to react. He needed to plan and approach this project like a complex operation. Weigh what was known against what was not. To explore the best avenues to go down. What challenges might he face? Where do his threats lie? He needed to have a contingency for every option before he even moved one centimetre.

This was like those moments where, as a surgeon, danger was ahead, and as he approached that tiger country, that place where all hell could break loose, every possible eventuality was covered. The first task was to observe and reflect. Ideally, reflect with someone he trusted. Someone with their moral compass switched on and perhaps also less affected by Henry at a subjective level. The answer was clear: he needed to observe things through the eyes and mind of Jemimah. Yes, he needs to find a moment to meet with her and talk things through. He had worried so much about it that it was affecting his every moment, even his time with his family. There had to be a way of putting this issue in the right space in his head. At that point, there was nothing else he could do, so he whispered a short prayer under his breath and focused on his children.

The next day started in the usual way, with his prayers and a light breakfast. He kissed the children goodbye and kissed the forehead of his wife, Aisha, before heading out to work at the usual time of 7.30 am. The day was beautiful, with morning sunshine bathing the red tulips in the garden. The air was fresh and fragrant, and he took a deep breath in, reciting Bismillah as he got into his car. God-willing today would bring his answers and comfort.

As he turned to the hospital, he spotted Jemimah's little yellow Morris. It was a car that looked almost alien in the consultant car park, which was otherwise saturated with shiny Mercedes, BMWs, Teslas, and Range Rovers. He loved that she didn't need anything showy. That little Morris was more stylish than any other car there, Ibrahim thought.

Walking into the trust, he was focused. He knew that Jemimah would be in her office. This was her admin morning, so there was a chance to speak to her. He walked down the corridor in a contemplative frame of mind. His brow was slightly furrowed, and his posture seemed to weigh down in thought. Bernie was there, starting the day as all days did, and for a second, he escaped his thoughts to say good morning to his old friend. Bernie was to Ibrahim a stabiliser, a trusted constant, and not seeing him at the start of the day was something that Ibrahim could not imagine.

"Ah well, good morning, Ibrahim. You look deep in your thoughts today. I hope everything is OK at home."

"Good morning, my friend. Yes, the family is absolutely fine. Thank you for asking. My thoughts are entirely on this place."

A knowing look showed on his face. "Well, I hope that you will fix whatever troubles you today."

"Me too, Bernie. Me too. Have a lovely day, and thank you for making this place so welcoming. I can't thank you enough. Sorry."

"That's very kind of you to say that. I'm just a small cog in this wheel, but seeing lovely people like you brightens up my day."

They parted with kind smiles and a feeling that both of them needed. That feeling of being valued and noticed. That feeling of mattering and knowing it. In their different ways, both men had struggles with that in the same workplace. They both passed the many wall-mounted copies of the trust slogan.

As Ibrahim approached the door of Jemimah's office, he stopped. There was someone in there with her. Henry was there with her. 'Damn! What is Henry doing in there?' He was now in an awkward place. The corridor was a long one, and his own shared office was nowhere near it. This was not a corridor where one could just hide. What if Henry came out now? He had to have a good reason. 'Think, think, Ibrahim. Think of a reason…ah yes!' He was running a medical student study afternoon that month and needed some help with the practical part. He would ask Jemimah if she was interested in helping. Why he hadn't just called her on the phone about it or emailed her was irrelevant. It sounded credible, and that was all that mattered. He walked towards the door, swallowed hard, and knocked rather more feebly than he had intended.

"Come in," she said. "Ah, good morning, Ibrahim. You're in early today. Sorry, can you give us two minutes, please, and I'll be all yours? Could you just wait outside for two ticks, please?" She smiled apologetically. "We are just finishing up."

Ibrahim stepped out of the door and waited in the corridor. He could still see Henry's eyes burning into him, but in his posture, there was a message of superiority as he walked out. To Ibrahim, Henry was the devil now, and he didn't care what he thought of him. All of a sudden, he felt strong, and he had no intention of bowing down anymore to Henry. This was a new and unusual feeling. Why had it taken him so long to realise that he had a right to be respected too? It was time to change the game. It was time for Henry to realise that there were other ways to be. If his expensive education had not taught him that, then life would now fill in the gaps.

The time spent waiting in the corridor felt much longer than the few minutes it lasted. Thoughts and words raced around Ibrahim's mind as he refined what he would say to Jemimah. It was difficult because, even now, his thoughts were pre-emptive, unsubstantiated, and risky. He worried that it might be too early to say anything, but at the same time, he knew in his heart that Eliza might be in danger. He had to do something.

The door swung open, and Henry charged out.

"What brings you here, Ibrahim?"

"Oh, just something I needed to ask Jemimah. Nothing to worry about."

"Right…" Henry was non-plussed that Ibrahim had not spilled the beans. He hated not knowing everything. "Well, don't be late for the clinic. We have 45 patients today."

"No, I won't be late, as you know. I will see you in clinic, Henry," his voice was stronger and more assertive than usual. His posture was taller too.

Ibrahim turned away from Henry and entered Jemimah's office. Henry was a little surprised by Ibrahim's tone. The cocky bastard would soon be back in his place if he had anything to say about it. He paced away, troubled by the change and curious to know what it meant.

"Sorry about that, Ibrahim. I was wading through the usual hospital treacle with Henry. How are you doing? I haven't had a chance to chat with you for ages. Is everything OK?"

"No, it has been too long, Jemimah. I thought I might swing by for just that reason. You seem swamped with work. Anything I can help out with?" Jemimah's desk was covered in small heaps of documents, notes, and letters. She was a proverbial organised mess, yet strangely, she always seemed to be perfectly on top of things. Jemimah never did things in the same way as everyone else, but she was brilliant at what she did.

"Yes, I've forgotten what colour the desk is!" she laughed. "When one pile is conquered, another magically appears. Is your desk like this, Ibrahim?"

"Sometimes it is, but I tend to plough through mine like a farmer. I like it clearly because I like to draw things, especially when I am planning study days and tutorials. I love the sight of a clear sheet of paper in front of me, ready to be filled with ideas."

"Yes, your tutorials are legendary, Ibrahim. Have you not thought about applying for a promotion to consultant? You do so much for this department, even up to on-calls and extra work; in every way, you are like a consultant minus the title and benefits. I would be happy to support your application if you were interested. I hear the Certificate for Eligibility for Specialist Registration (CESR) pathway is easier these days."

"That is so kind of you. Yes, I would love to, but the last two times I tried, Henry told me not to bother. As he is the clinical lead for the foreseeable future, I suspect that that is not likely to change for some time. I have collated all of the evidence, though, just in case."

His face demonstrated the despondency that had grown within him. The years of belittling had stifled his courage to dream of more. The familiar brick walls in front of every ambition had gradually eroded away, his courage to believe in something better. Jemimah could see that, and it angered her that the system could do this to such a capable person. She decided at that very moment that she would invest some of her time in rebuilding Ibrahim. Henry was not the only consultant here, and she fancied a new project. 'Project Lift Ibrahim.' Yes, she liked the sound of that. By the end of this year, Ibrahim will be a consultant.

"So, what else can I do for you, Ibrahim?"

"Well, there are two things I want to discuss with you. The first is easy. Do you remember the med school surgical study week I was running at the end of the month? Well, I need some helping hands with the practical stations on the second and third days. That would be the 27th and 28th of January. Do you think that you might be able to help with either of them, please?"

"Yes, it sounds like a great week and a huge project to make work. I would love to help. In fact, let me check my diary now and book you in before anything else sneaks in there. Let me see. The 27th is my admin day, and I don't have anything else booked, so you can have me all day on that day. Sadly, the 28th looks like a no. I'm doing an extra list all day. Would that be alright?"

"That would be more than alright. Thank you so much, Jemimah. I will email you a draft plan for the day. Please make suggestions for any improvements. The more heads, the merrier. I think it will be a fun day for all." His face lit up as he spoke about the study day. His passion for teaching was infectious.

"Now, what was the second thing?" Jemimah asked.

The colour and smile drained from Ibrahim's face. His posture changed, and Jemimah was suddenly worried.

"What is the matter? You look worried. Sit down and tell me."

Ibrahim sat on the chair next to Jemimah. He was tense and fidgety. His eyes wandered as he searched for the best way to start. Once it started, there was no going back. He felt anxious and swallowed hard.

"To be honest, I don't quite know where to start. Even mentioning it here at work feels wrong. Is there any way we could meet somewhere outside and talk about it over coffee, please? I think it is something that needs space. Are you free later today?"

"God, Ibrahim, you're scaring me. Yes, yes, of course we can meet. Let's go somewhere where we can talk privately after your list. Are you still on admin this afternoon?"

"Yes, I am. Shall we go to the Orchard Café? The cakes there are lovely, and the gardens are open at this time of year too, so we can talk without being overheard."

"Good plan I haven't been there for ages. Let's meet there at 1.30 pm shall we?"

"Thank you, Jemimah. I'm very grateful." A look of relief had spread across Ibrahim's face. He no longer felt isolated in his concerns.

"Don't mention it. That's what friends are for," Jemimah's warmth dissipated all of Ibrahim's tension at that moment. He smiled and left the office. It was clinic time, and he walked with an air of relief. Even though nothing much had been said, the sensation of not being alone in this nightmare was like a warm hand on his back. Jemimah had been the right person to approach. She was the voice of reason and knew well what Henry was capable of and how to handle him. If there was one thing that was certain, Jemimah did not worship Henry but had a crafty knack of not showing it.

The clinic was another opportunity for Ibrahim to observe Henry with Eliza. He felt calmer about it and, in some ways, was able to challenge his thoughts. Nonetheless, it was clear that there was a very different body language that Henry expressed with her than he did with any of the other juniors. Perhaps it was just familiarity? In the end, Eliza was in her second year with the team. He was hoping his suspicions would just go away. Wishing so hard, until the last ten minutes of clinic, when Henry walked out of clinic with Eliza and his hand reached out to place itself on the small of her back as they passed his surgery room. They were oblivious to everyone, talking happily together about a case they had seen at the clinic.

"Oh my God!" Ibrahim felt sick again. "I need to get out of here," he thought. He finished seeing his last patient, hurriedly completed the last few dictations, and rushed out without saying his usual thank you and goodbye to the staff who had helped with the clinic. The nurses noticed how strange he had been to the whole clinic and were wondering what the matter was. How could they not have noticed what he had? Were they, as a whole, so in love with Henry that he could do no wrong? Had Henry had his way with them too? Was there no limit to how low his position of privilege could go? Ibrahim was battling with so many thoughts. His mind raced, and he was consumed with resentment towards Henry that he had suppressed for years. In many ways, he had learned how to bury the pain of being ignored and undervalued, so long as all that was wrong was directed only at him. Now that the perpetrator of his misery was threatening someone else—someone vulnerable—the carefully buried emotion was overflowing from within. It was like correcting this would somehow also correct everything else. It was a battle between subjective pain and objective reason. Which would win?

Chapter 8
Unplanned, Yet Prepared

On-call days risk throwing the surgeon out of their comfort zone, being unpredictable and erratic, but training has in some ways compartmentalised that confusion into an opportunity to enjoy the stimulation of urgency, the opportunity to be the hero and save the day. For that reason, surgeons often thrive under the pressure of such periods, and today was Jemimah's turn. Because erratic and Jemimah did not go together on call days with her were like all days, understated and in her control. Having registrars help and leaving them to do the ward rounds allowed a little time to do a bit of admin before heading to emergency theatres. She had a heads-up last night that there was an ischaemic foot sitting on the ward that probably needed to go to theatre. A common problem in vascular surgery and in smokers and something that often ended up with amputation after a few attempts at salvage, this was what was waiting for her attention today.

Jemimah headed to the Oyster Ward, which was a vascular ward. It's a relentlessly busy place with that familiar, musty aroma of impending work to do with an ever-populated line-up of patients with failing blood vessels, excruciatingly painful ulcers, and palpable tiredness that accompany increasingly sleepless nights. It could be said without question that the ward was never the favourite place of any vascular surgeon but, like all waiting bays, provided an efficient way of processing work that needed to be done now, soon or never. Accompanying these were those patients whose consequent disabilities left them waiting seemingly endlessly for modifications at home, a care package, or discharge to somewhere other than home.

For cases like the one waiting for her attention today, Jemimah always wished there was a way to cure the problem, but as those ever-returning smokers inhale relentlessly on their cigarettes, coating their dwindling blood vessels with gristle-like atheroma and plaques, the battle was one she could never win alone. What could she do if the patient didn't care or couldn't fight the battle of addiction that wasn't curing their stress but now instead causing more? It was as if the battle was not surgeon against disease but addiction versus tired warrior. Addiction usually wins, and life or limbs lose.

For Jemimah, there was always a feeling of sadness when the findings of scans and examinations showed the end was nigh for a limb or worse. She had never lost her desire to do her utmost to help, but as maturity had grown, like all wise surgeons, she had also learned when not to operate. It seems almost odd to think of a surgeon who doesn't want to operate, but it is also the last benchmark of life's training as a surgeon. The measure of insight, reason, and experience culminating in a decision and a conversation that the patient often doesn't want to accept.

Today was not quite that bad, as Geoffrey Bourne, a 65-year-old male with a smoking history of 60 pack years, was delighted to hear. He was a retired miner, and as she looked into his tired, desperate eyes with heavy lids, she could see that his world was one that was so far separated from her own that she could only imagine what life down a mine was like and how fresh air was elusive even without cigarettes. All those years of toil for an industry that disappeared with the click of a politician's proud finger, leaving thousands impoverished and betrayed. Geoffrey was such a man with the double no-no of smoking and diabetes, and yet through all the years of hardship, he still retained a smile and sense of humour that made Jemimah admire his resilience and courage.

Today, she was going to do everything she could to save his foot. The foot was cold and pulseless, and early gangrene had started to set in. The pain over the last few weeks had kept him awake day and night. The scans showed extensive calcification of the arteries. A pretty appearance to look at, like snow-laced trees in the mountains, but also a sinister one. Only an emergency bypass would save the foot and potentially his life, so she sat with him and explained the surgery to him. The inevitable list of all that might go wrong and the benefits of trying followed the usual automated spiel of consent. A pause followed next whilst waiting to hear of concerns and arrival at the moment of consent and a signature. That little signature authorised the next step, surgery. Salvage or lose.

Thoughts of an earlier conversation with Ibrahim had been put to one side, and her resolve to get started subsumed all else. Jemimah was a meticulous surgeon, and an unplanned emergency operation demonstrated this more than anything.

As she walked down the corridor towards the theatre with Sarah, the registrar was quiet and focused. Surgical training had taught her to say little and prove much, particularly as a woman in a man's world where one mistake was a catastrophe. She thrived under pressure, excelled beyond all of her training counterparts, and developed a cool edge that many found both alluring and intimidating. Nonetheless, junior doctors loved working with her. She was an impressive surgeon, yet she was also elegantly understated. She had learned that hubris was largely a men-only item of attire.

As they reached the main theatre suite and met the team, she looked at the clock and remembered her plan to meet Ibrahim after her operation and his clinic. 'That leaves three hours, including anaesthetic time. Hmmm, tight but possible' she thought. She wondered what it was about. 'Had he had a complication he didn't want to discuss with Henry? One didn't associate Ibrahim with complications, though. He was a very solid and reliable surgeon. If that wasn't the case, what could it be?' Now was not the time to ponder possibilities. Now was Mr Bourne's moment.

As she scrubbed, she thought of the scans and all of the pitfalls she might encounter in a leg that was not only affected by atherosclerosis but also had the dreaded middle artery calcification that promised poor recipient vessels for the bypass and no easy solution.

"So, Sarah, as exams are approaching, what can you tell me about the limitations of the Rutherford System of staging in cases of chronic limb threatening ischaemia?" Jemimah was particularly well-read and loved any opportunity to teach the junior team. In many ways, the teaching not only evaluated the effectiveness of training but also kept her up to date.

Sarah was an excellent registrar and protegee of Jemimah. She was very intelligent, but she also had a great hand in surgery. She was going to go far; Jemimah knew that, and somehow, she reminded her younger self a little, and yet, she was hopefully going to live a more normal life than Jemimah hoped. Or perhaps she was to be another woman in surgery, ready to hand over her home life to her career in order to rise to the top and lead.

Sarah proceeded to present the latest research and papers in the way of the senior trainee. Every moment was a fellowship practice opportunity, and she commanded that moment. After citing all of the research, she went on to discuss trials, and in that one moment, it was crystal clear why it took so long to train a surgeon. It was not about what was printed on paper. It was clear that no test was absolute, no treatment was definite, that all evidence has limitations, and that this was significantly less easy to predict with concomitant advanced diabetes.

"A very good response, Sarah. So, what do you think is the likely outcome with Mr Bournes leg? And the rest of him?"

"I am predicting that despite the suggestion of incomplete calcification in the tibial artery, the clinical appearance is likely to be dire, despite collateralisation. I'm predicting that you will choose to amputate," she finished with an upward slant, her tone as though asking a question, but not.

"Yes, I fear that his risks of being unstable anaesthetically are high. We are in a quandary here, balancing the desire to save limbs and also to not end life. I have spoken to Dr Green, who is anaesthetising today, and he is concerned that, with poor exercise tolerance and other signs of more central involvement than anaesthetically, the risk of an adverse event is high. In light of his assessment, my threshold for a cut-and-run approach is high. I'd like Mr Bourne to not die today if I can help it," Sarah nodded in agreement as they approached the theatre in a subdued manner.

The team was ready, and the briefing was done. Images were put onto the screens, and Jemimah and Sarah scrubbed.

"Certainly, it shows again why AI and algorithms are crude measures and no answer for the many cases presenting like this, doesn't it?" Jemimah asked as she turned into her gown and handed the tab to the runner. She walked to the table. Autopilot was fully switched on. This was a consultant case.

As the cold leg was prepped and opened, Jemimah's fingers palpated the vessel.

"I will mark him for the Bruckner technique to close in light of the poor vascularity here, I think," she was talking aloud to convince herself rather than teach this time.

The only sound was the heartbeat sound on the anaesthetic team. It was irregular. Atrial fibrillation befits a man with advanced narrowing of his arteries.

Jemimah took a deep breath, and her head shook slightly.

"This tissue is too far-gone, Sarah. We cannot save this leg."

She looked up at Dr Green.

"Simon, how is he doing at your end?"

"I'm struggling to keep his pressure stable; I think the sooner we get him off the table, the better. What are you planning to do?"

The theatre thought ball was bounced back to her, and she had decided.

"Let's amputate and close. Give him a chance. Are you keeping him asleep after Simon?"

"We will have to see. I'm sending tropes off as he's just let flipped into heart block."

Things were not looking well for Mr Bourne, and Jemimah turned to the scrub team and instructed that the saw be ready as they were proceeding to amputate.

As if it were a normal thing, the leg was soon separated from the body, and the yellow bin was positioned to place it in. Thud! It was off. That toxic, painful, leg was no more. All bleeding was controlled, and the flap to repair the stump was sutured.

"How are you getting on, Simon? I'm almost done."

"Thanks. We need to get him to ITU ASAP and get an echo done on him. I think he has had an MI, but he is relatively okay. Let's keep things controlled whilst we assess the damage."

The case was finished with a feeling of tired resignation. Was there elation? No. Was there a sense of relief that the patient was alive? Yes. Was this really over for Jemimah? No. Not yet. Her brain was subconsciously working through the surgery and findings. Everything was recapped away from the zone of pressure. Now she would evaluate the outcome. She was pleased Mr Bourne was alive, but the next few days would determine if this was just a temporary window or a door through which he would be able to leave the hospital and survive this disease that was ultimately going to be his end.

In the one and a half hours of surgery, Jemimah was in that moment and only that moment. She was in command, and her goal was singular. Mr Bourne. As she stepped away from the table and threw her gloves into the bin, she stretched her back and took a deep breath. She looked at the clock and then at Sarah.

"Happy to write the op notes?"

"Yes, just doing that now."

"Simon, are you happy? Shall we do the time-out?"

"Yes, I'm as happy as I can be. Let's time-out."

The WHO sign-out checklist was carried out with answers given in synchrony like a well-oiled machine, and Mr Bourne was transferred to ITU.

"Right, I'll ring his wife and head off now, Sarah, if you're ok. Team, would you like a debrief?" All shook their heads and said that they would just carry on with the next case.

Sarah turned to Jemimah and said, "All is good, here. I'll finish up and will call you if anything else comes in."

"Thanks."

Jemimah was glad that she was meeting Ibrahim now. She needed the air and was also intrigued to know what it was all about.

Chapter 9
Briefing

The Orchard Café was a local delight situated in the orangery that crowned the beautiful lavender-scented parterre of Beaufort House. It was always a surprise to find a perfectly proportioned stately home at the end of the sweeping, lime-tree-lined driveway, just ten miles away from the heart of Saint's Bay. It was sitting at the top of the valley, looking out to the estuary beyond, and in every way, it provided the most perfect of positions to feel literally on top of the world. That mobile phone reception also worked; there was an added bonus. It was Ibrahim's favourite place, and he loved bringing his children there to run around the gardens. He loved walking through the old house and wondering what his own family home in Nigeria looked like with all its grandeur.

A replica of the life that was stolen from him and his mother. Somehow, he felt at home with this local substitute. Today it was his safe place, a place where he could share his thoughts with a trusted friend. He had known Jemimah since she was a registrar, and they had instantly liked each other. There was an effortless ease that circulated around them, as though they both shared a connection that they could not quite define. He knew that they weren't connected, but he also knew that Jemimah was not really English by blood. He felt sorry for her when she told him her story of how she was abandoned. She did not know where her family was from or, in fact, who they were. Who left her, and why? His loss as a child somehow made him a person whom Jemimah could relate to. She saw him as a person who understood what it was to not know something about their family. So many unanswered questions. So many feelings of incompleteness.

Ibrahim arrived first and chose his favourite table in the corner next to the tulip tree, which never failed to fascinate him. The luscious leaves, which were halfway between sycamore and fig in shape, created a beautiful shade in the glazed house that it had grown in for over eighty years. Surreal yellow tipped buds were scattered throughout its branches, and Ibrahim was visibly excited as he realised that in only a few weeks it would start flowering with its enormous tulip flowers. It seemed improbable to see such an exotically perfect flower in such a temperate climate. In many ways, he thought of how that flower resembled his mother. She was beautiful, delicate, yet hardy and strong, a survivor. As he gazed upwards at the tree, Jemimah walked in and joined him.

"Gosh, I forgot how amazing this place is. Great choice, Ibrahim," she had a smile that had the ability to touch any soul, and Ibrahim felt a sense of relief that he had sought her advice.

"It is my favourite place. Somehow, I feel at home here, and when things get to me, I escape here to heal. I seem to come so often these days that I know all the staff by first name. What is that saying about me? Apart from that I have a reason for getting fatter," he laughed.

"Well, that is a definite way to get the best cakes, I bet!" Jemimah laughed and had a teasing smile on her face. Her expression soon changed, though, and her eyes wandered around the room as she shifted her mind to her working life.

"There is something truly relentless about the NHS these days, and finding moments of opportunity for hobbies and life seems to be the only way to survive. You find peace with your family and here in this place; for me, I need the woods, going for a run or doing like we are doing today, and eating cake or great food. For Henry, it is hunting. We all have something to escape to, but in many ways, I feel that the human side of being a doctor is becoming more and more taboo. To err from the production line is a sign of weakness. That drives me crazy. I always wonder what would happen to me if, God forbid, if I ever had a bad day and made a mistake. Would they judge me as a human or as the robots they want us all to be? Do you ever feel like that?"

"Did the case go badly?" If there was one thing, what a surgeon says and what lies beneath are often incongruous.

Jemimah shook her head.

"Tricky case. I couldn't save a leg for every single reason you could think of. Calcified, necrotic soft tissues, unstable anaesthetically, etc., and he had an MI on the table. Depressing. He's in ITU now. Let's hope."

Ibrahim gave it a look that encompassed sympathy, shared experience, and knowledge. No words needed. Just that look.

"Regarding your question about the NHS, the answer is yes; I have never really felt like a visible person. I am an accessory to the few who are given the golden key to rise to the top. A long time ago, I learned that my path was carved very differently from the Henry's of this world and that I was destined to always exist in an echelon below. It has been my family and my faith that have kept me sane, as well as the knowledge that I am different. Knowing you has been a comfort too."

"I can see how badly you are treated by Henry and others, Ibrahim, and it makes my blood boil. He is clever and lucky, and his position in the trust makes it very difficult to challenge him. When I started here as a consultant, I tried to and soon learned that there were some battles best not fought. I learned how to compliment him and stroke his ego, and in return, he allowed me to develop my job plan and work in relative peace. I see how the nurses dote on him, and despite that, he keeps me relatively safe. It is as though he wants everyone to love him. The game, my friend, is to give him the impression that you admire him, even if you do not mean it. Make your life easy by keeping Henry at the top of the pile."

"If only things were that black and white. For years, I have played the yes sir, no-sir game with him. Still, he belittles me and crushes me. Time and time again, I have tried to look for friendship or even a glimmer of respect from him, and every time he beats me down. I cannot understand it. What does he gain from it all?"

"Ibrahim, you are thinking that Henry is a compassionate man. There, you are making the gravest of mistakes. He is a narcissist. He lives off the worship of others. His confidence masks his weaknesses, and everyone buys into the façade. Underneath is a man crippled by the hunger of his ego. There's a constant need for adoration and power. One day he will look around himself, and I fear he might only see the semblance of allies as everyone turns their back on him. As long as they think that pleasing him will get them what, they want they will follow him. One day they will see the other side of him, and that loyalty will disappear. One slip too far, and the worship will end."

"Ah, and I think that day may not be as far away as you think."

"Oh? What do you mean? Is this why you wanted to meet with me today?"

A smile appeared on Ibrahim's face. Jemimah understood everything. Perhaps this was not going to be so difficult to explain to her after all, following Jemimah's accurate synopsis of Henry.

"What do you think about the interaction between Henry and Eliza?" Ibrahim enquired.

Jemimah's expression demonstrated a calm, knowing smile. She was, as ever, not one to react but instead took on an almost psychiatrist-like enquiring posture, leaning forward slightly and fixing her eyes to his.

"I am suspecting you have seen something to make you ask that, Ibrahim. Am I right?"

"Haven't you? I wanted to speak to you about it because I was scared that my dislike for Henry might cloud my judgement. Now every time I see them together, I see something disquieting; I see it in their body language, in the way that he dotes on her, and in the blind admiration in her face as she looks up to him as TPD. But there is something more. Something more sinister, I fear. Oh Jemimah, it would kill me to just stand by and watch him take advantage of Eliza whilst she is distracted by her exams. She doesn't know what he is like." His voice seemed unusually impassioned, and Jemimah reached out and put her hand on his forearm.

"Slow down. Slow down. You are racing ahead of things. What EXACTLY have you seen?"

"Well, at first, I thought it was just a junior doctor admiring Henry, the surgeon and boss. That I can understand. He is in a position of awe, and she is in such a difficult space right now; but as the weeks have gone on, I have seen him putting his hand on her back, and yesterday I saw them get into his car together in the evening. Where could they have been going together? Am I seeing too much?" He looks imploringly at her, wishing for her to shake this craziness out of him.

"Ibrahim, what I want to say is that it is all fiction, but you and I both know that Henry is capable of some rather unorthodox things. This is not something you can just bring up, though. You need concrete proof and enough witnesses. In many ways Eliza needs to come forward and say that she has a problem with it. The problem is that if something is going on between them, they are two adults. What needs to be clear is whether anything has happened and whether Henry is abusing his position and role. Where the line is drawn is misuse of power, and there, Henry is a fool if he is playing this game in his role as TPD and a married man. It could land him in front of the GMC if Eliza is being put in a difficult place and speaks up, if this is coerced and not consensual. If they are, in fact, both willing parties, there is little we can do but be there to support her.

If it goes public, you know as well as I do that it will not be Henry that suffers most; it will be her reputation and her future. Neither of us wants that. We need to be clever and calm about this. Observe, document, and wait. Time will tell us how this will unfold."

"You are so right. I never thought about the consenting adults bit I confess, but that in itself is a grey area where one has power over the other. It will not be the first time a married consultant has wormed his way into the bedroom of a junior doctor or young nurse! I feel so sad for his poor wife. They have young children too."

"There you go again, anticipating the worst-case scenario! Stop it, Ibrahim. So far, what I see is a forty-something-year-old alpha male testing his virility as part of a premature midlife crisis. There's nothing particularly odd there if the target is a willing adult who is interested in a bit of flirting. Many marriages have survived worse and well, men are men. Apart from that, very little has happened worthy of escalation at this point, and it may still not evolve into anything much. It may just be one of those things that fades away as exams are passed, and Eliza moves on to her next job."

"You are so right. I think Henry has really crept under my skin. He has nibbled away at my common sense through his incessant nastiness. I need to keep my head up. I need to think more like you," he sighed slowly. "Thank you, Jemimah. You really are a great friend."

"Any time. Anyway, we have better things to put our energy into at the moment, like getting your portfolio up to scratch for that consultant promotion!"

"Do you really think I can get it?"

"Of course, I do. Pissing Henry off, however, might not be your smartest move. You know me, Ibrahim. When I get an idea in my head, I always follow it through. 'Project Lift Ibrahim' is on the top of my to-do pile, and we are going to make this happen! You mark my words. This is a project I think I need. The culture in the trust is becoming toxic and helping a friend rise, despite it gives me a sense of triumph in adversity. It will be good for us both! I need you as my consultant ally. Let's see if the two of us can't find a way to make Henry do what we need him to," she gave Ibrahim a cheeky grin and that wondrous smile that could stop him from leaving the room. Watching Jemimah, Ibrahim felt that anything was possible.

"Bless you. You really are the best. I shall take a calmer and more objective view of things and will immerse myself in my application. Now, onto cake! We have been so busy talking that we forgot to order!"

Jemimah laughed. "Forgot? Oh no, my dear friend. I didn't want anything to distract us from our cake moment. The delay was strategic. Cake cures everything. Now that was something med school forgot to teach us, but we know better," she had a broad, girlish smile on her face, and Ibrahim looked at her and wondered why no man had fallen for such a wonderful woman. Men these days were crazy if they could not see an angel like Jemimah. He looked around the room and spotted Deborah, the waitress. She smiled at him and came over.

"Ibrahim, where have you been? We have missed seeing you for the last few weeks. I was worried you had become bored of our cakes!"

"Dear Deborah, how on earth could anyone be bored of your wonderful cakes? I have been buried in work things for the last few weeks, and missing my weekly cakes was something that needed urgent redress. I'm here and hungrier than ever. This is my colleague and friend Jemimah, by the way. She loves cake almost as much as me."

They all laughed.

"Erm, Ibrahim, I think you may find that my love of cake is the greatest of all. I was distracted by the cabinet I spotted when I walked in. I cannot decide which one I want more. Debbie, which is your favourite?"

"Well, it is a tricky one as they are all good, but today, I'm going to be a bit biased and get you both to try the lemon, blueberry, and mascarpone gateau I have made. Let me know what you think of it. There is a little surprise in it that I think you will enjoy."

"Oh gosh, that sounds heavenly. Ibrahim, shall we order two slices of that one?"

"Yes. Absolutely. You will be astounded by Deborah's cakes. They are beyond perfect. Deborah, could we also have some filter coffee to go with the cake, please?"

"Coming up."

As ever, the magic of the orangery had worked into their hearts, and Ibrahim and Jemimah sat quietly with peaceful smiles on their faces. It was as though any problem would be solved by the wonder of that place.

Chapter 10
Money and Morals

The Hunters' Arms was Henry's local pub, and it was a place he liked to meet people. Even though he had his own office, some conversations were too private even for that. If privacy was needed, there was nowhere better than the Hunters' Arms. It was a unique place that was steeped in centuries of history and leant itself to conversation, discretion, and intrigue. The inn had been connected to the Monterriot estate that burned down during the 16th century. The smaller house that was built a century after the fire did not, however, retell the secrets that the inn had kept. The inn was the hidden gem of the estate, and that it fooled Queen Elizabeth I's men was something of a wonder. The Old Family Coat of Arms above the doorway was crowned with the date 1252, which was engraved at the heavy stone entrance. The ancient date heralded a place of mystery and atmosphere.

    Inside, it had evolved with the progress of the centuries that followed, as a testament to the wealth of the estate that it belonged to. The floor had worn flagstones that told of centuries of feet that had walked there before. Outside, the old coach house and stables were still standing, and today the stables housed the pub's own microbrewery that made its own ale, which was one of the gems of the region. Cooled in the cellars below the inn, Hunter's Pride was always served at the perfect temperature and quenched the greatest of thirsts. The dark oak beams of what would have been a great room in Tudor times framed the ceiling at the heart of the Inn and the large granite fireplace dating back to 1485 stood impressively, filling a large part of the wall at the end.

To the sides of the fireplace were insets in the stone, and on the right side, the inset marked the entrance of a mysterious spiral staircase that led down to a small room in a hidden cellar. The room was a priest hole, believed to have been designed by the ingenious Nicholas Owen himself, master of the priest hole who was some years later tortured for his role in hiding Jesuits and Catholics. Henry loved the stories of the old place, and had been at school with one of the descendants of the old family. He knew everything there was to know about the place and in some ways, it was an extension of his childhood and background. The Priest's Room, as it was called, could be hired out for meetings and romantic dinners as it was large enough to contain a small table and two chairs. In the corner was a glass display that contained a reproduction of a silver cross that was found there which reminded the modern visitor of the dark history of the nation and its turbulent relationship with the church.

Henry had reserved it for his chat with Dr Andrew McNair, his old university friend and colleague who also happened to be the Clinical Director (CD) of the surgical and anaesthetic division of the hospital. Andrew was a brilliant anaesthetist, and like Henry, was a keen hunter. From the day that Henry joined the trust, the two friends were on a mission to succeed in life, and both of them had a taste for the finest things and were chasing the money that afforded such a lifestyle. Although Andrew was greedy, he was not as devious as Henry, and in many ways, Henry had learned how to manipulate his friend to get what he wanted.

"So, Henry, are we making progress with getting the trust to outsource surgery to Holmfield Surgical Centre? I had Derek on the phone this week, asking about our progress. I'm guessing he needs capital for the extension he is building on the centre but can't make headway on the commissioning rights for vascular surgery work. The trust is holding control rather tightly, which isn't surprising, but the workload does keep going up. He keeps reminding me that he is promising us a rather good cut of the profits and a very interesting lump sum if we can get the commissioners and trust to play along."

"Yes, as long as we can look entirely independent of it on paper, it would be a nice little prize indeed. So far, I'm coming up a little stuck at the finance level. Remember, I told you that I was going to speak with Stacey in finance the other day? Well, she is a real stickler for the rules and is giving me nothing; if anything, she seemed unduly cagey. I'm not sure what that was all about. I also met with Rob to see how the waiting lists are looking from a divisional management perspective. Do you remember that I have been trying to get my varicose vein list to creep up, and all went well? Well, I've just found out that the bastard Ibrahim stepped in and offered to do some extra Saturday lists. I was completely kept in the dark about this! How the hell did that happen? I was trying very hard not to lose my temper, but mate, I was livid. Do you know anything about it? For God's sake, Andrew, you are the clinical director of the Surgery and Anaesthetics division; aren't you supposed to be the person authorising spending on extra lists? Surely one of us should have been told about them."

"Well, that is very interesting indeed. I am as unaware as you about it since I stopped doing weekend lists and the execs started talking about their new strategy called 'A New Way Forward.' Two months ago, the CEO was talking about it, saying that she was planning to give managers a bigger role in service efficiency drives. I wonder whether this is part of that. Her attempt to share the load may well have cut our arms off. If the management staff take control of the service, we will have little chance of making this work."

"Hmmm, well, their ideas only work if there are bloody surgeons to do the work. I need to get Ibrahim back into line. If he doesn't do the list, then maybe we can get management to look for resources elsewhere? The Achilles heel appears to be Ibrahim. Get him out of the way and this could still work out fine. Hmm, let me have a think about what to do," Henry pursed the corner of his mouth and looked thoughtful.

"Don't do anything rash, Henry. Ibrahim is a popular colleague and a good surgeon, and anything you do that affects him will earn the wrath of the managers and more. Be clever about this if you want to win the game. Let your head, not your fist rule this. I am still the CD, and the buck stops at my feet. Try not to get Mark involved because you know as well as I do that, he is the sort of Medical Director (MD) who will crush anyone who threatens that lovely retirement he is planning next year."

"Trust me. I will be positively Machiavellian about it. They will beg us to set up the service if I get my way, and Ibrahim can be distracted by other temptations that may send him to his own demise. I have a plan, and parts of it you probably do not need to know about quite yet." The glint of greed and power in Henry's eyes was intense, and Andrew suddenly was worried. Worried as much for himself as what Henry might do to Ibrahim. He wanted the plan to work but wished that it wasn't to the detriment of anyone.

"Henry, I need to know what you are planning if you want me to stay on board. I am not keen on breaking the law here. The money is good, but the cost must be measured. Keep me updated, and don't do anything I wouldn't approve of."

"Where is the hunting spirit I have always admired in you, Andrew? I would have never imagined you to fear a little excitement like this. Why have brains and influence if you can't use them? Besides, you have always known that we are stretching the rules by doing this. It is a game of how things are phrased, even if, ultimately, it is a conflict of interest in its truest sense. The way we plan to describe it and use Derek as our cover is still risky, but like all things, it is a measured risk. We are not the first to do this. I would rather we profit from this venture than from some bloody American private healthcare conglomerate or Whitehall crony that doesn't give a damn about any of us. This is the future my friend: privatisation by stealth. Let's get something out of it if we are to be the mugs doing the work."

"Yes. I agree with all of that except for the part where you plan to go after Ibrahim. What are you planning exactly?"

"Oh, I have a few ideas. Let's play a game of Russian roulette. Give Ibrahim a chance to win, but if he loses, we win. That way, he will have had choices, and nothing will have been forced. Let's dangle the poison cherry and see if he jumps and bites."

"Hmmm, that has not made me feel any easier about it. When you decide what you want to do, please tell me. Tell me everything, or I'm out."

Henry gave a perfunctory nod of his head without really making any promise at all. He was suddenly quite distracted with his plan. This could work out rather well indeed, and he would finally be rid of that presumptuous little Muslim. It's time to take back a little control of his patch and get the right people on the team.

Chapter 11
Hope and Wishes

Ibrahim knelt in Tashahhud, sitting at the end of his prayers with his hands held apart as he recited the last words of the Isha (nighttime) prayers. Today had been a good day; it had given him a lesson not to cloud his judgement with his emotions. What a blessing the words of Jemimah had been. They had brought calm to him again, and he thanked God for the opportunity to not err from the right path, the path of reason and respect. He felt focused again, and her words had given him a new lease of hope. It's a wonderful chance to perhaps finally be a consultant surgeon. He prayed for the courage to follow those dreams through to whatever that God wished for him and to always be grateful for the path that had been chosen for him. He prayed for wisdom and composure to never rise again to the torments inflicted by others. Ibrahim was once again himself, and peace returned.

He sat at the kitchen table with Aisha with a big smile on his face, and she laughed.

"What on earth is going through that mind of yours to bring out such a joyous face? You must tell me. I am bursting to know."

He laughed with her. "Am I not allowed to just be a happy man?"

"Now, Iba, my love, I have known you for many years, and although I know that I married the kindest and sweetest of men, I also know how to spot when you are hiding something. Today, that face says you are not telling me something. Something evidently lovely. Spill the beans!"

"Well, I might if you agree to make me my favourite eggy bread for breakfast."

"Sugar-coated blackmail!" She laughed out loud as she got up to prepare some eggy bread for him.

"Oh alright. You win. My stomach is already rumbling at the thought of that eggy bread. I hope you are having some too, so I don't feel too greedy." They were both laughing cheekily as the kitchen filled with the heavenly smell of hot, buttery bread.

With two plates full, they sat down opposite each other.

"Perfect! Absolutely perfect! You have won. So here is my secret: I met with Jemimah yesterday, and she has decided to support me in putting in a CESR application. At last, after all these years, I finally believe that I might be able to get there. Finally, become a consultant. That dream seemed so far away that I thought it would never happen. Can you believe it?"

Aisha's eyes lit up, and she jumped up to rush around and hug Ibrahim.

"Mashallah! Iba, this is wonderful, wonderful news! Now I can see why you had such a big smile on your face. Jemimah is such a lovely lady. Despite all of her own troubles in life, she always seems to do kind things for others. We should invite her over at the weekend for dinner. It has been far too long since she came here."

"Good idea. I'll text her today to invite her. You can make a big spread of her favourite food, and we can catch up properly with her. You are right, I feel awful that we haven't had her round for so long. I always forget that she lives alone. It is such a tragedy that she has never met a good man. Hey, perhaps we could invite Jeremy over as well and make it a bit of a double date? What do you think? I think they might be a good match, and even if they aren't destined for romance, she would have someone who might get on well with her as a friend."

"Do you know what it is? That is an amazing idea, Iba! I never thought of Jeremy, but now that you mention it, I think they could be a great match. They haven't met, but like we did, introductions through friends are always a good start. I know he is not a doctor, but he is in IT, is a keen runner, and is great fun to be around. They are about the same age, too. Yes, I think they have quite a lot in common. Let's try and get them together, shall we?" She had a cheeky smile on her face, and Ibrahim loved her so much for that.

Ibrahim and Aisha were feeling very happy that morning. After years of hard work and struggles that had at times felt relentless, it seemed that at last Ibrahim would be able to fulfil his ambitions in life completely. The impasse from associate specialist to consultant had over the years become like a millstone around his neck and, at times, weighed heavily on his mind and life. This new opening was like coming out of a coma. The world was the same, but this time it would be so much more. More, not because it was any different from other times, but because to him it was the unknown wonder of being treated with equanimity.

He was valued for all the hard work he had done without accolades, all the extra clinics and lists he had done that stole time away from his family; all the courses he had run without remuneration or gratitude, and all of the trainees he had supported, many of whom had become consultants over the years. He thought of all of the operations that he had done consistently to a high standard and never been acknowledged for, and the number of times people had looked at his ID badge and asked for a consultant at review despite him having done their surgery. He was tired of being seen as less than his white counterparts for reasons that had never made any rational sense to him. He wanted to stand in front of the photographs in the hallway and tell his father and mother that he had made it. That he was finally a consultant. He wanted to tell his mother and imagine the pride she would have on her face. Tell her that all those years of struggle and dreams for her had finally come to fruition. Her beloved boy had chased his dreams and reached them. Ibrahim dreamt of giving this last gift to her in memoriam.

Chapter 12
Power and Privilege

Jemimah had woken earlier than normal. The surgical day always started earlier than that of the physicians, and early risers were normal amongst them. She was distracted by her plans to sway Henry's prejudices and get Project Lift Ibrahim started. For her, the best way to gather thoughts was to run, so she slipped into her gear and set off into the woods behind her house. Yes, a few miles of running would give her ideas. Power hour.

Outside, it was one of those nondescript mid-grey days. There was little wind, and most people were still just stirring. There was the uplifting symphony of early morning birdsong that painted the air with the sounds of a hundred souls. The inquisitive robin darted from one branch to the next, teasing her as she ran. The river on the other side of the road tumbled along like the percussion to the birdsong, and there was a blissful air of peace around her. Jemimah loved the woods behind her house, and she turned off the road to enter the well-trodden path amidst the old mixed trees. Those rustling, sonorous trees gave the impression of a wind that she could not palpate on her skin, and ahead of her, a deer darted away. She felt so free amidst the nature that surrounded her.

A few minutes later, as her mind wandered happily, an unexpected sight shocked her back into reality. Yes Henry! He was running in front of her. Well, at least she thought it was Henry, but the outfit was definitely not his usual style. He looked rather flushed and uncomfortable, and his running style was at best unnatural. She wanted to burst out laughing but restrained herself as he bounced back in his baggy tee shirt, tracksuit bottoms, and bright white trainers.

"Good morning, Henry. Well, this is a surprise! I didn't realise you were a runner," Jemimah was in her element and not at all out of breath. Her skin was gently glowing, and her hair, tidily tied back. The contrast with Henry's more desperate and dishevelled appearance was like the reversal of their cars. The irony was blatant.

"Oh, erm hello, Jemimah," Henry was flustered and out of breath. "I didn't realise that you went running in the morning. I'm trying to get fitter. Back has been playing up recently."

Jemimah inwardly giggled awkwardly. Here, the great Henry had all his guards down and was standing here in front of and as she stood in front of her like this, she imagined him as a shy young schoolboy. Was all that he was just a lie? A show of bravado masquerading as a boy who never felt comfortable in his shoes. She had seen him with his son, Tom, and wondered whether Tom was more like Henry than Henry wanted to admit. Was the hunting and meanness just a remnant of his domineering father? A scar that had become, with time, a legacy in his persona? He had become his father. A man whom he resented.

"Yes, I woke up with loads on my mind, so I thought I would come out for a run to clear my head before my list. What about you? I'm sorry you are having a bad time with your back. Surgery is such a beast for that. Unlucky for you, who is so particular about posture too."

"Yes, it's a bugger. I am also realising that I am not a runner at all! This run has been painful. Any top tips for me?" They had both relaxed from the initial surprise of seeing each other.

"It is quite normal to hate running when you first start. Your body needs to acclimatise to it, so short, gentle runs and starting and stopping in bursts will help build your stamina and strength. Make sure you stretch out before and after, too, to prevent knots and pulls. Oh, and make sure you stay well hydrated. You might also want to get some proper running shoes because those tennis shoes are not great for mixed terrain like this," she looked down sympathetically at his now-muddy white tennis shoes. He grimaced and smiled apologetically.

"In many ways, I am rather pleased that it was you that I met here and not anyone else. Thanks for the advice. I shall get onto that right now. Oh, whilst I am thinking about it, I read your email last night about supporting Ibrahim in getting a consultant post. Yes, I think it may well be a good idea. Shall we meet up and look at his portfolio and application and see what he needs to do?"

Jemimah was surprised by this sudden supportive approach towards Ibrahim. She knew well how negative Henry had always been towards Ibrahim. What had changed? She was intrigued.

"Oh, er yes. That would be wonderful. Ibrahim has been working hard towards this, and if we can both support him in it, I reckon he will be eligible. When do you suggest we meet? I'm off next week, but I am just staying home, so if you have time to meet, I can pop by anytime."

"Great! Shall we say next Wednesday afternoon? I'm free after 3 pm. As you are off, shall we meet somewhere other than the hospital? Where would you suggest? Why don't you come over to mine and we can have a coffee with the documents spread out on the table? That way, we will have peace."

"Fabulous. I shall put it in my diary after my run. Have a great day, Henry, and thank you for doing this for Ibrahim. It means a lot."

Henry was basking in the compliment, and for a second, he forgot that his apparent magnanimity was all part of his plot. Ibrahim would fall for the trap as the enticement was handed out.

"Let's see how much of a consultant you really are," Henry thought as he bounced off towards his home.

Jemimah was still amazed, and she pondered what she had just seen and heard as she completed her run and drove towards the hospital for her theatre day. Could it really be that Henry was supporting Ibrahim? It sounded real, but something niggled under her rib. There was something that didn't quite sit easy with her. She just couldn't completely trust Henry.

On her way in, she bumped into Ibrahim. He looked happy, and his face showed a new brightness that she had not seen for a very long time.

"Ibrahim, good morning. You look very cheerful today. That is nice to see."

"Morning Jemimah. Today is a new day. I told Aisha about your kind offer to support my CESR application, and she was over the moon. It is like a dark cloud lifted yesterday, and our lives were lifted by your kindness. I revisited my portfolio and started rewriting parts. It is so strange how my despondency gradually crept into it over the years of failed attempts. This one feels different. Like somehow it might now happen."

"Yes, things are feeling more well-aligned. The Royal College also has a helpful guide for application, and guess what? I bumped into Henry on my run this morning, and he said he wants to help you get the promotion."

"Huh? You say Henry wants to support me? Was he drunk? I am astounded! Are you sure that is what he said?"

Jemimah was laughing.

"I was as shocked as you are. I confess that in all the years I have known Henry, he has never done anything altruistic. I'm still trying to work out what this sudden change in character might mean. Let's just enjoy the idea, at least, that Henry might have become a kind and generous man, shall we? Let's leave our suspicions and doubts until we have cause to pursue them."

Ibrahim slowly nodded, and his expression was now mixed with perplexity, suspicion, and surprise in equal measure. He wanted so much to believe that Henry had a little goodness in him. Jemimah was right. This was a time to be positive and focused. It was not a time to jinx this wonderful opportunity.

Chapter 13
Instincts

Eliza was suddenly feeling so much more positive about her exam after the last few study sessions with Henry. She had also taken the advice of Miss Withenshawe and joined a very focused and competitive regional junior doctors study group. It had taken her some time to muster the courage to find out what her peers knew. As time went on, she started to find computer screen reading easier, and her marks became consistently higher. Passing had become the norm, and she was no longer stressed about the exam; in many ways, she just wanted to get it over and done with so that she could start work on the clinical. Henry had been good luck for her. She felt grateful for his kind attention, and his daily WhatsApp messages to give her encouragement were now finished with an x that she thought was odd but probably something he does to everyone he knows well. Henry really was the kindest person on earth, and because of him, she was going to pass this exam.

    She stretched out as long as she could in her bed and reached her arm out to tug open the small floral curtain to her left. One of the many advantages of renting the smallest cottage on this planet was that everything was within reach from the regal position of one's mattress. The morning sun shone straight across the bedding, and its comforting warmth was palpable. The longer days of spring allowed for a decadent half hour extra in bed before the start of the day, and now that passing had become the norm in practice papers, Eliza felt a sense of calm around her. She glanced across to the wall in front of her and looked at the home-made calendar that she had made from old happy moment photographs; in the calendar boxes below, them was March 12th filled with a big red X for Exam Day. It was three days away, and she was ready. When she put that X on the calendar date for the exam, it mirrored her terror and anxiety about failing again.

Today, that red cross was a symbol of her passion, positivity, and determination. It had gone from a red alarm bell to something much more positive.

Dressed in her favourite orange dress, she smiled at her reflection in the mirror. One thing is for certain: Eliza Graham was not a stereotypical aspiring surgeon. She had about as much macho and narcissistic a persona about her as a lop-eared bunny. Her strength was her kindness, determination, and love of how surgery changed people's lives. She had loved crafts like painting and embroidery since she was a child, and the attention to fine detail had given her a good eye for surgery. Her suturing was always like a work of art, and she believed with all her heart in her dream to become a surgeon. She was not outwardly strong or impressive, like Miss Withenshawe, but she knew that she had the qualities to become a good surgeon. She just needed to convince everyone else of that. Now that Henry believed in her, she felt like the whole world would see it too. After all, wasn't half of the stereotype based on fiction and rumour? That was what her mum had told her, and her mum was someone who could have been anything she wanted if her parents had raised her to believe that there was more to life than just getting married at 21 and having babies. It was her mum who ignited her passion for doing medicine in the first place. Was it a vicarious dream of hers? Or was it just that she passed that little flame within her to her daughter when she gave her life? The passage of instinct and courage through the generations. Whichever it was, Eliza's mum was her greatest and loudest champion, and that was all that mattered. With her mum and Henry, Eliza could do anything.

The morning for Henry was not so peaceful. He crawled out of bed and put on his now more-appropriate running gear. He loathed running, despite having taken all the advice that Jemimah had given him. It made him so angry that he was not improving as fast as he wanted to. Was it age? No way! He was 46, for God's sake! He was in his prime, surely. He was good at everything, and he would conquer this sport or die trying! Maybe a personal trainer might work, although the idea of having someone boss him wasn't his first choice. The only advantage to this new discipline was that the morning runs helped keep his lust for pouncing on Eliza in control. He had become strangely used to messaging her, and his desire for her attention was no longer a devious thing in his mind. After all, he was a red-blooded man, and these feelings were normal, weren't they? He cared for her future, and there was an additional bonus in that he found her incredibly sexy, and he felt young being around her. He wanted so much to run his fingers through her wispy blond hair. It had been years since he had felt this way about anyone. His relationship with Vanessa was so different. They had been eager, passionate lovers in their twenties and married young. They had complemented each other in so many ways because Vanessa had given up nursing, let him do whatever he wanted, and made child-rearing effortless for him. With time, she had become like an accessory and comfort toy to him. Quiet, calm, and reliable. Always there. The excitement had faded into daily routines, and what he now craved was a little revival of some old fun. He saw that potential in Eliza. Her abundant positivity and passion had ignited a youthfulness in him, and he craved to explore this further. What he feared was that his feelings might not be reciprocated. Even if they were, how could he make it happen? His routine had become predictable, and Vanessa would soon become suspicious if things changed suddenly.

He jogged through the woods in deep contemplation. Perhaps the clinical exam sessions could become a reason for later evenings together with Eliza. After all, she would need to work on examination skills and anatomy. There is nothing better than palpating anatomy to bring it to life. He ran faster. His heart was beating strongly. The image he conjured of Eliza naked sent shivers of excitement through his body. Oh God, he wanted her so much. His instincts were completely clouding any common sense he might have had. This was the most exciting hunt he had ever done. Winning Eliza and not losing Vanessa. Pure and raw skills and risks. What a rush!

Chapter 14
Knowing

The alarm had been switched off, but still, Jemimah awoke at 6 am. There was a strange sense of guilt lying in bed, but today was a rare day off. She had to remind herself not to spring out of bed as she normally would. Annual leave was always a system shock, and Jemimah needed a few days to wind down when she took time off. Switching away from the urge to check emails and reply to them was a bit of an art for the established surgeon. Jemimah was instinctively meticulous about her work, and the idea of letting her inbox fill with unread emails was something that had tortured her in her first few years as a consultant. Recently, she left her trusted laptop locked in her work desk drawer on the last day. Her first day of leave was always carefully planned beforehand so that not a minute was left free to worry about work or other things.

The week before leave was always a frantic rush to ensure that every scan request, every pathology report, every new referral vetting, every letter, and every management task outstanding had been dealt with. Her secretary was as organised as her, and together they seemed to plough through the mountain of work like a well-oiled machine. Nothing outstanding was left to do, and they often took leave on, the same week so that the office of Jemimah Withenshawe was officially closed for the break. In the early years, her secretary felt compelled to message her and call her every day about new problems that needed her attention. With time, she learned that very few things needed her immediate attention. It was a discipline of life that was not taught. Training had demanded constant results and productivity. To work hard, play hard, and compete for the top was the culture of surgical training. It was engrained within all of her colleagues, and the 'soft stuff' was pooh poohed at.

Learning to pace herself was worked out the hard way, with the threat of burnout and isolation from overwork ringing like a loud wake-up call in year two of consultant life. 'It is a marathon, not a sprint' she often heard from her senior colleagues. It was so strange how those words seemed to just wash over her as she had dived into her philanthropic pace of life as a new consultant. It was her mentor who had helped her recognise that something within her was driving this desire to sacrifice herself. It was a battle within her to fix the things that she could so that the pain of never being able to find her parents would somehow shrink into oblivion.

Day one of leave would be a day of pampering and self-indulgence. The doorbell rang, and Jemimah ran down the stairs in her favourite ivory coloured Christy Bathrobe, and satin slippers. It was the DHL man who presented her with the parcel that she had ordered. She excitedly thanked him and took it to the kitchen. She would open it after her shower. This was something she had chosen for the day, and the first thing to do was freshen up and get dressed for a divine spa day at Beaufort House. This little treat to herself would complement that perfectly. She had booked a post-lunch massage so that she could get an early swim in before the pool filled with other people. Spa days were Jemimah's thing, and she had got them down to absolute perfection. After the shower, she put on her most floaty and pretty of maxi dresses and sandals, picked up a new holiday novel to read, and ignored the pile of letters that had just been deposited on the doormat by the postman. Today was spa day, and the post could wait.

Before leaving the house, she opened her present to herself. An exquisite box of Holdsworth Marc de Champagne truffles. It was only 9 am, but what the heck? The first powdery, intense chocolate landed on her tongue. Her mouth watered as it melted slowly on her warm tastebuds. It was like a perfect duvet of luxury embracing her. A satisfied expression erupted on her face, and all tension seemed to dissolve away. She popped the box into her yellow spa bag and set off in her Morris.

Like all of Beaufort House, a sense of peace and harmony was restored in Jemimah at the spa. The joy of sensuous aromatherapy scents and bubbling jacuzzis lifted her spirits, and the silence and warmth of the steam rooms replenished her. Relaxing with a decadent holiday novel was just what she had craved for weeks, and her mind soon forgot the pressures of her everyday life as a surgeon. Jemimah missed having someone to share her life with as she revelled in the fabulousness of the day.

Why had she not found that special someone? She had been rather surprised by the unexpected invitation from Ibrahim and Aisha to have dinner with them and meet a single friend of theirs. How intriguing! She pondered what this mystery Jeremy was like. If there was anyone she trusted at work, it was Ibrahim, so she was surprisingly excited about it. She pondered what she might wear. Should she take a cake for dinner? Would that look desperate? What if she couldn't stand him? How awkward would that be? She laughed at herself. For God's sake, Jemimah! You are 37 years old and a professional woman. It is not like you have never had a date before. This is serendipity. Enjoy it for what it might become.

On her way home, she sang songs and contemplated the next task in the day's diary. Phone her best friend Emma, whom she had not seen in over three months. Emma was Jemimah's oldest friend, and they were like sisters. They were so different in so many ways, but those differences were what had attracted them to each other, even in prep school. Emma was a bohemian, free spirit. Her life could not have been more different from Jemimah's, as she rebelled against every plan her parents set for her. She was a dreamer, and her imagination inspired the most beautiful sculptures and art. What she created resembled her. They were her dreams of living without barriers or labels. The women she sculpted were free and yet not brazen. Nudity was disguised behind exquisite carvings that looked like real silk or fabric.

The texture made the observer want to run their fingers along that fabric and imagine that somehow they could unravel the person behind them by pushing that cover away. The wonder of her art was in its mystery. Like her, she did not want her art to be fully exposed or understood. In many ways, that was why she had been drawn to Jemimah. In her closest friend was a mystery. An unknown. To her, Jemmy was like a beautiful sculpture. Perfect in every way, yet not like anyone around her. Jemmy was exotic and alluring, and her personality was as much a part of her upbringing as it was of the unknown genetic roots from which she had grown. Jemmy was the inspiration for Emma's life and creation, and the connection between them was profound and enduring.

"Em? Are you free? It's Jemimah."

"Hello. Tell me you are calling from a spa and are dressed in silks and smothered in oil."

"Oh yes. I followed all the rules. Laptop imprisoned at work. Work phone switched off. The post was ignored, and an extra-large box of chocolates was delivered. I just got back from the spa. I miss you. It's such a shame you couldn't be here."

"Complete bummer, and I'm so pissed off I missed out on the chocolates too. This exhibition in Munich is doing my head in. There are some big, big people here, so I am hoping for a few interesting commissions and to sell a few of my bigger pieces. OMG! You need to come here. It is teeming with rich people. There are lots of big, rich German men. Maybe we could grab one each and sort out the man thing in style."

They both laughed.

"Erm, have you had one bratwurst too many to inspire such thoughts of man grabbing? I confess, I have never quite got over my last experience of naked men in saunas. It just didn't quite set me off in the right direction, seeing all that unfamiliar sweaty naked muscle striding in and starting deep breathing next to me. NIGHTMARE! Nope, the English way suits me much more, thank you. Now you, my bohemian alter ego, might do quite well in Germany. I hope you took some pretty clothes with you for the exhibition."

"You really must lose the Victorian lady thing, Jemmy. It is not going to get you a man. Pretty clothes are so passé; these days, it is about letting the inner you hang out. No, this week I am wearing tight black leather garnished with silk and an anarchic hint of rebellion. I feel fabulous. I am one of the sculptures in my life! Besides, haven't you got a hot blind date this weekend? Have you managed to glean any more about the mystery man? What was his name?"

"Jeremy, and no, I know absolutely nothing about him. Ibrahim is a lovely person, though, and I trust him. He told me that I would probably convince myself that Jeremy was not for me if he only gave me a few facts about him, so this would be a blind date. He knows me rather well, doesn't he? This is the first time EVER that he has tried to match me, so I am thinking there must be something special about this one. As you seem to be far more style-savvy than me, what shall I wear?"

With Emma, Jemimah's guards all came down. She no longer exuded wisdom and composure. With her best friend, all her insecurities were exposed. Emma loved that about her. Her image was not all that was about her. She was her own fashion. The real Jemmy was so much more than just a surgeon. She was a complex masterpiece.

"Well, I know you won't feel comfy in something too trendy, but you must wear something that shows off your amazing figure and gives some room for temptation. Even if you don't fancy this guy, you have to make this evening one where you at least fancy yourself. You can't keep putting yourself down, Jemmy.

You need to show off what anyone with a brain can see. You are stunning. I say you choose a colour that brings out your best features. Why not wear that lovely light blue chiffon shirt and put on a skirt that comes just to your knees? That way, you can show off your amazing legs and an incy wincey hint of your breasts. Wear your favourite solitaire pendant to look expensive and dowse yourself in an exquisitely feminine perfume."

Jemimah made an awkward groan.

"Oh, Em, you know I hate meeting men. I always freeze and try everything to avoid questions about myself. I hate talking about myself and dread telling them that I am adopted. Who knows who I am? I feel like such a misfit. What if my parents are serving life in prison for murder or some other dreadful crime? Who knows? Being a surgeon gives me an identity at work, but as soon as I leave, everything floods back. Sometimes I go crazy with these restless feelings inside. Oh Em, how will I ever find someone when I do not know myself?"

"Jemmy, you have to stop this going round and round about it. Torturing yourself about a fictitious worst-case scenario is a crazy thing to do. Life has an uncanny way of revealing everything, and we both know well that answers rarely come when we want them to. What I see in my best friend is a beautiful, mysterious woman who also happens to be an amazing surgeon and friend. Your adoptive parents love you more than life, and every day you go to work and save lives. Sometimes the less is far greater than the lost. Trust me, Jem. The story will unfold in time, and until then, live life as though what isn't in this moment doesn't matter. One day, you'll see it never did. Love like you have it all, because what you do have is so much more than millions of people in this world. Now stop moping and start thinking of fab things to say to your hot date. This is an Emma order, and if you don't, I'm not coming to see you for your birthday. So, snap out of it!"

"You really are wonderful, Em. You're right. Whatever happens, I have it great right now. I am going to go and try on that shirt and think, DATE! I hope your exhibition is an absolute success and that Munich buys everything from your collection and offers you a German hunk for the week. Do tell me how you get on."

"That's the spirit. I'll send you pictures and updates. Tonight, I have the company of the magnificent Berndt. Oh gosh, he is HOT! Wish me luck."

Jemimah laughed again and wished her beloved friend much luck. Perhaps this week will be their week to find love.

On hanging up the phone, Jemimah went downstairs to make herself some tea. She stopped at the bottom of the stairs and looked at the pile of unopened posts. There was an envelope on top that looked intriguing. It was made of very high-quality paper and had 'STRICTLY CONFIDENTIAL' on the top. She picked it up and took it with her to read whilst drinking her tea.

She opened it slowly. It had a strangely weighty feel to it. The paper was thick, and the colour was ivory, not white. It felt significant. She was nervous, even handling it. As the flap peeled open, she could see a single letterheaded sheet of paper. The letterheads read Bevan, Levy, and Walters Solicitors, London.

Dear Dr Withenshawe,
THE ESTATE OF MISS VALERIE ETHINGTON

I have been instructed to be the legal executor of the will and testament of the late Miss Valerie Etherington. I would like to advise you that I have now completed the administration of the abovementioned estate in all matters except for the one most relevant to yourself. The instructions that she left in her will are of a delicate nature and would be best delivered in person. I would be most grateful if you could contact my office at your convenience to arrange a date to attend a hearing of the will and allow you the opportunity to discuss its contents, should you so wish. I would recommend that you do not attend alone, as the information is of a very personal nature and may be distressing to you.

I look forward to hearing from you.

Yours sincerely,
Rupert Levy
Senior Partner, Bevan, Levy, and Walters Solicitors
Lincolns Inn Fields
London WC2A

Jemimah reread the letter three times. She had a cold tingle on her cheeks, and her ears were ringing. Who was Valerie Etherington? Was this what she had been waiting for, for so long? So many questions flooded into her head. She felt sick. She felt faint. Her heart was beating hard in her chest, and for reasons that were difficult to explain, she burst into tears. She cried from shock, from fear, and from confusion. She did not know why the tears kept flowing, but she cried.

She had no idea what the letter was telling her, but in her heart, she knew. She knew that, in some ways, Valerie Etherington was a link to her past. Was she strong enough to go and find out what the will said, now that she had a chance to know some truth? How would she cope with it if it was not good news? Who could she take with her? Was it appropriate to take her adoptive mum? How would she feel if it was about her daughter's biological parents? What would her parents say if she didn't tell them? Would they forgive her? What was the right thing to do? Suddenly, Jemimah wanted to be anywhere else, but there. She rushed out of the house and got into her car. She was not in a good place to drive, but at that moment, it was not her mind leading her actions; it was her heart. She drove for an hour. She did not compute where she was driving, but her instinct was to take her home to her parents. The parents who had raised her as their own. Suddenly, the only place she wanted to be was in the arms of her mum.

"Jemimah! Darling. What's the matter?" Margaret Withenshawe was surprised that Jemimah had arrived unannounced and rushed out to her daughter. Jemimah climbed out of the car and tumbled into her mother's arms. Suddenly, she was a young girl again, and her heart was aching for security.

"Oh, mum, something came up today. I wasn't expecting it, and I don't know what to do. I don't want to hurt you or dad. I am so confused, and yet I need to know. What shall I do? What shall I do?"

Words poured out of her in no sensible order. She was inconsolable. Her mother and father rushed to surround her and console her. They were horrified. They had never seen Jemimah like this.

"Now, my love, you need to calm down and come inside. You are safe here. You are home," Michael, her father, was a calm and gentle man, and his words soothed her. His arm around her shoulder felt like a big blanket, and the tears stopped flowing. They walked into the house and sat down in the lounge. A glass of water was handed to her, and both parents sat beside her.

"Now, darling, you need to slow down and start again. I couldn't understand what you were saying outside, and trying to talk about it will hopefully help make more sense of whatever it is," Margaret had always been a practical and sensible mother. A lot of Jemimah's everyday habits had been learned from her mum.

"I'm sorry to have landed on you both like this. I couldn't think of where else to go."

"Oh, darling, this is your home. We are here for you."

"Thank you. I'm so lucky to have you both. I really am," she looked at them both with grateful, teary eyes. It was indeed the greatest of blessings that she had the parents she did.

She cleared her throat and blew her nose into a tissue.

"What I am going to tell you is not something I think any of us were expecting. Before I tell you what I received, could you go through again what you knew about my past before you adopted me, please? Have you ever heard the name Valerie Etherington?"

Her parents looked at each other initially, looking blank, and then the blankness was replaced with worried expressions, and her father went to the chest of drawers in the corner and took out an envelope. He handed it to her.

"This is all we have. We do not know anyone by that name, but this letter was left in your Moses basket at the hospital, and it does look like it was written by someone with her initials."

The envelope was aged and crumpled in the corner. Jemimah opened it and took out the small piece of paper inside. The writing was shaky and difficult to read.

Please take this baby girl and give her a home where she will be cared for.

One day she will know what happened, but until then please give her a safe home and tell her that her name is Jemimah, which means little dove. She was born abroad on the 9th May 1981, in a country far away. Tell her she was always loved.

VE

"Oh my God! The letter was written by Valerie. VE. Do you think she was my mother? Oh God, no! But she is dead. No, no, no! Why would she wait to tell me everything after she had died?" Jemimah's eyes welled with tears.

"Darling, we do not yet know who Valerie was, why, or even whether it was she who left you outside the hospital. Now tell us what you received today that gave you, her name. Please, darling, let us help you," Margaret looked imploringly into Jemimah's eyes and held her hand.

"Alright, but before you read it, you need to know that to me, my parents have always been and always will be you, and that I love you both very much. I do not want this to hurt you." As she said this, her eyes again filling with tears, she handed the envelope to her father.

He read it and handed the letter to Margaret. They seemed much calmer about things, and Jemimah felt a little better. She had done the right thing, coming to her parents. What a stroke of luck it was that this had happened during her annual leave week.

"OK, well, this letter tells us very little factually, Jemimah. It doesn't really give us any more information on Valerie, so to speculate is not a healthy thing to do. The only way to find out is to go and meet this Rupert man in London and hear what the will says. This is not our decision to make, though, darling, it is yours. We want to support you through this and would like to come with you if and when you decide to go," Michael had a kind and gentle expression on his face, and both parents nodded in agreement.

"Oh, thank you. You're right. We know so little. I wonder whether this week would be too soon to meet with him. What do you think? It is only four o'clock. We could try now and find out."

"Are you sure that you want to be so hasty, darling? Are you ready to hear what is written?" Margaret looked worried for her daughter.

"Absolutely! Mum, it is far worse than not knowing and letting my imagination and fears eat me up. We should call today and see if we can go this week."

"OK. Let's try. Here is the phone…"

Jemimah's hands were shaking whilst she dialled the number. The woman picked up the phone at the other end, and after explaining who she was, Jemimah was transferred to Rupert Levy's office.

"Hello? Dr Withenshawe, is it?"

"Yes, hello, Mr Levy. Thank you for your letter. I received it today and was wondering whether there might be a chance of meeting with you this week, please, as I am on leave and can come without too much trouble."

"Yes, absolutely. I am glad that you chose to respond to my letter. I am sorry if it was a difficult read. I hope that our meeting will answer some questions for you. Now, let me read my diary. How does Thursday this week look for you? I could give you a few hours in the afternoon to give you time to get here."

Jemimah had the phone on speakerphone, and her parents nodded and said that Thursday was good for them.

"Yes, Thursday would be perfect. Thank you, Mr Levy. Do I need to bring anything with me for the meeting?"

"Well, you will need to bring identification, and did you consider bringing someone along with you?"

"Of course. Yes. I shall bring my ID along with me. Is it alright if I come with my parents, please?"

"Yes absolutely. That would be fine. I shall look forward to meeting you on Thursday, Dr Withenshawe."

"Thank you, Mr Levy. See you on Thursday."

As she hung up the phone, Jemimah felt numb. All the emotion had suddenly fled from her body, and she slumped into the sofa. It was as though the last three hours had not happened, and she had imagined it.

"Your bedroom is all made up for you. Stay with us, darling, until we go."

"Thank you, mum that would be great," she smiled at her mother, and then suddenly her face dropped.

"Oh shit! I left Mutty behind. Who is going to feed him?"

"Why don't you ring one of your friends in the village and see if they can look after him for a few days? How about your colleague, Henry? Doesn't he live nearby?"

"Oh my God! Henry would probably shoot him. No way am I leaving him with Henry. Is there any way you might be able to drive me home so that we can put Mutty in the cat hotel, please? That way, I will know that he is safe and won't have to worry about him."

Jemimah's father laughed.

"Always thinking of others. Now that is why I say every day that we are blessed to have you. If Mutty being safe will make you happy, then I will take you back and we can book him into his executive hotel suite."

Jemimah put her arms around her dad's shoulders and gave him a kiss on the cheek.

"Thank you, thank you, dad. I am sorry. I am so hopeless today. I think I am not really in a good place to drive myself, but if anything happened to Mutty, I would be heartbroken."

"I quite agree, darling. Your driving is out of the question. I'm not quite sure how you drove here. Your father will drive you. I made a banana loaf this morning so you can take some with you on your mission to rescue the precious Mutty." Margaret was smiling, and she got up to fetch the cake from the kitchen.

Today had been a day of revelation for Jemimah. She sat silently for much of the journey home, contemplating the events of the day. The truth was finally going to come out, just as Em had said, and whatever the story of her biological parents, she knew that she had the best parents in the world already, and that was not going to end no matter what she was about to find out.

Chapter 15
The Devil is in the Detail

The monotony of seeing clinic patients was a grind for Henry. He was a surgeon, not a physician, and the talking-to-people part was never fun. Nonetheless, he had to go to clinics to get the patients for his lists, so it was a means to an end. Thankfully, the nurses got how he liked things to run, and they seemed so relaxed about time. "What a great team," he thought to himself.

These days were a little different for him, though, and he was distracted and more impatient than usual. On one side of his mind was the now obsessive planning to create an opportunity to capture Eliza in the biblical sense with a hint of the devil's influence, and on the other was the pressing issue of the deal with the Holmfield Surgical Centre and how to get Ibrahim out of his way whilst not letting anyone be suspicious of him. He needed a case. A case that would do the deed for him. Something that would make him look like a hero and make Ibrahim look like the one at fault. But which one? He had to find it, and he found it fast. It needed to be the sort of case that gets surgeons sitting on either side of the proverbial fence. It's one of those cases that tests the surgeon's ability to do what they instinctively do not want to do. Make the decision not to operate when an operation *could* be probable but possibly *should* not be done. Some say it is a trait of the mature surgeon who has done it all before and seen it all before. In many ways, because of opportunity and luck, Henry had seen a lot. He had grown wise early and had learned both first and second-hand what to touch and what not to. The fortune of a good reputation as a surgeon was to either be very lucky or pick and plan cases carefully to ensure that the statistics pointed to that surgeon being the best in terms of survival rates. What it also did was not necessarily tell the patients looking at the tally boards which surgeons took the greatest risks to try to help them.

Death had become the ultimate measure of excellence, and in return, many patients had been left to face the option they did not want; the option of doing nothing or facing the medical options available to bide time before an inconvenient demise. What Henry needed to do was pick a case that touched the heart. The sort of case that had survived near-death as if by miracle and was now facing danger again where the options were even higher risk. The thought of the case absorbed Henry, and then a face appeared in his mind. He knew just which case would fit the bill.

"Ah yes, poor Mr Potter," survived emergency AAA repairs six months ago, a repair that he had done with Ibrahim, so he was known to him. Mr Potter was a lovely old man with the crappiest medical history on the planet. The sort of poor soul with pleading eyes and a lovely wife that Ibrahim would feel compelled to help, if for any reason senior cover was not around when disaster struck. "Yes, Mr Potter would be perfect," he muttered under his breath.

Inadvertently, Henry had developed a sly smile on his face. Jackie, who was running the clinic, looked at him enquiringly.

"Is everything OK, Mr Blythe-Soames?"

"Yes Jackie. Everything is just hunky dory. How are we doing with the clinic?"

"Oh well, we are running a little late, but there is nothing you can't handle. You might need to up the speed a little."

"Sounds like a plan. Let's push the next few through a bit faster. No more of the chat. Next patient, please, Jackie."

"Coming up," she smiled as she turned to fetch the next patient in her usual happy mood when the lovely Mr Blythe-Soames was at the clinic. The late finish was no problem at all.

Whilst she was gone, he picked up his phone and called his secretary.

"Could you get a Mr Potter to Ibrahim's clinic this week? I'd like him to have a look at him."

"Yes absolutely. I'm glad you asked because Mrs Potter has been on the phone three times already this week. They really do want to see someone."

"Well, then let's get him seen. My clinics are full, and with me possibly heading off on study leave in a few weeks, it is probably better he sees someone with the diary space to help him."

"Good plan. Thank you, Henry."

"Pleasure."

"Oh, by the way, did you say you were off in a few weeks? I don't have anything in the diary."

"Yes, I have a course planned in London. Tell me you have booked my clinics off."

"Oh, erm. I don't have anything in my diary. Did you log it into the study leave diary?"

"No, I did not. You know me and admin. Besides, it is study leave, not annual leave, and I cannot miss it."

"B-But you need six weeks' notice."

"Well, I'm the clinical lead. There must be some sort of perk for the hassle of the job. I'll text you the details after my clinic."

"Right, OK, Henry. I'll look out for the text," she sighed as she turned back to face her computer.

Henry was suddenly feeling a lot more relaxed. Plan A is going as planned. Now for plan B. He picked up his phone and opened WhatsApp.

'Hope UR OK + ready for tomorrow. How is RU feeling? x'

The clinic suddenly picked up pace. The remaining patients were mere noise amidst his scheming, and he fancied a quick lunch before heading to the divisional meeting that afternoon. Andrew would be there, and he needed to keep him happy. The next project was choosing a good course to fill his diary with to make himself conveniently unavailable when the shit hit the fan for Ibrahim. A nice little two-day course might serve you well. Continuing professional development in a wider sense. Something profound and a little ironic, like a course on allyship. Yes, that would be quite nice. He would have a look over lunch and get things juggled around.

A gentle knock on his clinic door turned his head. It was Eliza with a beaming smile.

"Hello. I was just passing the clinic when your text arrived, so I thought I might deliver the reply in person. How is your clinic going? Have you seen any good cases?" There was an accustomed ease now between the two, and a very assertive new confidence had grown in Eliza. Henry loved watching that transition. To most surgeons, it was a privilege to admire from a distance, but this time Henry wanted to palpate it more closely. That confidence had turned the shy, timid girl like Eliza into an alluring woman. Even her body looked more attractive. Her posture had changed, and her breasts seemed more prominent.

"Ah, now that was good timing. I've just finished my last patient. I saw a few good cases too. We can chat about them over lunch if you fancy. I have an unusual half an hour free today before my meeting. Why don't we grab a sandwich and coffee at Costa's and see how your knowledge is shining the day before the big day?"

Eliza's face was beaming, "Oh, that would be amazing. I'm feeling very positive about tomorrow. What a contrast to a few months ago! I have so much to thank you for."

Henry loved the feeling of being admired by Eliza. In his mind, what he was feeling was perfectly acceptable. Both were playing along, and no harm was being done. He was just boosting Eliza's confidence, after all. What were the boundaries in such a positive relationship? There could be none, as so much good was coming out of it. It was not like Eliza was uncomfortable. She was positively glowing.

Henry had convinced himself absolutely that this was just a thing between two adults who needed each other's company for different reasons. He was a powerful man buried in the pressures of responsibility, management, and high-level surgery, and she was a woman and young aspiring surgeon who needed guidance and support in whatever way it was needed. It wasn't like it was going to go far anyway. Just a little fun, and God did he need some fun in his life.

They walked to the café together, talking about a few of the cases he had seen. Eliza was evidently interested, and her responses to questions were decisive and, more importantly, correct. She sounded like a surgeon, and this new confidence reinforced Henry's certainty that what he was doing was the right thing.

"You are ready for that exam, Eliza. I am so impressed by how far you have come. I knew you would do it. I have no doubts at all that tomorrow will go fine, and before long we can celebrate your success together." He looked into her eyes as he said this. There was a combination of paternalism and lust perversely mixed in his eyes, and she smiled at his comments. At that moment, Eliza's emotions exhibited a Jung-esque quality where Eliza seemed fixated on the father-like gestures of Henry. To her, he offered a safe and intellectual mantle to ascend towards. How lucky was she?

It was as though she was blinded by the devil's own liquor of awe and power, and the details of what it all meant were neither computed in her facts-saturated head nor did it matter as long as the result was that she passed her exam. Henry was her passport for that. Could it really be that, with time, the coquettish and self-doubting Eliza had acquired some of the spirit of Henry? Time will tell.

Chapter 16
The Realisation

With Mutty safely checked into his five-star cat hotel suite with a gourmet menu booked, Jemimah felt relieved. She had packed some sensible clothes to wear for the trip and felt like a schoolgirl again, sitting in the family car with her dad, heading to her first day at school. They were both munching on some of mum's delicious banana loaf as they drove back to the family home. Home had given her an enduring love of cakes and a much-needed place to belong. It seemed strange that so much of her life had been limited by inner doubts about her origin, and yet there she was, a member of the most wonderful of families and safe. She was angry with herself for being so concerned about her biological family. Whatever Rupert Levy was about to tell her, Em was right; she already had enough. This was just going to be the line to draw beneath the matter once and for all; after that, life was going to carry on.

"So how are you feeling about the meeting Jemimah?" Michael was driving the car, but half of his mind was on his daughter. He was still shaken at how upset she had been and was worried that there might yet be news that she was not ready to hear. The letter was slightly onerous, and he was not sure how to protect his girl from any more pain.

"Oh, I'm actually feeling surprisingly relaxed now, dad. Not sure if that is just pragmatic denial or the realisation that whatever I am told, nothing changes. I am still your Jemimah, and I have a family. I think the worst thing in life has been not knowing. Perhaps at last I can put to bed the fears and doubts I have had about my origins. At last, I will know if I am a descendant of a murderer or serial killer," Jemimah had a cheeky smile on her face, and her father laughed.

"I think we already know the answer to that last part. You are clearly not the product of deviant genes. You are the definition of loveliness and consideration. I imagine you will find that whatever their story, your birth parents bore some of those traits too. People give up children for adoption for all sorts of reasons, Jemimah. I suspect there will be a story to yours that will make the dramatic start you had make sense to you. I really hope that this journey will bring you peace and give you direction to pursue. Whatever you choose to do, darling, mum and I will always support you. I hope you know that."

"Oh, dad, it was such a blessing that I ended up with such great parents. I could not possibly wish for anything more. It is so strange, though, why we so much need to know where we came from biologically. I have always been troubled by how different I look to everyone else and the strange nuances of my mind. I have always felt foreign, and yet whenever I look in the mirror, my face could belong to many different countries. I have these weird grey-green eyes and dark hair. My nose is prominent, and my face is long. I could be Spanish, Arabic, or perhaps Italian. And then I have this olive-coloured skin. It must be Mediterranean. Just knowing that will be interesting, don't you think?"

Michael glanced at her with a loving smile.

"To me, you have always been absolutely beautiful. Even when you were a little girl, you stood out from the rest for all the right reasons. You have such lovely features, and I am so proud of you. Knowing your biological origin is interesting, but so much of who you have become as an adult did not come from that. Your home, your friends, and so much more have influenced the exquisite woman that you have become. Yes, you do look different, but for me, it has always meant that you are a woman of the whole world. You can be a part of it anywhere and fit in. That is a very valuable asset indeed."

"There is some truth in that, dad. I guess not being able to find out about myself made me someone who loved to find out about other people. I looked at others and listened to their stories, somehow finding mine in them too. The only sad thing is that, after so many years of wondering, I have grown to feel more and more like a misfit. Even at work, I have developed a strange worry about not fitting in and not being part of the 'club'. It is so strange. I'm British, I sound English, and yet I feel foreign."

Michael reached his arm out to her and held her hand.

"Darling, the NHS is hardly a normal place to work. Do you really want to be like Henry? If being like him is what you need to succeed, you need to count your many other blessings and attributes that meant you never needed that. Your patients love you; your students and trainees adore you, and you have so many friends. If work cannot see what a great asset you are to them, it is their loss, not yours."

"Oh, that is very kind of you to say that, dad. I am afraid I will always be my greatest critic. Perhaps I might soften if I could just find a bit of work-life balance. I wonder whether I will find it easier to let someone into my life after this trip. I seem to have avoided meeting men because I was so scared of telling them that I was adopted. I sounds crazy, I know, but it has been a real thorn that I couldn't remove. Perhaps this new man that Ibrahim wants me to meet might be a blessing in disguise!"

"Oh, is that why you haven't been interested in finding anyone? I had no idea," Michael was surprised.

"Well, it's one of those complex things about me that reminds me that I am not made from the same genes as you. You are so calm and accepting. In my body, there is this restlessness that has eaten away at me for many years. There is a strange sense of misplaced injustice and anger. I struggle to trust people and feel that, in some way, I am always at a disadvantage. Something does not want me to succeed. I do not know where that comes from. Part of me is itching to find out what Valerie Etherington wanted to tell me. Whether she was the one who left me at the hospital, and why? Perhaps by knowing about her, I can understand myself better. Who knows?"

Jemimah's posture is now upright. Her hands added to the emotion of her words, and in many ways, she demonstrated the hidden pain that she had carried with her throughout her life.

"And what is this about the new man that Ibrahim has for you? You kept that a secret!" Michael smiled cheekily.

"Oh, dad, he is just going to be another random man who doesn't fit. The only slightly interesting thing is that Ibrahim is a very sensible person, and this is the first time he has tried to match me with someone. I'm thinking that this man might be promising."

"Well, the key is to be calm and be yourself. He will love you to bits."

"Yes…but will I love him?" Jemimah shrugged and looked out of the window.

Michael asked her to put some good music on as they continued on their way home. Jemimah was surprised at how calm she was now about everything. Whether that would change as soon as she was on her way to London was another thing, but right now she felt in control of her emotions and eager to know the truth. The blind date had paled into insignificance.

Chapter 17
The Big Day

March 12th was here, and there was no getting out of it. Eliza sprang out of bed, having had one of those strange restless nights where questions popped into her head almost prophetically. Topics that she mostly knew well, but a couple that posed doubts in her mind. She dived into her file and looked up the correct answers. After a few minutes of eager fact-confirming, she closed the file.

"No more, Eliza. You are ready and just need to get this done. Today is Pass Day, and you need to dress."

The superstitions of exam days had become something of an art. Even choosing the right underwear carried significance. It was not like dressing for a date or a night out. Wearing the right knickers was crucial. Something comfortable, neither too small nor too tight. Something supportive. The next was the choice of trousers and top. The room that the exam was in was not something she could control. Too hot, and she needed layers she could take off. Too cold, and she needed a comfy, warm layer to put on. She had a lucky scarf that she always wore. After careful selection, she stood in front of the mirror and nodded. Today was so different from the last two attempts. Today, she felt like a surgeon.

Her phone buzzed. It was a message.

'Go and smash that exam. You are brilliant. x'

It was Henry. She smiled and felt like she was taking a part of Henry with her. She was confident and resolute.

The exam was in a driving test centre in the neighbouring town, so she decided to be absolutely safe and drive there early. There was a little coffee shop just nearby, and rather than eat breakfast at home, she decided that a toast and tea from there would be a much better idea. She checked the registration forms for the hundredth time to be sure of the time.

The start time was 9.30 am and doors closed at 9 am. No phones or electronic devices were permitted, and all paper and writing equipment would be provided. Pencil cases were banned. At 8.15, she parked her car in the public parking lot across the road, grumbled at the price per hour, and headed to the coffee shop. She was hoping that no one she knew would be there. She wanted to stay in the right zone and was anxious that other people would not help. She found a small table in the corner where she sat with an English breakfast tea and a warm, buttery teacake. Twenty more minutes of complete calm, and then it was time to go. She recognised a few of her study group colleagues by the window. Evasion was key, so she slumped into her chair and pulled her scarf up over her chin. As they left, she gathered her things and followed a few steps behind. She could hear their conversation in bits and decided to pretend she was unavailable in case they turned around. She put her mobile phone in her ear and called her mum.

"Morning mum. How are you?"

"Oh, good morning, Eliza. This is a surprise. I thought you would be doing your exam at this time."

"I'm just walking to the centre. It starts at 9.30."

"You are in a good time. That's great. Well, your father and I are sitting here with everything crossed. May all the right questions come up for you," she sounded so positive and encouraging, and Eliza was pleased that she had called home.

"Oh, thank you both. This time, I feel so much more prepared. I'm hoping it will be enough," she crossed her middle and index fingers at that moment and bit her lower lip. Yes, she was more prepared, and today was going to be a good day. "Well, I'd better go now, but I'll call later to tell you how it went."

Her phone beeped again. It was Miss Withenshawe.

'Good luck in your exam today, Eliza. Best wishes. JW'.

At that moment, she felt so supported and grateful as she walked into the centre. She was determined to show all her supporters, family, and team that she could do this! What she wanted most was to prove to herself that she could pass the exam.

After registering her arrival and briefly wishing her colleagues luck, Eliza went to her desk for the day ahead. A characterless grey desk with computers on either side is just far enough away to not be able to see their screens. In front of her chair was her computer. She sat down and stared at the screen with the title of the exam on it and a notice saying that candidates must only start when the exam time has begun, or they will be disqualified.

She opened her bottle of water and drank a little to moisten her dry mouth. She put her watch on the table in front of her and carefully placed the pencil that she had been given parallel to the screen. Everything had to feel just right. The adjudicator started to talk and announced the rules of the examination room and how a candidate could ask to go to the toilet. All visits to the toilet were accompanied, and mobile phones and electronic devices had to be turned off for the duration of the examination. They announced that candidates would be informed when halftime had been reached and when there were thirty minutes left before the end. No one was allowed to leave the room in the last 30 minutes of the exam, but if they had finished before then, they could leave.

9.30am. The exam began, and the first question appeared on the screen. Eliza took a deep breath and began. She had practiced the routine so many times before that today was just another day. Answers came to her fingers as she tapped the keyboard. Time seemed to disappear as she glanced at her watch between sections. Her mind was clear, and the other candidates interspersed around the room had become invisible. Even when one candidate started coughing, Eliza seemed undeterred. In previous exams, coughing had been a source of deep sighing irritation and distraction, but today she was deaf to it all. The only thing that mattered were the questions before her.

"Thirty minutes left. Any candidates who have completed their papers can leave now if they wish. After this call, no one is allowed to leave before the end of the examination."

Eliza had already completed the questions and debated whether she was brave enough to leave the room early or whether she should go through the paper one more time. This was a tricky decision to make, as in her practice papers, whenever she had gone back and checked and changed her answers, she more often than not, changed the correct answer to an incorrect one. She took a deep breath and raised her hand.

"I have finished and would like to leave, please," she looked at the adjudicator with a nervous smile. She had kept the pencil as a memento of the day. Was it theft? No, she had paid a fortune for the exam, and she had earned the pencil. She guiltily tucked it into her pocket.

"Yes, that is fine. Please make sure that you have collected all your belongings and complete, the feedback and leaving form outside before leaving the centre."

As Eliza walked away from the centre, she was relieved. She had done it and was also glad that she was leaving before the other colleagues left and started talking about the questions. She needed to escape and do something. Suddenly, she was overwhelmed with a sense of complete exhaustion. After all the months of hard work, it was over, and there was a feeling in the middle of her stomach of profound deflation. The unexpected anti-climax after the event. She avoided turning on her phone and drove home; what she wanted most was to put on her house trousers and lazy top, lie on her bed, and relish the silence.

Chapter 18
Obsession

Today, Henry was feeling quite rejuvenated as he pondered all that was going well during the morning run, which was now feeling less like torture and more like an asset. He pondered the benefits of his visible supportive role with Eliza, including possible benefits. He hoped that today's exam was a good one and that Eliza would pass with flying colours and move on to the next phase of her revision programme. The more hands-on clinical part.

He ran in a focused and empowered manner, actually enjoying this sport that he had hated so much at the beginning. In his new Nike outfit and stylish Bose Runners glasses, he cut a fine figure and was eager to bump into Jemimah. It was strange that his runs had not coincided with hers this week, but it could just be that she was running at different times because she was on annual leave. He was supposed to be seeing her that afternoon but hadn't heard from her, which was strange. He would text her before leaving for work.

As he ran, his phone buzzed, and he knew it would be Eliza replying to his message. He stopped and looked at the message.

"Great. Just Great. She is going to do just fine," he spoke to himself and popped his phone back into his pocket before setting off again with a slight slyness to the corner of his mouth.

As he reached his home, Henry walked up the driveway whilst texting Jemimah.

'Hi. Are we still meeting for our chat this afternoon? H'.

The message went off, but strangely, did not show the usual two ticks of being received. Perhaps her phone was switched off. He would check again later. He walked into the house to find Vanessa getting the children ready for school. She was like a machine operating around his life, and everything seemed to happen effortlessly. He was content that the mundane side of life was being handled by her so that he could get on with the important things like earning money and running the department. He was pleased that Vanessa was the queen of her own world, the home, and he very much left her to do it. Women, after all, were much better at those sorts of things, and who was he to get in the way?

"Morning all!" he shouted, and he bounced up the stairs for his morning shower. Jemimah was correct in her recommendation that running really was an amazing sport when you get used to it.

"Morning dad," all the family responded from the kitchen with breakfast laid out before them. All was indeed going well in the Blythe-Soames' household, and Henry felt satisfied. He had so much to focus on with his work and life that this part needed to run without issue. For the moment, Tom wasn't causing too much bother. Perhaps he was a late bloomer and needed a little roughing up. Yes, he thought rugby might be a good idea. Something to build his courage. 'Why was he so limp?' Henry was perplexed. Tom was not like any of his predecessors. Perhaps it was the school. Perhaps a stint in boarding school might help him; after all, his grades are good.

After his shower, Henry popped into the kitchen and grabbed a quick toast and coffee.

"Son, we need to talk about a few things. It seems like an age since we had a good man-to-man moment. Shall we put one into the diary for tonight? Is anything likely to clash with that?"

Tom looked up at him awkwardly and shrugged.

"I'll be here. What do you want to talk about, dad?" He looked worried and uncomfortable. His dad only 'talked' to him when there was something wrong, and he dreaded those man-to-man lectures.

"Oh, nothing specific. I'm just keen to catch up on things and hear how school is going from your perspective. Parents' evening never quite tells me your thoughts."

Tom was surprised. This was new. Perhaps it could be his chance to talk about boarding with his dad and finally escape the sense of eternal disappointment that he seemed to generate in his father. Maybe at boarding school he could be himself and pursue his own interests instead of rugby and shooting. At last, his father's obsession to turn him into a Blythe-Soames 'real' man would be delayed, and he could relax a little. The only proviso was that he was sent to the right boarding school. The Blythe-Soames had historically attended Eton, but this generation had been different because mum wanted everyone at home. There had been quite a bit of drama about it, but in the end, for the sake of peace, dad had backed down, at least for the prep school years. Those years were coming to an end, and it was like standing in front of a sand timer, wondering whether it would be simply turned over or if a new clock was about to start.

"OK dad. Let's talk tonight after dinner. Mum, is that OK? Will you be there too?"

Vanessa smiled. "No, Tom darling. I am not sure I can attend a formal man-to-man meeting," she winked at Henry. "I shall hear the feedback after."

"Excellent," Henry said as he got up to leave for work. Today was a day of waiting to hear from Eliza and Jemimah. It was also the day the Potters saw Ibrahim. The plan was unfolding, and with a nice two-day teamwork course booked in London in two weeks to coincide with the most likely date for an operation on the poor man, all was set. Which way would the dice roll for him and Ibrahim? Who would win their prize? Today was all about the premeditated alignment of all the things that mattered to him. Henry had learned well that if a gamble was to be taken, there had to be a very high chance that he was going to win. Was it an obsession? For Henry, it was more. It was a question of who was in control and who was winning.

Chapter 19
Facing Fear

Travelling to a will reading is not something that one quite knows how to prepare for, especially when you haven't ever met the person whose will is being read. The days preceding this day had been a rollercoaster of emotions and thoughts for Jemimah. On one side, her mind was focused on the positive perspectives; she would find out who this mysterious woman was; she would hopefully learn something about her biological family; she would be able to close a painful chapter in her past and let go of the 'what-if's' that had, over so many years, created barriers and obstacles to her life. On the positive side, there was much excitement and possibility. Those were the thoughts that she contemplated in the daytime. Then the night would fall, and as she lay in bed with her eyes open, she encountered fear, worry, and anxiety. In these moments, she toiled with the scenarios that could turn her life upside down.

Why was this mysterious Mr Levy being so cagey? What did he mean by "matters of a sensitive nature"? Clearly, there was something difficult about to be revealed because she was advised to attend with support. Oh God, what nightmare was about to unfold? Her heart pounded in her chest. At times, her eyes welled up with tears. She longed so much to know about her origins, but something inside of her was convinced that the story was not going to be an easy one to hear. Could it be that Valerie was, in fact, her birthmother? Why would she wait until she had died to let her daughter know whatever she wanted to say? Oh God, could it be that she was a criminal after all? How would she reconcile that? In one way, the life that her birthmother lived had nothing to do with her. Even if she had done something terrible, it did not mean that it was a trait likely to be passed on.

Suddenly, her medical mind jumped to the thought of a genetic trait. How much of the self is what you are born with, and how much is an image of who you grew up with? She had a lot of qualities from her adoptive parents. Her education had been excellent, and school had given her many of her personality traits. The not-knowing part of any journey is always grim. It was like waiting for results the day after an exam. You sit, pondering every single minute that felt a little wrong or difficult, and forget all the bits that went well. Human nature was torturing Jemimah, and the sleepless nights accentuated her emotional delicacy. The day of reckoning had to come. She glanced at the clock by her bedside. 02.30 am. She had to sleep. She had to. Clutching onto George, her trusted teddy of childhood, she rolled onto her side and started to recite her favourite poem. As the words rolled around her head, she finally drifted into a deep sleep.

Peep peep peep! PEEP PEEP PEEP! The vintage alarm clock shook Jemimah into the world of the living at 7.30 am. She was in the usual state of disorientation that one gets from waking up in a bedroom that is not the usual one after a deep, deep sleep. A few seconds of spatial orientation followed, with her eyes locating the light seeping from beneath the curtains. The awareness then shifted to the walls of the room and then to the door. It was her childhood bedroom, but how strange it was that she had felt disoriented in it! Suddenly, like a lead weight, she realised that it was THE DAY. Her heart started pounding again, and she felt nauseous. Today was the journey, and she was glad that she was not driving.

A gentle knock on the door made her sit up. It was her mum, like in the old days.

"Good morning, darling. Did you manage to sleep a little?" The welcoming, smiling face of her mum appeared around the door.

"Morning mum. No, it was not a great night again. In the end, I closed my eyes and recited the old poem you used to read to me. It still works. Do you remember it?" She smiled gratefully at her mum.

"Ah yes. The land of Nod. I loved that poem."

"But every night I go abroad."

"Afar into the land of Nod." They both giggled and remembered the old days. Jemimah had never been a good sleeper, but books and poetry were where she found comfort as the nights dragged on. Her mother had always understood her and had chosen Robert Louis Stevenson's poem to read to her as a comfort. It worked. As an adult, the gentle voice of mum still filled Jemimah's head when insomnia returned.

"Big day today," Margaret said with a sympathetic smile. "How are you feeling?"

"I'm exhausted. The last two days have felt like a month-long exam. I flitted between a sense of relief that I would finally get some answers and a sense of dread about opening what might turn out to be Pandora's box. Oh, I hope I can cope with whatever Mr Levy says to me. Thank you both so much for coming with me. It must be difficult for you too."

"Darling, when we adopted you, we knew that you were our girl, but unlike a child we had conceived ourselves, we also knew that this day would come. A journey where we would support you to find out the rest of your story. Doing this does not make us fear who we are as a family. You will always be the very best thing that came into our lives, and we will always stand by you no matter what. You will always be to us, our daughter, and that does not change by finding your birth parents darling. It just makes us a bigger family, which might be fun. In some ways, we also want to learn about your birth parents and thank them for bringing such a beautiful soul into the world," Margaret was sitting beside Jemimah when she said this. Jemimah flung her arms around her mum and squeezed her tightly.

"You really are the best mum in the world, and whatever we learn today, you will always be my mum. I will just have to give my birth mother another title if she is still alive. Hmmm, I wonder what, though?"

Margaret laughed.

"Well, you can ponder that tricky thought in the car on the way. Time to get up, or we will not have time for breakfast. I made something tasty for breakfast, so don't be long."

"Oh, now that sounds intriguing, and I can smell lovely smells coming up the stairs. I'll be down in a tick. Thank you, mum," she jumped out of bed and kissed her mum on the cheek enroute to the bathroom.

She chose a light blue dress and her lucky pearl necklace to wear, and she looked at herself in the mirror. Today was like heading for a big operation when things could go either way. For years, she had learned to revel in the thrill of surgery, where her skills and calm would see her through every eventuality, even though danger might be lurking a few cuts ahead. Today, there was no patient that she needed to hold her calm for; it was for her. This was not familiar ground, and yet it was. She learned the art of bottling up emotions and getting the task in hand done. That is what she needed to face today. With surgical mastery. Filter out the sounds that might distract her and keep focused on the end point. Today's end point was one thing. Answering the question, "What is the story of my parents?" With that thought in mind, she joined her parents in the kitchen to enjoy some fresh coffee and freshly baked banana and toffee muffins. Soon, they were on their way to London. Not long now.

Chapter 20
The Weighing Scales

Ibrahim was still on cloud nine that Jemimah was going to help him with his CESR application. In many ways, it would not change him at all, as he had never sought accolades, but this was his dream for his father and mother. He had dreamt of standing in front of the photo in the hall and telling his father he had made it. So many years of struggle and patience had passed, and in time, the rumble of defeat had become louder than the whisper of belief. Instead, he resigned to accept whatever he was destined to be and focus his dreams on his family and a stable, if limited, career.

As he drove to work, he pondered what would change if he became a consultant. He knew well that it was a double-edged sword to yield. On the one hand, there was the potential for autonomy and influence, but with these came risk and politics. Did he have enough support around him to be a success as a consultant? After so long in the department, was he almost too institutionalised to see a direction for the department beyond what he had always known? Would people expect more from him as a consultant? Was he expected to take more risks? Suddenly, the imposter within was filling him with doubt.

He felt cold inside, realising that although his surgical training and experience had taught him the skills of surgery, they had not taught him much about how to be a consultant and leader. What did he really know about politics? These were still precarious times in the NHS, with politics being unpredictable in terms of who was favoured and who was not. He had faced so many years of being undermined and overlooked that even his own self-belief had been challenged. He had to somehow prove his worth. Show people that he had the qualities of a consultant and that he was ready.

Today was a clinic day. Double math, and yet also a chance to ponder more about the plan that lay ahead. He headed into the hospital and stopped to talk to Bernie. Bernie looked different, and Ibrahim was concerned.

"Hello, my old friend. You look a little out of sorts today. Is everything alright?"

"Oh, hello, Ibrahim. How nice of you to stop and talk. Thank you for asking. I'm afraid today is not a good day. My wife, Penny, is not well and was admitted to the hospital yesterday. It looks like she might have had a stroke. I wasn't home when she called for the ambulance. I feel so bad about that part." Tears welled in his eyes, and he leant on his broom handle.

Ibrahim pulled his hand out and rested it on Bernie's arm.

"I am so sorry to hear that, Bernie. I am glad that she was able to call for help. You must not blame yourself, Bernie. Did the ambulance come to her quickly?"

"Oh yes, they were there in minutes. The Medicaid necklace alerted them, and it all worked. I am so relieved we got that for her last year. I just always hoped that we would never need it. We have been married for forty-two years; did you know? I don't know what I will do if I lose her," his red-rimmed, aged eyes looked almost tearful.

"Bernie you shouldn't be working like this. Are your daughters coming down to help you? You need to take care of yourself too, so that you are strong when Penny comes home. Can you not ask your managers to allow you a few days off?"

"My daughter Jane is coming tomorrow as her husband is abroad with work and Mel is in China for work, so I don't have anyone around, sadly. My neighbours have been lovely and were there with Penny when the ambulance came for her. I spoke with my manager, but they are short-staffed and cannot let me have time off this week. They said I could have a few extra days next week, though. In all fairness, what would I be doing at home? I would just be worrying myself with no one there, and besides, if I am here, I can pop in and see her around my shift."

"Well, you promise me, Bernie, that you will look after yourself and…" he rummaged in his pocket and brought out some paper. "Take this number. This is my mobile number. Promise me that you will call me if you need anything at all. OK?"

"Oh, Ibrahim, that is too kind. I wouldn't dream of disturbing a busy man like you. I'll be alright. We are tough where I'm from, you know. Tough and rather too proud for our own good!" Ibrahim smiled a sad smile.

"Well, where I come from, we are very proud of our elders. As both of mine are no longer alive, my concern is now all for you. Look, where do you live? It would be my pleasure to bring you some nice food to keep you strong until Jane arrives to take over. Will you allow me to at least do that?"

"Are you sure? I wouldn't want to impose anything at all. That would be so kind. Thank you, Ibrahim. You really are the kindest of men. I live just round the corner in the bungalows behind the hospital complex. Number 14 Cannon Road. Do you know it?"

"Yes, I do, and I shall swing by their later. What time will you be back from visiting hours?"

"Oh, I should be home around seven o clock."

"Well, shall I pop by around then? Is there any food you don't eat or like Bernie?"

"Yes, seven sounds good. It's quite easy, really. I'm just not much of a fan of spicy things, if that is ok."

"Of course, that is ok. We will rustle up a nice casserole for you to tide you over for a few days and keep you strong and fit for Penny. Please send her my best wishes, Bernie. I shall pray for her tonight."

"Thank you so much, Ibrahim. I really appreciate it," he grabbed Ibrahim's hand and shook it gratefully. Ibrahim was shaken at how frail Bernie seemed at that moment. For so many years, he had seen Bernie, but in reality, he had not really 'seen' him at all. He had just seen the eyes he knew whilst ignoring the body that, over the years, had aged.

That one single, grounding conversation had put the whole of life again, into context. Suddenly he remembered the importance of staying humble and never emulating Henry's of this world if he became a consultant. The day he lost his values and soul would be the day that he could no longer look at his father, no matter what his title. Whatever was to become of this chance that lay before him, he had to not let the desire for the elevation in status risk all that he was. Would it really be that easy? He doubted it. In his years, he had seen many gentle registrars rise to become enveloped in the bravado and façade of the big consultant surgeon persona. He called Aisha before entering the clinic to ask her if she would mind making a casserole for Bernie. As ever, she was delighted, and as it was her day off from work, it was no bother at all.

The clinic was a little different today because Henry had booked an "interesting" case for him to see and give an opinion on. He said it was Mr Potter, a lovely patient who had survived, against all odds, a complicated major bleed last year with the expertise of Henry and himself and a lot of blood and anaesthetic skill. The operation left him with failing kidneys and heart failure on the backdrop of his pre-existing diabetes, but as patients went, Mr Potter was one who did not want to die. He exceeded all expectations and, with dialysis and a cocktail of medication in a bag, left the hospital three months later, determined never to return. Sadly, despite his stoicism and courage, Mr Potter was not destined to stay away from the hospital, as late complications started to grumble.

First it was his heart, which the cardiologists and radiologists addressed with the wonders of interventional medicine and modern medicines; then it was his dialysis; an infected portal that caused a nasty case of sepsis that brought him back into ITU. He was not having any of it, though, and was soon back home. Over the course of this time, Ibrahim, and Henry reviewed him from the point of view of his aortic graft and stents. All seemed well until he had the infection from his dialysis portal, and then something was not right. He was feeling progressively more unwell. His infection seemed to wax and wane, and yet the exact site of the infection was not clear. Now he was starting to get strange-coloured stools, and his bowels were not right. His GP was getting worried about a sudden decline in the little bits of kidney that were still functioning, and he was sometimes quite sweaty. Mrs Potter was very worried and had pursued an urgent review.

"Mr and Mrs Potter, hello," Ibrahim always stood up and welcomed his patients with a handshake.

"Ah, Mr Baba. Thank you for seeing us so quickly. We have been so worried," Mrs Potter always seemed to do the talking. Meanwhile, her husband dutifully followed her with his Tilley hat on and his worn tweed jacket. He was not looking well today, and Ibrahim was concerned. In many ways, Ibrahim had grown very fond of Mr Potter and his wife, and although he was not ignorant of the prognosis of someone with such a complex medical history, Ibrahim still wanted this couple to have many more years together.

"You did absolutely the right thing. Mr Potter, you are not looking well, and we need to get to the bottom of things and see how we can get you back on track."

Whilst talking to them, Ibrahim was inspecting Mr Potter. The clinical signs were alarming. He was breathless and pale. His heart rate was high despite the medication to slow it down, he had lost weight and looked dehydrated. Mr Potter needed to come to the hospital. He was showing signs of sepsis, and Ibrahim was worried it was the graft that was causing it. Henry had helpfully organised scans the week before, and as Ibrahim looked at them, his heart sank. The graft was infected and had started eroding into the neighbouring bowel, and there was a lot of inflammation.

Like all things related to Mr Potter, uncommon things happen commonly and never seem to go as one might expect. This, if that was the case, required some difficult decision-making, and at the top of the decision-making pile was the patient, not the doctor. Ibrahim's face was an honest one, and it took one change in expression to alert the Potters that things were not good.

"Now, Ibrahim, you are about to tell me something I might not want to hear, aren't you? I can see it in your face," Mr Potter was squeezing his palms tightly, so tightly that his hands were blanched. Mrs Potter held onto her handbag as though it might hold secret powers to influence the direction of the conversation.

"Mr Potter, you know well that whatever we offer you, I will never be the one who makes the final decision. It was very helpful to have your scans last week, which helped confirm what your problems were suggesting. I am sorry, Mr Potter, but it looks like your graft has started to fail because of an infection around it. The infection is starting to cause problems with the part of your bowel that sits next to the graft." He took a piece of paper and drew a picture to explain the next part, a description of a fistula or communication between the graft where his aorta had been repaired and the bowel next to it.

"So, does that explain why I am getting blood from my back passage?"

"Yes, it does. It is likely that you have been getting little bleeds over time that have compounded your anaemia, which was always there from your kidney problems; that will get worse until you get a big bleed. This is something that is caused by a low-grade infection, which would explain your occasional fevers and the rather gradual onset of your symptoms. I suspect your anaemia is quite severe now, which would explain why you are so breathless and tired. We would need to do some blood tests to find out how bad things are."

Mrs Potter looked pale, "Does that mean that he is going to have another bleed like last time?" She had tears in her eyes. "Am I going to lose my Eric?"

Mr Potter put his hand onto hers and looked back at Ibrahim.

"What does this mean, Ibrahim? Can it be sorted?"

"Mr Potter, this is not an easy situation at all. This is not an emergency that we would operate on today, but it does need addressing urgently if we can. It is not something I can just deal with in an operation alone, though. You have a very complicated medical history, Mr Potter, and what might be possible for one person is not necessarily safe for you."

Mr Potter was more engaged and leant forwards towards Ibrahim.

"So, get me right here. What you are saying is that if you cannot operate on this, I am not going to make it?"

Ibrahim took a few seconds to answer and took a deep breath. In his heart, he wanted to tell the Potters that all was going to be fine and that he would make it all better. He could not, though. It was something he had always struggled with, despite his faith; knowing when to let go.

"I cannot answer that today because I need to discuss your scans with some colleagues and ask one of our anaesthetists to see you to find out what the risks are in the context of all your medical history. Remember, you have had heart problems, you have kidney problems, and you have diabetes, and all of that is on the backdrop of a chronic infection and anaemia. All of this will contribute to the overall picture. Anaesthetists have all sorts of clever ways of calculating your risks and helping you to come the right decision for yourself."

The Potters were nodding in synchrony, although they looked like they had just been bombarded with an entire foreign text and were processing the bits they had taken in.

"You need some time, and I will write you a summary in a second that you will be able to read and absorb. I will also give you Melissa's number as one of our secretaries, so you can get hold of me if you need to talk anytime, Mrs Potter. It is likely that you will need a few more tests on your heart and kidneys and possibly a transfusion, so I will write to your heart and kidney doctors as well as the infectious diseases team today. With everyone's expertise on board, I will be more able to give you an idea of what can and cannot be done. In the meantime, we need to start you on some antibiotics to try to get on top of that infection, but your kidneys pose some problem, with that, so we will need to try to find out what bacteria are causing this first to make sure that we give you the right antibiotics. We will take some blood from you today and hopefully get some answers back very soon."

Ibrahim looked at the two faces before him. They looked overwhelmed and a little confused. Not surprising since the brain never wishes to take in bad news. Not that it was all bad news, but it was serious enough to cause alarm.

Ibrahim turned to write a few notes to allow them time to think for a few minutes. Meanwhile, the Potters were holding hands, and both looked pale. This was a time they were not ready to face. Eric Potter was only 67. It was too soon. An intermittent unconscious shake of his head externalised the loud voice from within, and Ibrahim was able to palpate their distress. Keeping objective was one of the skills that every doctor had to learn, but it was so difficult sometimes.

"I'm sorry to give you so much information. This will be one of several opportunities to talk through things before a final decision has to be made, so please do not feel that you are being put on any spot or being told anything final. Today is the first of a few important days of information gathering, and hopefully all of that information will help you build a plan to make you feel stronger. Surgery is the last decision to make in this journey Mr Potter. First, we have to tackle that infection and get you as healthy as possible. It will involve your important input too, and I know you both to be the very best people in that department. You have exceeded our expectations before, so why not now? I'm going to speak to the haematology team and cardiologists today to see if we can sort out a transfusion plan. How does that sound to you?"

"I confess, I am rather overwhelmed, Ibrahim, so your idea of taking one step at a time and reading your summary sounds sensible; there's a lot of words in there that I need time to think about. Of course, I'm worried, but in many ways, we are also quite reasonable. We know I can't live forever, and surviving the big bleed last time was a gift of time we have enjoyed. I never wanted to be a burden to anyone. This time has allowed us to put everything in order. I think we just need a little time to absorb what we have heard today. Do you think we could meet up again next week to talk some more?"

"Yes absolutely. I will have you added to my clinic next week, and in the meantime, I will ask Vicky Mansell, our specialist nurse, to give you a call for support. Do you remember meeting her when you were in after the repair?"

"Oh yes, I remember Vicky. She was wonderful. I think we will need her help coordinating all the visits we will have. The bus journeys are getting rather tricky these days, and taxis are so expensive."

"We might be able to help you with that, Mr Potter. Vicky knows more. I will ask her to call you this afternoon. Is your phone number still the same?"

"Oh, well, Ibrahim, we have sprung into the new century with a mobile phone. Beryl, dear, do you have the number of the new mobile?" Beryl had red eyes and nervously rummaged into her handbag for her purse. She took out a little card with a mobile number written on it.

"Y-yes, I have it here. We don't always remember to keep the phone with us, though, so tell her to leave a message for us or try the home number as well."

Ibrahim copied down the number and held out his hand to Beryl.

"Mrs Potter, I'm sorry today has upset you. I know how much you have both been through this year. You are both so brave and have a courage that leaves me in awe. I promise to do all that I can for your husband," Beryl squeezed his hand, and her eyes locked with his. The depth of fear and pain touched Ibrahim's heart.

The consultation ended soon after that, and the rest of the clinic passed in a blur. Ibrahim was immersed in the Potter case, and he also realised that Henry had sent it to him as a test. Test to see if he can be a consultant. Was it a poisoned chalice, though? Time will tell.

Chapter 21
Inertia

The backlash to any intense lead up to anything is the inevitable crash that follows. Eliza was there right now, staring blankly at the ceiling of her bedroom as she lay in a starfish-like slump on her bed. The sunshine rested on her face like a warm flannel and made her whole body feel heavy and so tired that even lifting her head was too much. She could hear her heart beating in her chest. It was steady and almost hypnotic. Her phone and her bag were lying on the floor in the hallway, and she had absolutely no interest whatsoever in speaking to or texting anyone. Not even Henry.

That last thought lingered. Was she ungrateful? Surely he deserved to know how it had gone after all he had done to help her? Perhaps he was busy and had forgotten after this morning's text. 'For God's sake, Eliza, he has FAR more important things to do than think of you!' She shut her eyes and shook her head. Had she lost all perspective in the run-up to the exam? She certainly had felt strange, almost inappropriate feelings towards Henry in recent weeks, but perhaps that was just the consequence of the pre-exam adrenaline rush? What would it feel like to be a senior surgeon? Would people admire her as she did Henry? She had to go through these years, and any help was welcome. How almost pathetically needy she was.

The tiredness she felt was akin to an almost drunken feeling. She felt out of sorts and dizzy. Her stomach gurgled, yet she lacked appetite. She felt hot and yet her hands were cold. Perhaps she needed a walk outside. Yes, some fresh air would be good, and the village was so pretty at this time of year. The woodland at the end of the village was beautiful, and she had hardly been to it because work and revision had taken over her life for months.

She jumped up and changed into some jeans and her favourite floral top that she made for herself last summer but had not yet worn. It was a fabric that made her feel happy, and that was what she should have been feeling like, but instead she was dragging herself around like a heavy weight. This walk was going to sort her out.

Grabbing an apple in her hand, Eliza set off on foot. March was unusually warm that year, and her cardigan was poised on her shoulders like a sloth. She looked naturally beautiful, and a tired smile appeared on her face as the air touched it. The woods were a mile away, and her posture was palpably relaxed with every step she took. It was like she had been freed from a virtual prison, and for a little moment, life had restarted. Her blonde, wavy hair tumbled over her shoulders, and her step started to bounce. It was real. The exam was over, and slowly that strange sense of guilt that she had not opened a book or computer on returning home was fading away. For three weeks, until results came out, she was free to wind down, and she was not going to throw away this time for anything.

Turning into the woods, her eyes adjusted to the light. The heavy canopy of mixed leaves above her rustled and swayed, and the sunlight broke through the tiny gaps between the leaves like shooting stars. The ground was a mosaic of light and colour, and the birds filled the air around her. Nature was awakening her, and she basked in the luxury of freedom and time.

She looked below at the path that ran along the old railway line and noticed a person jogging there. Her eyes were still just glancing and not focusing. The runner looked familiar. A man with sunglasses, but his hair was familiar…His body looked familiar…He was familiar. It was Henry! For reasons that Eliza could not explain, she gasped and hid behind a big oak tree. Can one ever explain irrational spur-of-the-moment actions? This was definitely one of them. She couldn't believe it. What was Henry doing here? Did he live in the same village? She had never asked him about where he lived. OMG! He was here, and she had absolutely no idea why, but she did not want him to see her. She wanted to just watch him run and keep the moment, like her little secret. She leant around to watch him. How different he looked. Human. She twisted to keep him in sight, leaning carefully around the tree. CRACK! The log between her feet broke, and she fell. Suddenly she was tumbling down the hill until a tree abruptly stopped her helpless body.

"Ouch! Shit that hurt!" Her knee had caught something sharp, and her jeans were ripped. Her knee stung like fire, and she was disoriented lying diagonally headfirst downhill. A face appeared in front of her. It was Henry.

"Eliza? Is that you? Are you alright? My God, you startled me!" Henry looked worried and a little sympathetic as he looked down at the now soil- and leaf-covered Eliza.

"Henry. Hello…. w-w-what are you doing here?" She wanted to be invisible at that moment. She blushed, winced, and looked apologetically at him. "I-I was just taking a walk to clear my head after the exam, and erm well, I spotted something and tripped over a branch. Agh, I think I have done something to my knee."

Henry looked into her eyes and asked her with a heroic smile, "May I have a look? Hmm, it looks like you might need some urgent jean surgery there," she nodded with an embarrassed expression and laughed nervously.

He lifted the bloody flap of the torn jean leg, and it showed a nasty gash from what must have been a rock on the slope. It was bleeding and very mucky.

"I hope you are up to date with your tetanus because it has a lot of soil and rubbish in it. Luckily, my house is not far from here, so we can go there and clean it up. Can you stand?"

Eliza took his hand as he helped her stand. The injured knee was stinging and pounding, but she put on a brave smile and stood as straight as she could. She felt sick.

"Ouch! I must have been deep in thought to have done such a stupid thing." She took hold of his arm and limped next to him towards his home. They looked at each other and smiled.

"Well, now this was not what I was expecting. You didn't reply to my message after your exam, so I have been worried that you might not have had a good day. How did it go?" Henry looked at her enquiringly.

"Oh, I am sorry. I haven't turned my phone back on since the exam. I left and just headed home. I think the exam went well. I had plenty of time to finish and didn't struggle reading the questions. I feel much better about things, but we will only really know how well it went in three weeks' time. Until then, I am determined to do all things that is not about revision. Preferably without any more accidents!" She had a satisfied smile on her face, and Henry was pleased.

"That sounds like the Eliza I know and believe in. Great attitude too. Learning how to switch off is a bit of an art. Not something I was ever very good at except when I was out hunting or running."

"I didn't know you liked to run. Clearly, a surgeon thing I'll have to take up. You and Miss Withenshawe are so amazing. I hear she ran a marathon last year.

How awesome is that? I confess, I am not quite as impressed as you are." The imposter within had popped out again.

"Hey, what is this? Surely you do other things? Sport isn't everyone's game. What hobbies do you have when you aren't at work or revising?"

"Well, I like walking, even though today's fall might suggest otherwise. I like to make things. I sew and design clothes. I love to paint. I guess much of my talent is in imagination and creating things," she pointed to her top.

"You made this top?" He nodded approvingly as he stared at her chest and not at the top. "I'm impressed," he smiled widely at her, and she smiled back nervously with her teeth together. She loved how easily she and Henry could talk. Because of their relatively contrasting statuses, it still felt alien to her. There was a chemistry between them that was difficult to define, and she wondered what he had been like when he was her age.

They crossed the road, walked down the driveway of the Grange, and headed towards the house.

"You have a beautiful home, Henry," Eliza said.

"Thank you. We have lived here for a few years, and it has grown with us, I guess. I think everyone might be out, as my wife will be out with the horses and the children are at school. Let's find out."

He walked into the house and turned his face towards the staircase.

"Hello. Vanessa? Are you home?" He waited for a few seconds. Silence. They were alone.

"We had better get that leg sorted. Let's go into the kitchen, where I have some betadine to clean up that wound. Might sting. Sorry."

Eliza was silent and just nodded. Vanessa. That was his wife's name. What a beautiful home they had. He has children. She wondered how many. How old were they? What was Vanessa like? What sort of woman would a man like Henry go for? She was just taking in the house around her and following Henry in a state of silent observation. Could she belong to this sort of world? The kitchen was bigger than most of her childhood homes downstairs. She had come from a modest background. Henry was clearly, from something very different.

"Hmm, now how shall we get to this wound?" Henry was surveying the shredded jeans. Unbeknownst to Eliza, he was secretly wishing that she would suggest taking off her jeans, but that would be awkward if Vanessa came in. No, he had to be careful in the house.

"Perhaps you could cut the leg of the jeans off just above it. Would certainly make a very stylish pair of jeans," she laughed nervously. "We could do with some of those rounded, but very sharp scissors from A&E."

"Ah, you mean these tough cuts?" He presented a pair of them out of his box of first aid things.

"Yes! They are the ones. Brilliant. Cut away. I promise to be the very best of patients." She stretched out her leg with some discomfort and lifted the torn corner, revealing the now scabbed and dirty knee wound.

Henry was feeling oddly nervous. He carefully cut around the leg of the jeans and down the lower part to expose the whole of her lower leg. She had a slim and smooth leg beneath, with skin that looked like porcelain. He wanted to run his fingers up it.

'Focus Henry. For fuck's sake, what are you thinking? It is just a leg! A very pretty leg.' He wondered whether his thoughts were written on his face too. He didn't dare look up. He approached the process with surgical gravitas. His face felt hot, flushed.

"Hmm, well, there is a lot of grit in here, and if we don't get it out, you'll end up with a nasty tattoo on your leg. I'm afraid this is going to be rather sore. Let me see if I can find some topical local gel in my box of tricks. Hang on a sec."

He walked out of the kitchen through a door that looked like the entrance to a pantry or utility room. She could hear him rummaging around but dared not move from her perch on the table. She was glad for the momentary pause because Henry's hands on her leg had made her feel very strange.

Just as she looked up and blew a hair out of her eyes, a tall and attractive woman walked into the kitchen. 'This must be Vanessa! Oh God!'

"Hello. What is going on here?" She had a sympathetic smile as she approached the terrified Eliza.

Eliza smiled nervously and started talking quickly.

"Oh hello. I...I'm Eliza. I work with Mr Blythe-Soames, but today, something really weird happened because when I was walking after my exams, I saw him in the woods where I was walking, and then I fell down a hill, and he rescued me. I hurt my knee," she had clearly made no sense at all to Vanessa, who was now wondering whether this poor person had had a head injury. "Where had Henry picked this one up from?" she pondered.

"My dear, you aren't making any sense. It sounds like you have had quite a shock, and yes, that knee looks very dirty. Where is my husband exactly?" She looked around and then noticed the rumblings from the pantry. "Ah, that must be him."

The door swung open, and Henry, with his hands full, burst into the room and dropped some of the dressings.

"Hello," he said. Not a positive happy hello, but rather an awkward surprise. "You're home early. Sorry about the drama here. This is Eliza, one of our junior doctors. She had a nasty fall in the woods, and I was luckily out running and found her. Poor thing." They seemed to be talking over Eliza as though she was not there. Vanessa was watching him carefully. He was looking unusually awkward. Was there something missing from this story? One babbling lunatic blonde girl and Henry looking like a character from a slapstick movie…had the midlife crisis arrived earlier than expected? she wondered.

She let Henry struggle with his clumsy load and turned to the girl.

"So, your name is Eliza, isn't it? Are you working in the same department?"

"Yes, I am one of the junior doctors in the department. Mr Blythe-Soames is my boss and also the head of our regional training programme. I didn't realise that we were all living in the same village, which was why I was so surprised to see him today," she had started to sound more coherent after recovering from the shock.

Vanessa turned back to Henry. "Well, it looks like you are managing fine and don't need nursing expertise, so I'll just run upstairs and freshen up before picking up the children. I imagine you'll not be too long."

Glancing briefly back at Eliza, she said, "Well, it was nice to meet you, Eliza. I hope your knee heals fine."

It was a strange but empowering moment for Vanessa. She suddenly felt angry at Henry. The man who she had given up her career in nursing to please. There was something not right about what she saw in the kitchen, and she would be damned if a young girl like Eliza was going to threaten her home. Consciously or not. She knew Henry, and that was enough.

Henry tossed his armful of kit onto the table and walked round to face Eliza. They looked awkwardly at each other. Eliza was the first to speak.

"God, I'm so sorry if I startled your wife, Henry. I confess, I was a bit shocked myself. She must have thought I was mad or something," she bit her lower lip with her front teeth.

"I imagine she was quite surprised to find a pretty young lady with her leg out sitting on the table. Let's get this sorted for you," he had a smile on his face as he worked away. There was something deliciously, wild about the moment. The next twenty minutes were spent cleaning and dressing the wound. Having Vanessa in the room next to Eliza was an interesting and unexpected stroke of luck for Henry because he could compare them and reinforce his desire to snag Eliza. That leg was just too tempting, and Vanessa looked older. He needed to rekindle his fire.

After completing the dressing, Henry dropped Eliza off at her little cottage. He knew where she lived. She was close, conveniently close to his home. He was pleased. The trap would be easy to set. First, he had to convince Vanessa that all was well.

Chapter 22
Destinations

As they sat on the train into London, little was said. Today was a landmark day for them all, most of all Jemimah. The aura around them was pensive, and their eyes all looked far away in deep thought. Jemimah played with the gold heart-shaped pendant around her neck that her grandmother had left for her. The jostling in her mind between positive and negative had faded into a resigned acceptance. This was a day she was going to live through, no matter what, so the key was to keep focused on the things she could influence. She had told her mother all that she wanted to say to reassure her that there was no question, who mum was. She had dressed in a way that made her feel confident and appropriate for all eventualities. She had enjoyed her banoffee muffins and coffee with her parents, and the day had started as she hoped it would continue—that this door would finally be closed on her past forever and her lovely family would go on as normal.

As they came off at Holborn Station, there was the usual rush of noise and people. They were early, so their pace did not match the endless haste of London. It was as though the world stepped around her, and she absorbed the sounds and sights of the community. Every race, every gender, and every style imaginable rushed around them. This is such a fascinating contrast to the bland uniformity of the resident population of Saints Bay. Despite this, Jemimah felt more comfortable back home in colourful floral fabrics and bright shoes. Black, grey, and navy seemed to be the limited colour swatch of choice in London. How strange that diversity seemed to be diluted into monotony amidst the haste!

They stopped at a café nearby and ordered something to drink. Coffee was not a good idea, with tension lurking just a pore deep in each of them. A large pot of camomile tea was the universal choice, and the butter biscuits served on the saucer of each cup were just the right size to neither upset their poised stomachs nor too small to distract their focused minds with troubling rumbles below. Everything that day was about being on the edge of somewhere or something else.

The walk to the offices of Bevan, Levy, and Walters Solicitors was not a long one. They stopped for a moment at the park in the centre of Lincoln's Inn Fields. Like so much of the square, it was like stepping back into another time. Although the largest of London's many public squares, this one held a special place in Jemimah's heart as it housed, amongst its grand buildings, the Royal College of Surgeons of England. She had always loved that building and spent many hours walking around the breathtaking Huntarian Collection in absolute awe of the achievements and sacrifices of its namesake and founder. She had sat in the park in front of it, pondering the paradox of the history of the square, which changed from pasture to cows, to a place of execution, a plague burial site, and now tennis courts. How the world had changed, yet in many ways humankind had not. Being there was strangely comforting. What a coincidence that Mr Levy was in that square too.

They walked into the main foyer of Bevan, Levy, and Walters Solicitors, where they were greeted by a receptionist. Her name was Angela, and she was impeccably dressed in a black dress suit. Her perfectly manicured nails clasped their ID badges. It was like signing into a congress or institution. How official it all seemed. Jemimah felt conscious when writing her name, Withenshawe, down on her badge. Would this be her name when she leaves the building later?

They were directed down a corridor to an office with the name Mr Rupert Levy, LLB, on a brass plaque on the heavy oak door. They knocked.

The door opened to a stifled but welcoming smile. It was Mr Levy himself. The short, ageing man was dressed in a pinstripe, black suit. He had an unusual face. The one that made you want to look at it again. A sad face with a kind smile.

"Welcome all. Thank you very much for making the journey here today. I hope the journey was easy for you all."

He turned to Jemimah, and a melancholic change in his expression was noticed by all.

"Hello Dr Withenshawe," he extended his hand to her, and they shook hands. The handshake seemed to linger for a second or two longer than normal, and Jemimah was intrigued. He was looking at her with an expression of recognition. It was as though he had missed her. But she had never met him before.

After the initial pleasantries had been exchanged, they assembled on seats around a table. There was a small silver box expectantly located in front of Mr Levy's chair. Jemimah looked at it with apprehensive curiosity. Pandora's box, perhaps? Rupert Levy noticed her expression and pushed the box to the side.

"Today is partly a formality in the delivery of the last will and testament of my client, Miss Valerie Heatherington, and partly informal in my delivery of a story I have held for the whole of your life and longer, Miss Withenshawe. None of what I will say will land easily on the ear, but it is time to tell it, as my lasting promise to your biological parents."

Jemimah's posture changed from anxious and tense to upright, and engaged on the hearing of those last few words. Her hands gripped the handles and her knuckles were white. Did he know her parents? Does this man know her story? She swallowed and noticed a cold feeling creeping down her back like a finger. She felt in that same moment a paradoxical desire to stay, listen and yet also to get up and run out. She chose to stay. Time seemed to have frozen, and even swallowing felt laboured and palpable.

Rupert pulled out the documents for the will hearing. He gently cleared his voice and faced Jemimah. His voice had become clearer.

The Will of Miss Valerie Hetherington

I, Valerie Heatherington, once also known as Rachel Friedman, am of sound mind and hereby confirm my wish to leave, after all duties are paid, all of my assets (Glebe House and my financial savings and assets) to my only child, Dr Jemimah Withenshawe. I wish for my dear friend Rupert Levy to also give my daughter the box containing the little memories I have kept of her and tell the story of her birth and her family so that one day she might find it in her heart to understand the impossible decision we had to make to protect her. She is a symbol of the truest love and peace enduring in a world that never wished for us to live together. I would also like to extend my heartfelt gratitude to Jemimah's adoptive parents, whom I know gave her the very best of childhoods and a future that today would bring so much joy to her biological father, Dr Ameer Tuquan, if he could have seen her. From a distance, I have felt complete knowing that Jemimah was safe and free, and I will always be glad that I gave life to her.

I also left this message and prayed to her: "Live long and live well, my dear Jemimah. I hope that the gift that I leave to you in this will may, in some way, help heal your pain of never knowing me or your father in life. I am so proud of you and know that you will choose well with what I have left you. Your kindness is a gift that your father left for you and watching you, has been like watching your dear father come back to life. Two doctors in two different worlds. May you always walk together in Spirit. I will always love you both."

As I lie close to death, I say my prayers and read Psalm 121. With these words, which I know should be for my soul, I pray that the Lord will protect you always. That you lived is all that I prayed for. That my prayer was answered leaves me with peace. Live long and happily, my beautiful Jemimah. You were always loved and always will be.

Psalm 121 (translated from Hebrew)
A Song of Ascents.
I lift my eyes to the mountains—from where will my help come?
My help will come from the Lord, Maker of heaven and earth.
He will not let your foot falter; your guardian does not slumber.
Indeed, the Guardian of Israel neither slumbers nor sleeps.
The Lord is your guardian; the Lord is your protective shade at your right hand.
The sun will not harm you by day, nor the moon by night.
The Lord will guard you from all evil; He will guard your soul.
The Lord will guard your going and your coming from now and for all time.
End of the testimonial

Signed
Witnessed

Jemimah sat pale in her chair. Her eyes were filled with tears, and she was gripping the arms of the leather chair that she was sitting in.

"Valerie…. I mean, Rachel was my mother? Where is my father? The will suggests he is dead too." Her eyes emitted a tortured agony. Like she had lost her biological parents all over again. This time she was so close, but never close enough.

Rupert leant forward to her. He wanted to take her into his arms, but professionally, he could not.

"Yes, Jemimah, she was your biological mother. I am so sorry that you had to find out in this way."

"But why? Why did she never come to find me? Why did she give me up?" Jemimah's composure had cracked. Her arms rose up as though she was asking Rachel herself.

Margaret and Michael put their hands on her shoulders. They did not know what to say to her. Margaret was angry that Jemimah's mother had not tried to reach out until her death. What did they mean that they knew she had been well cared for? Were they spying on them? How cruel this all was! Michael was curious. Something more needs to be said. There was something more that might give answers to this story. He looked to Rupert Levy.

"Mr Levy, this story seems incomplete, and the will suggests that you have something else to tell Jemimah. Might that help her?"

"Mr Withenshawe, the story of Jemimah's parents is a story I have carried with me all of my adult life. I brought her to England with her mother as a baby. So yes, there is something more I can tell, but Jemimah, would you like to hear it?" He turned again to Jemimah. He had a kind smile on his face, and his eyes focused deeply on hers. She looked at him with her red eyes and nodded.

"Yes, please go on, Mr Levy. I need to understand."

"Your parents came from very different backgrounds. Your mother came from a Polish Ashkenazi Jewish family who emigrated to Israel after the war. I did not know them, as they lived in Jenin and my family was in Tel Aviv. The family had military connections and was very much against Arab existence in Israel or Palestine. Your father, Ameer, was a Muslim from a very old and wealthy family in Palestine. He had been educated in Oxford, and that was where we met when I was studying law and he was studying medicine. We formed an unlikely friendship, some might say, but in every way, we were like brothers.

"When we went back to our homes in Israel and Palestine after our university years, life was not so kind to him. As a doctor, he felt destined to help his people trapped in a world they did not ask for, and he faced the daily traumas of combat and disease in Palestine. We kept in touch as much as we could, but I was powerless to help him. We wrote to each other about our lives and our loves. Such different stories. One day, he wrote about a Jewish girl who had secretly crossed into Palestine to see with her own eyes what it was like. She was injured in the crossfire and ended up at the hospital Ameer was working at. She made him promise not to tell her family because they were linked to the Israeli military and would blame her injury on the Palestinians.

"Her wounds were superficial, so she was treated by him and sent back home that same night. She had taken down his name and promised that she would try to help in some way. The little escapade had opened her eyes to a world so different from what she had been taught to put her entire understanding of the validity of the State of Israel into question. The Palestinians she had met were not the animals she had been raised to believe they were. They were kind and educated. Human beings and with souls who had been trapped in a world they could not escape from. She was confused initially and later she hated what her family was condoning and doing. She wanted to rebel and seemed fearless in her intentions. She was glad for this introduction to the other side and was also fixated by the memory of her alluring doctor, Ameer. That was not surprising, as he was a very handsome and charming man. Let me see if there is a picture of him here."

He reached for the box and rummaged for a few seconds.

"Ah, yes, here is one." He paused to look at the face of his old friend, who was forever young. A nostalgic smile came over his face, and he handed the aged photograph to Jemimah.

She took the photo and stared at the face in front of her. It was the beautiful face of a confident, tall man. She could see that her wavy hair, eyes and face shape came from him. She wondered what his voice was like.

"What happened to him, Mr Levy?"

"The story is a sad one, I'm afraid. As the weeks and months went on, Rachel and Ameer met in secret, against all recommendations and without the knowledge of their immediate Palestinian families are normally very reserved and conservative, but in the case of your mother and Ameer, love transcended all rules and reason. I only knew and Ameer's closest cousin, Ahmed, in Jordan. Their friendship grew into a passionate love, and they were careless. One day, her brother spotted them together whilst patrolling with the IDF whilst on duty. He was furious. When Rachel came home that night, he beat her badly and told her that he would kill the Arab. It was over. The whole family was unforgiving of her actions and did not care how it started. They blamed your father for corrupting her. They did not, however, know that she was pregnant. A few days later, Ameer was found dead.

"A single sniper was shot in the head. No one admitted to the death, but Rachel suspected who had done it. Ameer had feared for Rachel and gave her my address in Tel Aviv in case anything happened to him. He was so frightened when he found out about the pregnancy. Not because of his family but because of hers. He wanted to marry Rachel and take her away to Amman. How naïve they were! In those days, and even today, Israel forbids mixed marriages, something called miscegenation. His fears were right. The next day, Rachel escaped from her house and appeared at my door unannounced. We had never met, but I knew who she was. She had been badly beaten, and her face was bruised and swollen, but still, I could see that she was so beautiful.

"I took her in, and my family cared for her secretly. Nobody would look for her in our home. Her parents posted adverts in the papers and put posters up everywhere, but our secret was not divulged to anyone. Posters said she had been kidnapped by militants. They did not find her, though. We kept her safe until the time came for your birth, and you were a blessed baby born on the Sabbath, 9th May 1981. How happy we were that you were healthy. Rachel cried tears of joy for your birth and also sadness that Ameer could not have seen you."

"B-But what happened to the person who shot my father? Who was it? Was it my uncle?"

"Sadly, nothing could be done as there had been no witnesses who admitted to seeing anything. We could not come forward as the risk was too great. If your uncle had known about you, he would have killed you, and Rachel could not go back to her home freely after giving birth to a half Arab baby out of wedlock. The only safe option was to get you both out of Israel. Ameer's family had strong connections with Jordan through his cousin Ahmed. With some fiddling of papers, we managed to get safe passage there as soon as you were strong enough, and we flew to London that week. I had acquired a place at a law firm here, and Rachel was enrolled in a correspondence English degree course. We rented a flat together and thought that everything would be safe."

"As the first few months went on, we started to relax. We did not see any danger and walked about with our daily tasks without taking any care. In many ways, we had hoped that Rachel's letter to her parents, telling them that she had to left to live a life elsewhere, would mean she was disowned and forgotten. How foolish we were! One day, I came home to find Rachel in tears. She had seen her brother walking on the other side of the road. She had hidden behind a tree, but there was no mistake. He was there and had somehow found her. He now knew she had a baby, and there was no doubt that he knew whose baby it was. We moved out of our flat that night and fled to a friend's place. The next day, we applied for her name to be legally changed to Valerie Etherington, and I did everything I could to make sure that all documents of her previous identity were erased. She cut and dyed her hair and bought glasses to disguise her face. I dyed my hair too and let it grow a little longer.

"Then we waited. I moved firms, changed my first name from Avraham to Rupert, and got a new place at a firm on the other side of town. As he did not know me, I did not think he would find me. I was wrong. A few months into my new job, I was looking out of my window in my office, and one day I saw him. He was standing outside. He had found me. We did not know how he had done it. He must have followed me from somewhere. I rang Rachel and told her not to leave the flat. I left work at the back of the block that evening after handing in my resignation. We left at night and made a decision that broke our hearts. We decided to give you up so that you would not be found by him.

"We had been careful and had not registered you yet, so you were effectively unknown to the authorities. If we had put you up for adoption, you would have been traced, so we did the unimaginable and left you on the front steps of the local hospital. I called the front desk from the phone box a few yards away so that you were picked up quickly, and we waited in the shadows until you were found by a nurse. We fled London that night in tears and did not come back for two years. I worked at a firm in Oxford, and we prayed every day for your safety. I know what we did when we left you was illegal, but it was the only way to protect you, Jemimah. The only way to let you live. The authorities would never have understood what we were facing. Culturally, it was not what people here when the media wanted to convince everyone falsely that the Muslims are nada md the Palestinians are dangerous and the Israelis are protecting themselves."

He gave the box to her. Jemimah was silent. She took the silver box and opened it. Inside were photos of her mother and father. There were letters written by both. There were little jewellery items and a lock of hair. Her hair as a baby. She stared at the photos of her mother. She had a beautiful, slim face and was fine-boned with green-grey eyes, just her father and her like they saw the world through the same eyes together. She looked happy, and her smile was the same as hers. In the two photos, she finally understood where her looks had come from. Green eyes and dark wavy hair. She put the photos together. Her parents. Her blood. Her past. All gone.

Rupert went on. "We knew that your uncle was not going to give up his search, as he had seen you. As predicted, the year we came back to London, he reappeared. He confronted your mother and told her that she was to come home right now and to bring the bastard baby with her. She refused. He asked her where the baby was. She lied and told him that you had died of an infection. Thankfully, I was there and corroborated and made up a story that she had married me after you had died. She wanted to be free now and did not want to see the family anymore. He tried to convince me to give her up, as she had been polluted by an Arab and was a wanted fugitive in Israel. I told him that I did not care and reassured him that it was all in the past and I had forgiven her. Thinking she was married to a Jewish man calmed him. He left, and we never saw him again.

"Rachel did not trust him, though, and we made the decision to never give anyone a clue about you. You were safe. That was all that we wanted. After that, I asked Rachel to marry me, but she refused. She told me that her heart would always belong to Ameer and that the rest of her life was to ask forgiveness for giving up her baby and exposing Ameer to her family. She worked as a publisher in London for the rest of her life and, in some way, found solace in reading the stories of others to comfort the holes that never healed in her heart. Neither of us married in the end, but we stayed friends for life. We wrote to Ameer's family and explained what had happened; being wealthy, they arranged for you to be watched to make sure you were safe. You never knew about this because we wanted you to be happy. We had reports sent to us as well, which comforted your mother, but we all knew that you were no longer part of us. You had a new life. Our pasts were destined to remain a secret. He sighed and looked up to the ceiling as though he was looking at someone else.

"And that is the end of the story, Jemimah. I hope that you will forgive us and, with time, understand our predicament. I will also accept whatever you wish to do. If you wish, you can report my actions to the Law Council and Police. I would understand. What I do ask you, if I may, is to think for a little while before you decide," he looked at her, and a tired expression appeared on his face. Jemimah could see that a great weight had been lifted off him after all those years, and in some way, he accepted that his job was done.

"But Mr Levy. You have sacrificed so much. All because of me. In some ways, you were lie a second father, the half of my own dear father that lived on through your actions, and I cannot thank you enough. Please do not worry. I wish nothing more than to have a promise from you, Mr Levy, that you will keep in touch from now on. You are my last connection to my parents. We cannot make the years we were apart come back, but that does not stop us from filling the years ahead with more stories together, does it?" She reached out her hand and rested it on the back of his. He did not move his hand. His tired eyes were filled with tears, and the façade of a lawyer was shed at last. Today he looked into the eyes of the girl whom he had saved, and he thanked God under his breath.

Chapter 23
The Limits of Altruism

The mind of the surgeon is indeed an armed weapon, and Ibrahim was very much aware of that. As he sat at his desk, staring at the scans of Eric Potter, he envisaged all that could go wrong. A secondary aortoenteric fistula was a rare thing to see for any vascular surgeon, and he could see why Henry wanted to get another clinician to see it. With Jemimah off, it seemed logical that he was next in line. Perhaps Henry was seeing him with more respect now. Ibrahim was feeling flattered to be involved in such a case. This was a high-risk case, and not something he wanted to tackle alone. If surgery was feasible, time was limited, and without doubt, Ibrahim wants another colleague to be in the theatre with him for this. With early bleeding already happening, it needed to be soon, or the transfusions will be wasted. Ideally, next week.

He swivelled his chair around and looked at the calendar behind him. Jemimah was on annual leave for two weeks, and Henry was going on study leave. This was not good at all. He needed one of them in theatre. Since blood had been spotted in his faeces, Mr Potter had been admitted to the ward for endoscopy, monitoring, antibiotics, and transfusion, and to get him ready for the possibility of surgery whilst trying to sort out a second surgeon in theatre. They would need an extra list, as the lists were already full. He picked up his phone and called the manager in theatres to explore options. The entire list was full, but this case could warrant an emergency slot if the bleeding started again in earnest.

Ibrahim picked up his phone and called Henry.

"Henry, it is Ibrahim. Is now a good time to talk about Mr Potter?"

There was a momentary pause of silence, and then Henry replied.

"Ah, Ibrahim. Yes, what did you make of it all?"

"Well, it is definitely looking like a secondary AEF, and cultures seem to fit with it being from the infected dialysis port a few months ago. He had an endoscopy yesterday, and it confirmed a high duodenal fistula with some evidence of acute bleeding, which I think warrants consideration for surgery. It is all very high-risk, though, and the cardiologists and anaesthetists are wary of his chances. He has had a good dose of antibiotics for the infection and seems more stable now."

"Interesting. I suspected it was so when I saw the first scan last week. Well done for bringing him in and getting everyone to see him. Doesn't bode well, though, does it?" Henry was being deliberately cagey and was not giving Ibrahim too many hints.

"No, Henry, you are right. The prognosis is dire if we do not operate, but the chances of a problem-free outcome for surgery with his medical history is less than 10%. He is such a young man, though. Do you think we should do it?"

"Do what? Operate?" Henry asked slowly.

"Yes, take him to the theatre and remove the infected graft and fistula and repair the segment. Could we take him back together?"

"Well, if he is bleeding, it needs to be in the next few days, Ibrahim. It will need to be on the emergency list, and you are on call. Tomorrow, I am heading to London for a course. It's your call. I'm rather tied up this week, so I can't help you with this one, I'm afraid. I'm sorry. Next week is rubbish for me too, as I have the regional meeting to lead and some other stuff. The key is managing expectations, Ibrahim. There is always the option not to operate. You decide. I have to run as I am going into a meeting right now. Good luck with it." He hung up.

Ibrahim felt sick. Henry dumped the case on him and ran. How typical! This was not a good case to demonstrate his skills, as the chance of it going terribly wrong was astronomical. He decided to organise a team meeting with the anaesthetist, the cardiologists, the upper GI team, the ITU lead, and the Potters. It needs to be carefully handled. If Henry was not going to be a part of it, he would go higher. The clinical director of critical care, Andrew McNair, was a sensible and experienced man. He would keep things balanced. Ibrahim started a group email for them all. This was urgent enough to be flagged with a red exclamation mark, and the plan was for the meeting to happen tomorrow during lunchtime. His hands were cold, and his heart was pounding.

Was this the case that would make or break his dreams for a successful CERS application? If it went well, it could herald him as a brilliant surgeon, but if it went badly, would he be branded as inexperienced or worse? Was there another option? Refer it to another hospital. The problem was that Mr Potter was potentially too high a risk to transport. Perhaps the challenge was to do what he did not want to do—to let Mr Potter die without operating.

He walked to the ward. Sometimes all the answers come simply from the patient. He had to know what Eric Potter wanted, now that he had been bleeding and on the ward for a few days. He wanted to hear his views after his transfusion and after he had had time to talk to his wife alone. St Jude's Ward could not have been more aptly named. The Saint of Hope and Impossible Causes seemed almost ironic in this case.

"Ah Ibrahim. It is good to see you. Thank you for bringing me in. I already feel so much better," Mr Potter was a much healthier colour than he had been at the clinic and was sitting up with a newspaper. His half-moon reading glasses were comfortably perched on the end of his nose, and he looked rather better than one might have expected.

"You look a lot better than last week, Mr Potter. I thought I might come and talk to you about things now that you are settled on the ward."

"Ah yes. I'm guessing you want to talk about the surgery."

"Yes." It was not an enthusiastic affirmation by any proportion but reflected Ibrahim's concern. "Having you in the hospital has been very worthwhile, as we were able to bring together all the right minds to look into things more closely. Do you remember much from our last meeting at the clinic?"

"Well, I was feeling rather rotten that day, but I did have a good read of your letter about the infection and the fistula I have. Your letter seemed to give the impression it was not good news, but is perhaps that better now that I've been in the hospital?" he paused and looked wistfully up at Ibrahim. "Is there something that can be done about it?"

"I'm pleased that you have a recollection of the consultation. What you have, the infected communication between your bowel and the big artery, the aorta, that we repaired last year is a very rare thing. It is something that is notoriously difficult to operate on, and the risks of that operation not going well are very high. I need to talk to you about those risks today, if I may, to see whether you would consider that or would prefer the second option, which is to keep you comfortable and support you knowing that another big bleed is inevitable. What we do know is that you have had some bleeding, which is heralding something much bigger. When that big bleed happens is a question of when, not if," Ibrahim paused and gave Eric Potter some time to assimilate words that he knew would not be easy to hear.

He continued, "Have you considered whether or not you would like us to resuscitate you in the event that that happened? Because of your heart and kidney problems, there is sadly a very high risk that resuscitation would not be successful," Eric was focused and nodding slowly to demonstrate that all was going on.

He took a deep, slow breath.

"Ibrahim, the last time I had a big bleed, I thought it was curtains for me, but against the odds, I pulled through. I know I was much fitter then, and this time is different. The recovery afterwards was slow, and I really did it for my Beryl. This time we had time to talk about things, and we agreed that the decision was wholly mine. I had a great life, Ibrahim, and although I wanted to live for more years, it seems I was handed a smaller lot than most. If I had a heart attack again, I would like to try to survive, but if it's not meant to be, then at least we tried. I will leave the decision about more than that to you, but if the chances are too bad, let me go."

"Thank you, Mr Potter. The other matter is related to the options with the fistula. Surgery carries an extremely high chance of complications. Those complications include failure of the repair, infection of the repair, heart problems, kidney problems, stroke, and death. Because of your bleeding, surgery is really the only option that gives you a chance of a cure, which may not be completely successful, but even that is fraught because of the infection you have. The alternative is to do nothing and support you in the event of a major bleed, which is what will most likely happen in the near future."

Another long pause followed as the patient considered the gamble on offer and the surgeon considered the risks.

"I am sorry the picture is so bleak, Mr Potter. I am trying to organise a meeting with the rest of the team involved tomorrow, but for me, it is most important to hear your views first. What are your thoughts?" Ibrahim sat still and looked at Eric Potter. He did not envy him at that moment. There was a connection between them that made this moment more difficult. The gold standard detachment of a doctor from the patient had never come naturally to Ibrahim.

"So, I've got two choices then. The first is to do nothing and die here from a big bleed sometime soon, or the second is to have an operation to deal with the fistula, knowing that my chances of having problems or dying are high. Hmm, what a choice," he stroked his chin with his thumb and fingers. His eyes looked at the wall beyond Ibrahim. His eyes then moved to meet Ibrahim's. "Well, if the choice is mine, I choose to take a chance and have the operation. If it all goes wrong in the theatre, let me go when I don't know anything about it. That is my decision."

Ibrahim looked at him and nodded slowly. "Thank you for that, Mr Potter. This was not an easy thing to consider, and this conversation will not be the last one we have where you can ask questions and even change your mind. I will try to see if we can have the meeting with the rest of the team tomorrow, and I wonder whether you would like your wife to be there too."

"Yes, I think Beryl would appreciate that very much. This is all so difficult for her. With the children all grown up, we have grown to depend on each other in old age. I hate this whole situation. She doesn't deserve this." The depth of sadness in his eyes was physically palpable.

"Mr Potter I really appreciate your honesty and contribution today. Thank you very much for that. I will document everything that we have discussed in the notes, and tomorrow we can revisit things with the additional context of the others. Is there anything else that I can do for you today?"

"No, everything else is fine. I shall see you tomorrow, Ibrahim. Thank you for coming down to see me."

Ibrahim retreated to the desk, completed his notes, and walked to his car. This was a test for him, and the right answer was not jumping out at him. He was swamped with self-doubt and questions. Was he good enough to tackle this? What support did he have? Can he delay it until Jemimah is back? The latter question stalled him. Jemimah was on leave for two weeks. That meant she would be back in ten days. Could Mr Potter hold out for that length of time on antibiotics? Yes, that could possibly work. He decided to break the code and call Jemimah on her leave. The phone went straight to the answer machine, so he left her a message.

"Hi Jemimah. Ibrahim here. Sorry to disturb your annual leave, but I need your advice and help with a case. Could you call me back, please?"

He drove home in deep thought and hoped that Jemimah would call back soon. Tomorrow, he would speak with Andrew and see if the right answer would become more apparent. As the hospital shrank behind him in the distance, he breathed in and shook his head. The whole thing had consumed him. What was he thinking? Jemimah was coming round to their house on Saturday for her blind date. He was able to speak to her then. He needed to keep his head cool for this. He needed to think like a consultant, even though he wasn't officially one by name yet.

Chapter 24
Clarity

Jemimah clutched the box as she sat on the train home with her parents. Her parents were seated opposite her, and they all looked tired. For years, she had filled her head with doubts about who she was; who her biological parents really were, and why they had given her up. Today, all her questions had been answered, and yet the outcome was just a little box of ghosts. A story so tragic that it warranted its own book. A story that extraordinarily explained her own inner feelings of inequity and injustice. Suddenly, in one day, she understood who she really was, and for the first time ever, she was looking forwards in a way that she never had before. The gravity of the revelation was so immense as to steal the very words from her mouth. On this train, she was surrounded by the love that had nurtured her into adulthood. But in her hands were the roots from which she had grown. She was complete.

The first to speak was Margaret. "Jemimah, darling, what do you say to us all packing our bags and going away for a long weekend to the Lake District? This week has been such an unexpected one that somehow the idea of a spontaneous trip away seems like a sensible idea."

Jemimah looked at her mother. She smiled. What great parents she had!

"Mum, that sounds great, but I need to wake my head up first from what feels a bit like a dream. Would it be alright if we got home first and pondered about it over a cake and some tea, please? For some reason, right now the only place I want to be is with you and dad at home."

"Now a cake is something I would love to make. I found a wonderful new recipe last week for a citrus explosion cake that I think might hit just the right spot."

"Wow! That sounds amazing. Yes please," Jemimah felt like a little girl again, and having her parents around her somehow comforted her soul as she grappled with the many questions yet unanswered about her new future.

As they approached Saint's Bay Station, Jemimah turned on her phone. It had never been switched off for so long before. A fanfare of alerts announced the revival of the screen.

"Crumbs, the world has missed me!" Jemimah sighed as she opened her messages. Ten Messages. Henry had five left; Emma had left three; one was from Eliza and one from Ibrahim. So much for the annual leave!

She had quite forgotten her plans to meet with Henry and talk about Ibrahim's application for consultant status. Was it this week? Perhaps they can do it next week. This week was almost over, and Project Lift Ibrahim had been put to the side. It was important to him, though, and she had promised.

"Hi H. Sorry I've not replied. I had a very unexpected week. Can we reschedule for next week, please? J." Sent.

Ibrahim's message seemed unusually brief and looked worrying; especially considering she was supposed to be going round to his house on Saturday for the mystery blind date. Perhaps the mystery man had cancelled. This was a text that warranted a reply.

"Hi Ibrahim. Sorry, I've been silent. Had a very interesting week. Just read your message. Is everything OK? J." Sent.

Eliza's message was short.

"Hello, Miss Withenshawe. Eliza here. Just to say thank you for your good wishes. The exam went well, I think. Eliza."

What a relief! It went well. Jemimah smiled and then remembered Ibrahim's words of concern. Hopefully, the exam will put an end to that.

Then there was dear Emma.

"Where the F#8k are you? I tried calling you, but you aren't answering! Did you go to London to meet that lawyer guy?!"

"OK, this silence is crazy. Are you OK? CALL ME!!!"

"Lying here with my legs wrapped around B but I'm thinking of you. WTF?! Where are you???".

Jemimah laughed. This was going to be the first call of the day, without a question. Emma was about to explode, and she had been remiss in not updating her.

Jemimah looked up at her father. He was intrigued by her expression.

"Is everything alright?"

"Yes. Everything is just as I left it. I've just had a string of messages from Emma. I forgot that I had texted her about going to London. She's dying to know how it went. I don't blame her. My birth parents have been the subject of many conversations between us over the years."

"Well, I'm guessing a few hours will be spent today filling her in with all that has happened," he laughed and seemed relieved that Jemimah had taken things so well. Even though every adoptive parent accepts that their children might want to find their birth parents one day, nothing quite prepares them for how it will feel. That gnawing feeling of fear of losing the person most precious to you. He loved Jemimah more than words could tell, and today he was so proud of her.

"I'll call whilst mum is making her super citrus cake so that I won't disturb her and eat all the cake mixture." They all laughed as the train rolled into the station, and they walked off towards the next phase of their lives.

Chapter 25
The Final Position Before the Shot

Text: "How is the knee? Hx."

Text: "Sore and red. You cleaned it up well. Thx. Want to have a look at it?"

Text: "Does it look like it needs my attention? x"

Text: "Yes, I think so. I am on call until 8 :-/."

Text: "OK. Shall I swing by this evening on my way home if this meeting finishes soon?"

Text: "thank you. I didn't fancy going to A&E."

Henry sat back in his chair. He was pleased. Everything was falling into place. Eliza seemed oblivious to his intentions but seemed happy to engage. This was a very amenable sort of prey to chase; Ibrahim was heading for disaster; the investment was on track, and he felt fit and young. This next step, though, required delicacy. He was in a senior position in the trust and his little hunt for Eliza was high risk. It excited him and also stirred an emotion of delicious fear. It was almost better than a hunt. The prize this time was to be kept alive. To savour.

The knock on the door startled him. He had been deeply immersed in his thoughts. It was Andrew.

"Hi Henry. Is it OK to talk?"

"Ah, Andrew, good to see you. This is an unexpected visit. Is everything OK?"

Andrew purposefully pushed the door closed to ensure that no one else could hear their conversation. He was not in the mood to beat about the bush and launched right to the point.

"When we met at the pub, we talked about the lengths you might go to to get the deal sealed on the service expansion. We also talked about what I would and would not agree to be a part of, if you recall." There was a hint of irritation in his voice, and his face was flushed. Henry stayed calm whilst sitting positively in his chair with his hands on his chest.

"Yes, we did. What is troubling you, mate. Spit it out."

"Today, I met with Ibrahim and a team of other doctors to discuss a case that you had given to him. The case was Mr Potter, who we all know from his unexpected recovery from a complicated Triple A last year. Ibrahim wanted to discuss the risks of the case, and I confessed that my alarm bells were ringing. This is not the case for Ibrahim, Henry, and he told us that you were not available to help him. This is a case for two consultants, not a lone associate specialist, no matter how experienced he is; and you bloody well know that. In any case, it is a case that should not happen here. We are not set up for this sort of case. Was this the case you wanted to set Ibrahim up with? Tell me the truth."

Henry leant forward, and his eyes narrowed. He looked uneasy.

"Mate, Ibrahim wants to be a consultant. In this case, I am showing him that I am happy to treat him as one. My being away has nothing to do with it. I have a course booked for next week, and I'm tied up in meetings that were planned by your team two weeks ago. Don't try to make this look like I am the devil here. I told Ibrahim that not operating was an option with Mr Potter. If he still wants to operate, that is his issue, not mine! I've told you lots of times he is not ready to be a consultant, but as you and Jemimah seem determined to make him one, you can pick up his shit too! I'm not God. I cannot be expected to be everywhere for everyone," his voice was raised, and his body language in earnest, despite his words being untrue and overflowing with the aura of gaslighting at its best.

Andrew stared at him. He was annoyed because he could see that Henry was lying.

"Well, whatever the story, I have advised a hospital transfer for Mr Potter. He will be operated on at a tertiary centre, and we will hear no more of this case. Ibrahim is a good man, Henry, and he does a lot to help us. Find another way of getting the business plan through. I will not help you screw up the career of a man who is innocent. What exactly were you planning—that he does the case and be suspended when it all went wrong? That would never work because Ibrahim has done everything by the book. The questions would fall squarely at your feet, Henry. Clinical lead and lead consultant for this case. If you think playing the suspension game with Ibrahim will work, you are seriously wrong. Perhaps in other, more toxic trusts, that might work, but not here. We don't have the sort of medical director here who would fall for that. It would land at your feet."

Henry sat back in his chair and folded his arms. His face was flushed, and his lips pursed. Damn Andrew. He had ruined everything.

"Well, regarding the deal, it cannot go through whilst the extra work is being done by Ibrahim. Do you have any ideas what we can do to shift the game?" Henry lifted his eyebrows as he asked Andrew.

"I have been thinking about it, Henry, and there may well be a case for bringing Ibrahim in on it. If we take him on as an additional consultant, he might understand the strength of having a bigger capacity and choice of different environments for patients. The key is to convince him that this is what the service needs after a few minor tweaks have been made to make it sound plausible. Perhaps he can develop another service here to fill the capacity he has been using for the extra lists. There are many options."

Henry, who had been tense and defensive, started to relax. What Andrew was saying was credible and not easy to oppose. Perhaps this was another way. Sadly, he would have to tolerate the idiot Ibrahim as a colleague, but if he could turn it round to his advantage, he might be able to cope with it and also possibly come out of it looking like the hero. His head was nodding slowly. After all, there was something to be gained here.

"Yes, that is viable, Andrew. I will let you lead on it if that is OK."

"No, Henry, this is your baby. You need to prove to me that I am not teaming up with a bad deal. I want to see you improve your relationship with Ibrahim. If you can do that, I will stand by you in this project."

He stood up and walked to the door. Enough had been said.

Henry sat back and swallowed. He hated losing. He hated it when things did not conform completely to his plans. He felt betrayed by his friend, and all common sense at that moment escaped from him. As Andrew walked out, Henry mumbled under his breath, "Ibrahim, you may have got away with it this time, but mark my words, your day will come, and I will get rid of you. Softly, softly, catchee monkey." Rising anger filled his body.

He launched out of his chair and strode into the corridor towards the clinic. He was distracted and angry, and he needed to regain his sense of power and control. Submission was not his style.

Walking out of the clinic at the time was Ibrahim.

"Ah Henry. Hello," he looked pleased. "How are you today?"

"Ibrahim. Hello. Today is busy as always." There was a slight air of hostility in his voice.

"I had a chance to have an MDT discussion about the patient you asked me to see. Andrew McNair felt it would be better to transfer him for surgery, so we have set the ball in motion for that. Hopefully he can be sorted out to give him a chance of surviving this."

Henry just stared at him. He knew that he had to play a clever game here. Perhaps he had lost this one, but he would get another chance. The key was to play supportive.

"Yes, I heard about it. Good call, Ibrahim." Compliments to Ibrahim were never easy for him, and he was keen not to let his face belie his true feelings. He turned around and walked off towards the clinic.

Ibrahim smiled inside. He knew that this was not Henry's plan. Now he just had to hope that Mr Potter would get through the next few days without a major bleed and survive the transfer to the tertiary hospital. Either way, surgery was not in his hands anymore, and his angels had looked after him once more.

Chapter 26
The First Droplet of the Storm

As the long day of work reached its end, Eliza looked at the time on the computer as she typed the last comments onto the handover file. It was like all on-calls, a relentless day of rushing around, endless clerking of patients, non-stop talking, to-ing and fro-ing from theatre, and once again forgetting to eat properly or drink enough water. Her mouth was dry, and her body felt tired. It was nearly home time, and she was ready. Her colleagues taking over for the night shift were pouring into the room as she printed off the job list and added it to the folder. Still, so much to do, despite so much having been done. The life of a junior doctor was like a machine. Relentless and intense. A sore knee didn't help matters at all.

As she changed out of her scrubs, she caught a glimpse of her face. It looked pasty and pale, almost oily. The hospital air did something dreadful to her complexion. Her hair, which had been tied up sternly in a bun off her face, looked dishevelled as she pulled her band out. Home time was approaching, and she needed to freshen up. She remembered Henry coming over, hopefully to work some magic on her throbbing knee. For the first time all day, she noticed the stinging and pain in it. There hadn't been time to think of anything before that. Her limp had become her walk from one ward to the next.

She took her first step out of the hospital as she walked towards her car. The sun had set, and the dusk air was cold on her face. She shivered as she tucked her face into the scarf wrapped around her neck. She longed for a hug and a nice meal at that moment. Today, she missed her ex. She missed having someone to come home to who she felt safe and cosy with. It had been a long time since her last relationship, and there were still clinical exams to pass. Romance would have to wait.

She drove home in the usual post-on-call stupor. Music, which she loved, was a source of irritation that evening, so the radio was turned off, and the white noise of the car accompanied her to her tiny cottage. As she reached the front door and entered her house, she sighed and smiled. Lovely home. She looked at her phone. It was 8.30 pm. Time for a quick shower and change into a dress.

She raced upstairs. The shower revived her, and as she stood in front of the mirror, she looked pretty again. Her long, wavy blond hair was wet and smelled of the latest patchouli and vanilla shampoo, and her cheeks had regained a pink colour. She chose a sand-coloured floral dress to wear and some matching dolly shoes. She looked like a woman again.

The doorbell rang. Perfect timing, Henry. She hobbled down the stairs with her limp and opened the door.

"Hello Henry. My knee is glad you're here. It has been a distraction today," she was smiling with her sweet smile, and Henry looked at her kindly.

Eliza looked so beautiful with her tumbling, wet hair, and youthful smile. Henry felt a rush of excitement go through his body. He had to be calm and not act too fast. It was a game of trust and stealth.

"You look surprisingly well after an on-call day, Eliza. I'm glad your knee has missed me." He winked.

"Ah, that is the wonder of a good shower rather than a good day." She laughed.

Henry imagined her in a shower.

"You are still limping, though. Is that knee causing you trouble?"

"Yes, it hurts when I put any weight on it. I did a rather good job with my tumble." She looked guiltily at him.

"Well, we can have a good look at it and see how to get it better."

"Would you mind if I just grabbed a little something to eat first, please Henry? I haven't eaten all day, and I'm starving."

"Oh, of course I don't mind." He followed her to the tiny galley kitchen. This place was a matchbox, but the closeness was convenient for his intentions.

Eliza went to a big tin labelled "BISCUITS" and opened it. She offered the tin to Henry, and he took one of the chocolate chip cookies inside. Eliza grabbed another one and held it between her teeth as she closed the box. Henry laughed.

"You are hungry."

"Famished. I have always had a fast metabolism. Family trait, I'm afraid!" She said with the biscuit poised between her teeth. He loved how relaxed she was. What a contrast to Vanessa, who was all prim and proper and watchful of calories.

"Is this the sort of food you eat?" Henry had a perplexed face.

"Oh no. I have a pasta bake in the fridge, which I will warm up in the microwave in a bit."

"Put it in now. You need to eat."

She smiled and popped the ready-cooked pasta dish into the microwave. 2 minutes later, it was out, and she poured it eagerly into a plate. She picked up two forks and offered one to Henry. "You can have some too. There is too much here just for me."

"Thank you. I have food at home, but I'll take a few bites to keep you company."

They headed for the little lounge room. Tucked in the corner were a small table and two chairs, but Eliza thought it would be easier to share the plate if they sat on the two-seater sofa together. They ate the pasta and talked about the day. It felt lovely to have company. Some tomato sauce had escaped past the angle of Eliza's mouth as she talked. Henry reached forward and wiped it with his finger.

"You are hungry! Some got away," he smiled and was now sitting very close to her. She was conscious of it but innocently oblivious. Eliza blushed as he touched her face, and for the first time, she really noticed his eyes. It was his intelligence that she had been inspired by before. God, he was good-looking. She shuffled back, a bit embarrassed by her emotions.

"Now, shall we look at that knee?" Henry quicky, said so as not to lose the moment.

Eliza nodded. She rolled up her dress a little to expose the knee. Her porcelain-coloured legs were smooth and toned. The wound on her knee looked angry and red. There was a swelling on one side that looked infected.

"Hmmm. You have a little infection here. It is, hopefully, superficial." He took her leg with both hands and moved her knee. How soft her skin was. How warm her leg was. He wanted to take his hands further, but he stopped himself. He focused his eyes on the knee. Then he looked up at Eliza with the intensity of a focused surgeon...plus something more.

"Do you have pain in the joint when I do this?" She shook her head.

"No, it is just sore around the edge. I am hoping it is just inflamed and not infected, but I didn't notice the swelling yesterday."

"Well, I think it might be worth you getting some antibiotics for this." Instead of releasing the leg, his hands still held onto it, and Eliza did not feel she could even though she felt a little awkward. She was flushed and breathing a little deeper than normal. He was so strong and so imposing. Of course, he was. He was her boss!

As he put her leg down, he leant towards her.

Henry was the first to speak.

"Why are you single, Eliza?"

"Oh, I don't know. Too busy? Wrong time? Who knows? I have been focused on my career, I guess." She wanted to move him back into perspective. "What stage did you meet your wife at?"

Henry looked a little startled by the question.

"Oh, Vanessa and I were very young. I guess we just worked. She was a nurse, and I was a registrar. We just clicked." He wanted to change the focus back to now.

"The problem is that over time people grow used to each other, and sometimes something is missing and there is a need for more." It was a loaded comment, but his expression spoke many more words that Eliza partly comprehended as he suddenly leant forwards to her. His strong right hand crept around her head, intertwining his fingers with her hair, and he planted his lips onto hers.

Eliza wanted to resist, but she felt unable to. There was a feeling that she could not. A feeling that this was something outside of her power to control. She did not want him to hate her, so she let him kiss her. It wasn't as though he was a troll after all. It wasn't as terrible as she thought it could be.

OMG what was she thinking? WHAT was she doing? She pulled away abruptly and looked at him questioningly.

"I'm not sure if this is right, Henry."

Henry put his hands on her arms and smiled.

"We are adults, Eliza. This is just normal. We have such a connection. This is what we both need. You should see that. Shall we keep it our secret?"

He leant forwards before she could answer, and he kissed her again. She was helpless. His hand crept up her leg, and she tensed and yet also felt stimulated by his moves. This wasn't right, but he was strong, and also her boss. She had to pretend it was ok. She had to.

She gasped as he touched her. His strength scared her, but he also paradoxically aroused her, and she was helpless. He forced himself into her body, and there was nothing she could do. One hand pushed him away, and the other held his shoulder. She had let him in. Who would believe her? What could she do but yield to her fate? Intercourse was brief and urgent, but both were entwined in silence. One was relieved; the other was trapped and confused.

Henry had won his prize, and also revelled that she had not refused him. The power was like nothing he had felt before. A living stalk positioned and willing; how new and exciting this was.

"You are so beautiful, Eliza," he said as he moved the curls from her flushed face and kissed her again. "Now, we must keep this our little secret, OK? A sort of working relationship with benefits."

She smiled nervously at him, whilst inside feeling trapped.

"I...I'm not sure it is right to do this, Henry."

"Oh, Eliza, Eliza, you invited me here. You responded, didn't you? It's not like I forced myself on you. It isn't like you hated it, is it? Unconsciously, you see the connection that has grown between us." Gaslighting at its finest. He was the king of manipulation and charm, and this was his moment to shine. "Let's enjoy it for what it is. It's a bit of hard-earned fun for two adults. A celebration for a good exam done and all the hard work. Still friends?"

He had that winning smile on his face, but his eyes were assertive and probing and reminded her that their alliance was about her future, and he was a powerful man. She was trapped and had to play along with it. She nodded timidly.

Henry got up from the sofa and put on his clothes. He needed a good excuse when he got home so late. As he jumped into his Aston Martin that was parked around the corner, he was flushed. This was the best stalk he had ever done, and he was pleased with day one of his conquest but also there was an internal niggling feeling of anxiety. What if she spoke about it?

He needed this. He was on top of his game again as he strode out of her cottage. Andrew had no control over this. Eliza was his.

As the door shut, Eliza sat still on the sofa, confused about what had just happened. Had she wanted to have sex with Henry?

No, absolutely not. Her finger was poised anxiously between her teeth as she saw images of her in her head of him kissing her. Then she remembered him on top of her. His strong arms. She was powerless, but she said nothing. Did she respond to him? Was she aroused by him? Did she want this? She was so confused.

Could she stop it?

No. She could not.

Why didn't she try harder to push him away? She felt guilty. Part of her did try, didn't she? Maybe not, she was so confused.

Would anyone believe that when she had invited him into her house?

Of course not.

Was it their secret?

No. It was Henry's, but her future was in his gift, so she was trapped. If this was what Henry needed to get her through the exam, then she had no choice. One day perhaps she would have power, but today she had none at all.

She felt scared and sick.

Chapter 27
Impossible Decisions

Nights in the hospital constitute a strange time where corridors seem wider and the view out of the windows seem more apparent. Tonight was no different for Ibrahim or any of the on-call team. Vending machines were a focus of sporadic activity, sustaining the life flow of busy junior doctors as they rushed from one end of the hospital to the next with empty spaces in between. Ibrahim liked the calm of those corridors. In contrast, the vascular ward was like a beating heart. Relentlessly mobile and active. The beeping of pumps and call bells came from every direction, and the nurses' station was occupied by on-call doctors reviewing notes and imaging or talking to other doctors or nurses elsewhere. In many ways, it was a mirror of daytime, and yet in another way, it felt calmer, as though there was more space to think. In the evenings of his on-call days, Ibrahim enjoyed going up to the vascular ward to see all of the patients handed over to him.

It was something he had always done, and it reassured him that he knew everything about each patient just in case something changed overnight. As he sat down to review the blood results and observations for Mr Potter, he said a little prayer under his breath. If there was a sudden bleed, the right decision to make was going to be one of those dreaded moments where support and inactivity were all he could advise since the decision was made that treatment had to be at the larger centre. Mr Potter was on borrowed time; he knew that. But over the last few weeks, there was a deeper accord between doctor and patient. The cross-team discussion Ibrahim had requested (much to the irritation of Henry) that operating in the event of a major bleed was not something that should be done at Saints Bay. If it happened before the transfer to the tertiary hospital, they would have to let him go.

All measures had been put in place for that in the notes and on the drug chart, and lines were kept patent to allow the administration of drugs to support Mr Potter in his final moments. The transfer was set for two days' time, but Ibrahim was staring at the blood results. The haemoglobin was falling, and the platelet count was rising. Blood pressure was compensating, and his pulse was rising. Mr Potter's body knew it was in danger. Ibrahim knew a bleed was just around the corner. All the signs that the slow trickle of blood was gradually getting worse were glaring at him. It was a matter of time and luck. Was Mr Potter going to make it to his last chance location, or would it be the last night they saw each other? He prayed for the former. He prepared himself for the latter. The team had been briefed on what to do.

Walking up to Mr Potter's bed, it was noticeable how pale he was looking again. He was tired, and he looked older and more drawn. He was resting but opened his eyes as Ibrahim approached.

"Hello Ibrahim," he said in a slightly laboured voice. "Had a good day at work today?"

Ibrahim smiled and sat on the chair next to him.

"Hello, Mr Potter. I hope I did not wake you. Thank you for asking. Yes, I had a very good day. I thought I would just pass by and check, how you are. How have you been today?"

"Well, I feel like I'm tied to the bed with all these things coming out of my hands and arms. They must be doing some good because I am still here," he had a gently teasing smile on his face. Ibrahim smiled sympathetically back.

"Yes, it does seem like a lot. I guess it wasn't colloquially called a Christmas tree for nothing. Each one is necessary; I am afraid," he was reluctant to say anything to worry Mr Potter.

"So, do you reckon I am going to make it?" The look of hope was apparent in his pale eyes as he asked his daily question to the doctors.

"It is impossible to say, Mr Potter. You know well that I am crossing everything that you will make it to the transfer in two days' time, but with this scenario, the risk of that big bleed is high. I will not lie to you."

"I trust your word, Ibrahim, and value your honesty. Tell me, if I do bleed, how long will it take before it's curtains for me?"

"With a bleed of the size anticipated in you, it would just be a matter of minutes before you would no longer be aware of anything. I have also prescribed some medicines for you to help make that event as gentle and peaceful for you as possible. In many ways, you will not be aware of much." There was a pause. Both men looked at each other. Mr Potter broke the silence with a big sigh.

"Well, you make that sound like quite a nice way to go. I hope I can make it up the road to the operation, but if I am not meant to, then that is a pretty acceptable option two. I have seen my wife every day, and we say goodbye each day as though it is our last. She is such a wonderful woman. I could not have asked for a better life, Ibrahim," Ibrahim nodded slowly.

"Mr Potter, you are both lovely people, and it has been my absolute privilege to care for you." It was something that tugged at the heartstrings to have such a wonderful patient. Having a faith was Ibrahim's only way to reconcile the brevity of some people's lives and how unfair it seemed sometimes.

Ibrahim slowly stood up. He touched Mr Potter's arm.

"I shall be heading off now. I hope you can rest tonight and also hope that we will see each other in the morning. Good night, Mr Potter."

"Good night, Ibrahim. Thank you for passing by."

In many ways, Ibrahim instinctively knew that that would be the last time he would see Mr Potter alive. He wished so much that he could have done the operation with Henry or Jemimah. There was something unjust about being in the wrong place at the wrong time. The centralisation of care made financial sense and also made some sense in the concentration of specialist expertise, but Mr Potter brought home the case for where it was potentially less good. The limiting of hospital resources had limited what the team, a capable team, could do. The delay in transfer was because the central resource was not big enough to accommodate demand. The result was that all too often, patients like Mr Potter were held on a wire. Reach the end and make it. Don't reach the end and die.

As Ibrahim drove home, he felt flat. He thought of what would have happened had he not consulted the wider team. That was never an option as an associate specialist, but perhaps had he been a consultant, he would have made a different choice? Was being a consultant any different when the responsibility was squarely at his feet? Would it make him more daring or more cautious? He pondered these thoughts. He questioned whether becoming a consultant would change him. Would it make him more or less like Henry? Was this case an example of the difference between them? No, he thought not. After all, Jemimah was nothing like Henry. In many ways, she embodied the very image of reason and reserve. Yes, he would model himself on Jemimah as a consultant. If, of course, that day ever comes.

Just before he exited his car, he inspected his phone for messages. No texts, no missed calls, and one new email from the directorate manager.

Title: Extra Lists
Message: Dear All,

Following the divisional services meeting this week, a decision has been made to stop all extra listings on Saturdays as part of a service efficiency move and also to try to address the higher sickness rates and short staffing rates of nursing and allied staff from theatres during the week. It was decided that there is currently scope for better use of elective lists, and this will be trialled over the next two months. A new tracker will be embedded into the booking system to ensure that no lists are under-booked and also, that cancellations on the day of surgery are avoided. We hope that this will produce a 20% reduction in waiting lists alone.

A separate email will be sent to each of you this week with the details of the new plan, and I would like you to comment on it and email me any suggestions or your support by the end of this week. No reply will assume that you are happy with the plan.

Targets and actual data will be presented at monthly consultant meetings, and it is hoped that all teams will strive to reduce the burden of extra lists.

Yours sincerely,
END of Email

Ibrahim read the email, perplexed. He was taken on the weekend list because the waiting list was too long. The extra money was welcome too. Now they want to stop this and ask teams to make magical space appear on the already fully booked lists. It made no sense. Who on earth thought it would be a good idea to push teams to the brink this week to save a few pounds at the weekend? Sometimes the disjunction between management decisions and staff needs could not be further apart, but this time it seemed that this was a consultant-led decision. But why? The trust was not short of money. It was one of the few trusts in the country that had managed to balance its books, albeit using a skeleton workforce working like dogs. It epitomised short-termism in the height. Was this the sort of thing that he would be dealing with every day as a consultant, rather than just having to follow the rules without question? This would be something he would have to learn. The email had managed to distract him from Mr Potter. Home time was calling.

As he sat in the lounge at home that evening, Ibrahim thought and wondered. He was quiet and contemplative. His phone was sitting next to him at the table, and his conversation with the family had an air of distraction to it. Part of him was thinking of Eric Potter, and part was ruminating on the content of the email he had received. What was going on? Was this a Henry trick again? What did it mean? He knew well that he had been set up with the Potter case. Henry was not a man to take losing anything easily. Was the cancellation of the weekend lists a punishment? A message to remind Ibrahim that he was under the control of others and not to forget it? Yes, that sounded like Henry. The decision was a bad one, though, and risked putting waiting lists up not down.

If there was one thing that rattled Ibrahim, it was backhanded politics that put the agendas of individuals before the needs of the patient. But if this was the case, what could he do about it? The voice of Jemimah came into his head: "Pissing off Henry would not be your smartest move." Yes, this was not his battle to fight. Well, at least not yet. He needed to think like Jemimah and gather the information with stealth first. Then, with everything to hand, weigh it all and make a decision in the cold light of day whether there is something worth going after or not. Ibrahim had never been an astute politician. Part of him was pleased with that because it was a testament to his raw honesty and integrity, but part of him regretted his apparent naivety and lack of ability to spot the wolves amongst gentlemen.

As he lay awake in bed, he listened to the gentle breathing of Aisha. She was his strength and his one absolute in life, and even when sleep eluded him, he could find some peace in just being beside her. He tried to close his eyes and recite some Dhikr, the form of silent meditation in Islam that he found daily comfort in. Subhanallah, Subhanallah, Subhanallah…The words went round and round in his head. He felt the tension rolling off his shoulders and back. The furrows on his brow relaxed, and his ears seemed to fall back a few centimetres. His teeth stopped clenching, and his face felt the tiredness of his tension. He slowly drifted into sleep.

BZZZZZZZ! BZZZZZZZ! BZZZZZZZ! The mobile phone beside the bed lit up and awoke him with a jolt. His eyes were wide open, but for a second, his body remained asleep. He clumsily stretched his arm to the bedside table and in an almost dyspraxia manner knocked the phone to the floor. He sighed and realised that it had awoken Aisha too. He looked at the clock, and it read 03.23. Grabbing his phone and swinging out of bed. Tiptoeing out of the room, he answered with a whisper, "Hello. Mr Ibrahim's phone. Give me a second; I'm just going into another room."

In the study, his voice returned to normal volume, and his brain was alert and switched to autopilot. It was the nurse on the ward.

"Hello, Mr Ibrahim. I'm sorry to disturb you, but we have been trying to get hold of the junior doctor and the registrar, but nobody is answering. It is Mr Potter. He has a MEWS score of 4 and we are worried he may be bleeding internally. He is not rousable, but he is breathing. SATs are normal, but his blood pressure is low. Should we start the haemorrhage package?"

"Oh, I am sorry you cannot get the team. They may be in the theatre or at A&E. Yes, you are right, it does sound like he is decompensating. How is his temperature? Is he septic?"

"No, if anything he is hypothermic. Temp 35.5."

"Well, sepsis can shift the temperature either way, so it might be. Call the outreach team and see if they can get blood and do a septic screen whilst I come in. Put a bag of normal saline up for over 4 hours. If it is a bleed, he will not be with us by the time I get there. Remember, he has a TEP form active. He is not for intubation," he was putting some clothes on whilst talking. "I'm on my way."

"Thank you, Mr Baba."

He rushed to his car and dialled A&E whilst starting the car. Bluetooth hands-free kicked in as he raced out towards the hospital. He drove fast, as the roads were empty. Normally, it would take fifteen minutes to get there. This time, it would take less. The call was answered.

"Hello, A&E"

"Oh, hi, it is Mr Baba, a vascular surgeon. Do you know if my SHO and registrar are down there? The ward has not been able to find them."

"Yes, they are in resus. Trauma call with a bleed. They have their hands full. Do you want me to get one of them?"

"Oh, right. No, let them deal with that. I will be in the hospital shortly and will go to the ward."

It was turning into one of those nights that might not end anytime soon.

He parked by the entrance and walked with speed to the ward. There were several people around Eric Potter's bed, and he stood at the end of the bed to assess.

Eric was white as a sheet. The monitors around him heralded the one thing he had wished wouldn't happen. This was not sepsis. He said hello to the team and introduced himself. He walked to Eric and pulled the sheet back. There was bruising all over his flank. Eric's hands were cold, he was unconscious. His time had come.

"I am afraid it is the bleed we were hoping would not happen. I am afraid there is nothing we can do. Poor Mr Potter's time has come. Has he been this settled all along?" He looked at the nurse opposite him.

"Yes, he has been very calm. We have diamorphine and midazolam ready in case that changes. Shall I give some?"

"Yes, a little of both would be a good idea," he looked at the outreach team and said, "Thank you for coming out. I think we can let him have a little peace now."

They smiled gently towards, Mr Potter and walked away. Jane the Nurse and Ibrahim remained. A few minutes later, Mr Potter passed away. It was peaceful and calm, and there was silence around him.

Ibrahim looked at the nurse opposite him. Her name badge said, 'Hello, my name is Jane.' "Are you alright? Sorry, you couldn't get the team here sooner. They are stuck in a resus with a trauma patient. Thank you for all that you have done."

She looked sad. "Eric was such a lovely man. I can't believe he didn't make it to his operation. Was there really nothing you could do, Mr Baba?" She looked achingly at him.

"Sadly, not Jane. An operation here would not have been successful with the facilities we have, and going this way was much more kind. Surgery is a big insult to the body, and Mr Potter was not a well man besides the fistula. There was little hope even with the operation that the tertiary hospital was proposing. He knew this might happen and seemed at peace with it. Sometimes the greatest power we have is to allow a person the right to die with dignity. Tonight, you and the team did that for him. Thank you," he smiled kindly at her. She reciprocated.

"Would you call Eric's wife at 6 am please?" She nodded. "Thank you, Jane,"

He was the last person remaining with Eric. He leant forward and squeezed one of his cold hands. Under his breath, he whispered, "Rest in Peace, Eric." His phone rang, it was A&E. The night was going to be a long one.

Chapter 28
Life Reset

"Fuuuuuck! That is heartbreaking Jemmy. I have no idea how you can sit here and be so calm after going through that," Emma was perched on the edge of the chair she had sat on. Jemimah sat opposite her on the edge of the bed. She had told the whole story of her biological parents for the first time since returning from London, and it felt good. She wanted to tell it over and over so that somehow, she could reconcile herself with the heart-wrenching fact that she would never meet them in life.

Emma jumped from the chair to sit next to her best friend. She stretched her hand out and held Jemmy's. They were uncharacteristically silent as each weighed the meaning of the words that had filled the air between them. For years, Jemmy had tortured herself about her background as though it was the key that would open the door to her existence, and now that they held that key, they were almost afraid to turn it and find out what had been denied for so long.

For Emma, there was a sense of bereavement for the mystery that was now gone. The mystery that had fuelled so much of her work. Yet here her darling friend was exposed, and also still in so many ways, a paradox. The lovechild of two sweethearts was never allowed to live in peace. It was as though that tragic story left a tale in her eyes and her soul. She felt anger for the lovers lost, pain for their lives not lived, and gratitude that this wonderful gift of a friend had been brought safely to grow beside her. How the universe perplexes her sometimes. It made all of the wars and prejudices pale into insignificance when the product of love that shatters those boundaries can produce a phoenix like Jemmy. She was a beacon of hope for all. A symbol of how the world should be and who we could all become. Emma was the first to break the silence, and it was not just with a few words; she let her thoughts pour out.

"Shit! this one moment has defined my art for a decade! Your story is how I see triumph. The tragic love story of your parents is the story of the faults of this world, and yet their friendship with Rupert shows that so much can be conquered where there is belief, courage and great friends. Your story is like a living opera, Jemmy. It is like this door waited to open because it was just too fucking massive to deal with when you were young. Your parents thought they were protecting you from your uncle, but in actual fact, they saved your story until you were old enough to really live the life they wished for you. How fucking profound is that?"

Jemmy was looking at Emma with a sad smile. Her eyes were tired and also receptive. She loved Emma. The eternal glass, half full, could turn every situation into a piece of art that remembered that moment forever. It was as though she had chronicled the story of Jemimah Tuquan in beautiful creations that allowed others to interpret her story as their eyes saw it. Some might have found it intrusive, but for Jemimah, it was a way to see what she had not been able to comprehend for years. The story that was trapped within her stifled her breath. Now that story was free, and she wondered whether she was free. Free from what? She wondered. Her doubts? Her fears? Or perhaps it was just her insecurities. There was a strange burden that came with being an orphan. It was a constant aching, for something great that had been lost before consciousness, as we define it had started. She wondered whether there were in fact different types of consciousness and that, in fact, we never forget the first moment our newborn eyes see our mother and father. Those eyes in which one trusts implicitly. A tear rolled down her cheek.

"Oh Em, how I wish I could have known them, heard their voices, and seen them look at me. I know that my father never got the chance, but I hope that today they are both looking down at me from heaven and smiling. It seems so strange that I love them even though I do not know them. Looking at their photographs has filled my mind. I imagine them alive and imagine what our lives might have been had the prejudices in Israel not existed. So many years have passed, and still the people of Palestine and the tolerant in Israel suffer. My whole life and longer. It's inconceivable. Something within me suddenly wants to go there and help them. Was that why I became a surgeon, I wonder? For years, I have felt like a misfit, wondering what my purpose is. Perhaps this is what has been missing in my career."

Emma's facial expression showed she was not convinced. "Well, my advice is this: take it slowly, Jeremy, because you know well that it is a very risky thing to do. There are other ways you can help without going there. Perhaps you should meet up again with Rupert and talk through things. It sounds like he is a lovely man. He did so much to protect you. I have a feeling he will be distraught to hear that you want to go into the same firing line that killed your father. Also, you have no idea if your uncle is still alive. Leopards rarely change their spots. Let them go on thinking you died as a baby. So many people sacrificed their lives for you to survive. You help people every day here. Keep doing that, lose the bloody Mother Theresa outfit, and for God's sake, loosen up and go on some dates! You don't need to become a martyr. I would much prefer that you focus on finding a man and having some babies of your own."

Suddenly, Jemmy laughed.

"Oh, Em, you have such a good way of resetting my mind. Where would I have been without you? Whenever my head fills with thoughts of things I cannot change, you seem to say just what I need to hear to snap out of it. You're right. Why am I planning so far ahead? I have my hot blind date at Ibrahim's tomorrow. I don't need to screw it up. I'm so glad that you came home early, Em. I needed you."

"Ah it's alright babe. I was so distracted with worry for you when you weren't answering my texts that I gave up playing with my German stallion and came home. Besides, I sold loads at the exhibition, and guess what? I have three big commissions, too! Things are looking great. There was absolutely no way on this planet, I was going to miss being here for you. As you can see, your dumb idea of going far away won't work as you can't live without me, and there is absolutely no bloody way in hell; I'm going into a war zone!"

The two women laughed and hugged. It was as if Jemimah's mind had found new clarity, and she realised it was her duty to live and enjoy life. The life that so many had sacrificed so much for. Today was the turning point, and her bigger and more colourful family had filled in the last pieces of her jigsaw puzzle of identity, and she was happy with what she saw.

They spent the afternoon talking about outfits for the date and telling jokes about what might happen. The journey ahead was not one of doubt, but instead one of enjoying her identity and meeting more of her family. She wanted to meet her family in Jordan, who had helped her mother and Rupert escape to England. She wanted to get some frames and hang up copies of the photos of her full family. Her biological and adoptive parents all filled a big wall in her home so that she could look at them anytime and feel like the luckiest woman alive. Complete and alive.

Chapter 29
Power Misguided

'Andrew, you pompous man, cornering me like a naughty schoolboy and telling me to be nice to Ibrahim. You patronising fool! The deal was my idea, and now you want me to sort out the trust as well!' Henry was absorbed in his anger whilst out running. One half of him was pure fire, and the other was pure power from his recent conquest. Yes, he needed more of the latter. He ran faster than usual, and after freshening up at home, headed out in his car. He drove mindlessly towards Eliza's cottage. He was driven by impulse. A toxic mixture of anger and power consumed him. He reached the door and took a deep breath.

Eliza opened the door and looked surprised. This time there was no invitation, but again, she was powerless to refuse.

"Henry, hello. This is a surprise. I'm just in from shopping," she felt a bit awkward. She could see that he was rather flushed. Was he angry? Her long wavy blonde hair tumbled over her shoulders and partly masked her enquiring expression.

"You look frustrated, Henry. Is everything alright?"

He was breathing deeply.

"Right now, Eliza, everything is better. I needed to see you. Today has been difficult."

"Oh, I'm sorry you've had a bad day," she replied sympathetically, although she was confused as to why he was in her house.

"How is the leg?" Henry needed to appear to have arrived for a purpose. His inquiry, she knew, was about more than her leg.

"Much better, thank you. The antibiotics did the trick. You worked your magic on it," she smiled nervously.

The door shut behind her, and Henry launched forward to kiss her. This was not a gentle kiss, though. He was in earnest, and his eagerness frightened Eliza.

He pulled her towards the sofa and pushed her onto her back. This was not the tender man who had kissed her and confused her before.

"Henry! This is intense. Slow down. Is everything alright?" She was shaking. She was breathing heavily. "Henry, please, this isn't right. Henry, please stop."

He did not reply. He held her down. He kissed her neck. His body rubbed over hers. He was hard and aroused. His hands reached between her legs, and she gasped. He forced her legs apart, and she was helpless. He thrust into her like a wild animal. It hurt her, but she was too afraid to stop him. She closed her eyes and tried to imagine it was over. She was not strong enough to push him away. The ordeal came to an end after what seemed like an eternity, and she stared at him, confused, and scared.

"What is wrong with you? You hurt me, Henry. Why are you being like this? I asked you to stop." She looked straight into his eyes. They were close to her. She could feel his breath against her. He was breathing heavily, but the animal in his eyes had previously gone. He stared into her eyes, into her soul.

Her words had disarmed him. He pulled back and looked at her as though the beast had left him and the gentleman she knew and loved was lying on top of her.

"I'm sorry, Eliza. I thought you'd enjoy a little rough sex. I did not mean to hurt you. You know, I think you are wonderful. I could never do anything to hurt you. You know that don't you? God, you make it sound like I raped you. I'd never do that to you," Eliza pulled herself free from beneath him. Her arms were wrapped around her breasts, and her ruffled hair shadowed her tearful eyes.

"You scared me, Henry. It was like you were venting some anger at me. What made you do that? Has something happened?" She did not want to show him her naked body, so she turned her back to him.

"Oh, Eliza I am a fool. I had a rubbish day yesterday and woke in such a mood that the only thing that I wanted was you. Even a run didn't help me, and I could only think of one thing. That, I wanted to be with you. That's what I needed from you. I would never wish to hurt you. You know that don't you? Forgive me?" His heart was beating strongly. He felt a sense of profound worry for having hurt her. He was also scared that this little venture of his could sting him professionally. He had clearly lost the plot and was unravelling it. What was the matter with him? He was angry with himself and with Andrew. But taking it out on Eliza was a rubbish thing to have done.

Eliza stood still. She was shaking.

"Henry I am no enemy of yours. I am so grateful for all that you have done for me, but you had no right to do what you just did to me. Promise me that you will never hurt me again, and I will try to pretend it didn't happen."

"I promise. I hope you believe me. You do, don't you?" His reply sounded desperate. Pleading. Pathetic. She pitied him but was also wary of him. Could she end this without making things awkward at work? He was her boss. He was her route to finishing the exam. Once she had passed the second part, she could leave. She managed to escape. It was just a case of bidding time and trying to give the impression that everything was the same.

"Henry, these visits to my home need to stop. I want to continue our session together, but only at work. Can we agree to that?" She looked at him with a combination of pleading and fear.

He was worried. He had to make things better. He had to reverse his error somehow.

"Oh, er yes, sure, that would be fine. Have I ruined everything?"

"There is nothing, Henry. You are a married man and my boss. What has happened between us needs to stop."

Henry had to concede. What Eliza said was right, even though it wasn't what he desired. He had crossed a very serious boundary and risked everything for a moment of thoughtless impulse. A moment of selfish venting.

Eliza had wrapped her arms around her waist to hide her hands, which were trembling. She needed to keep calm—well at least calm externally. Her head was racing. What had she done by getting involved sexually, willingly, or not, with her consultant and training programme director? A married man on top of that! I was wrong. She was blaming herself.

Henry walked up to her gently. "You are an amazing woman, Eliza, and I respect you. I promise I will get you through your exams, and I promise I will never hurt you again. I do not know what came over me. I apologise. Truly, I do," he smiled nervously.

Henry quietly stepped back from her and looked at her. He felt sick. Had he just forced himself on a junior doctor? 'Oh God, what have I done? She was able to report me. I need to smooth things over.' His mind was racing. His heart was beating strongly. He slumped back, tense and upright, on the sofa. The pale light coming through the window highlighted his flushed complexion. He needed air but he could not leave. Not until he had checked Eliza was really ok. How could he do it? 'Think, THINK!'

Eliza's head raced. There was a lump in the middle of her chest, and it felt like it could not move. She was somewhere between bursting into tears and complete despair. She was trapped. He could not see her cry. What could she do?

Henry was the first to break the moment of awkward silence. Suddenly, the fierce consultant was replaced by a gentler face. "You have made me think about myself. I used to imagine that the world was my oyster. I could have everything I wanted, and nothing could get in my way. I have become complacent, and I am not proud of that. You have become such an important part of my life. I guess that is why I ran first to you. I had no right at all to force my feelings on you. I am so sorry. I just misinterpreted what you said and your response to my advances. I thought of it as what you wanted. You seemed to enjoy it."

Was he really trying to suggest that she had made him do this to her? Eliza suddenly felt an unexpected anger rising inside her. She needed to stop herself from shouting at him for suggesting that any of what had happened was her fault; she resisted calling him all the things she wished she could. He was still useful to her. She had to play this cleverly. She also recalled that she had allowed him into her house. In some ways, she felt partly to blame.

"Henry, I think enough has been said today. Let's shake hands and promise me that you will never do that again, and we can start over, but professionally only." They had to work together, and somehow this nightmare had to be buried. At that moment, she had to set some boundaries.

He took her hand and gently shook it. Never before had he been in such a grovelling situation. He hated that feeling. His brain could not compute the concept of being disarmed, even if the mistake was all his. He had always been on top. His cunning side was momentarily disabled, and his only instinct was to plead pity. He had a lot to lose. Come to think of it, so had she. Even his posture had changed. His towering presence appeared shrunken. Eliza had noticed it, and although there was a little pity for him, she was also wary. If he could do this after a few days of getting closer, what else would he do to her? She was scared. She had trapped herself in a corner. He could ruin her.

Another silent, awkward pause followed.

Henry realised that this was his moment to turn around and leave.

"I will make it up to you. You can trust me, Eliza. I hope you know that." He looked sad and sincere.

She stared at him with her soft blue eyes. Her eyes were still showing alarm, but her fear had subsided. If ever there was motivation to pass the exam, it was this. Now her freedom and future depended on her success and surviving this torpid moment intact. Nobody could know about it. It was, as Henry had said, 'Their secret.'

Chapter 30
Faces

Sitting on the bed with Mutty sprawled across her lap and purring to the strokes after his return from the holiday hotel, Jemimah stared out through the window. A mere two days had passed since her day of revelation, and every emotion imaginable had passed through her body. It was as though she was living through an accelerated bereavement for people whom she had never met and yet was a part of. The agony lingered for the part of herself that had died. There had been an initial shock associated with profound despair at knowing that her mother had been here in the country but had never met her. She ached, thinking that they had never talked or laughed together and that she had never heard her mother's voice. Although she would have seen her eyes as a baby, she could not remember them. It was like being abandoned all over again, but this time she felt as though she knew her parents. She felt guilty for Rupert, who had loved her and her mother but who could never enjoy a full life because of his sacrifices. She wanted to reach out to him, but she needed time. She knew that this journey of many questions was only just beginning, and she needed to be conscious of how this might affect her at work. Now was a time when she was distracted and could make a mistake. After all the years that she had been meticulous at work, she feared now that she might take her eye off the ball. Perhaps she needed time away. A tricky prospect lay ahead, trying to convince Henry that she needed compassionate leave to mourn her parents, whom she never knew. Yes, that would need to be thought through. It was not difficult to imagine his face and words if she told him that. She would be more likely to get compassionate leave if something happened to Mutty.

Jemimah stepped off the bed, much to the disgruntlement of His Royal Fluffiness, and stood in front of the mirror in her bedroom. She had spent hours looking at old photos of her biological parents, and now she looked at her own face. A face that she had grown up with, and now at last she could see where the features came from. She held the photos of her parents up in a mirror on either side of her face. There was no doubt that she was the child of these two beautiful and innocent lovers. She had worried for so long about what her lineage was. Whether there were criminals in her past. Here the truth lay in the smiles and written words of two innocent people torn apart by an injustice that stole their youth; it stole their right to be a couple; it stole their right to raise their child; and in the end, it stole their lives. One thing that lasted, despite all of that, was their love for each other. It had never died, and just knowing that gave her new strength. She pondered whether to do like her mother did when she came to the UK and change her surname, but she also found out on the internet that often in Palestine, women keep their maiden names after marriage; conversely, it was normal for a Jewish man to give his name to a woman he marries. Also, the love between Rachel and Ameer was not a normal union. Choice was not something they had. So, knowing the history of her mother and father, she imagined that Rachel would have chosen to give up her surname and become a Tuquan. With this in mind, she pondered the idea of becoming Jemimah Tuquan-Withenshawe. Yes, that sounded quite good. Workwise, though, she would probably stay with Withenshawe because she was known for that professionally. This change would be just for her. A symbol of the blood that coursed through her veins and the love that had raised her.

She turned to Mutty, "So my darling, how would you like a new surname? Mutty Tuquan-Withenshawe." Poised regally between her two pillows, he blinked as though in approval, and his tail wagged sinuously over the headboard.

"So that looks like a yes from you, and it is a yes from me. That is what we shall do." She took her beloved cat into her arms and kissed him.

Although she was restless and tired, Jemimah had received strict instructions by text from Emma to make sure that she went on a blind date at Ibrahim's that night and to make sure that she looked stunning. The first part was difficult enough, but the energy to dress to impress was one step too far. No, the mystery was that Jeremy was going to meet her au naturel, without any fancy makeup or suggestive clothing. Just Jemimah. That, she could cope with. Before any of that, though, she needed to go for a run, so she jumped into her running gear and set off with Le Trio Joubran playing through her headphones. It was a new album she had downloaded earlier that day. An album of traditional Palestinian music. The mystical sound of the oud, played by people from Palestine, took her to a world she was yearning to discover. Images of her parents flickered in her mind as she ran. She ran faster and faster as the anger over what happened to her family played again and again as images she had formed of the past.

How she ached for all that they and Rupert had suffered as they courageously and innocently lived in fear and confusion about injustices that none of them had created—senseless injustices that had engulfed the love and friendship that bound them all across the man-made barriers. Faster and faster, she ran as the trembling, rhythmic strumming of the ouds permeated through her ears. She seemed to instinctively relate to the music of her origin, and it reached out, telling her the story of her culture embedded in history, tragedy, and faith. It answered her memories of the yearning sense of displacement that she had carried with her throughout her conscious life. The song *As Far* was telling of a journey, and she felt that was starting a journey of her own. One to trace her family in Jordan as Palestine was impossible to get to and she did not know whether her Israeli uncle was still looking for her. It was not safe for her to cross into Israel even with her westernised name, so locating her uncle, who had helped her mother and Rupert escape to England, was going to be as far as the journey could go for now until peace, that ever-elusive peace, could return to Palestine. It was her land by blood, but not one she could enter unless she went there as a doctor, and Rupert would never let her do that. How could she come to reconcile that, having grown up as a free citizen of the United Kingdom? She pondered what freedom really was. Was she really free here? Her mother had not been free to keep her. How could an Israeli assassin just cross into the country with no questions asked? Just because he was Israeli. Was the world really that black and white? She had not seen it as having grown up in a bubble of UK ignorance and distorted stories. In a world where Palestinians were classified as terrorists and Israelis were the victim. 'Oh, the irony!' she thought. In a way, she felt triumphant as a half-Palestinian who had made it through the net. How had they done it? It was because her mother was an Israeli Jew, and Rupert was too. There were clearly different kinds of Jew, but no questions were asked in the West. The Israeli passport was all that was needed. Even if her parents had managed to escape together, she suspected that her father could never have come here easily. She suddenly had a hunger to learn more. To read more. To talk to people more. It was as though she was about to be reborn. The new Jemimah emerging was a survivor, a remnant of a great legacy of love undeterred and triumphant through the persistence of life within her. There was no wall or barrier that could hold her back now.

As she reached home, she caught a glimpse of her face in the mirror in the entrance hall. She was glowing and looked altered. There was a lightness to her brow where furrows had resided before, and she appeared younger and more alive. There was a post-run warmth on her cheeks, and she could palpate her new self-confidence. Tonight was a great night for a blind date, she thought. For the first time ever, she was able to introduce herself and talk about herself without the innate feeling that she was in some way telling a lie.

As she dressed for the date, her apathy was replaced by a new optimism. Instead of her original plan to go in a very unembellished way, she rummaged around the dressing table for some mascara and lipstick. It was heavy makeup for Jemimah, as her olive-coloured skin was without a blemish and the run had given her a natural rose colour. She put on one of her favourite yellow dresses and some black and ivory shoes. She recited the rhyme "yellow on black…venom lack; black on yellow…Kill a fellow." Yes, the colour scheme was the right way round and no man was dying tonight. She smiled. It seemed that even the air of melancholy that had lingered behind her old smile was no longer there.

"Mr Mystery Jeremy, here I come. You had better be worth all this fuss."

Driving to Ibrahim's place on the other side of the village, she hummed one of the Arabic tunes that she had listened to whilst running. There had been some beautiful words alongside the music, and she had found the Arabic language so lyrical to listen to. It was not a language she could understand yet, but that would soon be changing. The truth was that although she had a name for her origin, she knew little of the culture. She pondered as she drove.

Ibrahim's house was truly picture-perfect. A pretty, double-fronted stone cottage. The sun shone on the stone, giving it a glistening golden pink hue, and the fuchsia-coloured rambling rose climbing along the wall exuded an intense aroma all around the garden. Entwined amongst its leaves, white jasmine flowers glistened like stars. Aisha had kept the gardens immaculate, and, in every way, it was a welcoming home that resembled its occupants. Jemimah knocked on the door and sniffed deeply to absorb the smells around her. She looked at the name plaque next to her on the wall as she waited. Fatima, Ibrahim's mother, had named the cottage "Gidan Wardi" which was translated as "House of Roses" in her native Hausa language from Nigeria. Jemimah said it aloud. She loved that name.

The door opened to the sparkling smile of Aisha. Despite being only five feet tall, she seemed to fill the doorway with warmth. Her love of bright Nigerian colours was a feature of everything around the house. She wore a bright green, embroidered Nigerian tunic and slim trousers with a coordinated headpiece. She was a lady of Nigeria to look at, but her accent was plain English. Jemimah loved how she seemed to smash stereotypes into pieces and yet, at every level, exuded a depth of her culture that left no doubt about her identity at heart.

"Ah Jemimah. Do come in. You look very pretty." They kissed on the cheek.

"Aisha how lovely to see you! I love your outfit. It is simply stunning."

"Oh, gosh, thank you. It comes from my home in Nigeria. I love wearing this sort of thing. We call it an agbada. They are made for women who move lots and want to look stylish. It suits a dinner party rather well."

"I think I need one in my life," Jemimah remarked.

"Well, then allow me to choose one for you, Jemimah. It would be my pleasure."

"Oh, I would love that. Thank you, Aisha. So, is the mystery person here? I confess I am unusually intrigued, but I imagine part of that is because I trust you and Ibrahim to have good taste." They both laughed.

"Well, Jeremy is an old friend and someone like you. Single for reasons that no one can figure out. I suspect he is rather particular about his women, as he is a man who has a lot to offer."

"How enticing," Jemimah smiled cheekily. They walked through into the lounge. Ibrahim was there and stood up to greet her.

"Jemimah, hello. At last, we have managed to organise something outside of work. Do come in and make yourself at home." He stepped to the side to reveal the mystery man behind him.

"This is my old friend Jeremy. Jeremy, this is my friend and colleague Jemimah."

There was an eager nervousness in each of them as they stepped towards each other to lightly shake hands. Although the idea of love at first sight was not something that either of them believed in, there was a definite connection between the two strangers, and both blushed. Well, Jeremy blushed, and Jemimah, whose olive skin tone meant blushing was not visible, felt flushed. This was indeed going to be a good evening. Ibrahim made a rather feeble excuse and followed Aisha into the kitchen to 'help'. The two Js were left alone, and as if they had known each other for a long time, they just began talking. Everything seemed effortless, and the evening passed by with a sense of knowing that something very special had begun.

Chapter 31
Newton's Law

Every action has an equal and opposite reaction, and thus, it also occurs in humans who instinctively exhibit a naturally reactive response to an unexpected event. Henry was such a person the day after his misdemeanour. Although internally he was worried and angry with himself about the possible repercussions of what he had done, he was also paradoxically remorseful and softened in his general tone. He was like a great tower that had just crumbled a little on one side. Still an impressive man, yet weakened. To say he was humbled would have been one step too far, however, as his thoughts remained solidly fixed on himself and what might happen. He was focused on making the world see nothing. Possibly, a flawed approach, as when one tries to hide something, it is usually written all over their face with the big black marker of guilt. Henry was not a good liar. He had never had to be because he had always got what he wanted and been admired by all around him.

There were several people whom he needed to convince that all was well. Firstly, there was Vanessa, who was no man's fool and had already been rather twitched after finding Eliza sitting on the kitchen table. He had been somewhat mistaken in believing that she was blindly in love with him. It was what he had convinced himself of, and now he was being forced to think of himself as a husband rather than an infatuation. This self-reflective exercise was not something that he had ever had to do, and he hated it. The discomfort of the idea that he was in any way flawed. After all, it was his hard work and wealth that had afforded the comforts that Vanessa and the children had enjoyed.

There had to be some understanding that he was just a man and that it was natural for him to want to be that red-blooded man occasionally. So the fact was that this was the easiest of the tasks on the list, as flowers and perhaps a nice new diamond ring should reinstate him as a loyal husband. After all, his time with

Eliza was just something that was about keeping him healthy. It was not as though he was planning on leaving Vanessa. Eliza was an adult and had her own life ahead of her. This was just an interlude.

The second person was Andrew McNair. He was angry with him, but after what had happened with Eliza, he knew that he needed to control those emotions just in case the truth broke out. He had lost perspective and had said things to Andrew that revealed his deeper thoughts. What a fool he had been. A fool to believe that Andrew would simply get his views. Now that he was exposed, he had a lot of work to do to convince Andrew that he was a man to be trusted. The task he had been given was not an easy one. A task where he would have to support a colleague who was a damn nuisance Ibrahim, becoming a consultant colleague in order to reach his current desire to get a deal through. Oh, the irony! The sheer pain that would be needed to pretend that he was fully behind a man he had loathed since the day they met. How would he do it? How COULD he do it? This was his nightmare, and he risked his inner anger breaking out again. The flip side of losing an ally like Andrew was dangerous in itself. He knew well that part of his status in the hospital stemmed from his association with him. How tightly that knot of solidarity was tied. A true club that was, in reality, as brittle as the morality that was the foundation on which the tenuous membership stood.

The last person to convince him was Ibrahim himself. Now this was something that Henry felt sick just thinking about. He could not quite explain why he disliked his colleague so much, but some of it was related to his sickening sycophantic politeness. Who on earth was that polite and meant it? He was British-born, so surely it was not a cultural thing. No, he was just a fake person and did not fit in. OK, that he was not a bad surgeon had to be acknowledged, but that was not what made the team. It was the fitting in that mattered most. The team was something much more related to understanding each other. There were just some people who didn't fit into Henry's team, and Ibrahim was one of them. Why on earth Andrew and everyone else seemed to like him was beyond him.

He was also a clinical lead, and that was what mattered. If Ibrahim had not already been a permanent fixture before he started there, there was one thing that was certain: Ibrahim would not have been part of the team. To think that now he, Henry Blythe-Soames, was being forced to support Ibrahim in becoming a consultant was something that was akin to torture. He had to do it. Not for Ibrahim, but for himself. To give everyone the impression of how reasonable he was, even Eliza might like him again. This was going to be the hardest thing he had done. And then there was Eliza, whom he needed to keep close. What had he done? He needed her admiration and understanding. He needed her approval. Why was this? He could not explain. It was part of his plan, and one thing—just one thing that he had wanted needed to go according to plan. His response needed to be swift and carefully constructed. The first thing he needed to do was phone Jemimah. Where the hell had she disappeared?

He picked up his phone and texted her.

Text: Hello J. Sorry, last week did not work out. Are we still planning to catch up and talk about Ibrahim? Are you around? H

Henry sat back on his chair and stared out of the window. He was stressed, and he felt that the world was caving in around him. He had never felt so disempowered, and he hated it. He hated that people were watching him and questioning him. He had always been the one everyone looked to as an example of how a surgeon should be. This whole experience was alien to him, and he was perplexed. Letting go of control and power was not in the master plan.

His phone beeped. It was Jemimah.

Text: Hi H. Sorry, I haven't got back to you. I had a difficult week off. Can we meet to discuss it pls? J

This was not the reply he was expecting.

Text: Sorry to hear that. Yes, call anytime to arrange. H

The reply came quickly:

Text: Thank you. J

He wondered how Eliza was. Should he call her to touch base? This was the first day he had not instinctively messaged her and felt awkward. He looked at his phone and their messages. There was a hiatus in the messages between before the event and now. This was an important matter. Should he send one?

He was uncharacteristically confused. Is it too early to say hello, or is it the right time to restart the conversation as though nothing had happened?

Text: Hi. How are things? Hx

Delete, delete, delete...

He stared at the phone and then threw it down on the table. Give her space, Henry. You just raped her. Oh God, no, it wasn't rape; it was just a bit of rough sex, wasn't it? Give her time.

By reflex, he turned on his computer and checked his emails. There was work to be done. That is what he needs to do before the clinic to get back into the moment. Focus Henry, Focus. His heart was beating fast, and he knew that it was not the coffee that he had drunk that morning. Fifty-four new emails later, and he was calmer. He took a deep breath and headed to the clinic. It would be the first time since the big change that he would see Ibrahim. Let the game begin.

As he walked into the clinic, he felt strangely uncomfortable. A sense of wariness and being exposed had crept into his demeanour, and it did not go unnoticed by the staff. The first to approach him was Nurse Jackie.

"Hello Henry. You seem serious today. Is everything alright?"

Henry looked at her and faked a smile.

"Ah, good morning, Jackie. It's good to see you. Thank you for asking. I'm fine. I'm just swamped with things at the moment. Have we got a busy clinic today?" The rapid deflection to the subject of the clinic was strategic and worked.

"Oh yes, it is a standard clinic. Forty patients for you and Ibrahim to see. He got here early and has already started, so I'm thinking all is well," she smiled kindly.

"Oh, that is kind of him. Good, good," he said whilst clenching his teeth and smiling. This whole thing was going to be exhausting, but he imagined that day one was always going to be the hardest. He immersed himself in his work, and the clinic passed without any more strain. At the end, Ibrahim popped his head around the door.

"Hello Henry" He smiled with his usual kind and slightly sad smile.

"Ibrahim hello. Thank you for starting the clinic. We seem to have finished at a good time, with enough spare time for lunch. Now, that is rare. Fancy joining me?" His eyes told what his fake smile did not, but Ibrahim was willing to go along with this new style of conversation. Could it be that the story of Henry supporting his application was in fact true? He was not going to absorb himself into the whys and wherefores. This was a chance not to miss.

"That would be nice. Yes. Let me just grab my jacket."

As Ibrahim walked out of the room, Henry took a deep breath. He pondered where Andrew might see them and used the opportunity to demonstrate his efforts. The main canteen was the most likely spot.

The two men walked out of the clinic, and Henry was conscious that Eliza had not come to say hello. Was she going to report him? He felt sick. He needed to message her. He needed to see her.

Chapter 32
Fear

Eliza sat at the doctors' station on the ward and stared at the notes she was writing in after the ward round. Images flashed back of that terrible moment when she felt that she no longer had control of her own body. She could not get it out of her mind. She wanted to cry and shout it out. She could not. Suddenly the response, that pent-up volcano in the chest, was on the edge of erupting, but she was at work, so it could not. There was an overwhelming weight that seemed to lie in her chest as she fought away the tears. There was no possibility of help. This was her own mess. It was a situation in which she had convinced herself that she was as much an instigator as Henry. Somehow, she and Henry had to forget it. There was a bigger picture. The exam. With Henry by her side, she was going to pass that exam and move away.

All she needed to do was put the thought away. Far away in the back of her mind, and focus on the task. This was not a fair world, and she knew that if she did speak out, it would wreck her chances of becoming a surgeon. Henry was a high profile and respected surgeon. The world would believe his story, not hers. He had far more than she did to lose. His defence would be more convincing. Her thoughts were abruptly broken, by a voice.

"Hi, are you using that computer, Eliza?" It was one of the other junior doctors.

"Oh, er, no. Sorry," she jumped out of the chair and rushed out of the room. Her colleague had noted the strange behaviour and wondered what was going on.

Eliza felt that the oxygen in the hospital was thick and unbreathable. She needed air. She walked fast towards the side exit and pushed open the door. She gasped and clutched her chest. How was she going to get through this? What was she going to do when she next saw Henry? He had to think that everything was alright. It was a forgotten moment. She had never felt so alone in her life. At that moment, she missed her ex-boyfriend, Simon. He had always been predictable. At that moment, someone dependable was what she needed. Perhaps she could call him. She needed to talk to someone. If anyone knew her, it was him.

She pulled out her phone from her pocket and dialled the number. Her hands were shaking, and her face was pale.

"Hello? Simon, is that you?" Her voice was trembling and weak.

"Eliza. Are you OK? You sound terrible," he was concerned, and his voice came down the phone to her like an enormous hug.

"Is it OK to talk to you? I just really needed to talk to you." Tears were running down her face as she spoke.

"My God, Eliza. What's happened? Are you alone? Do you need me to drive down? I've just finished a week of nights, so I'm off."

"Oh Simon, I have done something so stupid. I'm in a mess. Could you come down? Please?" She started weeping and put her hand over her eyes. After trying to bottle everything up, the shock was just pouring out of her. She was scared.

"Who is with you, Eliza? Is there anyone there? I cannot get to you until tonight. Will you be okay until then?"

"No, I'm alone, but I'm also at work and need to finish my day. I'm OK. Really, I am. It is just a ward-based day, so I am OK. So far, all seems quiet. I just needed to hear your voice." At that moment, her bleep went off. It was A&E.

"Oh, I have to go. Thank you, Simon. Thank you. I'll text my address to you." She hung up before Simon could say anything else. She wiped her eyes and sniffed hard to try to stop her face from looking like she had been crying. That day was going to be an almost impossible day, but it was also a test of her resilience. Four hours to go. That was all.

She rushed to the nearest phone and took the call. From that point onwards, whatever emotions she wanted to express, there was no time for any of them. The job was the priority, and she didn't need to mess up.

As she rushed to A&E to see the emergency patient, she wondered whether anyone would notice that she had been crying. Her face did not have a good tone for crying and tended to get very blotchy. She tried to blink a lot and put on her glasses, which were so weak in prescription that she hardly needed them, but they covered her blotchy cheeks. She tightened her hair back and coughed. She could do this! Even though she felt anxious and scared, she had to do this.

Every task, every note, and every question were considered. It was as though she was taking a history from outside of her own body. Her ears were ringing, and it was as though the mouths of the patients were moving slower than usual. She needed to concentrate, but her mind was distracted. Three hours to go.

Suddenly, an alert came through the A&E speaker phone. A call for vascular surgery to resus. She looked up. This could not be happening, so she rushed to resus. The trauma team was preparing to receive a complex road traffic accident case that was bleeding. She switched to autopilot, phoned Sarah the registrar, and donned her gloves and gown. Sarah arrived and looked at Eliza. "Are you OK? What has happened?"

"Oh Hi. I'm really not feeling well. Terrible migraine, and I feel like I'm going to pass out," she lied.

"You need to go home, Eliza. I'll take over here. Will you be OK driving home?"

"Erm…yes, I think so." Her eyes had welled up again.

Sarah looked at her. She was not so convinced by the story but didn't have the time to ask more.

"I hear what you are saying, but that doesn't quite fit with what I'm looking at. Go and get yourself some water and sit down in the staff room. I'll come and see you in a bit. Don't drive home like this. It would not be safe," she put her hand on Eliza's shoulder and squeezed it.

"OK?"

Eliza nodded and looked at Sarah apologetically.

"I'm sorry," Eliza said.

"No need. These things happen. Go and sit down. I'll see you in a bit," she turned away and headed towards the resuscitation team. Eliza turned and walked obediently to the staff room. She was numb but also rather paradoxically angry with herself. If this was how she was going to cope with it, she was being absolutely rubbish at it. The anger with herself seemed to break the cycle of tears, and she sighed deeply. This was day one. Yes, it had not gone well, but tomorrow she would be stronger.

Instead of waiting in the staff room, she phoned her colleague, who was taking over for nights, and asked whether he might be able to start his shift early to help her. He was happy to and came to pick up the bleep. She was free and rushed to her car. It was time to go home and rest. A conversation with Simon would sort everything out. It was not as though she could ring her mum and tell her that she had been assaulted by her married consultant. That would not help the situation at all. No, Simon was a safe bet. He worked far enough away from her that her story could lie safely with him. Also, she trusted him.

The case in A&E required consultant input, and the consultant on the call that day was Henry. Five minutes after Eliza had left the department, Henry walked in. His presence in the resuscitation room was as commanding as ever, and in this role, he was calm. It had not crossed his mind to look for Eliza. The focus was on the patient at that moment. It would not be something he thought about until he was scrubbing for theatre, and at that moment, he missed her. Over the last few months, she had made it her task to be in his company as often as possible, and he had got used to her. What a damn fool he had been.

Arriving home, Eliza jumped into the shower to wash off the stress from the hospital. As she walked into the bathroom, images of Henry flashed back into her mind. Images of him, his breathing, and his smell consumed her thoughts. She stood frozen and pale. Memories of fear and pain produced a deep pain in her throat.

After a quick functional shower, she walked to the bedroom and flopped onto the bed. She curled herself into a tiny ball and held her knees. Her eyes were wide open, and her heartbeat palpably in her chest. How was she going to face him again? She had to. She had put herself in this mess. It was her mess to unravel. She flitted from distress to anger to confusion. So many feelings, so many thoughts, all tangled in a knot that lay uncomfortably in her chest. Without noticing, and possibly out of exhaustion, she fell into a restless sleep. Day slipped into the night, and the front doorbell awoke her. It must be Simon.

She walked downstairs, ready to fall into his arms, but it was not Simon. It was Henry. Henry was at her door with a big bunch of flowers and a smile that looked kind but still guilty. It was no use; his futile attempts to make amends were not helpful. Both had made mistakes, and it would take time to recover from them. She was as angry with herself as she was unsure of him.

"Oh, er… Henry. Hi. I was not expecting you. I…er…have a friend coming over," she stood at the door and did not move aside.

"Oh, that is good. I just wanted to check that you were alright and not alone. Is someone from work coming over? Sarah told me that you had left early because you were not well, so I thought I would pass by after the case was done to see you."

"Yes, I had a horrible migraine. To be honest, I'm still a bit spaced out. Would it be alright if we met another day, please, Henry? I'm afraid I won't be in good company tonight. I think we need a little space for a while, if that is OK." She avoided answering questions about who exactly was coming over. Why was it any of his business? Her body was shaking behind the door, and her hand gripped the edge of the door tightly. Outwardly, she tried to retain her smile. She still needed Henry. She didn't need to upset him. She was powerless, and somehow she had to make it all right again. It was just that it was too early. This was not supposed to be happening. She took the flowers.

"Thank you."

He leant forwards gave her the flowers, and kissed her cheek. She responded with a tentative tilt of her face to receive the kiss, but then moved away carefully. Why did she now hate this? She had loved how he smelled before.

"Of course, it is fine, Eliza. Do message me if you need anything. Rest up tonight, and we can chat another time when you are ready. Good night," he smiled a sad smile and walked away.

"Good night, Henry," she closed the door.

She closed her eyes and took a slow, deep breath. Her heart was racing, and she felt nauseous. In a perverse way, Eliza pitied him. He was a confused soul who did not know how to apologise easily. She was going to have to gradually let him back in, but the few weeks until results day for the written exam would give them time to have space. She needed that time to figure out what had happened. Henry's words, telling her that he had responded to her signals, made her wonder whether the whole thing could have been her fault. Was it fair to blame him when she was the reason it happened? Yes, it was her fault. She let him in. She led him to hold her wounded leg for longer than he needed to. She had led him on. "Stupid, reckless Eliza," she thought to herself.

As Henry drove home with a second bouquet of flowers for Vanessa, he was deep in thought. Eliza didn't suffer from migraines. This was all his fault. She was upset, and he had been the cause. He had much to mend; first, Eliza, and secondly, Vanessa. Would Eliza spill the beans and tell someone? What if a colleague was coming over? Was the story going to come out? Oh God, Henry. You complete IDIOT! You knew this could happen, but still, you ploughed recklessly on, and now you're scared about the consequences? He slammed his hands on the steering wheel. At least he had to ensure his marriage was not about to end too.

As he drove up to the Grange, he was not his usual confident self. In some ways, he felt like a lesser man. This escapade that was meant to be a bit of fun had in fact derailed him and left him questioning everything about who he was and what drove him. Was it just the consequence of his actions that scared him? Was he really so baseless that his sole raison d'etre was himself? No, surely not. He had, after all, provided well for his family. Vanessa and the children had wanted for nothing. He had that to be proud of. Gradually, he convinced himself of who he was as a man. This was just a little blip. He had allies. He was going to be OK, even if Eliza said something. There was always another side to every story, and he was a respected consultant. Questions would be raised about her. Surely? It wasn't the first time a consultant had slept with a junior doctor after all. He exited his car feeling a little more stable.

As he walked up to the house, his previous guilt was buried inside, and he launched like the performer he was into the hallway to announce his arrival. As Vanessa came over to see him, kissing his cheek and saying hello, she looked at the flowers with an expression of slight perplexity. Henry never bought her flowers. What could have brought this on?

"This is a surprise. Is there a special occasion that I have missed?" She asked him.

"No. Not at all, darling. I saw them in the shop outside the hospital and thought you might like them. It has been too long since I last bought you any." He tried to maintain as genuine a smile as possible on his face and hoped that she would be convinced. Trying to dupe the person who has shared your life for the last twenty years is not an easy task at the best of times, but now he was enshrouded in guilt. Was it written across his face and in his eyes? He could not tell.

"Well, I think I might have a shower before dinner. Today was a long day. Do I have time to do that, darling?" He quickly moved on from the subject of the bouquet and turned his face towards the stairs. Vanessa was still standing facing him with the bouquet in her hands.

"Yes, if you are quick."

As she turned to go into the kitchen, she pondered. Did this have anything to do with that girl who was in the kitchen the other day? Could she trust Henry? She pondered whether this was the expected midlife crisis for Henry and a challenge they would have to work through. Was it something she could deal with? Time would tell.

Meanwhile, at Eliza's house, Simon had arrived. As she opened the door to him, she rushed into his arms in tears. It was as though all the shock and fear that she had kept inside were released in one go.

"Shhhhh, now. I'm here, Liza. I am here. Shhhhh. I'm sorry it took me so long to get here. What has happened?"

"Come in and take your coat off. You will need a stiff drink before you hear what I have done. I'm in big trouble, and I need your help."

"That sounds like a big ask. I'll try my best." He looked into her eyes with concern and then followed her into the cottage.

They went to the lounge. Eliza poured them both a gin and tonic and sat down next to Simon. He was the first to speak.

"Now, if tonight is going to be helpful, we need to set some ground rules. Number one, we do not get drunk. Number two, you need to tell me the whole story, not just the end bit. Number three, we need to find an answer to your problem in the next three hours because I need to be up at the crack of dawn to get back to work tomorrow. Do we have an agreement?"

Eliza smiled at him. How she missed her sensible ex-boyfriend. Simon had been a balancing force in her life, and in many ways, they were very good together. If only geography and training hadn't got in their way. None of this mess would have happened because she and Simon would most probably still have been together.

Eliza stretched out her right hand towards Simon in a gesture of agreement. How strange it was that not long ago she and Henry had done the same, but the context was so different. With Henry, it had been about drawing lines and creating false promises to make things feel better. Now she was doing it to ensure that a solution was found.

"Agreed. Let's find that solution. Thank you, Simon," they shook hands like committed businesspeople.

She went on to tell Simon the whole story. Nothing was left out, and time ticked by as the details mounted in one pitiful moment after another. Simon listened quietly. He sat next to her but was careful to give her the space that she needed. The last thing that she needed was another man taking advantage of her. His head was spinning with anger at Henry, but he restrained himself from commenting. He reserved his responses for nods and expressions that were aimed at comforting Eliza. Eliza, whom he had loved since school days. That innocent, silly girl who had now been thrust into the cruel world in such a way that she could never be the same again. He hated Henry. He felt guilty that he had not been closer and protected her in some way. As Eliza cried, tears flowed down his cheeks too. Imagine how she felt about being effectively raped in her own home by a man she had trusted. A consultant. A doctor. A married man. It was too much. As the story came to an end, he asked her if he could give her a hug. She nodded weakly, and he gently opened his arms, which she fell into like a child.

Simon broke the silence.

"I want to punch the lights out on that bastard! How could he misuse his position of power in such a way? Please don't think for a minute, Eliza, that this was anything at all to do with you. It was not your fault at all."

"I don't agree, Simon. I led him on, I think. I must have. We were both to blame. We are both adults, after all. Nobody would believe my story when I let him in, and he left without a struggle."

"Eliza thinks like a doctor, not a bloody victim here! He raped you. His story of why doesn't matter, Eliza. It is only the action that counts. You know as well as I do that rape is often carried out by people whom victims know, not strangers. Henry will have carefully groomed you. He used your exam and the revision sessions to worm his way into your trust. He knew exactly what he was doing. He sounds like that sort of alpha male psychopath, and you are one of the most unsuspecting people I know. Please try to understand that you need to report this. Not only to defend yourself but also to protect others. He is a predator in a surgeon's outfit. A privileged, upper-class git who thinks he can have whatever and whoever he wants on tap. Well, this is not a day when he is going to get his way. Not with you. No way." He was getting more and more heated as he grappled with the horrific truth of what he was saying. Not just saying but recounting to a woman he still loved.

Eliza looked into his eyes and smiled sadly.

"You are so kind, Simon. I know you mean well, and I guess that is why I trust you more than most. Reporting Henry is not something I can do right now, and I am not sure that he is as bad as you say. He is very powerful, both in the hospital and outside. You know as well as I do that the hierarchy of surgery does not always bat on the side of women. My key to escape is my exam, and sadly, Henry is now very much entwined in that journey. He would not have walked away from this guilt-free. I suspect he will be treading very carefully from now on and I need to be someone I have never been. I need to be cleverer than him. I need to use him and then deliver the blow in a way he is not expecting. Somehow, I need to survive the next few months; I hope that I can pass the exam and get a training number a long way away. If I choose not to report him, I need to think of another way to win. We have to figure that out. My head is such a mush at the moment that I cannot think clearly. Can you help me, Simon? Please?" Her beautiful blue eyes looked imploringly into his. What she had said was not what he wanted to hear. It was all so terribly wrong.

"Eliza, going to work and seeing that man is not what you need. Where will you get support from? Apart from me, who else knows? Have you told anyone?"

"I don't know how I will cope, but I have to. I cannot tell anyone here. They will say what you have, but that cannot end well. I am trapped. I must find a way to survive this. My exam results from part 1 come out next week, and if I have passed, that leaves only a few months of hard work to the clinical, and I am on the escape route out. I need to play a game with Henry by bringing others into our revision sessions and making excuses to prevent him from coming to my house. Perhaps we can find a place we can meet together that in every way prevents him from doing anything sexual to me but at the same time allows me to give him the impression that it is no big deal for me. That way, I stay in control, and he may, in time, naturally walk away. That could work, couldn't it?"

"It all sounds very unsafe to me, Eliza. You need to have a clearer idea of where that secret place will be. Promise me that you will never go alone in his car with him and always carry a mobile phone with you. Uh! I hate this, Eliza. I just can't sit comfortably with it. Why do you have to do this when he has done such a terrible thing to you?"

"Why? Because I am nothing, Simon. A little trainee and he is the big consultant. He is a popular man, a leader, and respected, and I am perceived as a dizzy blonde woman who hardly anyone knows. The stereotypes alone are enough to answer your question about why I cannot just report him."

"Eliza, the GMC has clear regulations about this sort of thing. He would be hung high and dry if you could prove it."

"Yes, I see that, but I didn't call the police, did I? I didn't go to the hospital and cry rape, did I? No, the next day, I went to work. I went to the same place where I knew Henry would be. Yes, I went home early with a migraine, but that is hardly a case for rape. Do you not see that this is not as black and white as you are saying?" She sighed deeply. Her posture slumped into the chair next to him, and for those few hours, she felt safe. If only she could carry Simon in her pocket with her for the next few months to talk through things, she would be able to cope.

"You still haven't told me who your support network is going to be through these next few months. I am not going to be happy going back to my place if there is nobody here to support you, Liza. We need to find someone you can trust," he looked at her with a look of intense concern. "Is there not a staff grade or another doctor you can talk to?"

"That would be as good as reporting Henry myself, and even if they chose to respect my wishes, it would put them in an impossible position as they would have a duty of candour to report anything that put me at risk. No, there is nobody here that I can tell."

"By that argument, Eliza, I should report it. It's not fair to just dump this on me and say it's OK because I work at a different trust in a different county. It is still the same NHS and in the same country, both of which exercise strict rules on rape and misuse of power. Can I not say something? What about his wife? Is she safe?"

"Vanessa? Yes, I feel terrible about what it risks for her. In some ways, I was hoping that I could just disappear after my exam, and hopefully Henry would just return to being a married man with his two children and loving wife and forget me. Can you not see that that would be the best outcome for all?"

"No, I do not see how that would be the best outcome for all. It would have been the best outcome for Henry, and he would have walked away from a heinous crime with no reprimand at all and therefore be as likely to do the same again to someone else. No, I do not think that just walking away would be a solution. And what about you? You have to carry that terrible memory with you for the rest of your life. Will it affect your future relationships and how you look at other men? Eliza, this is not something you can just walk away from. You need support and help, and we have to find a way to do that."

"I know you are right, but I have you as my friend. What more do I need? I know it is selfish of me to burden you with all this, but in you, I have an absolute confidante. In that, I am lucky and supported. There is no rule book on what you can do in the closed world of the medical profession. You and I both know well that justice is rarely served to the right people, so the greatest win I could have been was to become a consultant and from there help to steer the change we all need to happen. This will have been my wake-up call. The moment when Eliza grew up and proved to the world that not only was she going to be a surgeon, but a great surgeon and advocate for vulnerable surgeons in the future. That will be my goal, and it will give me the courage to see beyond this trauma to a day when I really can do something. If not, I will just crumble into a failing heap, and Henry will have won in another way."

"Oh, Eliza, you are beyond brave. I don't know whether what I am hearing is the bravado of a survivor or the voice of a triumphant survivor, but whichever it is, you are convincing me. Yes, you do have me. You will always have me at the end of the line. Promise me that no matter how dark the moment or how bad the day, you will phone me or text me to talk about it. Yes, it is a burden, but like you say, it is a finite one, and as the days pass, you may see things a little clearer and realise that something else might be done. I'm a great believer that even Karma needs a little helping hand now and then," he smiled at her and held her hand.

Eliza felt as though the lump had lifted from her chest. She could breathe again, and she no longer felt the pain of loneliness that she had earlier that day. She was feeling guilty, though, at the same time, for burdening Simon, someone she had finished with two years before, with such a heavy weight. It was strange, but the one thing that she did not have any doubt about was the sincerity of his word. She trusted him not to tell anyone, despite all that was written in the GMC Good Medical Practice Guidelines. This had to be dealt with in a much more discrete way, and they would figure out how one day at a time.

It was past midnight by the time the conversation reached a natural pause, and both of them were tired. Tomorrow was just seconds away, and in many ways, Eliza felt stronger and more able to face a new day than she had been earlier on. It was just a case of getting through one day after the next. Aim for results day; create a safe revision plan; figure out how to interact with Henry whilst staying safe; study so hard that time itself would lose meaning. Fill every day and night with preparations for the clinical exam because that was her exit plan and the only option she had. That sounds feasible. Yes, she could do that and restore a sense of control to her life.

Simon was taken to the spare room. Like everything in the cottage, it was tiny. Barely enough room to turn in, let alone swing a cat around, but cosy enough to fall into a deep sleep if only his thoughts were not exploding out of his head. No, that night would not be a good night for sleep, but he was glad to be there for Eliza. Once again, the anguish of their job allocations so far apart hit him hard, as he wished that he did not have to leave the next day. Eliza needed him, and he wished that they had not split up. Somehow, he had to convince Eliza to speak up about her ordeal. He could do little, as he had made a promise to her and was her only support network at that moment. She was so scared when he arrived. Could this nightmare tip her over the edge? Was she strong enough to get through this? Oh God, he hoped so. 'Please don't do anything stupid, Eliza' he thought as he stared up at the ceiling.

He did not notice himself falling asleep, but at 5.30 am, his phone alarm played its familiar jingle, and he awoke in a disoriented haze. Where was he? The room felt wrong. Where was the window? What is this bed? His heart was beating fast, and then suddenly he remembered where he was. It was still dark, and the stress of last night had not left him. He felt uncomfortable leaving Eliza as she slept, but he had to get back to his job. He tiptoed to the bathroom and washed himself as quietly as he could. He didn't shave, which was very unlike him, but his mind was distracted. He could only think of Eliza and how she would feel waking up in the empty cottage. He walked to her room and opened the door gently. She was asleep. He looked at her silhouette, and in the quietest voice he could muster, he whispered, "Don't worry, Eliza, I am here with you even when you cannot see me. Until then, be strong." He closed the door and headed out to his car. He would be back soon.

Chapter 33
False Impressions

The daily routine was broken, and Henry was troubled. He had not slept for much of the night. He was worried about Eliza and what she might do. Was he going to arrive at the trust for a situation that he needed to manage, or had she kept her promise and kept quiet? She would indeed be a very ungrateful person to say anything. Especially after all that he had said and done to apologise. This was not a good situation, and he needed to sort it out quickly. The key was to start ticking the boxes to win the trust of all around him. The first was to sort out the Ibrahim matter. As much as it wasn't what he wanted to do, it would win him much respect from the hierarchy and would also sort out the outsourcing plan, leaving him much richer and with plenty of excuse to see even less of Ibrahim than he did now. Yes, it could work out very well.

He turned to look at Vanessa, who was asleep next to him. She was a good wife to him and someone who had never let him down. He felt a pang of guilt for what he had done by betraying her trust. It cannot have gone unnoticed how awkward he had been when she found Eliza in the kitchen. Vanessa was no fool. She knew him better than anyone, and yet she seemed oblivious to his transgressions. Was she just hiding her feelings and hoping that it would end? What would he have done had she had an affair? He would have been furious; he probably divorced her and had not given her anything. Yes, that was the problem. He expected Vanessa to deliver what he could not. Was that his prerogative as breadwinner, he wondered? A sort of natural privilege born of the need to escape from duty and the grind of a hardworking life. Yes, he could see how his actions were understandable. It was not as though he wanted to leave Vanessa. He was just trying to stay happy for her.

He rolled out of bed. No press-ups today. He just walked to the bathroom and turned on the light. There in the mirror was his face. Not the usual strong and confident face, but instead a tired face. He could see the truth. The wrinkles he had not noticed around the corners of his mouth and the crow's feet by the corners of his eyes. He had greying hair, and despite all of the exercise he had been doing, his body was no longer what it had been as a younger man. He was a man just toppling over the edge of his prime. Was this what a midlife crisis was like? Was his foolish episode with Eliza just him trying to prove to himself that he still had it? Was that it? He could not cope with the idea of losing the edge. Losing control? He splashed some cold water on his face. It stung his cheeks and felt like ice as droplets tumbled onto his naked chest. He turned towards the shower, and suddenly he remembered the scared face of Eliza. What had he done? There was no justification at all for what he had done, whether he consented as an adult or not, however much relief he had needed. She had encouraged him, though, hadn't she? Was it really about two consenting adults after all? Did she consent? Oh, it was all such a mess.

As he drove to the hospital, he retained his troubled expression. He did not play any music. He drove slowly and deliberately. Was today to be his day of reckoning when the world would look at Henry Blythe-Soames and judge him? Would Eliza be able to face him at work now? Would the rest of the team see through him even if Eliza hadn't spoken to anyone? So many questions. Should he just give himself up, like a fugitive? No, absolutely not. It was a private matter. How would he explain to Andrew that he had effectively taken advantage of a junior doctor to vent his midlife issues and frustrations about Ibrahim? What a bloody psychopath that made him sound like! It wasn't like that. No, it wasn't. He tried hard to find cause to pity himself and find reasons why it was just feeling worse than it was. He just needed to act normally. Show everyone what a nice person he was. Yes, today was just another day at the hospital and a busy day too. So much to be done.

He parked in a different space than usual because he had arrived slightly later than his normal hour. He stepped out of his car with a heavy, almost nervous step and headed towards the front entrance. Bernie was there. Something familiar.

"Good morning, Bernie. How are you today?" He did something that he had never done before. He stopped to speak to Bernie, and the response was one of surprise.

"Oh…er…good morning, Mr Blythe-Soames. I am well. Thank you for asking. Busy day ahead for you?" Bernie was perplexed. A leopard surely could not change its spots into stripes, could it? Before him stood a different man than the one he had loathed for so many years. Here was a troubled-looking man. Something must have happened. Something possibly to do with that nice junior doctor he had seen him leaving with, perhaps. As Bernie was listening to the great man before him, he was thinking.

"I'm so glad. I never seem to stop and ask you. I just want to say thank you for all that you do..." The smile was partial to his face. Body language, uncomfortable. Nonetheless, the compliment was much appreciated.

"You are too kind; you're embarrassing me, Mr Blythe-Soames. I just do my job so that important people like you can do yours."

"Don't put yourself down, Bernie. Each of us is needed to keep this place going. You are needed very much," he put his hand on Bernie's shoulder, smiled, and headed off.

For a good five seconds, Bernie remained standing in the same place, clutching onto his mop, and rubbing his left sideburn. He thought he had seen everything. Today he had seen something new, something unexpected, and he did not know what it meant, but he was intrigued to find out.

For Henry, a brief conversation with Bernie helped him relax a little. That was all. It was a momentary thing that had passed as quickly as it had happened. Each task that day, or come to think of it, that month, had to be carefully constructed and deliberate. No temper, no rash comments, no false moves of any kind. He had a plan, and it needed to be conducted meticulously. He was going to repair what he had done wrong. So, many mistakes, yet he was not without support. This was his test to see how much his friends really had his back. Whatever lay ahead, he needed to jump through the hoops and rise again. It was just a tricky patch.

As he sat at his desk, his first slightly stressful task was the opening of his emails. This would be the first sign of whether Eliza had said anything. An email would be sent from Mark Smith as the medical director, or perhaps from Andrew McNair as clinical director if the trust hierarchy was to be followed by the book. When it comes to consultant misdemeanours, either can be the first port of call. He logged in. His mouth was dry, and he held his breath.

Inbox: 89 new messages

He scrolled down and then scrolled back up to the top. One generic medical director notice to all staff but nothing else. Nothing yet. He would check again at lunchtime. He had to get to his list. Ibrahim would be there. That was his second test. He needs to catch up with Jemimah to discuss Ibrahim's application.

Why had she not replied to his messages? It was not like her at all. Did she know something? He wondered. Perhaps she was avoiding him. Maybe Eliza had approached her woman-to-woman. Surely Jemimah would have spoken to him if Eliza had approached her. He picked up his phone.

Text: Hi, J. I hope you had a good holiday. Shall we catch up this week to discuss Ibrahim's application? H.

He picked up his surgical clogs and headed to the theatre. Thankfully, it was not a too onerous list today. This was not a day for a distracted man to be challenged; everything had to go by easily. He was engrossed in his thoughts and his plan. He had to get to the end of the day and feel more like himself. Unconsciously, his brow was furrowed. The inconvenient truth is that what lies in our deepest thoughts presents itself first on our face, not in our mouth.

He arrived at the theatre department a little later than usual. Everything was out of sorts, and he was annoyed with himself but needed to contain those feelings. 'Calm Henry, calm.' He sighed deeply and walked into the admissions lounge. Ibrahim and Eliza were there. He approached Ibrahim first.

"Good morning, Ibrahim. Sorry, I am a little later than usual. Is everything looking good for today."

Ibrahim was rather surprised, but he responded eagerly to this unusually pleasant version of Henry. It was now spanning days. That was definitely unexpected.

"Good morning, Henry. You are not late at all. The anaesthetic team have only just arrived, and all patients are here and have consented, so we have a little time this morning. Would you like to go see the patients?"

"Ah, that is a relief. Thank you, Ibrahim. Yes, lead the way, and we can see them." He smiled and extended his arm out towards the admissions bay to usher Ibrahim in to lead the way. He could see Eliza busily typing away on the computer in the corner. She had not taken her eyes off the screen, so he decided not to disturb her. He felt unexpectedly comfortable walking around with Ibrahim. Why was this man, whom he had hated, not irritating him today? He actually felt safer walking beside him. What had got into him? Was he so fickle? He was perplexed. Was guilt so much of a drug that it could alter the whole person so easily when need prevailed?

As they reached the last of the patients, Ibrahim took them towards Eliza. Henry walked behind him, feeling awkward. He had no doubt at all that those feelings were also etched across his face and body language, but he could not control it.

"Ah, Eliza, how are you getting on?" Ibrahim asked her.

She looked straight at him and smiled.

"All good, Mr Baba. I am almost done. I have one more drug chart to complete, and I am ready. Is there anything else you need me to do?" She focused intensely on him to avoid looking at Henry. She knew that she would have to, but for a few seconds more, she could delay the inevitable.

"Thank you, Eliza. No, I think that should be fine. Henry, is there anything else we would like Eliza to do?"

"Oh…er…no. Thanks Eliza. Are you coming into the theatre with us today?" He sounded diminished and humbled. As he looked at her, he felt sad. She was particularly pretty today, but what stood out more was how young she looked. He thought of how old he had looked in the mirror that morning, and suddenly perspective hit him like a lead weight in his stomach.

"Yes. I'm timetabled to be here. I've read up on all the cases, and I am ready. Just give me five minutes more, and I will join you both," she smiled nervously at him and then turned back to the computer. The strange body language between the two had not gone unnoticed by Ibrahim. He tried to hold onto Jemimah's advice, but deep down he felt that there was something wrong. Part of him was hoping that they had ended whatever was between them and that this was the normal response. Was it normal? Nothing was normal at all that morning! He was on high alert.

Ibrahim and Henry went to the coffee room and sat down whilst the team assembled. Henry's phone beeped.

Text: Hello, H. Sorry I didn't reply sooner. Some unexpected things are happening. We need to talk, please. J

'Oh Shit.' Henry felt a cold shiver go down his neck. What did Jemimah want to discuss that was urgent? This sounded more like her last message. Was this the message that he had been dreading?

"Is everything alright, Henry?" Ibrahim had noticed Henry looking suddenly pale. Henry looked up at him with worried eyes.

"Erm, yes, Ibrahim, could you possibly get the list started for me, and I'll join you in a moment? Um, I need…I need to sort something out. Thank you, Ibrahim," he stood up and walked out quickly. Everyone in the room had gone quiet. They had all noticed his change in demeanour.

"I hope everything is OK Ibrahim; do you know what is going on?" Jane enquired.

"I am not sure, Jane, but I imagine he will not be gone for long. Shall we go and do the morning introductions and get the list started?" He smiled gently at her and tried hard not to exacerbate any of the palpable anxiety that had just enveloped the team. She sighed and nodded in response. The mystery would have to remain unsolved, as there was work to do.

Eliza slipped into the anaesthetic room and looked around. No Henry. Where was he? Was he hiding from her? No, that was not how he operated. Perhaps something else was happening. She introduced herself to the team and smiled at Ibrahim. If it was just them, it might be a positive day 2, after all. She could do this. She had to. At some point, she had to try to face Henry and suppress what had happened. After all, they had had some lovely revision sessions together as well. She was making excuses, but that was her way of surviving this nightmare. To make what happened look less terrible. Yes, that was what she needed to do. After all, she needed Henry's help with the exam. Focus Eliza.

Ibrahim approached Eliza and smiled.

"Are you going to do some operating today, Eliza? We have some great cases today for you."

"Yes, I would love that, Mr Baba. I read up on them last week. Thank you," she smiled gently, but Ibrahim could see that she looked exhausted.

"You look tired today, Eliza. Are you OK? Sarah told me that you went home early yesterday. If you want to talk about anything, you know I am always here to talk." The question had clearly derailed Eliza, and she looked towards the door as though someone was coming through it. She then turned back to him and smiled weakly.

"Oh, no I am fine. I always feel tired after a nasty migraine. Didn't sleep very well last night either, which was not helpful. I think I will have a coffee at lunch time." Her migraine story was proving rather helpful, and it also provided a plausible excuse for why she looked so pale and drained that day.

"OK. Well, make sure you tell me if you are not feeling well. Mr Blythe-Soames will not be long, so if you need to sit out, just tell us," she nodded and walked to the scrub room to hide the tears that had started to fill her eyes. Ibrahim's kindness had turned on the wrong Eliza. Just hearing Henry's name seemed to trigger the opposite response to the one she needed to show. Tears were for home, not work. She needed to hold herself and focus on operating.

The scrub was more prolonged than normal, but the sensation of the warm water splashing over her arms and running up to her elbows seemed to calm her for a few minutes. The image of Henry appeared in her thoughts. Those intense eyes tortured her. That is different from Henry, whom she did not know. She quickly stopped the tap with her elbow and turned away from the stainless-steel sink to dry her arms and don her gown and gloves. There was at least something safe about that blue scrub suit. Nobody could touch her when she was wearing it, and even if Henry was in the room, they stood separately, and that professional boundary would be her safe zone. A space where she could learn and work and not contact skin to skin. Don't look eye-to-eye. Just focus on the one thing that matters most. The patient.

"So, Eliza, are you going to start this case? Do you want to run through with me the sequence of what you plan to do?" Ibrahim kept focused on the case with one eye watching Eliza. He could see that asking her about herself had unnerved her. He needed to not scare her. She was unlikely to talk if she found him a threat. It was going to be a test of patience, but he wanted to be there for her and support her.

"Yes please." She looked up at him and positioned herself on the right side of the patient, over the groin. This was a routine case of a high tie-off of the long saphenous vein in the groin to treat varicose veins. After preparing the site, she discussed the anatomy and marked the incision line. Ibrahim allowed her to talk, and she nodded positively as she talked her way through the case. He did not interrupt her. He let her enter the surgical mind zone and escape from whatever had troubled her. Surgery gave her the space that she needed, and he was there to make her feel safe. With a little advice and assistance, Eliza carried out the whole procedure herself, and the thrill of the moment finally brought a smile back to her eyes. This is what would save her. Surgery.

Ibrahim nodded and smiled. "Eliza, that was brilliant. Imagine where you started, and I see you now. Today, you look like a pro. Well done. Now, let's check everything and close up," he turned to the anaesthetic team and told them that they were closing. Case one was nearly done, and Henry walked back into the theatre. He looked more relaxed.

"How are we getting along, team?" His voice was more positive, as was his body language.

"Well, Eliza just did the whole case herself, and there were no issues at all. It was very impressive. We are just closing up," Ibrahim was beaming at Henry.

"Oh, that is great. Can you give me a peek in?" He walked up to the table, and Eliza stepped aside to let him in without touching her. With the gown on, that was the natural thing to do, and he would not read into it in any other way. "Very nice. Are those knots all secure?" He looked at Eliza.

She smiled nervously and replied, "Yes, Mr Blythe-Soames. Two knots, both checked by Mr Baba. We also did a Valsalva at the end, and there was no bleeding."

"Well, an expert job done," he turned to look at the clock on the wall with the viewing panels. "Excellent timing too. Brilliant. I think I'll go and sit in the coffee room, as I am rather supernumerary here," he had a smile on his face and turned to leave the theatre, but stopped to check that the anaesthetic team was happy too. Nods all around. First conversation done. No drama. Jemimah knew nothing too. It was just a request for some leave, which was fine, if a tad over the top, but it was not time for any big fights with the people he needed as allies.

Eliza thought about herself as she did the subcuticular suture. That was not so bad. He had been nice. This was the Henry she had been in awe of and looked up to. Could she forget what had happened? Should she forget what happened? Would she be letting someone else down if she said nothing? What would happen to her if she spoke up? She would be slaughtered. Her career would be over, and she would be labelled a marriage breaker and not serious about her career. No, it was never going to look good. She could not say anything. She had managed to push herself into a corner all by herself. What an idiot! Stupid Eliza.

"OK, that is a little tight, Eliza. Gently… gently," Ibrahim's voice pulled her back into the moment, and she realised, with frustration, that her emotions had overflowed into her suturing. She eased the suture before tying the Aberdeen knot and dressing the incision line before undraping the patient.

'Don't turn a positive morning into an emotional mess, Eliza! HOLD IT TOGETHER!'

The second case was a more complex one, and Eliza was the assistant for Ibrahim. She loved watching him operate. He was as good a surgeon as Henry and taught her some great pearls of wisdom, which filled her mind for a few more hours up until lunchtime. Today was actually going better than expected. Henry was quite kind and kept out of her way. She could see herself coping now. They had been positive once. That could come back slowly with time and space. One day at a time. Simon's advice was at the front of her mind, and she knew that her number one priority was to stay safe. Rather than asking whether the same could happen again, make sure she was never in such a position again. The right thing to do on paper, which was to raise concern, was not the right thing to do in real life, where people could get in the way of the intended outcome. Besides, it was a private matter. It was not something that had happened at work. It was not like she was going to report Henry to the police! That would be extreme, or so she had convinced herself. She was trapped, perhaps more in her thoughts than reality. He had just been in a bad place that day. He wasn't a predator, really, was he? Was Simon exaggerating?

Henry had decided to go and sit in his office instead of joining the team for lunch. All of the extra effort to please everyone had been exhausting and challenging for him in equal measure. How long would he need to sustain this for? He wondered. He sat at his desk, thinking about the sense of panic that he had experienced when he called Jemimah back. A deep-seated terror that was all about to unravel. It was as though he had been destabilised, and the predictable, controlled man that he had been before was suddenly like a crumbling bridge. A little more water beneath the pontics, and he would fall into it to be washed away and forgotten. Suddenly, his usual position of complete control over all around him had been lost, and he hated it. This was not how it was supposed to be. He needed some positive action, so with Jemimah off for some time, he decided to make Ibrahim plan to come together on his own with Andrew's support.

He picked up his phone and stared at it as he thought about what he wanted to say.

"Hi, Ibrahim. Is the second case out of theatre?"

"Hi Henry. Yes, it is all done. No concerns here."

"Excellent. Have the team broken up for lunch yet?"

"Yes, they have just now. We are sending for the final case at 1.30."

"Great. Could you pop by my office a bit, then? I need to have a chat with you about a couple of things."

"Yes absolutely. I'll head there now. Do you want me to pick up some coffee for you on the way?"

His kind offer caught Henry's thought stream by surprise.

"Er…no. That is kind, but no. No, thank you. Do grab one for yourself, though."

It was like all of these niceties were an unnatural extra that Henry was just becoming aware of today. They felt artificial and seemed to stop him from his natural flow of pace and control.

Ibrahim rushed to the tea shop in the hospital and grabbed a quick latte. As he walked to Henry's office, he wondered what today was signalling. It was clear that something had happened. It may not be what he was thinking, but something rather dramatic had changed. The atmosphere had changed. Henry was being nice. That in itself would have been momentous enough, but the distressing observation of Eliza, unnerved, was troubling him. He needed to talk to Jemimah again. One of them needed to speak with Eliza. He hoped that it was just a simple breakup and nothing else, but his suspicion of Henry was not abated by one morning of uncharacteristic pleasantries.

He knocked on the door and went straight in. Henry was sitting in front of his computer, looking deep in thought.

"Ah Ibrahim. Thank you for coming in."

He pulled over a chair next to him and invited Ibrahim to take a seat.

"Before Jemimah went on leave, she came to see me. She told me about your plans this year to try to get consultant status and said that your portfolio was impressive. She asked if I might support your application, so I went away and had a long think about how that could work. I know Ibrahim that things have not always been easy between us. Probably largely due to my own interpretation of things I agree. I would like to change that and would like to support you in this venture. For a long time, we have recognised that we have a need for another consultant as the workload has increased and the team likes you a lot. I would need the support of CD and MD, and for that, we need to make sure your application is as good as it can be. Sadly, Jemimah is now off for a while for personal reasons, so I wonder whether it would be OK if I team up with Andrew McNair to make this happen."

Ibrahim sat listening to Henry in a state of complete shock. Could this really be happening after all the years of insults, slights, and humiliation? Was this man, who had turned his life into misery, really now his saviour? Could he trust him, or was he just dangling the sweetest of cherries in order to pull it away from him before he could jump up and take a bite? He had to have faith. Alhamdullilah, his prayers were being answered.

"Oh my. Yes, it would be wonderful to have such help from you and Andrew. Thank you very much, Henry. I have a copy of my portfolio with me. I can email it to you today if you would like." His eyes were wide, hopeful, and not a small bit surprised.

"That sounds like a good place to start. Is it OK if I forward a copy to Andrew later, and we can arrange a good day to meet together next week to talk it through?"

"Yes, of course. It is in PDF format. Would that be alright?"

Henry feigned a genuine smile at Ibrahim. "Yes absolutely. Let us make this happen and see if we can tick all the boxes so that no nasty surprises catch you out on the way. I have printed off the Royal College guidance about it, and it all seems quite straightforward," he sat back and smiled at Ibrahim. In a way, it had been far easier to do than he thought, and the gratitude returned made him feel good. He needed to feel liked again. If only so that he could like himself.

"Well, I had better get back to theatre. Will you be joining us for the last case? It is Mr Palmer. It might be a tricky endarterectomy. Fancy doing it together?" Ibrahim thought he might try to step up and be more consultant-like in his conversation. He was nervous doing that, so his body language did not quite match his words.

Henry picked up on that discomfort and secretly enjoyed that he still had power over this man. It was not a game of love he was enacting here; it was all about politics and business. It was necessary.

"Why not? I will join you in two minutes. I just need to send a couple of emails off, and then I will have a free mind. Do get that CESR portfolio out to me before the day ends, Ibrahim. I want to send a copy to Andrew to give him plenty of time to read it. What day shall we suggest for us all to meet next week? Is Thursday afternoon good for you?"

Ibrahim checked his diary on his phone and replied, "Yes, that should be fine."

"Great. See you in five minutes, Ibrahim," he turned back to his computer, and Ibrahim left the office.

As Ibrahim walked towards theatre he was perplexed. Today was indeed a strange day. Such a long time had passed waiting for this moment, and now everything was moving so fast. He wondered why Jemimah was off. He would call her that evening. The Eliza issue he needed to deal with himself. "Give it time, Ibrahim. Stay calm and don't be too hasty. Let the story unfold. Give Eliza time to approach him. Just be there for her."

Chapter 34
Little Steps

It is hard enough to have never met your parents, but to have missed your mother's funeral as well added further discomfort to the already difficult circumstances that Jemimah found herself in. It was like being handed a jigsaw puzzle that was open, then discovering that there were key pieces missing as you tried to complete the picture. Were there enough pieces in her hand now to satisfy her that she knew all that she needed to, or would she forever be tortured with questions about those missing pieces that she could never find? One good thing was that she knew that she did not have evil biological parents. In fact, quite the opposite. How much of what she now knew about her beginning would change what she was yet to become?

She had talked to Jeremy about it. He was such a blessing in her life. He was calmer than Emma and more detached than her family. A perfectly neutral soul to bolster her and help her contemplate the void that had troubled her for so long. It was uncanny how easily their conversations seemed to roll. He was attentive, calm, considerate, and kind. In every way, she was surprised by this new feeling of being a woman in a relationship that made sense. Was it a relationship that made sense to her, or was it just that she was able to see how she fit into it now that she really knew who she was? She suspected that that did not matter.

Her project for the leave that she had taken was to go and see Rupert in London and show him that she meant every word when she asked him to be in contact. Repeatedly, she tried to imagine how he and her mother had felt as they left her at the hospital. It was an unimaginable thing to comprehend. Life is full of difficult decisions, but that was not just a decision; it was an act of the truest kindness and love. She could not even imagine what she would have done in their shoes. Did she have the courage of her mother to let go of the only lasting link that remained of her love for Ameer? To give up her baby not because she could not raise her but because others would not allow her. The injustice of it all. Tears welled up in her eyes. She carried photographs of her biological parents with her in a wallet that also had pictures of her adoptive parents. Her little home parcel in her bag. This had been a time of dramatic readjustment, and talking about it was what she needed to do. Only Rupert would understand.

She wanted to take the journey to London alone, but Jeremy insisted on being her travel companion and supplier of a necessary hug and kiss afterwards. He had work that he could get on with in London, and all he wanted to do was be there in case it all became too much for her. It was as though her whole life had been blessed and protected by the kindest of people. Even those who had suffered oppression and fear had never stopped putting others before themselves. What an example they were to her.

Whilst Jeremy worked on his laptop on the train, Jemimah played her Arabic language course on her headphones. It didn't quite stick as she had hoped, but she was determined to have the basics covered before her trip next week to Jordan, when she was planning to meet the Tuquan family. Rupert said he would accompany her if she wanted, and she was delighted to accept his kind offer. What an adventure down memory lane it would be for him to almost reach home! It was always going to be incomplete, as he had been banished from Israel for smuggling a criminal woman who had intermarried. Not being able to enter Israel had pained him, as his family had remained there and died without ever seeing him again.

As they arrived at Paddington station, Jemimah kissed Jeremy and looked into his eyes.

"Thank you, Jeremy, for coming with me today. You were quite right. I am not yet as brave as I would have hoped to be and, if I confess, a little scared to go back to that office where so much pain seemed to pour out of me last week."

"Jemimah, all that you are feeling is perfectly natural. My mother was a wise lady and was a great exponent of the "when you fall off the bike, get right back on" motto. This is one of those situations. You think you are scared because you are remembering your previous journey. This is not the same journey. This time, you know your story. You are not expecting surprises. Today is a day of re-reunion. This time, you can really get to know Rupert, the man. He sounds like an incredible guy, so soak up that greatness as you sit with him. Your being there will no doubt make him very happy." He held her hand in his, and she was comforted by his generous eyes. He was right. Today was not a day to fear. It was a day to relish. She hugged him and rushed off, shouting out behind her, "See you later. Have a wonderful day." He waved at her.

Jeremy watched Jemimah as she ran off, and at that moment, he adored her. She was, in every way, the perfect paradox. She was staggeringly intelligent and composed as a surgeon, and yet underneath that façade of strength lay a self-doubting and sometimes vulnerable woman. He wondered how many of her work colleagues and patients could see this side, or was it his secret part of Jemimah to care for and protect?

Walking up to Lincolns Inn Fields, Jemimah felt positive and unexpectedly excited about seeing Rupert. She had bought him some of her favourite Holdsworth chocolates and had a thousand things that she wanted to say to him. The main challenge was not drowning him in questions all at one go. She walked into the foyer and was greeted by the usual stern receptionist, who this time even feigned a little smile of recognition and guided her down the corridor to Rupert's office. He was already at the door when she arrived.

"Marhaba, dear Jemimah. Shalom," he gently placed his hand on her arm. It was strange that, although Jemimah had only met Rupert once in person, there was an ease between them that was more typical of two people who had known each other for a long time. Perhaps Rupert had a good reason for that familiarity, as he had been updated about her throughout the course of her life. That would, to many, have been a little creepy, but Jemimah found it actually very endearing. It was their way of feeling that although they had left her behind, they were still a part of her life. She could understand that easily.

"How was your journey here?" He asked.

"Oh, it was lovely. I came up with another surprise in my life, which is Jeremy. My new boyfriend. I think you would like him," she blushed and looked almost girlish when she said that.

"Boyfriend, you say? And where did this very lucky man spring out from? Is he someone you knew before?" He looked very inquisitively at her. This was news that he had found out not through reports but by doing the one thing he had longed to do for so long. By simply talking to her face-to-face. It was such a beautiful face. He could see both of her parents in that face, and it was like a reunion every time he looked at it.

"Well, he was a blind date. We met through my friend and colleague, Ibrahim. I was rather worried about meeting him, but strangely, it was as though he had been quietly waiting for me to sort out my own hangups. I had always struggled with relationships because I was so confused about who I really was. When you told me about my parents and my past, it was as though that knot in the middle of me just unravelled. He was the first man to meet me as the real me, and luck would have it that he is a wonderful person too," she looked so happy that Rupert was thrilled.

"This is like hearing the words of my prayers for you answered. Your mother always wondered what sort of man you would meet. I think secretly she hoped that he would be as kind as your father and as committed to your happiness as we all were. Would you say that at this early point you might have found that man?"

"Oh Gosh, those are big things to expect from anyone," she laughed. "If he is even half of you and my father, I imagine I would still be blessed with a wonderful man. Let's see how things go, shall we?"

"Yes, yes, absolutely. Now, tell me how you are feeling about meeting your uncle and your family in Jordan."

"Oh, I am a little scared. I have been trying to learn Arabic, but it is taking longer than I wanted. I want them to like me. I want them to be glad that they were a part of saving me. I am hoping that they do not blame me for my father dying."

"Oh, Jemimah, please do not say such things. Firstly, your father did not die because your mother was expecting a baby. He was killed because your parents were in love and because of all that is bad in Israel. Your Palestinian family is lovely. Although I just met them briefly as we were getting passage to England, I remember the Tuquans being a truly generous and kind family. They lost Ameer, and you were their link to him. The last part of his life. They were so glad that they could help you, and meeting you now would make them feel like it was worth all the risk," he had a reassuring face as he spoke to her. "I am glad that we are going together. It will be a great reunion for us all."

"Oh yes, I don't think I could have done this journey without you, Rupert. I hope that it will be a happy experience for you too. What should we take as gifts for the family? Do you know what is traditional to give in Jordan in such circumstances?"

"Well, your situation is not a typical one, I must say. The Tuquan family is a very large and old family, and they value culture and education. I wonder whether you might like to make something for them. Something that they cannot buy might be nice, as this is such a personal visit." He sat back in his chair and thought deeply.

"Make something. Hmm, that is an interesting thought. I cannot take food, so that is out. I like embroidery, although I haven't done it in a while. Perhaps I can make a small embroidery depicting my home and its flowers and write something to accompany it that tries to express how grateful I am to them. Are there any etiquettes, I need to follow?

"Well, they are Muslims, so it's probably best to avoid putting anyone in your picture. The idea of your home is an excellent one and will give you a focus to talk about. Embroidery is a very big tradition among the people of Palestine. It is called Tatreez. I think they would love that. When you write something to accompany it, try to avoid any western affectations like kisses and words like love. The key is to show respect and gratitude. Your uncle Ahmed, who arranged your transfer, was educated in Britain, so you have nothing to worry about there. He was not married when I met him, so his wife and two children will be new to us both. People of the Middle East are very generous by nature, Jemimah. I think you will feel at home with them, as your own nature will sit very naturally amongst them," he looked at his watch. "I am hungry. Shall we go somewhere for lunch?"

"Oh yes. I am rather hungry, too. I was so nervous this morning that I did not eat anything, and right now I think I could eat a horse," she put her hand on her stomach and laughed with Rupert.

"Well, I'm not sure where you can get kosher horses at this time, but there is a lovely little restaurant not far from here that might satisfy that hunger. Shall we?"

"Yes, that sounds great." They walked out together and talked like uncle and niece. It was for each of them a bridge that connected their pasts to their present, and that connection between them seemed to complete them both. The afternoon was spent planning the Jordan trip and talking about her parents. So many stories filled the time, and yet there were so many more to tell in the future. Jemimah looked at Rupert. He was not a young man anymore. He had a slightly bowed posture and a very typical face from Jerusalem that had wrinkled with the years. Biologically, he looked old and tired. She hoped that he would not be stolen from her. Not yet.

Chapter 35
Hidden Obstacles

Although day two had gone better than expected, just seeing Henry had been an emotionally taxing event for Eliza. She had wanted to tell Ibrahim about her struggles, but she was scared that it might end up being too much for them both and make the problem worse. In her mind, managing the damage was far more sensible than unleashing a reaction that would topple both herself and Henry in one go. If there was one thing that she had observed in her few years in the NHS, it was that the processes were very black and white and used somewhat crude and excessive tools to address "problems." Little seemed to ever get sorted, although a lot of emails and meetings seemed to happen to fill the time that could have been filled better with solving the problems with the right people in the room. She granted that her experience of this had been somewhat limited to the problems linked to the on-call rota, but she had often overheard the consultants and registrars moaning about the unyielding bureaucracy of the system.

She was not sure if she wanted to test it in her case. Besides, her time there was finite, and she had to just keep focused on that and try to survive what had happened to her. She was not the first female surgeon to be taken advantage of, and she was sure she was not the last. Henry had given a reason for what he had done, and his behaviour since then seemed to be better. If she could use his guilt to her advantage, perhaps this nightmare could be somewhat reduced in her memory. Right now, she was in a vulnerable place. Her future depended on the references and kindness of others. This was not the moment to be a Joan of Arc character and charge out to her death. She needed to move with care.

Simultaneously, she was feeling annoyed with herself that she had not spoken up, as she had seen so often on trainee forums talking about bullying and sexism. Her situation was not about the odd snide comment or being put down. This was much more complicated to unravel, and for every single thing that she could say about it in truth, it would not be at all difficult for Henry to twist it to the contrary and make things look rather bad for her. No, she had to stay focused and remember that her goal was to pass her exam and become a surgeon. The world was not a fair place, and she knew well that surgery was not yet an equal playing field as far as men and women were concerned. Come to think of it, nor was the world.

Staring at the computer in front of her, Eliza realised that she had work to do, cleared her throat, and logged into the computer to complete all the jobs that she had gathered from her evening rounds. She was way behind with her jobs as her mind had almost frozen into reflective mode. Before her was a long list of catch-up to-dos, discharge summaries, medication updates, and fluids. The jobs would fill a couple of hours, and between bleeps, she would fill the rest of the day, as long as she stayed focused. Could she stay focused? Correction: could she wake up and start focusing?

Buzz… Her phone signalled that a text had arrived. She looked at the screen; it was Simon.

Text: Just checking in. How are you? How did today go? Been thinking of you. S

She smiled. It was the best thing she could have done to tell Simon. He was someone whom she could trust.

Text: Hi. Tricky day. Saw H. It was awkward at first, but he stayed out of sight, and we got through the list. Mr Baba helped a lot. Picked up on my stress, and I wanted to tell him. Just couldn't do it. Worried about what might happen. Glad you know at least. Thx. Eliza x

She put the phone in her pocket and started making the first request on the computer. She was distracted and felt like her eyes were not fully focusing on the screen. She typed away and clicked the necessary buttons, and just as she was about to click 'Complete' her heart stopped.

"Shit!" she said audibly, and the other doctors at the station looked up at her, enquiring what had happened.

"Oh…er nothing. Just remembered something," she shrugged, and they turned away. Delete, delete, delete…"How could I get the wrong bloody patient? What is the matter with me?" She sighed deeply and started again. This time with the right patient credentials. Her heart was beating hard in her chest. Was she fit to work, or was she too distracted?

"Beep," her phone buzzed again. She completed the form on the computer and rechecked the patient details for the third time. Rechecked what she was meant to request and pressed 'Complete'. It was going to be a long list of jobs. She looked at her phone. She thought it would be Simon, and her face went pale when she realised that she was looking at a text message from Henry. She couldn't believe him. She stared at his name in the inbox for a few seconds before swallowing hard and clicking on it to open the message.

Text: Hello, E. Was just thinking about you. Are you OK? Here to talk. Talk anytime. I'm not far away. When do you get your results? Hx

Her hands were shaking, and her body tensed up. She was not over it. Why was she being so weak? 'For God's sake, Eliza, pull yourself together. Stop being so stupid. Put the bloody phone away and get your work done. You have already made one mistake. Ignore Henry'. As she berated herself, her emotions got the better of her, and her eyes welled up with tears. She got up and walked fast to the toilet. She looked down to avoid the gaze of anyone. Her arms were wrapped defensively around her chest. She needed to get off the ward. She rushed down the corridor. She did not see Ibrahim walking towards her. He had noticed her.

"Eliza. Are you alright?" he said. She looked up, startled, and nodded as she walked past him.

In an almost whisper, she replied, "I'm OK. Sorry. I have to go, Mr Baba. I will be back in a minute," she could hardly see him past the tears in her eyes, and she turned away from him before he could speak. She started running and was gone from the ward a second later.

Ibrahim remained in the corridor, deeply concerned by what he had just seen. The awkwardness in the theatre that morning had not just been about a lovers' tiff. Something was very wrong. Something had happened. How could he reach out to her and help? Was she safe to work like this? He suspected not. He decided to wait for her return, however long that would be. It was getting late, and he would need to message Aisha that he was unexpectedly delayed.

As Eliza ran to the toilet, her mind raced. She was gripped with a sense of anger towards the mistake that she had nearly made on the ward and disgust with herself for what happened with Henry. Why was he messaging her? Hadn't she made it clear that she needed space? Little things added up to big emotional responses that seemed disproportionate, and she was angry with herself. She hated how silly she was being. In every way she hated herself and felt trapped. All the confidence that she had built over the months of being with Henry had suddenly evaporated, and she felt exposed. Although nobody there apart from Henry knew what had happened, she felt frightened that people might have sensed that something serious had gone on between her and Henry. She wondered who had seen her. Perhaps the nurses were talking about them. They were not as discrete as they should have been. She thought about the ways in which their association had changed at work as they became more familiar and relaxed, and suddenly a sense of terror filled her mind. If people saw her upset like this, they would add two and two together and make a hundred, wouldn't they?

As she sat on the lid of the toilet, staring at the locked door, the anxiety slowly eased, and she took in some deep breaths to gather herself. She had to go back to the ward and try to finish the day's jobs, but now there was also Mr Baba waiting for her. She turned on the selfie screen of the phone and looked at her blotchy face. She looked up at the ceiling to drain her tears and sniffed hard. She blinked several times and then looked again at her face on the screen. 'A little better.' She could do this. She managed to get to the end of the day without killing any patients. 'FOCUS Eliza, Focus!'

She flushed the toilet, not because she had used it but because she had sat on it. Her brain was clearly still mush, but the mindlessness of that action made her shake her head. She exited the toilet, washed her hands, and splashed some cold water on her face. The hand dryer had one of those turning heads, so she adjusted the vent of the hand dryer upwards to redirect the air to her face. It dried her tears and was actually quite refreshing, in a hot way. Her body was no longer shaking. She needed to maintain this composure and figure out what she was going to say to Mr Baba. In her head, she could hear Henry's words, "This will be our secret."

On the ward, Ibrahim had sat down next to the sister at the nurses' station. Melanie was a very astute, if somewhat blunt, nurse, but she had always been pleasant to him. He turned to her and smiled.

"Melanie, can I ask you something in confidence, please? You notice everything on this ward, so I know you will have noticed something if it was going on."

Melanie laughed. "Do you imagine Mr Baba spending my days spectating the ward from my throne here in the nurses' station? You doctors seem to swan on and off and don't notice that most of the time I am rushing around doing ward duties, management meetings, or paperwork, like I am now."

Ibrahim smiled back. It was a big red button he had just inadvertently pressed. "Now, Melanie, where did you get such an idea from? I know you think we doctors are oblivious to what you do, but that could not be further from the truth. You are like our arms. We cannot do what we do without you. No, I am not at all suggesting that you sit there all day, but I am hoping that you may have seen something here that I need to know about."

"Oh, now that does sound intriguing. Do you want to go into the sisters' office to talk? It is a bit more private there."

"Yes, that would be a good idea if you have the time to talk right now."

"I always have time to talk to polite doctors like you; come with me, Mr Baba," she smiled the familiar smile of a colleague who had known him for a very long time.

They walked to the office and closed the door. Even before sitting, Ibrahim started talking. It was as though he was bursting with something.

"Melanie, do you know our senior house officer, Eliza?"

"Yes, I know her well. A lovely young doctor. Why do you ask?" As she asked that, a knowing expression appeared on her face, as though she knew something and wanted to find out how much he knew.

"I am a little worried about her. She seems upset, but I am struggling to find out why. I don't mean that in a nosey way. I need to know that she is alright and that she is safe to work."

Melanie nodded and leant towards him in a pose of secrecy.

"You are right there. We have all noticed that over the last few days, she has been distracted and upset. Several jobs have been forgotten. Over the past few months, she seemed to be spending a lot of time coming to the ward alone with Mr Blythe-Soames. I found that quite odd, as they seemed rather close to a consultant and junior doctor. At first, I just put it down to her having been here for longer than most junior docs but then I noticed that he would sometimes touch her in an overly familiar way—nothing more than a hand on her back—but I thought it was a bit unprofessional. I confess, I was wondering whether there was something going on between them, but it was clearly none of my business, so I dismissed it. Today, however, she ran off the ward in tears, and that did concern me. She has done virtually none of the jobs she was meant to do this afternoon, and the discharge summaries for tonight are not completed, so a few patients will not be going home as planned," Ibrahim nodded slowly but gave away nothing as far as the Henry-Eliza issue was concerned.

"Yes, I saw her leaving the ward. I didn't realise that there were issues with her work today as well. She was distracted but did well in theatre this morning. I need to get to the bottom of what is wrong. Thank you for telling me that." His brow was furrowed, and he rubbed his beard as he sat back. "Hmmm, let me try to find out some more when she comes back to the ward. May I use your office to speak to her, please, Melanie?"

"Yes, yes, of course. Give me a shout if you need me to be there with you as a chaperone."

"Thank you," he smiled and stood up to leave the office.

Melanie also stood up and said, "I would prefer that you don't tell Mr Blythe-Soames what I said about him. You know how he can be," Ibrahim nodded knowingly.

"You have my word, Melanie. This conversation was just between us," he smiled reassuringly at her and opened the door. Just as he walked out onto the ward, Eliza passed him. She looked more composed but was still preoccupied. He approached her steadily to avoid alarming her.

"Hi." He looked at her and thought it was best to let her speak before continuing with his request.

"Oh, hello, Mr Baba. Sorry about earlier. I'm just having a difficult week. Did you need me to do something?" She spoke as though nothing had happened before.

"No, not at all. I was wondering whether it would be okay to have a chat. My sister says her room is free, so we can go in there. Would that be alright?"

"Oh. Erm. Yes. Is everything OK?" She looked worried; her body language was suddenly defensive.

"Thank you, Eliza. Don't worry; I am not here to tell you off. I just want to talk to you about something."

Ibrahim opened the sisters' office door and let Eliza walk past him. She took a chair in the corner and looked very diminutive and scared. Ibrahim closed the door and sat opposite her, trying to keep a good space between them.

"Eliza, I think we both know that things have not been right for you recently. Until this week, you seemed to be managing just fine with all your work duties, but now I can see that you are struggling, and I want to know if there is anything that I can do to help you. Is there something you want to discuss with me in confidence?" There was a noticeable pause as Eliza looked around her and then back to him. Her eyes started to well with tears again, and as she looked at him with an almost desperate expression, she felt broken.

"I'm sorry I haven't been doing my work so well today. My problem is not work-related; it has to do with…er…with my private life outside of work. God, I know that sounds unprofessional and that we should not bring our private lives into work. I think that has been part of the problem. I've been trying so hard not to, that ironically, I failed." A tear rolled down her cheek, and she looked down at her hands, which were tightly interlocked on her lap.

"I'm so sorry that you are having such a difficult time. Who is supporting you outside of the workplace?" Ibrahim enquired compassionately.

"Well, I have my ex-boyfriend Simon, who calls me. He has been lovely."

"Is he here in Saint's Bay?"

"No, he lives in Wales."

"Do you have anyone nearby?" There was a pause as Eliza tried to think of someone. Just one person. There was no one.

"No. No, I do not," she looked at him. Her reddened eyes stared at him pleadingly. "I cannot really talk about it with anyone, Mr Baba. I am sorry."

Ibrahim sat back and took a slow, deep breath. He cleared his throat gently and rubbed his beard with his hand.

"Eliza, may I ask you a rather direct question, please?"

"Uh-huh." A nervous affirmation quietly came from her.

"Is this 'problem' (he gestured with his hands) related to work?"

She looked up at him. Her eyes were wide. He knew. Oh God, he knew.

"W-why do you think that, Mr Baba?"

Ibrahim knew that he only had a short window here, and if Eliza's bleep went off or his phone rang, it would be lost. So instead of a slow introduction, he came up with the big question.

"Eliza, as your educational supervisor, I am here to help you and support you. I can see that something is wrong, and if it is work-related, that is why I am here. To help you. I am not going to beat around the bush, Eliza. People have been talking, and I would like to know whether something has been going on between you and one of the consultants in this hospital. One of the surgeons here?"

Eliza sat up and put her hands on the chair handles.

"Oh God. Who has been talking? What has been said? I cannot tell you. I'm so sorry, Mr Baba. I cannot. It is a personal matter. I will sort it out. I promise, but I cannot tell you." Tears started flowing from her eyes, and she pushed herself back as far into the chair as she could. Her arms were wrapped around her stomach, and she was shaking.

"Eliza, I cannot force you to tell me what is happening, but I do have an obligation as your clinical supervisor to make sure that your practice is safe, and you are safe. I am very concerned with how you are at the moment, Eliza. It is not like you at all. I need to know if you are OK. How can I help you? This conversation is confidential, but if you will not let me help you, I will have to bring in some additional support for you. Having an ex-boyfriend hundreds of miles away is not enough when you are like this. What about your family? Can they help you?"

"No, I don't want to upset my mum. I wouldn't do that to her. Who are you going to talk to, Mr Baba? What have you heard?" She was scared that he wanted to talk to Henry. If Henry found out that people were worried about her, he would be angry.

"Eliza, there are a few things that we need to do. The first is that you need to be signed off as unwell for a little bit so that you can be away from here. The second thing is that you need a more formal support network to talk to here in Saint's Bay. If you are not happy having me as your support, is there anyone else here that you might be happy to talk to in confidence? What about Ruth? She saw you upset the other day and was worried about you."

His suggestions of discussing it with others frightened her. She had to tell him.

"If I tell you the truth, can you keep it a secret, please? I trust you, Mr Baba. The other day, I wanted to tell you so much about what was going on, but I couldn't find the courage."

"You can trust me to support you, Eliza, but if there is something serious going on that either puts you or patients at risk, I am obliged to confidentially escalate my concerns. What I can promise you is that whatever is discussed will be done with the strictest confidence and only with senior people on a need-to-know basis. Is there a particular person you want me to avoid discussing things with, Eliza? Is that the problem here?"

She nodded nervously. "It wasn't all his fault. It was mine too."

"By 'his'…do you mean Mr Blythe-Soames Eliza? Has something been happening between you?"

She nodded again, so slightly that it was barely noticeable. Her blue eyes looked at him with pain and guilt.

"Yes. He has been helping me with my revision, but last week things changed," the details were too acute to mention, "Th…things have changed between us, and it has become a bit awkward. That is all." She felt that this was the best way to tell him the bare minimum of what had happened so that it sounded better.

Ibrahim nodded reciprocally. He was suddenly struggling to find the right words to say. He needed to come up with a question he was dreading to know the answer to but needed to ask.

"Eliza, has Mr Blythe-Soames, I mean Henry, ever taken advantage of you, or done anything that you did not want him to in that relationship?" He looked at her without moving. He swallowed but stayed very still. There was a palpable silence between them as Eliza realised that Mr Baba had guessed what was going on.

"I cannot tell you, Mr Baba. I won't. I'm sorry. Henry has been so kind to me helping me, with my exam and giving me the confidence that I needed. Whatever happened between us, we need to sort out ourselves. I'll take a week off and go home to my mum, but I will not speak to anyone else about it. I'm sorry, but I have too much to lose," she seemed resolute in her response and had even surprised herself with her words.

Ibrahim sighed deeply.

"Alright. I will not push you today, Eliza, to discuss the details, but I am glad that you are going home to your mum. Even if you don't tell her the facts, being with her is what I think you need. Can you please report to me within the week to let me know how you are getting along? I'm here for you, Eliza. You are not alone. Do you want me to change your timetable so that you don't have to see Henry so much at work?"

"I guess part of avoiding telling my mum has been guilt, but you are right, I agree that I need to go home for a bit. It won't be for long. Results will come out next week, so hopefully I will return feeling better if I have passed," she gestured with crossed fingers and a little smile, which Ibrahim was pleased to see, even if it was short-lived.

"Regarding me avoiding Henry at work. No. I do not want him to have any idea at all that we had this conversation. We are speaking to each other, Mr Baba and hopefully, with time, all will be well again. What happened, happened, and to be honest I am not entirely sure how it happened. Henry is a very impressive person, and I guess he is my boss, and then things just happened," she shrugged and bit her lower lip. How innocent she looked at that moment, and Ibrahim hated Henry so much for taking advantage of her. This was not going to pass. Somehow, he needed Henry to learn his lesson. He just needed to find the right way without anyone suspecting his involvement. Henry had to get his CESR application through first, but there needed to be some way of cornering him. He would have to think about it. He wished that Jemimah was not off. He leant forward and put his hand on Eliza's arm.

"Eliza, this is not your fault at all. Henry should have known better than to do this. I promise I will not speak to him, but Eliza, if things do not improve for you, I may need to find help from others. Promise me that you will be safe and will not meet Henry outside of work anymore. Shall we arrange a time to meet when you are back?"

"Thank you, Mr Baba. I don't want to cause too many problems for the team. We are all adults, and no matter what it looks like from the outside, there are always two sides to the story. I don't think I can go through any inquiry into it, but I agree that I need to stop meeting him outside of work. I guess I just want to pass my exams, move on from here, and have a future as a surgeon. It is hard enough to be a woman as a surgeon. Any blemishes, and I would be doomed. Do you understand that, Mr Baba? The world isn't fair. I think you understand that. I may appear naïve, but I do know a little of what the NHS can be like. I am glad that I have you to turn to and I am also glad for your confidence. I can trust you, can't I?"

She was appealing to him to stay silent when whatever Henry had done was an abuse of his position. If he promised to stay silent, Henry might do this again. What could he do?

"Eliza, I do know what you mean about the world and the politics of the NHS, but you also need to understand that as a senior doctor, Henry has many privileges and also a duty to adhere to the boundaries of professional behaviour. There is something that I think you have not told me about in this story, and that does not rest easily with me. I hope that you can stay safe, Eliza and promise me that you will tell me if you are ever scared or feel trapped. Can you promise me that?" He tilted his head enquiringly.

"Sometimes, there are things that just need to not be said, Mr Baba. You are right that there are more details to the story, but Henry and I need to work it out together. We will, but first I need a little time away. I promise I will speak to you if I need help, and I will stay safe. Anyway, I need to get the jobs done for today. I am rather behind."

"No, Eliza, you don't need to be doing any work now. I can sort out the last few bits for you today and tomorrow, so we can sort out the cover for you. You need to go home. I will inform occupational health tomorrow morning, and they will call you. Tell them how you are feeling and that you need some time off."

"I will do that. Thank you, Mr Baba," she stood up and smiled at him. She felt worried that he had guessed what had happened, but also, in some way, she was glad that he knew. The weight of the secret had been too much for her.

She nodded and smiled weakly. She wondered what things would have been like if she had had the strength to stop Henry. Was it possible to trust Henry again? What did she want? Did she want to still see him? Mr Baba was right. She needed time out. What had happened earlier with the mistake on the ward was one near-miss too many. She needed to clear her head and find a way to cope. The meeting ended, and she headed to her car.

Sitting in the driver's seat, staring at the fence in front of her car, her heart was beating heavily. She could not believe what she had told Mr Baba. Had she done the right thing? Would he keep silent? Was a week off enough to regain her composure? She suddenly remembered that she had not replied to Henry's text. What was she going to say to him?

Text: Hello, Henry. I am feeling a bit unwell, so I'm heading home for a few days to recover. See you next week. Eliza

It was a bland text, but so much about it spoke far more than the words it contained. Henry instead of the Hx. Eliza and No. x. the vague nature of the content. She felt that a huge rift lay between them at that moment, and she wondered how he would take the cold shoulder. It did not take long to find out.

Text: That's a rather distant message. H

He was worried. She could palpate that. Would he react?

Text: Not distant. I'm just a bit off-colour. No problem. Speak next week. E

She turned off her phone. She needed to turn off Henry and gather her thoughts. She needed to make sense of what had happened without the fear of seeing him, or hearing from him every day. She needed her home and her mum.

Chapter 36
Seeking the Root

Flying to Amman was like travelling to a new world for Jemimah. She had been nervous about telling her adoptive parents about her plans to go to Jordan, but like always, they had been unreservedly supportive of her choices and understood why she needed to do it. How lucky she felt at that moment! She could not bring back her biological parents, but she was still blessed to have loved adoptive parents to whom she felt she belonged as much. It was a strange obsession to seek out her biological family when she already had one and knew that both of her parents were dead. She was chasing branches and the last fragments of her family tree. It was not about moving on or away from what she called home, but rather about completing the circle of her life's own purpose and meaning just by simply knowing herself completely.

She pondered how many people, even when they were not adopted, knew as much about their background as she now knew about her own. How many people could say that they truly know their parents? She reflected that in most families that she observed, it was typical to merely be aware of the presence of parents and yet to just live alongside one another without really understanding the story of each individual. It represented to her a non-intrusive co-existence that just worked because differences were simply accepted, and the innate lack of curiosity reigned as a definition of normality itself—a space that allowed individuals to grow within it. That was not how Jemimah's mind worked, however. She was someone who had always sought the whole story, whether it was in the diagnosis and treatment of a complicated disease or in the exploration of her past. She had never been the sort of surgeon to merely treat the symptoms. She wanted to find the root of what stood before her and then decide the best course of action to achieve the desired global outcome.

Rupert had done something that he had not done for decades as he embarked on this journey with Jemimah. He had left all outstanding work in London and packed only clothes, toiletries, gifts, and a good book to read. It was as though he had suddenly rekindled a part of himself that had been buried beneath the traumatic story of his past, and he was not going to allow anything to distract him from this long-awaited moment. He needed to repair the wounds, or at least some of them; in particular, the loss of his close friend and the lifelong fears that he had held for Jemimah's wellbeing. Every time a report arrived about her, he held his breath. Each time the news was good, he breathed a sigh of relief.

Jemimah defined the union between himself and Rachel, and although she was not his daughter, he loved her as though she were. She had filled the void of not having a family of his own and, in some ways, also helped reconcile the injustices of Israel, where he had grown up. His almost exile-like existence had left a feeling of loss that was impossible to describe. Yes, he had a home and a life in London, but the deepest connection to his identity had been lost. As he stared ahead in the plane and looked at the headrest in front of him, faces of the past appeared in his mind, and the journey he was now on was like relighting an old candle. What would he find? What was left of the past? Little steps each way, but he would complete his journey by reconnecting the loose ends.

He had convinced himself that this was the final decade of life, and he reminisced about how so much of his life had not been completely his own. It was a web of interconnected people, events, and circumstances out of his control. It was as though life, as he knew it, was about an evolving community, not an individual. Would he make it back to Israel one day? He was not sure why he would, as ther was none of his family there anymore. Was it just the soil that he wanted to touch? That feeling of reunion? Spiritually, he had a journey to complete as well. Would his country of birth welcome him back one day? He knew deep down that it would not. He would be forever branded a traitor and criminal.

The new Israel was not a forgiving place, despite honouring the Pikuach nefesh and his obligation to save a life. The problem was that the lives he had saved were not considered valid in the new Zionist Israel that had risen post-Nakba day, where the Mitzvah's of Jewish life had been distorted by the new laws of the land, where the lives of Arabs and anyone associated with them had become worthless. His Israel had become, in his eyes, a morally barren place of possession for him—a place where love was only valid if it avoided people of cultures that the ideology of Zionism deemed invalid. It was no longer a place he related to; this was not the Judaism that he loved and had adhered to all of his life. Reconciling that was something that he would probably carry with himself to the grave.

This journey to Jordan was as close as he could get to his homeland, and in some way, it might be just enough, as he was there with Jemimah—the one life that epitomised all that he believed love could produce—and his reunion with her had kept alive his one true love: Rachel and his greatest friend, Ameer. Reconnecting with Ahmed would complete the story and unite the strands of his shredded web of life. He turned to look at Jemimah. She was sleeping. What a beautiful and kind woman she had grown into; what a legacy from each parent to leave to this world.

As they approached the landing strip in Amman, the sky was a pinkish grey. Where Jemimah had expected clouds, there was a silvery haze that softened the walls of the tiny white cubes that represented houses scattered amidst the roads and desert below them. She took a picture of it from the little window she was peering out of. They were nearly there, and the excitement within her resonated through the twinkle of her blue eyes. Her cheeks were flushed, and a spontaneous grin had appeared in the corners of her mouth. Rupert looked out, and memories flooded back to him. The last time he entered Amman, it was as a scared young man fleeing in the night by foot. It was a much bigger city now, and he was entering it without fear. He was returning with a treasure that exists today because of Amman. That treasure, that tiny, innocent life that Rachel clung onto in desperation, had grown into a beautiful woman who was sitting smiling next to him. The significance of this approach to a city that had represented salvation for them could not be underestimated.

A small tear welled in the corner of his eyes as he recalled the expression of relief on Rachel's face as she believed that they were safe from her family. Ahmed had met them at the border that night, and they climbed silently into his car. Even Jemimah did not make a sound. The combination of fear and exhaustion was enough to steal the words from everyone's mouth.

"Nearly there," Jemimah whispered. "I wonder what it will be like. The airport looks huge."

Rupert looked at the enlarging airport on their approach.

"That is quite a new airport, and I hear it is very beautiful. I think you will find it an experience when you arrive. Don't expect the guards to smile, though.

They have a reputation to keep. Their frown even has a name. People call it 'Kashra' and when they stand in corners watching you with their cigarettes, they remind me of Italian mafiosi. I remember it well. The last time I saw it, I didn't find it as funny as the locals do. Those stares bore through me as we waited to board our flight to England. Today, I intend to not let it trouble me. I might even try staring back." A childlike, cheeky expression spread across his face.

"Now, Rupert, I'm not sure having a staring contest with a security guard sounds too safe!" she laughed. "Do you think they do it as a powerful thing? The stare of superiority? I hear people of Jordan are very welcoming people in real life, so this surprises me…although come to think of it, the Queen's Guards in London never smile, even though they are marching around with giant pompoms on their heads, defending the head of state. Maybe it is a requirement of the job. Part of the training is to be a guard anywhere and look convincing in your uniform."

Rupert laughed out loud.

"Oh yes, the people of Jordan are lovely, but many of them also bear the scars of oppression and war, so they value life more than most. It is a place rich with culture, and what I remember most about it is its incredible diversity of faces. I think you will feel quite at home here, Jemimah. You will blend in without any difficulty."

"That sounds surreal, Rupert. I have never known what blending in means in my life. In England, I have always stuck out like a sore thumb," she said this whilst staring out of the window.

"Oh Jemimah, here I have no doubt at all that you will feel welcome. The people of Jordan epitomise hospitality at its best and absolutely love food. There are many traditions that they hold on to, although I am not sure how much of that has been lost with time. It will be interesting to see."

"Mmmmmmm! The sound of lots of food is making my mouth water," Jemimah said, and she licked her lips. "Who do you think will meet us at the airport? Do you think my uncle Ahmed will come?" Jemimah was almost too excited to wait for the plane to land. She was restless in her seat, and her eagerness made Rupert giggle.

"Jemimah, being so excited is not going to land the plane any quicker. You are even making my heartbeat fast," he simulated the heartbeat on his chest with his hand as he laughed.

"Oh, I'm sorry. I am simply too excited to describe. What an unforgettable week this is going to be. I can't wait!" At that moment, the calm surgeon Jemimah could not have been less apparent. The beauty and purity of her smile were something to behold. It was not difficult to understand why she turned heads everywhere with a smile like that. The plane landed just a few minutes later. They were there.

Rupert was calmer and wondered if he would be able to recognise Ahmed. In some ways, Ahmed resembled Ameer a lot when he was younger. He wondered whether he would be looking at Ahmed that day and remembering his dear friend and the life he never had a chance to complete. He never stopped missing him.

"I imagine Ahmed will come to meet us and may bring his wife, whom I haven't met. They are a very influential family here, so I imagine that they will have made arrangements to make our time at the airport very easy. We need to look for someone with our names on a banner. They will be the people asked to help us."

"Gosh, that all sounds very official. Do you mean we get treated like VIPs? What an honour. Are we expected to tip people?"

"No. Everything will have been sorted out for us."

As they exited the doorway of the plane, the warm, dusty air of Amman touched their faces. It was June, so that meant it was springtime. It was an excellent time of year to visit, according to the guidebook that Jemimah had downloaded for the trip. She had failed in her plans to learn Arabic in time, so at that moment she felt like a complete tourist. That was not good in her books. This was supposed to feel like coming home, not another Brit on tour expecting the perfect English language from the natives. She sighed. In her pocket, she had put a small sheet of key introductory words. The absolute must-know things like 'please' and 'thank you' and the essentials like 'where is the toilet?' All the other words and phrases that she had learned were just a fog in her head.

As they went into the grand new Amman Airport with its iridescent windows and white walls, she was surprised. In her mind, she had imagined a much smaller airport and a lot more dust and heat. What she found was heavenly. As they entered, a man waved at them as he held up a banner with their name on it. They were guided through all of the check areas very uneventfully, and their baggage was collected effortlessly. They made their way into the arrivals lounge next to each other, and as they came through the double doors, standing there, with a tearful smile was a man who was unmistakably Ahmed. Rupert waved to him, and they rushed towards each other shook right hands enthusiastically and kissed each cheek.

"Asalamu Alaikum, my dear friend, Avraham. It has been too long. Alhamdullilah, you made it here at last. Welcome," Ahmed held Rupert's slight arms between both hands and smiled kindly at him.

"Thank you, my friend. Although it has been many years since we have seen each other, our communications and correspondence have helped keep our lifelong bridge connected. I am so happy to be here at last. You look so well." He turned to face Jemimah and extended his arm to bring her forwards. "May I introduce again to you Jemimah, daughter of Ameer and Rachel. Now a beautiful doctor and woman."

"Alhamdulillah . Can it really be you?" By custom, he did not kiss her cheeks but put his hand over his heart as a symbol of welcome. She reciprocated by mirroring his actions and saying, "Ahlan wa Sahlan Uncle Ahmed. Yes, it is me. I am so pleased to finally meet you." His eyes were the same as her father's, and she felt an instant connection to him.

"You look so much like your mother, but Masha Allah you have the smile of my brother. Alhamdulillah you came here, Jemimah, and this is your home. Welcome. There are so many people who have prayed for you for many years. At last, their prayers have been heard," she wondered how many other members of the family she was going to meet that day, but felt it was wise not to ask too many questions at that point.

Ahmed extended his hand to introduce the beautiful woman with almond-shaped, dark eyes standing next to him. "May I introduce you to my wife, Zaynab? We were not yet acquainted when you were both briefly here."

Jemimah moved to kiss her on the cheeks, and Rupert raised his hand to his heart. They both said, "Marhaban Zaynab, it is wonderful to meet you," in synchrony.

"Marhaban, both of you. I have heard so many stories about you that I feel like I already know you. It is my pleasure to welcome you to my country."

"Let us go home and meet the rest of the family," Ahmed said. He ushered them towards a large black Mercedes. The driver had already loaded their bags into the back. Jemimah, Rupert, and Zaynab sat at the back (Jemimah had read in her guidebook that women typically sit at the back of cars), and Ahmed sat in the front. He took on the role of tour guide for the journey home.

"We are rather pleased with the new airport we have here. They planted these green areas less than ten years ago, and today they look like they have been here for much longer. I always think it is a good way to welcome visitors and travellers."

Jemimah was admiring the airport through her window and taking photos with her phone.

"Oh, Jemimah, one thing to be wary of in Jordan is taking photographs of women, even if you did not focus your camera at them. It is to protect the modesty of the more-strict Muslims here, and although I am almost as western as you, having spent many years there in my education in Oxford, I do try to respect the many customs here."

Jemimah felt embarrassed. She had not thought of that. "Uncle Ahmed, I am so sorry. Thank you for explaining that to me. I am sure I will keep making mistakes unconsciously this week, and any advice is gratefully received," he turned to look at her with that kind smile that he had.

"It is alright, Jemimah. Jordan is actually a very easy country to live in, but like all countries, it has its traditions and sensitivities. You are safe with your family. We will help you as you get around and visit places. We have so many things to show you."

"Thank you. If all I do this week is spending time with you and hear the stories of my family, I will indeed be very pleased. This is like a dream. I feel like it is a chance that I have to understand the father that I never had a chance to meet. I have seen some photographs of him that my mother left for me. Is it polite for me to say that I see much of his face in you, uncle?"

He laughed gently. "My dear Jemimah, that is the kindest compliment to give to me. Avraham, do you agree with what Jemimah sees?" Rupert was deep in thought as he looked out of the window at the city.

"oh, I am sorry, my friend. I was lost in memories watching the city go by, and I missed that. What were you saying?"

Ahmed laughed.

"Always the deep thinker. Even when you were a young man, you could lose yourself in those thoughts of yours. I was just asking you whether you agree with Jemimah's observation that I look like Ameer. What do you see?" Rupert looked into Ahmed's eyes through the rear-view mirror. He smiled nostalgically as he inspected the face of his friend.

"You and Ameer always looked more like brothers than cousins. Jemimah is quite right that you have a lot in common with him. Especially the eyes and hair and that smile. I always told Ameer that he could cure any disease just by smiling. That was the sort of man that he was."

Zaynab, who had not said much, turned to look at Jemimah. She smiled at her and looked at the necklace she was wearing.

"That is a very beautiful necklace you are wearing, Jemimah. Do you know what it is?"

Jemimah reached out to touch the pendant. It was a necklace that she had found in the box that Rupert had given her from her mother. She loved the gold hand with the blue gemstone eye in the centre, but she had no idea that it signified anything more than just an object her mother had owned.

"Oh, thank you. It was something that my mother left for me in her will. I thought it was very pretty. Does it mean something?"

"MashaAllah. It is the hand of Fatima Al-Zahra, the daughter of Prophet Muhammed, sallallahu alayhi wa salaam. The five fingers represent the five pillars of Islam, and the eye represents protection against the evil eye. It is a pendant that is meant to symbolise the keys to faith and protection. Although in Islam we do not believe in superstition, this symbol has been worn in many cultures for thousands of years. It is a symbol worn by both Jews and Muslims, interestingly, but the stories that go with them are slightly different. It is the perfect thing for you to have Jemimah. Masha Allah," she looked into Jemimah's eyes, and Jemimah reached out and touched her hand.

Rupert looked at it and smiled, "Ah yes. In Judaism it symbolises the hand of Miriam, the sister of Moses. The essence of its connection to God and protection are the same in both religious depictions of this hand with an eye."

"Oh, how amazing! This little pendant is, in effect, a symbol that connects the two different faiths of my parents and two important women, Fathima and Miriam. How apt and beautiful! I will always treasure this. Thank you for telling me about it. I wonder whether my father gave it to my mother as a symbol of his love for her," she held it again between her fingers and smiled as each little interaction unwrapped more details of her past.

Ahmed restarted his mini guide to the city. "We are entering the main street, heading to Jabbal Amman, where trade is the beating heart of the city. If you roll down your window, Jemimah, you will smell the Shawarmas and falafel cooking and hear the bustle of the shops and people. Jemimah opened her window, and the warm Jordanian air gushed into her nose, filling it with the smell of warm flatbreads, meat, spices, and also a small bolus of city pollution that had been filtered by the air conditioning of the car. She looked at all of the stalls by the footpath and the clothes of the people walking there. There was no single code of dress. Western clothes were as common as Islamic ones, and the contrast from the oligochromatic predictability of Saints Bay to the kaleidoscope of fabrics, styles, and colours that she could see now was dramatic. She hoped that she would be able to walk there and soak up the details more slowly as the week progressed. She longed to taste the foods and hear the languages spoken.

"It is a delight to see Uncle Ahmed. I am getting hungry just seeing all those stalls with fresh food."

"Well, Jemimah, we have a lot of food at home, so you will get the opportunity to taste some of our local favourites soon."

"This is a dream. Thank you so much for all you are doing. Every minute I am here, I feel more complete." All the others in the car smiled. Each had smiles with different thoughts attached. For Rupert, it was love and sadness; for Ahmed, it was memory and gratitude; and for Jemimah, it belonged.

"We are now entering our part of Jabbal Amman in the first circle. This is the oldest part of the modern city, and what you see here started in the 1920s in the Emirate of Transjordan, which preceded what you call Jordan today. Our family first moved here with other old families, keen to find a place that was safe to live. We brought wealth and investment to the Emirate when it was a poor place largely populated by Bedouin nomads, and in return, we found a new home as our own in Palestine was occupied and destroyed. There is a mixture of houses here, and many are now protected to keep some of our history alive. Our own home, Beit Tuquan, was built in 1928, with elements that reminded us of the house in Nablus. When you see the house inside, you will see more of our heritage, Jemimah. Our wider family is a very educated and large family with a long history in business and many professions, but today, we are scattered all over the world." Jemimah watched the white houses as they drove past. Now they were looking more individual and larger. All of the windows and doors had wrought grills that were either plain and straight like bars or forged in different patterns. She wondered whether the patterns were cultural."

"Why do all the windows have grilles? Is that for safety?"

"Ah Zaynab is the expert in all things architectural, Jemimah." He replied.

"Are you an architect, Aunt Zaynab?" Jemimah asked as she turned to her aunt.

"Yes, I am. Although I did my studies in England, where I met Ahmed, a lot of what I design is with Islamic influence, and I am pleased that you noticed the windows here. Although most houses have plain barred grilles for security, a few of the older houses and buildings have decorative ones, which represent a part of ancient Islamic architecture known as mashrabiya. Our house here has a particularly good example of it, and it is one of only a few with such an ornate design. They vary depending on the country and the purpose of the building, but as well as decorating the windows, they are there to provide shade, security, and privacy. For me, they also allow you to decorate the view that you see from every window and reflect beautiful shapes into each room." Every word that her aunt told her filled her ears and soul. 'Mashrabiya'. Such a lovely name. Far more beautiful than the word grilles. She was falling in love with this culture and country.

The car turned onto a side road and passed through some tall wrought gates into a courtyard. They were home. Beit Tuquan was an impressive two-story house with pillars at the entrance and a balcony in the centre on the first floor. The building was all white, like all of the houses in Amman, but its grandeur made it stand out from the houses she had seen before.

"Welcome to our home Avraham and Jemimah. Come in and meet the rest of the family."

Jemimah felt emotional and a little overwhelmed. There is a great difference between the excitement and curiosity to discover the roots of your family and that feeling that engulfs you when you have found them. The realisation that all that she was connected to by birth was here in this magical place. The air in the courtyard was heavily perfumed by the honeysuckle that grew along the walls and Jemimah took a deep inhalation and memorised that moment of arrival. She followed her family and Rupert into the house. A member of the household staff opened the glass doors at the entrance and stood by to let them in.

The floors and walls were covered in white marble, and their feet made a pleasing sound as they walked on it. In the centre of the entrance hall, there was a large round wooden table displaying an impressive vase of exotic flowers, and on the walls, there were portraits of family members, most of whom she had not met. As she stared at the pictures, a maid came up to her with a tray of tea. It was served in a glass cup decorated with intricate silver embellishments. 'Shukran' she said as she took one. She sipped on the dark tea and was rather taken aback by the sweetness of it. She could taste cardamom in it too, which she loved. Rupert spotted her face and came up to her with a knowing smile on his face.

"Ah, your introduction to Arabic tea. What do you think of it?"

"Well, it is strong and full of flavour, but oh my God, it is too sweet! Do they have any milk?"

"No, no, no, don't ask for milk. It is not the done thing," he adored her complete naivety about the customs of Jordan and the Middle East. Even though he had lived in London for most of his adult life, he had strangely never lost the customs of his origins. Three sugars was still a bad habit he had clung onto in his tea and coffee, although thankfully in Israel cream was another important additive that he was glad to have.

Ahmed approached them and invited them into the main reception room. In contrast to the old wooden furniture and gilded picture frames in the hallway, this room was brighter and had gold and glass furniture and a modern white sofa suite. It did not seem to fit into the style of the house, but Jemimah presumed that it was a modern redecoration. There were at least ten other people in there; uncles, aunts, cousins, nieces, and nephews. It was overwhelming to see so many people that she was related to but had never known about. Rupert toured the room with Ahmed, and Zaynab gave Jemimah a tour of introductions. So many new names. So many faces that just seemed to fit. Here, she really did blend in and, at last, understood where she belonged. Everyone spoke English beautifully, and she felt guilty that her own efforts to learn Arabic had been so paltry. It was a goal now to learn how to speak it properly, if only to show respect to her and her family.

"Jemimah, there is one person who we want you to meet above all. Hajjah is in the next room, and she is your grandmother."

"My grandmother? Do you mean my father, Ameer's mother? She is here?"

Her broken questions reflected the surprise that was on her face. Her heart was thumping, and she felt dizzy.

"Yes, Jemimah. She is the last of our elders to live, and I sometimes wonder whether she has lived to this old age just to meet you. Come with us," Ahmed and Zaynab directed Jemimah and Rupert into the next room through tall, gilded doors. It was like entering a different house. The room was darker and laced with a film of fragrant smoke. It was filled with old wooden ornate furniture, beautiful mother-of-pearl vases, crystal ornaments capturing the light, and ornately carved lamps. On the walls were pictures of Mecca, Al Aqsa Mosque, the Dome of the Rock, and other Islamic places that she presumed her grandparents had visited in their lives. The room and everything in it were touched by a heavy perfume of oud coming from a central ceramic tray with oud chips smouldering in it. To the side, with her face lit by the lacey light coming from the decorated window opposite her, an old lady sat with her legs raised on the divan. She was wearing a beautifully embroidered velvet thobe. The embroidery was detailed and almost Aztec in its formation. Jemimah had read about the Tatreez embroidery that was from Palestine and how it told the story not only of the place it originated from but also of the status of the person wearing it. The embroidery on Hajja's clothes was impressive. She walked up to her grandmother and knelt beside her so that their eyes were level. Hajjah placed her hand on Jemimah's cheek and smiled at her.

"Asalamu'Alaikum Hajjah."

"Wa'Alaikum Salam Jemimah. Alhamdullilah, you are indeed the child of my boy Ameer. I can see that now in your beautiful face."

She leant forwards and took the pendant on Jemimah's chest between her fingers.

"Masha'Allah, you have it now."

"Yes, my mother left it for me. Do you know this pendant, Hajjah?"

"Yes, I do, it was mine, then your mother's, and now rightfully yours. Your grandfather bought it for me," she pointed to a photograph on the side table next to her. Jemimah stood up to look at it. Her grandfather stood as an elegant Arab man in an old black-and-white photograph; next to him was a younger Hajjah and when she examined the photograph, Hajjah, was wearing the necklace. They were standing outside a beautiful house with olive trees around them.

"Oh, you are wearing the necklace here. How lovely. Where was this taken, Hajjah?"

"That was our home in Nablus. It was a beautiful place then. Now it is all gone. All the trees have gone too," she looked at the photograph with sadness in her eyes. As her gaze turned to Rupert, there was a moment of recognition.

"It has been a long time, Avraham. I last saw you as a young man with my son. We have all grown old now, haven't we? Do you not come with a wife?" Rupert swallowed and played with his index finger.

"No, sadly, not Hajjah. I never married, but I have worked hard in London and made sure that Jemimah's mother was safe."

"That is a shame, Avraham. You would have made a good husband. Why did you not marry Jemimah's mother? She was a Jew, was she not?" She had the directness that only an elder could have, and Rupert had been expecting it.

"Yes, she was a Jew. Our marriage was not meant to be Hajjah. Rachel never stopped loving Ameer, and neither of us ever married. She stayed loyal to your son always."

"My dear eldest son. My Ameer. What a pure and good man he was. How I miss him. Inshallah, I will meet him again Inshallah; but first I wanted to meet my grandchild, and may Allah always bless you, Abraham," she turned to Jemimah and said, "I prayed that I would meet you, Jemimah. Come closer to me so that I can see you a bit better."

For the next half an hour, Jemimah talked to her grandmother, and they shared tears and stories. She gave Hajjah the embroidery that she had made for her, showing her home in England. Hajjah loved it and signalled to Zaynab to bring a gift for Jemimah. It was a beautiful thobe with golden thread, silk, and velvet entwined with ornate embroidery. The sleeves were heavily embroidered and shaped like long petals. Hajjah explained the meaning of the embroidery to her, and Jemimah did not want the moment to end. She then gave her a rosary chain known as a Sibha.

"Jemimah, use this in your prayers. It was your father's, and I want you to have it now."

"Oh, Hajjah, these gifts are so beautiful. Thank you. With all my heart, thank you." She did not know if it was allowed, but she leant forwards and hugged her grandmother. There were tears in both of their eyes and a love that was now complete. Jemimah had found her roots.

Ahmed came in to invite everyone to the dining room, where a grand table burgeoning with every delight imaginable was waiting. "Time to eat now, everyone." A tray of food was brought through to Hajjah first, and then everyone went to eat.

The dining table looked fit for royalty. It was a long, ornate wooden table that was completely covered with dishes of food. The smell was heavenly. Jemimah tasted the wonders of food she had never eaten before all of her senses came to life. Zaynab gave her a tour of all the dishes: mezze, Palestinian olives, hummus, musakhan, mansaf, shush Barak, wara'dawali, kubba and many more. They ate, talked, and laughed together, and on that day, the web of life was complete.

Chapter 37
Like Mercury Beads

As Ibrahim sat in his office at his laptop completing the jobs that Eliza had not been able to do, his mind was distracted thinking about the conversation he had just had with her. He knew well that the reaction that Eliza was having was not just about a simple breakup. Henry must have done something bad … or could Eliza be pregnant? He was feeling uncomfortable with his situation where he was bound to a promise to not tell anyone, and also to the quandary that he could not say anything without knowing the complete facts. Jemimah had a point that if it was the case of two consenting adults in a relationship there would be a case to say that all was not as bad as it looked, but there were reasons why it was discouraged for consultants to be involved with junior doctors; especially one who was the training programme director.

It was the balance of power and its potential for misuse. Who would he talk to if he wanted to ask for another opinion now? Jemimah was off and the next person to speak to was Andrew McNair, who also happened to be a close family friend of Henry. That was a risky avenue to take as he did not know how close the two friends were and how much they would protect each other, no matter how bad the transgression. He then recalled how Andrew had protected him when Henry tried to set him up with Mr Potter. It suggested that Andrew was no man's fool and also knew Henry better than most. Perhaps he would be a good person to speak to after all. Then came the next problem. Escalation was only valid with enough verified facts to hand. Eliza was not happy to talk to anyone and she needed Henry's support in the hospital.

Breaking that trust would leave Eliza exposed and alone. That was a risk not worth taking until more information was offered by her. He needed to think like Jemimah, be calm and considered, and above all, not be reactive about allegations related to the clinical lead and a colleague breaking the code of practice of a consultant and abusing his position of power. How on earth could he reconcile that? This was an absolute mess and at the heart of it was poor Eliza whose life was likely to never be the same again and equally bad was the problem that she was still in communication with the perpetrator on the loose. Henry was protected by her silence and the fortune of having friends in all the right places. The injustice of it all made him feel sick. In the background was also his own selfish need to keep Henry's alliance in his application for a consultant position. He had waited all of his life for this but morally, the dilemma and hypocrisy were tugging at his soul. He needed to consider things in prayer tonight after the shift was completed. I have a few more blood tests to request, a quick handover to the night team and then home.

....

In Wales, Simon sat at the edge of his bed. He was still furious about what had happened to Eliza. He hated that she had not given him authorisation to speak up about the sexual assault and he hated Henry so much that he wanted to punch him. He still loved Eliza and she did not deserve to go through this. God, what was he thinking? Nobody deserved to suffer what she was going through. Thankfully his emotions were not a reflection of his character, and the idea of punching Henry was just that. A thought. He had agreed with Eliza that he would not say anything to anyone in the trust. Perhaps there were other avenues he could take. After all, Eliza had told him everything; or at least he hoped so as what she had said was already more than enough. He knew all about the people involved in that knotted web of deceit and betrayal that Eliza had become entwined in. She had not left any details out and had also reminded him that Henry was a powerful man and with allies in many places. There had to be a way of helping Eliza move on from this without leaving her reputation and consequently her future irreparably damaged. There must be a way. Think Simon, think!

....

Henry looked at the text that Eliza had sent. Something was very wrong. So far, there was no evidence at all that she had spoken to anyone, but the potential for disaster was just too real. He needed to work faster at completing the things that would reassert him as a popular and supportive colleague. He needed to keep his allies close and somehow work on Eliza to get her trust back. What an idiot he had been to take such a risk and make such a mistake. How did he get here? He kept reading her text over and over. Vanessa had entered the room, and he put his phone down. Was there guilt on his face? He smiled at her and told her to come and sit down with him. There was so much that he had neglected in his relationship over the last few years. He had taken for granted all that Vanessa had done for him, yet she had remained loyal to him. Even if there was no guilt on his face, he felt it gnawing inside of him. She walked up to him with a concerned expression on her face.

"Henry is everything alright? Yesterday you bought me flowers. You never buy me flowers. Today you want to snuggle on the sofa. I cannot remember the last time we did that. I know you darling. Something is wrong. Tell me what is going through your head," she was sitting next to him. Their legs were touching but she kept her hands on her lap. She looked deeply into his eyes. Something went wrong. Would he talk about it?

"Yes, I'm OK. I just feel guilty that I have rather taken you for granted for too long. It seems that with work, the kids and everything else I have forgotten about us. Work has taken over my whole life and somewhere, I forgot to be a husband to you. I had told myself that all I needed to do was bring in the money and somehow my role was complete. You never complain. You have just been here. I'm so sorry Vanessa. I have let you down." How those last words meant so much more than he could explain.

Vanessa's hand moved to hold his. How long had it been that she had waited for the love that she had felt for Henry to be truly reciprocated? His words filled her head with intoxicating thoughts. Suddenly she felt guilty that she had been suspicious of him. How could she have doubted him?

"Oh, Henry what a beautiful thing to say. Everything we have we have built together, and it is because of you. You gave me a home, this beautiful home, to raise our children in. We have needed each other to make this dream a reality. I love you more today than I have ever loved you. Thank you, my darling,"

She leant towards him and kissed him. He did not know whether it was the guilt or the desperation to hold onto one certainty in his now-turbulent life, but Henry reciprocated with a passion that he had not expressed with Vanessa for many years. They walked upstairs together and made love like they had during their honeymoon and for those hours, he let go of his anguish and worry. This was the woman he needed in his life and Eliza had just been a blip. He needed to close that episode quickly and fan this new flame between Vanessa and himself. Tonight, he could see why he had married her.

....

Reaching home, Eliza had finally figured out what she would tell her mother. This was an unexpected visit, and she needed a good excuse that was anything but the truth or the real reason why she needed to be home. There was a sense of growing relief that she felt as the miles grew between Saint's Bay and her final destination. How right Ibrahim had been to convince her to get away! She needed space. She needed to start looking at herself with less disgust. She hated herself for what she had done. When she told Ibrahim that she was involved with Henry, just that word alone made her feel tainted and dirty, more so because she did not want it. It was in her eyes partly her fault and that she had been assaulted because she had allowed it to happen. She had let him into her home and therefore she was the cause for all that had happened. How could she have allowed him to take advantage of her? What sort of doctor was that stupid? She needed to get away and find a way to forgive herself, or at least come to terms with her errors. Was the week that she had planned to be away enough? Would she return to a storm after telling Ibrahim? Could he keep the secret? She was scared and needed her mum.

....

Back in his cottage in Hampton-Astley, a mile away from Henry's house, Ibrahim knelt in prayer and questioned himself. Was this a test? To see if he would put his own progress in front of protecting Eliza? The other problem was that she had invested her trust in his silence. Doing what was right was also risking going against his word to not speak up. If he knew more, perhaps the decision would have been an easier one, but the partial picture that Eliza had delivered to him gave as much a justified reason for not saying anything as speaking up. This was not an easy decision and he asked Allah to guide him and show him the right path to choose in the coming days. Until then he had to be supportive of Eliza. He and Jemimah had both agreed that that was the primary objective. To protect her. He felt more at peace now after what had been a rather sad day. He had hoped so much that his suspicions about Henry were wrong. Now, he knew that they were not, he was angry. 'Damn you, Henry. Don't you have enough?'

....

It had been a long day of work for Andrew McNair, who was reading Ibrahim's portfolio in his study at home. He was surprised by Henry's eagerness to do as he had said and reverse some of what he had done to Ibrahim. He had known Henry for a long time. Their friendship had at times made work life a little difficult, especially since he had been appointed as clinical director and effectively one step hierarchically above Henry. As young men at medical school they had been ambitious and at times reckless. In many ways that was more a reflection of Henry's character than his. He thought it ironic how by some fortune he had climbed faster than Henry in the hospital management structure but still he felt in some way in awe of Henry. As a man, Henry was like a beacon to walk towards and yet as a person he was as flawed as the rest of the world...perhaps even more flawed and yet, impressive.

It was Henry who had spotted the potential for a deal with the Holmfield Surgical Centre that convinced Derek to take the risk and somehow spun a story that sounded only moderately shifty and on paper very sensible. Throughout his years, Andrew always played things safe and this was the first time that Henry had tempted him to question that and take advantage of the opportunities in NHS that were evolving somewhat by stealth with privatisation and external investment. There was a constant niggle inside of him that was deceitful, but if it did work out, they would both make enough money to start planning an early retirement and for the first time in a long time, relax and let go of the daily relentless stresses of life in the NHS. He felt tired and craved peace. Perhaps there were ways to balance the wrongness of his plans with rights elsewhere.

He looked at Ibrahim's portfolio, and it was a testament to a career of hard work. As a doctor, Ibrahim had done far more than anyone who had followed the usual path to a consultant appointment, and yet the system seemed to have held him back. Andrew pondered for the first time about his own biases. Was he part of the problem in that system? Had he been part of the limitations that Ibrahim had faced without even realising it? It was all over social media that healthcare is full of racism and prejudice that was "unconscious." Was he part of that? No, surely not. He had no prejudices that he knew of. This project of lifting Ibrahim to his rightful place as a consultant was something that he felt pleased to be a part of. Whatever Henry was not, this time he was doing something right, and that was something that Andrew had long wanted to see. Henry had finally become a better person. He turned to his computer and wrote a recommendation in support of Ibrahim's application, citing all of the evidence that was clear for all to see. It was his time to join the ranks of consultants.

....

Vanessa woke up in the arms of Henry. She felt like it was a dream. A beautiful reverie that she was afraid at some point she might be shaken out of and realise that it had all been a lie. When did she become so negative and doubtful? This was not like her. This was not who she was inside. She was someone who had always believed in good things and had always loved Henry and the home that she had nurtured. It was time to start enjoying this surprise. The best sort of midlife crisis to behold is when a husband wakes up one day and looks at his wife with the eagerness of newly revived youth instead of chasing a younger woman, hoping to relive years gone by. What a delight it was! A bright smile was on her face as Henry's eyes opened to meet hers.

"Good morning, darling. What a gorgeous smile to wake up to! What is this for?" He kissed her and held her face gently between his two hands. "You look perfect today."

She just smiled and soaked up the moment. Many moments in life had made her happy, but it was possible that that very moment was the happiest of all for her.

"If only we could make today Sunday and not Wednesday, we could stay like this in this perfect moment all day. Sadly, you have work to go to and I have two lovely children getting ready for school. Don't let go of it, though, because I want us to continue later if that's what you would like."

"Yes, life does keep chugging on, but what we have rekindled is not just about one day, it is about every day from now on. Perhaps our hours will go by faster because of it, and before we can take our next conscious blink, we will be back in each other's arms."

Vanessa kissed him and rolled out of bed. He admired her naked body. It was a beautiful body despite its age, and all that he needed was there in her. He was the luckiest man, and letting go of Eliza was going to be the easiest thing he had ever done. She needed to move on, and he would make sure that she passed her exams and left before too long. He had to ensure that she stayed silent about the mishap. It was only a momentary blip…or maybe two blips. Surely, she could forget them, couldn't she? Today was about getting Ibrahim's plan sorted. Andrew would hopefully have read the portfolio and application by now. It was time for a coffee and a chat with him. That was his first text of the day. As Henry headed out to work, Vanessa picked up her phone and called her younger sister Claire, who was having a tough time with cancer. She hadn't seen her in too long.

....

Eliza's mother, Justine, was visibly worried when her daughter arrived unexpectedly at her home. This was not her brave and brilliant daughter who was standing at the front door. This was a fragile and scared woman, she was horrified.

"Eliza, darling, this is a surprise; a lovely surprise to see you. I have to say, though, that your face does not say that you are here for a celebration. Is it the exam?" There was something rather ambiguous about Justine Graham, who exuded an almost military grade of strength and lamb-like kindness in equal measure. She was a solution-finder rather than a sympathy-giver. She had raised her daughter to push herself and believe in herself enough to not let anything stop her from chasing her dreams. Today she was looking at her daughter, worried that she had not quite achieved her aims.

"Hello mum. I missed you. No, I'm not here because of my exam. The exam results come at the end of the week, but I've just been feeling a bit lonely and fed up with life. I've gone through some upsetting things at work, and they seem to have shaken my confidence. I needed to come home. I hope you don't mind." She smiled weakly at her mother.

"What a silly thing to say! You are always welcome here, and I can see that you need rebuilding." She gave Eliza the hug that she needed so much. There were only two people she could trust to touch her at that moment, one was Simon, and the other was her mother. She had felt violated by Henry and was now scared by the smallest of things. What was happening to her was confusing and seemed extreme in some way. She had, for just a short moment, lost control of her body and self, and yet the aftermath seemed to have produced a far greater impact. She was experiencing a psychological outcry to make the horror go away and for her body to return to being universally her own. It was not the physical pain that had lingered with her; it was the fear. It was like a thick cloud that shrouded her thoughts, stifling her confidence.

Small tasks provided niduses for the propagation of fear. Scrubbing in the theatre reminded her of his string hands; looking at herself in the mirror filled her with a sense of disgust and revulsion; hearing Henry's voice incited a physiological sequel that was akin to a fight or flight response with tremors and palpitations; even reading a text from Henry caused her mouth to dry out and her vision to blur. She felt angry with herself for being so weak, but it was not she who was the destabiliser; it was the memory and the impact that Henry had left. She had no idea how she would be able to see him and return to work in this state, but this week, with her mother, she needed to find a way without telling her the whole truth. The one thing she would not do was hurt her mother and make her think less of her.

"We need to sit down and talk, Eliza, darling, and make some sense of this knot you are tied up in. I want to see my strong daughter again, and home is just the right place to find her."

She smiled and took the bag from Eliza's hand. Eliza was happy to be home. She needed the pragmatism of her mother right now. Ibrahim's sympathetic tone had just propagated her tears and sense of self-pity. That was not going to be where her solutions lay. She needed some pragmatism, and her mother was the queen of that.

As they sat down over a cup of tea, Eliza started to concoct a pseudo-truth that had enough truth in it to lay a platform for relevant solution finding without mentioning the words sex or assault.

"Mum, I am going to try to tell you what has happened. It might sound odd at times, but what I need is to find a way out. Give me a chance, as my head is a bit confused."

"Alright, you get five minutes to blurt out all you need to say, and I'll butt in then. Sound fair?"

"Yes, that sounds fair. Thank you, mum. OK, here goes. Well, you know that I stayed in Saints Bay to get my exam done, and that breaking up with Simon left me rather alone. Anyway, I was rather lucky because Mr Blythe-Soames, the training programme director, decided to take me under his wing and started teaching me and helping me prepare for the exam. He gave me loads of extra revision sessions and encouraged me in theatre. Over time, I started to become rather more confident and really looked up to him. Anyway, in the last few months, he and I became more like friends than colleagues, and more recently, he started wanting me to be more than that, but in the last few weeks, things happened. I feel rather uncomfortable about it now.

"Anyway, forgetting all that, I have started to become really worried about seeing him at work, and it is affecting how I work. I nearly made a stupid mistake on the ward yesterday, and I think it is because I haven't been sleeping well and have been distracted. Being in the theatre with him is so awkward. I don't want to tell anyone at work because he is a very powerful man, and people will think that I led him on, so instead I have been hiding away, feeling frightened and stupid. What should I do?"

It was as much as she was willing to say to her mother, and she was hoping that there would not be more probing questions to follow. Underneath the table, she crossed her fingers. There was a momentary silence as her mother assimilated what had been said. On her face was an expression of concern and anger. If there was one thing her mother hated, it was misogyny, and the story as Eliza had delivered it portrayed just that.

"Eliza, it sounds like your colleague has overstepped the boundaries of his role. Is he a married man?"

"Yes. He is married and has two children. They live in the same village as me. Down the road, actually."

"Have you met them?" She looked alarmed.

"Er…well yes, I met his wife Vanessa after I had a fall in the woods, and he found me. I had injured my knee, and he had things at home to clean the wound. Nothing else happened on that day." The story sounded as implausible as it had been when she explained it to Vanessa, and her mother was not totally convinced either.

"Right…and how was his wife when she met you?"

"Oh, I think she was fine. She was a nurse before she married him, so I guess she understood why I needed help." There was a slow nod from her mother.

"I confess, if I were her, I might have been rather alarmed to find a young lady in my home with my husband, but perhaps that is just me," she shrugged. "When you say that he wanted you to be more than friends, what did he mean, Eliza?" Her enquiring eyes bore into Eliza. The dreaded questions were starting.

"Oh, er, well he told me that he found me attractive and wanted to kiss me. I have to admit that I was attracted to him as well. He is a very handsome man, mum."

"That is irrelevant, Eliza. He is your consultant and colleague. Did he kiss you?"

Eliza just looked at her and nodded ashamedly. "Y-yes." Her eyes filled up with tears. She did not want to say any more but felt like she was sitting in front of an investigating officer.

"Did he kiss you because you wanted to kiss him? Eliza, did he do anything else for you? Tell me the truth, please."

"Mum, I cannot tell you the whole story. I'm sorry. All I know is that whatever happened, it was wrong, and now I do not know how to get out of it. We were both adults, but somehow right now I feel like we are not equal adults and I have so much to lose. This could screw up my whole future if it gets out. Tell me what to do. Please."

"Eliza, this is a situation where both of you have a lot to lose; not that I care two hoots about Mr Philandering Blythe-Soames! We can all make errors of judgement, but some errors are easier to forgive than others. We need to do something, but detail matters, and we will need to be particularly creative about it. I am guessing that you have not told anyone because you are afraid of what he might do in retaliation as your senior. Am I right?"

"Yes. I was upset yesterday on the ward, so I told a half version to Mr Baba, who asked to speak to me. I made him promise not to mention it to anyone, and he is very trustworthy. He is my educational supervisor. Nobody else, apart from Simon, knows about it. I am worried that telling anyone higher up will result in a backlash from Henry that I cannot control and that risks being turned against me. I cannot handle that, mum. I just can't." Tears streamed down her face, and she clutched her elbows, protecting herself.

"Eliza, if nobody finds out, this will not just go away for you. Mr Big Surgeon's consultant can walk away and return to his family, but look at you. It looks like it has broken you. You have to face the fact that somehow there have to be consequences for him, or you will never get the peace you need to move on. No consultant should take advantage of a junior colleague. It is wrong, Eliza. You were alone and vulnerable. I suspect that is why he chose to target you. Irrespective of what he did to help you in your exams, there is no justification for this. None. Did you consent to what was going on, Eliza? What did Mr Baba say to you?"

Eliza felt as though she was hearing echoes of Mr Baba's speech and Simon's words as her mum spoke. She knew well that all that everyone had said to her was right. Somehow Henry had to face consequences, or he would think that what he had done was alright. She did not want to ruin his career, though, any more than she wanted to ruin her own. She was not ready to take such a risk. Not at the moment. Her mum was thinking quite differently though about it, and it was written all over her face.

"If I was you, Eliza, I would try to hurt him where it would hit him the hardest. You say that you met his wife. Vanessa, was it? Well, perhaps she deserves to know the truth. I suspect she would sort things out without anything reaching your work environment if she was given the chance. I'm sure she doesn't want to lose her husband over an affair, although your face suggests it wasn't something much worse. Am I correct? but at the same time, she deserves to not be taken for a fool by him. She needs to know so that she can handle it."

"what? Do you want me to tell Vanessa and break her heart? I can't do that, mum. I feel guilty enough as it is. She doesn't deserve that!"

"Eliza deserves to know what her husband is capable of doing. The truth has an uncanny way of coming out, Eliza. It is better that it is the whole truth and not a Chinese whisper. Now you are stuck with the problem of being worried about work, worried about rumours, and not being able to address the problem through the normal channels because of a less-than-ideal system and hierarchy. If you do not find a way of offloading this from your chest, you are going to explode. I cannot force you to do anything, but you are asking me for a solution. In my books, the truth is the greatest weapon there is to fight injustice. If you cannot speak the truth at work, let him deal with the impact at home anonymously. You can tell her in such a way that she will have no idea who wrote it.

"That way, her darling husband will get to feel a little of your insecurity. I could write it for you, and in that way, if he challenged you, you could honestly say that you did not write it. He only needs to know what he needs to know. Make this your chance to rise from the ashes around you, Eliza. What do you call it when your surgeons get into a sticky place where your choices and preparation can get you out of danger?"

"Tiger country."

"Yes, right now you are approaching tiger country and looking for a safe way through it. Let's set a trap for Mr Blythe-Soames that will free you. No daughter of mine is going to be treated like this by some misogynistic idiot who thinks he can have anything he wants without consequences. No, this is where you go out intact, and he falls. Shall we put a few thoughts on a piece of paper? Strike whilst the iron is hot."

Her drive and determination to conquer this was empowering, and Eliza felt a little like an oarless boat being blown towards the shore by a powerful Scirocco wind full of heat and determination. The courage that her mother personified was not inside her, however.

"Mum I can see that there is a good idea in what you say, but I am not quite in the right place to write a scandalous message and just send it to the Grange for Vanessa to read and deal with. Not yet, anyhow. He is going to help with the clinical, and I need that, mum. I really need it."

Her mother extended her neck, looked at the ceiling, and then her eyes came down and focused on Eliza.

"Well, perhaps today is a bit early, but I am going to write down a few thoughts, and you can read them when you are ready. You have to do something, Eliza, or this will not get easier for you; it is not like some switch you can just turn off. The natural response of any successful woman to being cornered or trapped should be to draw a sword and fight her way out. Henry is not moving aside for anyone. He is going to be just fine where he's at. To make him move, you have to create a distraction that sends him running elsewhere. If that distraction is the fear of losing his wife, then that should work. The most important thing is that he does not think that you caused it directly. We have to be clever about things. Being here has given you an alibi," Eliza was astounded by this side of her mother. She knew she had a strong mum, but this was an almost Catherine de Medici side that she had never witnessed before. It was almost as though her mum was enjoying the whole moment.

"Mum, you seem to be enjoying this. What has got into you?"

"Eliza, there is one thing that Mr Blythe-Soames has done that is very bad. He has undermined you. I will not allow that on my watch. You are my flesh and blood, and I will defend you tooth and nail. If he has power to hide behind, so do you. You have me, and I will help you through this."

Eliza smiled. She loved her mum so much at that moment.

"Wow mum I sometimes wonder whether you should have been the surgeon in our family and not me. You are impressive! I needed to share in your strength today. Would you allow me a few days to gather my courage, please?"

"My courage runs through your body too, Eliza. You just forgot it was there. Promise me that when this is over, you will never dip your pen in the work ink well again. I want you to find a good man to share your life with. It was such a shame that you and Simon split up. I liked him very much."

"I promise, mum. I have more than learned my lesson, and if I can survive this, I will be forever more on the straight and narrow. Regarding Simon, I agree with you. He was perfect. Perhaps we will get back together after my exams. Who knows? He is still single so that is a start." Her face demonstrated her sense of shame over what had happened. If her mother knew the whole truth, she was worried that Henry might not survive the night. Sometimes just enough truth is enough.

Eliza got up and kissed her mum on the cheek. "Thank you, mum,"

"My pleasure, darling. Now go upstairs and freshen up before tea. Enough has been said for today. Let's eat something nice and watch something pointless on the telly."

"Good plan." This conversation alone had just been the start of Eliza's recovery. She wondered what thoughts her mum would put down whilst she was having a shower. There was no stopping her now that the bee had entered her bonnet.

……………………………………………………………

Three days of bliss followed in the Blythe-Soames household. Even Tom had been able to enjoy the new side of his father, and Vanessa had convinced both that boarding school was not the best plan. She wanted her boys at home. They had both willingly agreed, which had surprised her, and this newly found sense of influence in the home was great. Henry had managed to get the application for Ibrahim fully signed off and submitted, and even Ibrahim was not irritating him as much as he had before. It was as if he had risen from some sort of cloud, and the newly found clarity was enlightening. He was palpating how this game of conviviality was making everyone around him love him. That felt good and was also creating the necessary bolster in case the Eliza matter ever came out to try and bite him. Allies were plenty, and he felt strong again. Eliza being off had provided a space that he needed to achieve a great deal of positive action. She looked like a troubled soul, and nobody knew why.

He can make anything up if he needs to. When she returned, he would be able to keep things professional and above board, and in some way, what had happened between them could just fizzle out. She had been a surprising and late, messy little interlude. Nothing more. It was over, and he had not lost any control. If this nicey, nicey Henry was working on others, it would surely work fine with Eliza too. A few more months, and she would either pass her exams and move on; or fail her exams and be made to move on. The end point was all that he cared about.

He gave Vanessa a long, lingering kiss as he headed out to work. 'God life is good' he thought as he strode to his beloved Aston Martin. The world was in his hands again, and the next task of getting the surgical centre deal through was on track. Andrew was happy that he and Ibrahim were getting on and all of the management had swung in favour of plans to expand the service. Derek had prepared everything for the commissioners, and the right faces were on the panel. What could go wrong? 'Money, money, money' he sang as he grasped the steering wheel strongly and sped away.

....

Vanessa was preparing breakfast as the postman pushed the daily letters through the letterbox. She walked up to the doormat with a slice of buttered toast in her mouth. "Junk mail, bills, more junk mail…and this." The letter was addressed to her. It provided no sender details and gave no indication of where it had been posted. She took it back to the kitchen with her and sat down before opening it. It was a typed letter:

Dear Vanessa,

I am sorry if this letter causes you alarm, but you need to know that your husband has been unfaithful to you and has done things that could put into question his fitness to practice through what he has done to one of the junior doctors. At this point, only you know about this as it has not been discussed higher in the trust, but I will give you the time and the discretion to choose how best to deal with it. Lives have been affected by your husband's actions. Yours is now also affected. Do the right thing. Please. I will wait to see how you choose to act before I do.

A friend who knows everything.

A cold shiver went down her back. She dropped the toast on the table and reread the letter several times. Her heart was thumping in her chest, and her head was shaking.

"My God. Henry, what have you done?" A painful lump filled her throat, but she stifled it. Her mind raced with questions. Was all that she had revelled in over the past week just a lie? A cover-up for this? For an affair? Oh Henry, please no! How stupid she had been. All her fears had been justified. Was it that twenty-something-year-old that had sat on her table? On HER table, in HER house? Had he brought that girl to their home when she was out? When could he have done this? She was thinking fast and in a disordered manner. She threw the rest of the mail onto the floor and shouted out loudly into the empty hallway. That house that she had been a slave in for so long. His puppet, to do all the house duties so that he could galivant around playing Casanova behind her back.

'Well, Henry Blythe-Soames, you are not going to get out of this marriage. I intend to do just as this letter says. I will do the right thing, except you will have no idea at all that I did it. Let's see how much you like playing games, Henry. I WILL NOT lose my family. That little presumptuous upstart can take her hands right off you. You are my husband.' Her hands were shaking; her tears had dried. She was focused and furious. She did not care who had written the letter, and Henry would not know that she had received it. She needed an excuse to take the children away for a few days. She needed to act fast. He didn't need to suspect her. She needed to speak to Andrew.

....

Andrew was just waiting for the next case to arrive in the anaesthetic room. Normally, his phone was switched off, but not that day. It vibrated in his pocket, and he glanced to see who it was. Vanessa. Now that was someone who didn't call him often.

"Hello. This is a surprise."

"Hello, Andrew," her voice was unusually flat and serious. He could palpate the tension in her voice.

"Is everything alright?" He was trying to be discrete as his team members were in the room. He had known Vanessa for almost as long as Henry had. They had both fancied her as house officers, but she had preferred Henry, of course. The next patient arrived in the anaesthetic room just at that moment, and he needed to hang up.

"Can I call you in a bit, please? I have a patient in the room," her reply was not what he had expected.

"I need to meet with you urgently, Andrew," her voice was wavering and broken. "Can we meet somewhere private after work? You must promise me that you will not tell Henry about it. Do you promise, Andrew?" Andrew popped out of the anaesthetic room, gesturing an apology to the team and that he would be back on a tick. He spoke outside with a whispered voice.

"Er…yes. Of course. God, you are worrying about me, Van. He is playing golf tonight with Mark and me. I'll make some excuses that I'm running late, and we can meet at the Hunter's Arms at a quarter past six. Can you do that? I can't meet for long, as they will be expecting me. Would that be OK?"

"Yes, that is fine. Thank you, Andrew. See you later," she hung up, and Andrew paused for a pensive second before returning to theatre. 'What the hell was that all about?' The list passed uneventfully, and he then texted Henry to say that he was running an hour late and would join them in the bar later. Henry replied instantly with an oblivious affirmative, and Andrew headed out to the pub. In all the years that he had known Vanessa, he had never heard of her like this. She was always the one to be calm and composed. The image of an immaculate lady. She fitted well into Henry's life as a landed gentleman, and she had learned to ride horses like a natural. Even when she had fallen once off her horse, she did not show any misplaced emotions. Today's audibly shaken Vanessa must have been caused by something terrible. A distracted working day, but it was soon over.

He arrived at Hunter's Arms and walked into the dark main room. In the corner, Vanessa was sitting, wearing sunglasses, and looking down at the wine glass in front of her. She looked up as he approached her, and she stood up to greet him. He kissed her on the cheek and squeezed her arm. She had been crying.

"I'm sorry I could not come to see you straight away. Thankfully, the list went to plan, and I managed to escape on time," he lifted her glasses from her eyes and winced. "I hate seeing you like this. What has happened?" she urged him to sit down.

"No. Don't apologise, Andrew. Thank you for meeting me this evening. I think you need to sit down before I show you something. I need your help. It is not something that you will find easy to do, but you are our oldest friend and right now the only person who can help me make this right," she swallowed hard before passing the envelope to him. He cautiously opened it, scared to see what might be inside. Henry and Vanessa were his oldest friends. Something bad had happened to them, and he hated that thought. Nothing could have prepared him for what he read.

"What the hell? Henry has been having an affair. At work? With a junior doctor? Which junior doctor? I don't know anything about this van. I promise I don't," he looked at her with wide, horrified eyes. She knew that he did not know about it. This was not something that Henry would have been able to tell anyone about because it broke the code of practice.

"I know you didn't know about it, but I suspect you might have seen him with her."

"Her? Who do you mean? Do you know who she is?"

"The junior doctor, Eliza, I have met her. I just didn't know what was going on between them. What a fool I have been, Andrew. A damn fool. I can't lose him. Not after all these years. I just can't." Tears welled up in her eyes. She spoke quietly, so he leant forward to hear her. He took her hand into his.

"Oh my God. I thought he was just helping her with her revision, and I was so damn busy that I didn't notice anything untoward between them. Vanessa, I am so sorry. You don't deserve this."

"Yes, I suspect that was how he caught her, although the note doesn't exactly say that. It implies that Henry has done something terrible. What could it mean? He can be so determined sometimes, as we both know. She was a rather childlike, innocent girl when he brought her to our home. The story she told was completely gibberish. Something about Henry finding her after she fell over in the woods. I was so stupid to imagine that it was a coincidence that they were there together by accident."

"Do you have any idea how long it has been going on for and what that comment has done things that could put into question his fitness to practice might mean?"

"No, I have no idea what it means and also have no idea who sent this. There is no suggestion of where it was posted. Can you help me, please, Andrew? I want Henry to be punished for this. I don't want to lose him, but he needs to be taught a lesson that will give him a little of the pain he has caused me without destroying my family."

Andrew nodded.

"In all the years I have known Henry, I knew that he had a slightly distorted view of boundaries but never thought he would do something as terrible as this to you. He seems to have become more arrogant since he became a consultant and, strangely, more like his father—something that you and I both know he would deny in a second. The apple never falls far from the tree, I guess. I do have an idea, what can be done, but first I need to investigate the facts discretely and find out how widely known they are. In a just world, if he had done anything terrible, he would be suspended and investigated, but that would hurt you as well as him. I would not do that to you, Vanessa. I promise. Let me go and think about things. May I keep this letter, please?" she agreed.

"You are a true friend, Andrew. I am sorry that I am asking you to do this. I just don't know who else to ask."

"You did the right thing, Vanessa. Leave it with me and find a way to get a bit of space from Henry. Make up a story and go up to see your sister. Be out of the scene as his world crumbles so that he will not suspect you. Don't give him any idea."

"Thank you, Andrew. I'll call Claire right now. She has just started chemo for a recurrence of her breast cancer, so in actual fact, it would be a great idea to go and see her. I can drop the children off at their grandparents' house on the way. They would like that," she reached over to hold his hand and squeezed it. "I cannot thank you enough," she whispered.

Andrew kissed her cheek again, and they walked out of the pub. He watched her get into her car before getting into his own. 'How could you hurt her, Henry? How could you?' How would he be able to face Henry now without raising suspicion? There were questions that needed to be answered before he could act, and Vanessa and the children needed to be safely out of the way. He had to bide his time and look like nothing was unusual.

Chapter 38
The Reckoning

Vanessa had packed all of her bags and the children's things into her car before Henry was home from golf. 'Act like nothing is wrong, Vanessa. He cannot see that, you know.' Those words circulated in her head as she rushed around, gathering things and clearing up. Dinner was in the oven, and the children were at the table eating their evening meal.

"Now, children, you and I are heading up to Northamptonshire tomorrow. You get to stay for a few days with Grandma and grandpa, and I will be going to see Aunty Claire, who is not very well."

Amelia was the first to say, "Yes! I can show Grandma my new puzzle too."

"I thought you might want to, so I packed it in the car. Tom, is that alright for you?"

"Yes, I guess so. Why so suddenly? Weren't we going for a picnic tomorrow? Dad said we were." Vanessa had not been told about any picnic. This was evidently a plan that Henry had made to surprise her.

"Oh, er no. I did not hear anything about a picnic. I'm sorry, Tom. Can we go for one when we are back, please? I need to see your aunt tomorrow."

"Alright. I guess so," Tom looked disappointed, as the new friendly side had given him some hope of a better relationship with him.

"Thank you both. All done with your food?" They nodded in synchrony. "Well, then it is upstairs, you both go. I'll be up in a few minutes. Don't forget to brush your teeth." Autopilot was switched on, and for once, she was happy with the routine. It kept her calm. Just as she closed the dishwasher, she heard Henry walking into the hallway.

"Hello hello, everyone. Daddy is home." He sounded happy. Andrew hadn't raised suspicion. Good. She walked out to meet him, and seeing him made her feel sick. 'Don't make him suspect Vanessa. Convince him everything is alright.'

She felt anger welling up inside of her, but she suppressed it and went up to him. She closed her eyes and kissed him on the lips. Those lying, deceitful lips that had kissed another without caring about her.

"Hello darling, how was your day today?" he asked.

"It was a difficult day, Henry. I called Claire, and she is not well. I need to see her. She needs me. I want to go tomorrow and be with her for a week or so until she is feeling stronger. Would that be alright?"

Henry was visibly disappointed but determined not to be unsympathetic, even though he had arranged some surprises for the weekend.

"Oh, that is sudden. I'm sorry about Claire. Do you want me to drive you there?"

"Er…no Henry I think she just needs me, and as it is on the way I thought I might drop the kids off at your parents' place for a bit of fun on the estate during the holidays. They haven't seen your parents for a long while."

"Yes, that is a good idea. I might swing by there on Sunday to join them, as I will be home alone here. We can chat, and if you need me to bring anything else up, I will."

She tried to stay calm despite the annoyance that he was going to effectively follow her to Northamptonshire the next day. Thankfully, the story she had given about Claire's health was likely to discourage him from joining her at her sister's place.

He walked up to her and put his hands on her waist. She loathed him at that moment but knew that she needed to stay calm.

"I'm going to miss you, darling. Don't be away for long."

"I won't, Henry. Just enough time to help Claire through this difficult patch." The oven peeped at just the right moment, just before he kissed her, and she smiled and turned to take the food out and lay the table.

"You seem rather edgy tonight, darling. Can I help?"

"Henry, my little sister, is struggling with her cancer treatment. She has three young children, and David cannot cope with his work and them. My family is not as rich as yours, and they need my help. It broke my heart to hear how upset she was this morning. If I am not all love and cuddles tonight it is because I am upset that Claire is feeling that way. Do you understand that, Henry? Can you?" The tears in her eyes and the anguish in her voice were not just about Claire, who was doing rather better than she portrayed; she was allowing a little of the sense of betrayal in her chest to escape. Henry needed to feel a bit of her pain. He stood there, looking guilty. She was glad.

"Vanessa I am sorry. I'm being selfish. I guess I was looking forward to a weekend with our family, and you know well that I never take disappointments well. Forgive me."

His reply slightly disarmed her. Over the last week, she could not recognise the Henry that stood before her. How much of it was a lie and how much of it was true was unfathomable. He had become, in one week, an enigma to her, and she needed to get away, just to think things through. She trusted Andrew to help.

The night was a sleepless one for Vanessa. As Henry's arm rested over her chest, she rested her hand on his. She had loved him since the day they met, and she had not wavered once in her commitment to him. Perhaps if she had chosen to keep working, so much of her life would not have been about her marriage. The pain of betrayal had spun her into a state of self-doubt. Why had he strayed? Had she not loved him enough? Did he no longer find her attractive? What did that girl offer him that she did not? What had he done that warranted that letter? Did she really know Henry after all these years? She thought he was a good man, but she had seen how cruel he had been towards Tom. Perhaps her love for him had blinded her and prevented her from seeing who he really was. Had he tricked her in other ways, and she didn't let herself see it? 'Oh, Henry, how could you?'

The next morning, she woke up early and left Henry in bed as she fed the children and packed the last few things. She went up to see Henry, who was by then awake and in the bathroom. She popped her head around the door.

"I'm heading off now Henry. Have a good weekend. We can chat later."

He went to her and kissed her briefly on the lips.

"You're off early. I will miss you. Drive carefully, and let me know when you get there. Bye darling. Are the children in the car?" He was just putting his gown on. "I'd like to say bye to them."

"No, they are downstairs waiting for me."

He walked downstairs with her and hugged Amelia, "Have a lovely time with your grandparents, my princess. I will come and see you tomorrow and join you for lunch."

"Grandma is going to do a big puzzle with me. Mummy has put it in the car."

"Oh really? A big puzzle, you say? Well, you definitely need Grandma for that. She is brilliant at puzzles," he laughed and kissed Amelia on the cheek again.

He stood up and rubbed Tom's head. "Have a good time, Tom. Perhaps your grandfather will take you out for a drive in the Morgan. There is nice weather at the moment."

"Thank you, Father. I'll ask him."

Within minutes, Vanessa and the children were on their way, and she clenched her teeth. She wondered what Andrew would find out and how he would organise Henry's punishment.

A little further down the village, Andrew was awake early and sitting in his study with a pen in his hand and an empty page in front of him. He needed to find a way of gleaning answers without stirring suspicion in the trust. Who else might have noticed what was going on? A list started to form on the page:

Eliza

Ibrahim (educational supervisor)

Jemimah (friend of Ibrahim)

'Who else might know something?' he scratched his head and put the pen between his lips. There had to be others. Who would have written that letter to Vanessa? He stared at the words. It did not look like the words of Eliza. Jemimah was away. Perhaps it was Ibrahim. Perhaps it was someone close to Eliza.

Who knows Eliza?

The most logical place at that point was to speak with Ibrahim. He checked the on-call rotas on the trust system. He was in luck. Ibrahim's weekend was on call. He picked up his phone and dialled.

"Hello?"

"Ibrahim. Andrew McNair here. Are you on call today?"

"Yes. I am. Are you?"

"No, thankfully not, but I'm sitting at my desk at home doing admin and wondering whether I might be able to swing by and chat with you about something later."

"Yes, of course. I have to get the ward round done, but assuming we don't have too much to sort out, I should be free around 11. Would that be any good for you? Shall I call you after the rounds in case we pick up cases for theatre?"

"That sounds like a good plan. Speak in a bit. Bye."

"Speak soon." They hung up.

Now Andrew needed to figure out what he was going to say. He had to be mindful that others might not know anything, although the letter suggested that perhaps more people knew about Henry's actions than was evident. He decided that a spot of weeding in the garden might help him find the answers. There was something cathartic about taking one's stress out on a deep-rooted dandelion in the wrong spot. There were lots of dandelions this year. The garden was where he needed to be. Angela, his wife was already out with son George at his tennis lesson, and daughter Jessica was at a stayover with friends. There was no distraction. Just him, the dandelions, and his thoughts. He marched to the shed, deep in thought, to get the trowel and a bucket, and headed determinedly to the rose bed.

At 11 am his phone buzzed in his pocket. Ibrahim said:

Text: Hello, Andrew. Just done on the wards. One short case for theatre then likely to be free around midday. Where shall we meet? Ibrahim

Text: Great. Glad it is OK on the wards. Shall we meet in my office?

Text: Good idea. See you then!

Text: OK.

He looked at the time on his phone again. Two more dandelions, and he would go in and clean up before heading out.

At 11.20 am after a freshen-up and drink of water, Andrew headed to the hospital, ready to meet Ibrahim and start his plan to help Vanessa. He had not heard from her but hoped that she had managed to get away. The next couple of weeks could turn into a bit of a storm, and she and the children needed to be far away from that.

Ibrahim arrived at Andrew's office at midday, as agreed. He was dressed in his scrubs from theatre and, as ever, was pleasantly smiling. Andrew liked Ibrahim very much. A steady sort of chap who worked as hard as a bee. What was not to like? He had never understood Henry's problem with him. Ibrahim had always been immensely polite and deferential towards his senior colleagues, no matter the insult given. The hierarchy, driven largely by men like him and Henry, was all very old-fashioned and, in his opinion, a little artificial. He knew well that his position was not necessarily a permanent one, even though there was never a queue of people vying for that position of human punchbag between clinicians and higher management, known as clinical director. He had always found it more of a political role than a clinical one, with the wholly euphemistic title of Clinical Director. Perhaps it should be the clinicians' director? He was pondering that as Ibrahim gently knocked on the door and came in.

"Ah, Ibrahim, good morning," Andrew stood up and shook hands with Ibrahim. Even on a weekend day, there was always an element of decorum that came with interactions with hierarchy. "How is the on call going?"

"Good morning, Andrew. So far, so good, but who knows what the day will bring in," he smiled and raised his eyebrows in a gesture at the unpredictability of on call.

Andrew thought he could start a bit off-track and ease into the topic he wanted to discuss. "Well, I have read your excellent portfolio. It seems to meet all the requirements of the college and more. I passed it on to Mark yesterday, and he will give the final sign off to send the application to the GMC. At that point, who knows what will happen? You and I both know that there is no rhyme or reason for decisions made there, but I reckon your application is as strong as it gets, and I know of several successful CESR applications in the last few years. Let's stay hopeful, shall we?"

"I am so grateful to Andrew for all the support that the team is giving me. It has been a portfolio that has been built over many years in the hope that one day I might be here. As a man of African and Islamic background, I confess that any interaction with the GMC, either through application or otherwise, is rather daunting. The history is not good, but let's hope that things are getting better, shall we? Like you, I know of a few successful applications regionally, which has bolstered me. God-willing, my application will be accepted without too many obstacles."

"I hope so, Ibrahim. I hope so, too. We have quite a good track record with them here."

"I am never sure where exactly my sense of doubt comes from, but the fear of struggle influences the individual's courage to try harder. Nobody wants to receive bad news. That is why I am so grateful to you all, because I would not have tried had I not had such wonderful support from Jemimah, you, and even Henry. Just listening to your positivity, Andrew, has given me a sense of real optimism today. Thank you." His expression was one of true gratitude, and Andrew was pleased. Now that the initial softener had been delivered, he needed to get the conversation back on track before Ibrahim was called away. He looked momentarily at his coffee cup and turned it a few times as his head assimilated the progress of the conversation and then planned his next step. Ibrahim watched him silently for those few seconds.

"Yes, I have to admit that Henry has surprised even me with this," he extended the first feeler.

"Hah, that was a surprise for me too. You know well that for some years our relationship has been a difficult one, for reasons that I have struggled to understand. This sudden change in Henry must have been precipitated by something. I wonder what." They were playing psychological ping pong, and Andrew was pleased. This was a good start.

"An interesting thought, Ibrahim. Yes, as we say, a leopard does not change its spots. Do you have any idea what might have changed?"

"Well, Jemimah has been keen to push my application through, so perhaps she has greater leverage on his actions than we thought."

Damn, that wasn't the right direction.

"Although Jemimah has been rather distracted of late so, I cannot imagine she would have had a great deal of time to do that," Andrew tried to move away from Jemimah and back to Henry.

Ibrahim suspected nothing and was openly pondering. "No, no, you are quite right. I haven't heard from her this week. I hope she is alright."

"I hear she is in Jordan addressing some personal problems," Andrew said, somewhat frustrated.

"In Jordan? How strange," Ibrahim's thoughts had thoroughly moved away from Henry, and Andrew needed to shift the conversation. He just needed to come out with it.

"So, Ibrahim, you have worked hard with the trainees I can see from your portfolio. I understand that you are currently, educational supervisor for one of the junior doctors. Eliza, is it?"

Ibrahim's face suddenly changed, and an expression of interest appeared on his face.

"Yes. Why do you ask?" Ibrahim was curious about the sudden change of topic and the slightly uncomfortable body language exhibited by Andrew.

"Well, I may be stabbing in the dark, but I imagine Ibrahim that you know something about the reason why she has gone off sick. Am I right?" The tone of the clinical director had altered, and Andrew changed from relaxed to earnest. Ibrahim leant forwards. This was a strange conversation to be having with the clinical director of the division.

"Andrew, this is an unusual topic to be discussing. Correct me if I am mistaken, but are you possibly asking me a question that you may also have an answer to? What have you been told, and I will see whether our stories align." Ibrahim's new evasiveness was unexpected. Andrew was tired of the game.

"What do you know about the interaction between Eliza and Henry, Ibrahim?" There, he had said it. The cat was out of the bag, and there was no going back.

"So, you do know, Andrew. I have been asked not to say anything, so I have not, to protect Eliza, who is rather scared and upset. She has not told me the whole story but has told me that something has happened between them. I am sure that there is something else going on because in the last week she has been terribly distracted, and it has started to affect her work, which is why I got involved. I advised her to go home to her mother, as she is rather isolated and alone here. What have you heard, Andrew?"

Andrew sat back and sighed deeply. So, it was true. *Henry, you idiot*, he thought. He reached into his pocket and took out the letter.

"Vanessa, Henry's wife, received this in the post this week." He slowly handed it to Ibrahim.

As Ibrahim read the letter, he was astounded.

"She received this in the post? Poor Vanessa. Did she have any idea at all?"

"Well, it appears that she met Eliza once at the house. Henry took her there a few months ago, although the story was rather odd. Something about cleaning up an injury after a fall somewhere. I cannot remember the details, but Vanessa had been suspicious at that time."

"No, I don't know anything about that, but Eliza seems to be more upset than one might expect if, indeed, the right thing had happened and they had just split up. I am worried that something more sinister might have happened. Eliza would not let me escalate things, but it seems that someone else has intervened first. Who do you think wrote this letter, Andrew?"

"I thought it might have been you, but that was a stupid thought. Why would you? You would have taken the normal path to escalate things to me, wouldn't you?"

"Yes absolutely. It must have been someone close to Eliza who perhaps we don't know. I wonder who it was. They clearly know more than we do about what has happened. What do they mean that Henry had done something that puts his right to practice into question?"

"That is something I do not know. I've known Henry for longer than Vanessa, and he has always been a slightly unpredictable man. This, however, goes way beyond that, and I worry that Eliza may not want to tell the whole truth about it. The poor girl is probably scared about the repercussions, and I don't blame her. When she is back, I will need to speak to her without frightening her. Damn, this is a bad time for Jemimah to be away. We could have used her woman's touch right now as a chaperone and support for Eliza."

"Well, to be honest, I had been suspicious of the Henry-Eliza thing for some months before this, and I spoke with Jemimah in private about it. At that point, we were rather lacking in evidence, and we all know that it is not unheard of for relationships to happen, and even occasionally marriages, between consultants and junior doctors. This feels different, though, Andrew. It has an air of something more sinister. The issue is, however, in my mind, the risk of predation and misuse of power. Do we have an idea when Jemimah might be back?"

"Interesting. I did not know that she knew about your concerns. You have all been keeping this very quiet. As far as I can see, there is little we can do until I have spoken with Eliza. I suspect we may never find out who wrote this letter to Vanessa, but before I speak to Henry, I need more facts. Thank you, Ibrahim, for this. We will have to keep things very quiet, so I hope I can trust in your confidentiality in this matter." His expression was one that Ibrahim knew meant many more things. Henry was his friend after all, and Ibrahim could see that this was not going to follow any usual pathway.

"Yes, absolutely. You have my word. Let's wait for Eliza and Jemimah to return."

"Regarding Henry, don't raise his suspicions just yet. Leave him to me. Act like nothing has happened."

"You can be assured that I have no intention of saying anything about this to Henry, or anyone else, for that matter. That ball is very much in your court."

Chapter 39
Consequences

After four days of pragmatic reasoning from her mother, Eliza felt a phoenix-like resolve to return to work and not let Henry crush her. She had rejected several drafts of letters that her mother had wanted to send to various people, although reading them did help. If only she had the confidence to send one. She wished she was more like her mother sometimes, but the last few days had reminded her that she did share some of her strength but just needed to believe that. Exam results were coming out on Friday, and she decided that it was wise to stay home until then and then arrange to meet with occupational health on Monday and get back to work. There had been enough disruption; she needed to focus and make her exit plan and future work for her.

Henry was a thing of the past, at least in her house, but he had his uses that she would be able to figure out in time. He owed her that much. She turned on her phone for the first time that day, and there were just a couple of messages from Simon checking if she was OK. Nothing else. All was well, and she was going to try to return to work life as normal.

Text: Hi Simon. Feeling much better after a few days with mum. She wishes we were still together. You must have done something to impress her. Ex

A few seconds later, he replied.

Text: I've been worried about you. Have you heard anything more from the trust? What have you decided to do? You can't let the bastard get away with it. Sx

What a strange reply. She felt bad that she had upset him. He must have been thinking about it all alone for the last week. She felt guilty.

Text: Feeling bad that I dumped all my rubbish on you the other day. Sorry Simon. I agree that I will not find peace without saying something. I just need to find the right time and person. I will, Simon. I promise. Ex

Text: Perhaps they have noticed something and said something already.

Who was 'They'? she wondered. Did he think that Ibrahim would have spoken to someone? She was suddenly worried again. What if he had. Would she be facing a storm on her return? The façade of a stronger woman suddenly fell off her. How could she find out?

Text: I made him promise not to say anything. Why would he? I think it will all be OK.

She wrote that more to calm herself than Simon.

Text: Do U want me 2 come down next Mon and Tuesday? I'm off post nights. That way you will not be alone. Sx

Text: RU sure? x

Text: Wouldn't have asked if I wasn't….

Text: Then yes pls. x

Text: x

Eliza felt more relaxed knowing Simon would be around for the first few days. She was certain she didn't need it, but Simon was always someone she could relax with. She trusted him. Even her mother was pleased that he was coming. Her common sense was cutting sometimes though Eliza had to admit it. This was just one of those moments, "Why on earth you got mixed up with that older married man when you had Simon to be with, I will never understand. I hope you two will talk things through and help you make the right decisions. Whatever happens next week, I am happy you have Simon there."

"Why do you say that, mum? Simon and I split up ages ago. You know that. We are just friends, and anyway, what do you mean by 'Whatever happens'?"

"I mean, whatever you do or however you feel, you will not be alone. That's all." She looked at her daughter, a little worried that this stronger daughter before her might actually be no less fragile than Eliza, who had come home a few days ago. She was so naïve sometimes; it was not a surprise that Henry had targeted her. 'He needs to pay that complete devil. How dare he mess with my Eliza?'

Sitting alone at the Grange, Henry missed Vanessa and the children. He hated not having people around, and he was restless and perturbed that his great plan was not going exactly as he had imagined. What a nuisance that Claire would be sick at this time. What was the rush to get there so fast? It all confused him. Vanessa seemed to be alright with him. It must be a sister thing. Vanessa was always a kind person, forever the palliative care nurse of old, so it was quite in character for her to rush to the needy. He was just missing the physical side of their newly rekindled marriage. This sudden arrest of events frustrated him. He enjoyed the lovemaking and the feeling of being back in control of things. He wondered when Eliza was coming back to work. The week with her out of the way had been opportune for him. A lot of progress been made at work. Time had been his friend, and no one would notice anything if he could sort out the Eliza drama quickly when she returned. That was what he would focus his mind on, trying to forget the momentary rush of ultimately controlling her.

Monday morning was the start of a week that was not likely to be a routine week for anyone. Eliza was back; Ibrahim was worried for her; Andrew was contemplating how to talk to her; and Henry needed to iron things out with her and make sure she stayed quiet about things. Amidst all this, Jemimah was returning to work after a self-affirming trip of a lifetime and completely oblivious to the events of the last fortnight. It was a timebomb ticking, and who was to be the first to move on this dynamite chess board approaching the decision point?

"So, Eliza how are you feeling after your week away?" Dr Philip Greenway, the occupational health physician, sat opposite Eliza and was poised to write notes.

"Oh, I think I am much better, thank you. I think I just needed a break. Everything had got on top of me."

"Good. So did you have a chance to think about what the cause was for you feeling overwhelmed?"

"Oh, er…well yes. But that is probably going to be all sorted now, so I'm less stressed about it."

"Oh, is it related to your work, Eliza?"

"No, well not directly. No, not really. Is it OK if we don't talk about it please?" She was sitting defensively in the chair, and Dr Greenway could see that it was clearly not something that was OK.

"Eliza, you do know that this consultation is confidential, don't you? Please don't feel that I will say anything beyond this room. Do you want to tell me something in confidence?"

"I'm sorry, Dr Greenway, I can't. It is something I need to sort out myself, but if it is alright, I would like to come and see you again if I am struggling. Would that be OK?"

Dr Greenway had taken his reading glasses off and was looking at her, concerned. There was something that had clearly frightened this junior doctor, and she was scared to talk about it.

"Eliza, we do have a confidential counselling service here if you might find that an easier environment to talk in. I see that you are still quite anxious, so please do reach out to us if we can help. Would you like me to make some recommendations for reduced working hours or anything else to help you?"

"I haven't thought about that. Perhaps if I could not be on call for a few weeks, that might help, as I haven't been sleeping very well and I think tiredness may have been part of the problem."

"Yes, that should be fine. I will contact the managers today to arrange that for you. When are you next on call?"

"Oh, I'm on call on long days from tomorrow. Is it too soon to change things?"

"No, not at all. I will send an email as soon as we have finished here to sort that out for you, and the managers will call you to confirm. What are your thoughts on the counsellor?"

"Can I have a think about it, please? I'm not sure talking about things will help me right now."

He took a deep breath in and a slow sigh out. During the silent pause, he looked at her.

"Alright. Call us anytime if you change your mind. Shall we arrange to meet again next week to see how you are getting along?"

"Yes, that would be a good idea. When will that be?"

"Shall we say the same time next Monday?"

"Great. Thank you." She stood up to signal that for her the consultation was over and Dr Greenway had finished the meeting.

As Eliza left the room, Philip Greenway felt uncomfortable. There had not been enough to warrant a breach of confidentiality to protect her, there had been not enough detail at all, but instinctively, he was worried that Eliza was in some trouble that might derail her again. He had to wait and see, but thought it might be an idea to suggest that the departmental manager keep an eye out for her and check that she is OK without giving any details in particular. He picked up the phone after Eliza had left the room.

Eliza was half-wishing that she had not arranged her timetable to fit around Henry's. The first thing in her day was a clinic with Henry, and seeing him that morning would tell her whether anyone had spoken. She had to face him, and somehow she had to not make it too awkward. She had to find a mantra to empower herself with. Something from a strong woman. Opening her phone, she scrolled through a few pages to find one for the day. For some inexplicable reason, it needed to be by a woman. Scroll…scroll…no not that one…scroll…a ha! That is it: 'Grab the broom of anger and drive off the beast of fear' by Zora Neal Hurston. Yes, every single time she felt scared, she needed to harness the anger she had for what had happened to her and turn it into courage. She could do this! She had absolutely no idea who Zora Neal Hurston was, but at that moment, she was glad that she had said those words. She could look her up on Google later. 'Thank you, Zora,' She looked forwards and walked into the clinic. Even her posture had changed. 'Drive off that beast of fear…drive off that beast of fear…' The first person she met was Nurse Jackie.

"Oh, hello, Eliza. It is so lovely to see you back. Are you feeling better?"

"Hello Jackie. Yes, thank you, I am. I've never taken time off before, so it felt odd, but I really needed it. It was Mr Baba who convinced me to go. He was right."

"Yes, Ibrahim will have your back. I'm glad you listened to him," she smiled kindly at Eliza, whilst her comment concerned her that Mr Baba had said something to her.

"Now, are you with Mr Blythe-Soames this morning or with Mr Baba? You get to choose today as we have a full clinic."

"I think I might go with Mr Baba for a change, if that is OK."

"Of course. I'll give you the surgery next to his, and you can go to him for help and discussion."

"Great. Thank you, Jackie,"

So far, so good. Jackie was absolutely fine, and there was little suggestion that she suspected anything in detail. Next to arrive was Henry. She could hear him talking in the corridor. He was with Ibrahim. They were discussing a case. Both sounded fine. She decided to hide away in her room until she heard Henry say, "Jackie, has Eliza returned today?"

"Yes, she has. She is in surgery next to Ibrahim's. She wanted to work with him today for a change."

"Ah good. Yes, absolutely. We have plenty of patients today at the clinic, so both of us will have cases for her to see," he cleared his throat, and she could hear him walking to his clinic and closing the door. Just the sound of his voice started her heart racing. It was as though the thought of speaking to him scared her more than the action would. Was it all irrational? She needed to remember her mantra for the day and stop being so feeble! 'Grab the broom of anger and drive off the beast...' A knock on her door broke her thoughts. It was Mandy, the departmental manager.

"Hello Eliza. Sorry to startle you. Do you have five minutes to talk with me please?"

"Oh yes, absolutely. The clinic doesn't start for ten minutes. Come in." Mandy walked in, closing the door behind her.

"Dr Greenway called me yesterday to explain that you needed a little break from on-calls as you return to work. I thought I might pop down to see you to see if there was anything else that I might be able to do to help you."

"Oh yes, he mentioned he would call you. Yes, please. I would like a couple of weeks off from on-call if possible. I think I was a bit overtired when I went off, and I don't want to dive straight back into a week of on call. Is that going to be possible, Mandy?"

"Yes, absolutely. I've managed to cover the shifts with a swap for you, so you'll cover one of your colleagues, Martha, in two weeks. Would that be alright for you? If you are not ready as that time approaches, we can explore other options."

Mandy was one of those rare managers who really wanted to know the team. She knew the whole team, and the fact that junior doctors knew her by first name was a testament to her character. Eliza really liked her and was glad for this conversation.

"Mandy you are so kind. Thank you. I was starting to panic about the idea that I would have to work on call tomorrow because of the short notice. You have taken a load off me."

"I'm here to make things work, Eliza. We can all be under the weather sometimes, and it is my job to make sure that the system has some give for that. Promise me you will come and talk to me if you need anything else. I don't just move rotas around," she looked endearingly at Eliza, and this connection was just what Eliza had needed.

"I will, Mandy. Thank you again," Mandy left the surgery, but in the back of her mind were the words of Dr Greenway. "She needs support. I'll keep an eye out for her. I worry that she may not be quite well enough for work, but she is putting on a very brave face," she wondered what he meant. To her, Eliza looked well. Was there something in the department that was the cause of her illness? Why were so many details missing? She was intrigued.

Eliza sighed a prolonged sigh of expectation and frustration. Although nobody had said anything, she was tense. An impeding sensation of what might happen. She logged into the computer in front of her and, by habit, opened her email. It was not as though she was particularly expecting anything, but there was a habitual need to check the inbox anyway. Twenty-three new messages were sitting there. The majority would trust generic emails, but as she scanned them, her eyes stopped abruptly, one with the simple heading CONFIDENTIAL. It was from the clinical director, Dr Andrew McNair. Her heart made a palpable thud in her chest. Her mouth went dry. 'Shit. Clinical Director.'

It took a few seconds for her to build enough courage to press the 'OPEN' button…'click' there, it was done.

Dear Eliza,

I am sorry to hear you have been unwell. I hope that you are feeling better and have returned to a reasonable work plan for the next few weeks. I was wondering whether we might be able to meet tomorrow to discuss a matter that I wish to keep confidential. I am sure that attending any meeting can be stressful, so please contact the occupational health team if you need support. I understand that you have already seen Dr Greenway today. My PA has suggested tomorrow at 10 am. I hope that this will be convenient for you. If you would like a colleague to accompany you, please feel free to do so.

Could you please reply to this email and copy my PA so that we can add it formally to my diary?

Yours sincerely,
Dr Andrew McNair

She reread the email three times. The screen was blurred as tears welled up in her eyes. 'Someone must have spoken to him. Did Henry know?' She checked her phone to see if he had sent a text message. Nothing. 'Oh God, I don't understand. Why does Dr McNair want to see me? I don't understand.'

She stood up abruptly, dragging her chair across the floor. She was in a panic. She needed air. She rushed out of the room and looked at Jackie with an expression that was able to replace her words. She shook her head.

"I'm sorry. I can't do the clinic. I'm sorry," her voice was almost a whisper. Jackie rushed to her, but Eliza turned and ran out of the clinic. Henry heard her voice and came into the corridor just as she left.

"Was that Eliza? What happened?"

Jackie looked at him. She put both hands up and replied, "I have absolutely no idea; she looked very upset though. Something must have happened. I need to go after her. Can you start at the clinic without me?"

"Oh, er, perhaps I should go, Jackie. Give my apologies to the patients. I shouldn't be long. Ibrahim can start seeing them." With that, he rushed out to find Eliza. He had his phone in his hand and dialled her number. She didn't pick up. Where could she have gone? Perhaps she was in the ladies' lavatory. He looked at the receptionist.

"No, she rushed out of the department Mr Blythe-Soames. Went left at the end of the corridor as far as I could make out."

She had gone towards the side entrance of the hospital, and he knew where she had gone. There was a small, enclosed courtyard garden to the side of the building. It was one of the few places onsite, where you could feel like you were no longer in a hospital. Landscapers had rather cleverly planted it with tall grasses and broad lavenders and cleverly placed leylandii to obscure windows and doors, and in its heart, the only thing you could see whilst sat on the circular bench, were leaves and flowers.

He walked slowly towards her as she sat with her back to him. She looked ahead as he walked around to find tears streaming down her cheeks. What had he done? Although the forefront of his mind was filled with the repercussions that could happen if the cat got out of the bag, there was, a little further back in his mind, a looming sense of guilt. His blind need to pursue her had been, at best, primitive. So had his actions been. Spontaneous and impulsive, and the result was this. A blubbering wreck in the heart of the hospital. 'For fuck's sake, Henry, sort this out!'

"Eliza? Are you alright?" What a dumb question to ask, but for some reason it was the right thing to do. Say the blatant opposite of what is apparent to you to incite a desired response.

She looked up at him, somewhat confused. Of all the people to follow her out of the clinic, Henry was the very last person she imagined would deign to come considering the circumstances.

"What are you doing here, Henry? This isn't the time. People will talk," he didn't move.

"I think it may be a perfect time to talk about you."

"Me? Henry. We should be talking about you and who you really are. But no, I think that may not be something you wish to talk about in the hospital. No, you feel that it is better to talk about me and the crumbled wreck I am at the moment as I try to figure out how to make everything that happened between us disappear and life return to normal."

"Well, I am not sure we can make things that happened in the past disappear, Eliza, but we can draw a line beneath them and find a way to create a semblance of normality again. I hope that you will agree that what happened between us is in the past. Can we do that, Eliza?" A necessary pause followed as he looked into her eyes.

"I want you to know that I still care for your future. I still want to help you get through the exam and become a surgeon. I hope you can see that. I hope that you will let me help you."

She looked into his eyes. Even with her red, saddened eyes, she was beautiful both in looks and her vulnerability, and Henry felt sad that he had messed things up so much.

"Do you really mean that, Henry? Do you think it is possible for us to just forget you assaulting me in my home and act as though nothing happened?" Her expression was one of tortured perplexity.

"Yes. Yes, I do. But what I believe is less important than what you think. I am the one who screwed everything up by misinterpreting your advances and not controlling my own emotions. I should have known better, and I am sorry, Eliza. I truly am."

His honesty disarmed her, and she turned to him. There was still a strange pseudo-attraction that bound them together, and their mutual desire to find a feasible way forward was apparent, even though the reasoning was quite disparate between the two parties involved.

"You know, going away was good for me. Whilst I was away, I went through such a tirade of emotions. First, I was so angry with you. Angry and abused. Then I felt hurt and saddened. Now I am in that strange confusion that follows, and I am scared. Scared about what it all meant and how we could possibly work together. Hearing your voice this morning scared me for reasons I cannot fully explain, it was like an unconscious reaction to a moment that has ended. For you,

Henry, it was just a moment, an impulse, but for me, it was an assault on my very person. I don't imagine you will ever comprehend what that means—being the stronger of us physically—but when a person says stop, that isn't meant to be ignored. I mean, you wouldn't touch a patient without their consent, would you?" Her red eyes looked questioningly into his. He sat there with a more diminutive posture than he had presented her with on arrival.

Hearing her words was profoundly sobering for him. This was the first time in his life where he had to face his own shortcomings and the truth that he had raped her, and it felt terrible. Why had he not realised who he had become? Why had nobody told him that he had become a complete idiot? Perhaps it was just not the one thing, or perhaps even if they had, he would have thrown it back at them with some smart retort that dampened their comment.

"Eliza, there is nothing I can say that can reverse the errors of that day. It is my actions now that I hope will convince you that this has been a real eye-opener for me and that, in some way, this terrible episode will possibly make me a better man. I know that that does not erase the gravitas of what I did to you, but I would be grateful if we could find a way together through this. I never thought I would ever say that to a junior doctor, but in many ways, I look at you today as so much more. You are sitting here talking to me like an equal, and your ability to even do that is very grounding. We have much to teach each other. Perhaps that was why we clicked in the first place. The person you have blossomed into over the months we have spent together has been a joy to witness."

Eliza's assertive body language relaxed, and she turned to him.

"Henry, if you really mean that, then yes, I do want to make things better. Thank you for saying that. I didn't tell you that I passed the written exam, did I? The results came out on Friday."

"No, you did not tell me," he suddenly had a big smile on his face. "Oh, Eliza, I am beyond delighted for you. I am not surprised, as you were more than ready for the exam, but just hearing your good news has made my day."

"Thank you, Henry. Our hard work paid off. Before…what happened…I found my confidence…even if you took it away again afterwards." She looked at him with narrowed eyes.

"What I did was unforgivable, but I wonder whether you might consider forgiving me, Eliza. Could you do that? I do not expect you to trust me easily again, but your suggestion of us not working alone together might help you rebuild a little trust." His eyes were pleading and the animal who had launched at her was nowhere to be seen. There was a pause and silence as Eliza considered her response. She didn't want him to touch her, and she kept a distance between them. He still scared her.

"Perhaps. I think we can, but there would have to be strict ground rules. Firstly, there would be no physical stuff anymore. Secondly, we should meet at work, not at home, but only with other people there."

"That sounds fair and sensible. We have a few months until the clinical, and I am presuming there is a group of you preparing for the exam."

"Yes, there are three of us, although getting us all together will be tricky with rotas and shifts."

"That is true, although I imagine you can study together and call on me if you're stuck with things or need a little extra help."

"Yes, that sounds possible. I would be more comfortable with that."

Over the few minutes that the conversation had occurred, the atmosphere and body language had shifted between them. An air of professionalism had returned. A boundary had formed. Suddenly, the two found a compatible domain to coexist in. Both seemed relieved. A moment of silent thought followed.

Henry sighed under his breath. Instead of the animalistic urges he had produced in the past, his feelings at that moment had evolved into a passive malleability, and he felt like something dramatic had shifted within him. In this one day, he had been reminded of what he was capable of, and he was not proud of it. Perhaps he was not such a great guy. The image in the mirror had cracked. He had ensnared himself in his own unleashed ego. Had he done enough to survive the repercussions, he wondered? Could it be that he might have got away with this terrible mistake without consequence after all? Time will tell.

He turned to Eliza and said, "Shall we go and rescue Ibrahim at the clinic now? I imagine he will be swamped with patients," Henry smiled at her.

"Oh gosh, I had forgotten about the clinic. Yes, let's go and help Mr Baba."

They walked together back to the clinic. Eliza walks in front of Henry. Eliza had forgotten about the meeting with Dr McNair at the time, and they headed back to the business of the clinic.

Chapter 40
Perspective

As Jemimah parked in the carpark, she felt revived. For so many years, she had worked with a sense of insecurity and displacement but no way of solving the insecurity within herself, and today, for the first time ever, she was walking into the trust complete. She was the richest of people, with two families and new friends who defined her true tribe, filled with love, unity, and a story that made sense to her. She no longer questioned how she fit into the world she lived in. She knew. Her world was so much larger, and she was proud of it. She wanted everyone to know her story and embrace her uniqueness. Her new self-confidence had bolstered her relationship with Jeremy, and for the first time ever, she felt complete. Work was just a part of her now, rather than the whole of her.

Walking to her office, she came across Ibrahim. He looked happy to see her. I'm very happy. Almost relieved as he strode towards her.

"You're back. Welcome back Jemimah," he looked like he wanted to hug her, and she was almost overwhelmed by the rapturous reception.

"Gosh, you look like you've missed me Ibrahim," she laughed jokingly.

"You have no idea! You could not have picked a stranger fortnight to be off. We have a lot to talk about. In fact, there's so much that you'll need to sit down to hear it."

"Right, now that is far too mysterious and intriguing to leave like that, and you're going to tell me you can't talk now because you have a clinic, aren't you?" She shook her head.

"Yes, you have it spot-on. Henry and I are in the clinic. I think this is one to discuss after work. Are you free this evening?"

"Sadly not. Jeremy and I are going to the cinema," She had an almost girlish smile on her face as she said it.

"Ah, Jeremy, you say? Am I guessing that you two are getting on well then?" He had an almost-brotherly delight on his face.

"Oh, Ibrahim, he is wonderful. Yes, it is going very well indeed. We definitely need to talk. Let's talk and eat cake. Does tomorrow lunchtime sound like a plan?"

"Definitely. Excellent plan. Have a good first day back. I hope your inbox is not too oppressive."

"I hope the clinic goes well."

This little conversation had not triggered any particular alarm bells in her, and she walked to her office feeling genuinely pleased to be back. The usual inbox of 289 unread emails did not surprise her as she sat down to a large pile of paperwork stacked around her desk. There was something pleasant about returning to routine.

As she ploughed through her emails, her phone rang.

"Andrew, hello," she was surprised to hear Andrew McNair's voice on the phone. He was not a frequent caller.

"Hello Jemimah, I am so glad to hear you are back. I am sorry to hear about your mother. My condolences to you."

"Oh, thank you, Andrew. Yes, it was quite a rollercoaster of a fortnight, but in the end, it was a journey that I needed to go on. Now, tell me, to what do I owe the pleasure of your call?"

Andrew cleared his throat.

"Er, well, whilst you were away, something unfolded that I think was more of a surprise to me than it will be to you. I wonder whether we might be able to speak today, as I need your help with it, please."

"Another intriguing conversation. What on earth has been going on whilst I was away? Yes, of course we can meet. I have a few things I need to finish first here, but what do you say to me coming to your office at 11? Would that suit?"

"Yes, that will be great. See you then." They hung up.

Jemimah's brow furrowed in perplexity. What on earth had happened whilst she was away? Everyone seemed so charged and clearly, they seem to have needed her for some reason. Her progress through her paperwork was at rocket speed efficiency, and she was done before 11 and ready to see Andrew.

As she walked down the corridor to his office, she tried to guess what the drama was about. What had been grumbling in the background before she left? Well, there were overruns at the clinic, but that wasn't really a CD issue. Was it about the service reconfiguration that Andrew and Henry had been talking about? Perhaps. Just as she reached Andrew's office, another thought came to her mind. 'No, surely not…'

Andrew looked deeply at his computer as she walked in.

"Looks like you're engaged in something gripping. Is it still a good time for me to pop by?"

Andrew laughed. "I always look like I am doing a complex procedure when I'm reading my emails. Angela always teases me and calls me Gollum when I'm working from home."

"Harsh! but perhaps partly true," Jemimah winked teasingly at him and giggled. "So, what is all the drama I have been picking up on since I got back today? I clearly seem to have missed something big. Is that why you have called me here?"

"Why, what have you heard?"

"Oh, nothing in particular, but Ibrahim looked rather more delighted to have me back than I think I deserve and told me that he has a lot to tell me about. Are you both on the same theme in your comments?"

"Erm, yes, I think we are. I think you will need to sit down for this," he ushered her to a chair beside him. She sat in it eagerly and looked curiously at him.

"Right, spill the beans, Dr McNair. The suspense is killing me."

"OK. Well, whilst you were away, we seem to have had some problems with one of your junior doctors. Something that I think Ibrahim discussed with you some months ago," he paused to allow Jemimah to fill in.

"Eliza, you mean?" She did not give any more details. Her eyebrows raised, and she tilted her head.

"Yes, Eliza. Eliza and Henry. What do you know about them?"

"Well, I don't know a great deal. It's just that Ibrahim was concerned that there may be something going on between them. There was not much of an issue when we spoke, so I suggested that we wait to see if it was just a thing or consensual. Why? Has something else happened?"

"Yes, something has happened. Whilst you were away, Eliza was not coping well and went off sick. She mentioned to Ibrahim that she had been working from home with Henry and that things had gone a little wrong. We were all very alarmed, and she was reticent to give any details, so we could not really do a great deal. In addition, Henry has been excessively nice, which has worried me most of all. What concerned us about Eliza was how upset she was. She did not want us to take it further." He turned to his desk drawer and opened it. He pulled out a folded letter. "Well, we were getting nowhere for a bit, and then this was delivered to Vanessa. She called me and was devastated," he handed the letter to Jemimah, and she opened it cautiously. Her facial expression changed from calm and business-like to alarmed.

"Henry's Vanessa, you mean?" He nodded. "Oh God, Andrew, how terrible! It must have been such a shock for her. Did she have any idea? What does it mean? Do you know who wrote it?" Questions seemed to flow uncontrolledly, from her.

"I have no idea, and I need to try to glean more information from one of them. Nobody has admitted to writing it, and in all fairness, it might not have been anyone here; it could have been anybody who saw Eliza whilst she was off, so we may not ever know who sent it. Vanessa is very upset, as one might imagine. She wants to find out what Henry has done. I am meeting with Eliza next Monday. I wanted you to be here to support her if you could. She has also engaged with occupational health, but I need to ascertain whether we need to put in place other measures. Henry has been such a fool."

"Hmm, well, there are a lot of unknowns. That Eliza and Henry were having consensual out-of-trust study sessions is hardly a sackable crime, albeit risky on Henry's part; but the comment in this letter about his fitness to practice is rather concerning and definitely begs further inquiry."

"Yes, I agree, it does. The only problem is that Eliza seems to be protecting Henry and is, for some reason, reticent to share any details with anyone. I wonder whether anyone can glean anything, or whether I can. I'm meeting with Eliza next week and will try to meet with Henry before that."

"Well, I can offer support to Eliza. She is closer to Ibrahim than me, but perhaps a woman-to-woman approach might help her open up about things. Perhaps not. Who knows? What are you going to do about Henry?"

"Leave Henry to me. I've known him long enough to understand how to handle him. What an idiot! Poor Vanessa did not deserve this. Come to think of it, neither did Eliza."

"Yes, you two do go back a long way, but I do not envy you in this, Andrew. If you need to talk, you know I am here. I am suspecting you want to keep this out of Mark's ear at the moment," he nodded as she looked at him. "I do hope Henry will learn a lesson from this, though. It seems he has caused a lot of unnecessary pain and worry," she said the words, but at the same time felt slightly ashamed that she had appeared seemingly supportive of Andrew covering things up. Was this how the old boy's network made bad things disappear under the proverbial carpet? Was she like that now?

Andrew sat slightly awkwardly in his chair, "Oh yes, Mark would have an apoplectic fit if he found out. Let's see if it can be managed more discretely and, at the same time, make sure that Henry learns a good lesson from it. One more thing, how do you fancy being clinical lead?"

She laughed. "So, I am to be punished too, am I? You are not selling your strategy to me, Andrew, by offering me the headache of taking over as clinical lead…any other suggestions?"

"Well, you know I cannot let Henry just walk away scot-free from this, and what better than to take a few titles from him, knock his ego down a few rungs, and get him to prove his good behaviour?"

"Yes, I can see that. Hmm," she pondered for a few seconds whilst looking straight at him. After taking a sharp breath in, she replied, "Well, what about this as a compromise? Assuming Ibrahim is successful with his consultant application, I would be happy to be the clinical lead for two years and hand it over to him. We could all do a two-year rotation, and that would give Henry a four year 'good behaviour' window before he returns to his role, if he returns to it. How does that sound? He would also need to give up his training programme director role, as this transgression with a trainee is a big no-no."

"Yes, now you are singing from the same hymn sheet as I am. Henry reverts to the jobbing consultant on probation, and the team carries on. Eliza doesn't end up in the spotlight. We help her with her exams, and she moves on. No questions asked. All the paperwork has gone in for Ibrahim's CESR, and I cannot see a reason why he won't get it. Sounds neat and tidy. So do you agree?" He held out his hand to her, and they shook on it.

"So, when are you speaking to Henry? Wouldn't it be better to speak with Eliza first? If she talks, then you have him. Don't give him a chance to wiggle out of it, Andrew. Speak to Eliza beforehand," Andrew nodded in agreement.

"You are right. I'll get onto it. I'm glad you are back, Jemimah. How was your trip, by the way?"

"Oh, crumbs. My trip deserves a chat over drinks, as there is a lot to say. In a nutshell, it was an adventure worthy of a book," she smiled in satisfaction at what she said.

"Then let's make that happen. We can't just meet over work. Once this sticky patch has been sorted, why not do drinks with Ibrahim somewhere?"

"Yes, that would be great. Good luck, Andrew."

"Thanks."

Jemimah got up and started heading back to her office. As she walked, she wrote a text.

Text: Hi Eliza. Just met with Ibrahim. He told me you have had a difficult time. I am sorry to hear that. Would you like to meet up and talk? JW

Eliza just finished her notes on the last patient in the clinic. It was as though a huge weight had lifted from her shoulders after she had spoken to Henry. To see him so deflated and humbled was indeed disarming and in some ways, cathartic. She felt guilty but also a little pleased that Henry was feeling a little of the discomfort that she had suffered. It had been a horrible time for her, but somehow the fragile Eliza of before had toughened that day, and she felt, at that moment, resolute that she was not going to let this ruin her future. Exams and her job were her focus, and now that she and Henry were talking and had agreed on a way forward, there was hope. Her phone pinged, and as she read Miss Withenshawe's message, her heart sank. She had forgotten that she had been summoned to the clinical director next Monday. The nightmare was not over yet. What would she tell him?

Text: Hello. Thank you for your message. I am doing OK today. Happy to meet if you would like. Eliza

Text: I'm glad you are OK. Fancy meeting for a coffee after the clinic? Are you in theatre this afternoon?

Text: Yes, I am in theatre with My Blythe-Soames this afternoon. Can we meet tomorrow after the ward round, perhaps, please?

Text: Yes, that is fine. See you tomorrow on the ward. J

Jemimah was pondering about Henry. Henry and Eliza were in theatre together that afternoon, which concerned her. She texted Ibrahim to see if he could pop by and check that Eliza was alright or swap in someone else to do the list. He was onto it in a flash.

What on earth could have got into Henry? Come to think of it, what exactly had he done? Nothing was clear yet. Men and midlife crises, she imagined. Henry was certainly in 'that' window when letting go of youth was just that little bit traumatic for many men. He had certainly taken to Lycra when running, so perhaps his MAMIL years had begun, and this was his way of expressing them, whatever 'this' means. He knew the rules and had a lot to lose. They all did, but on top of it all, he was married to a lovely person and had two young children. Why on Earth would he risk all of that? Now that Vanessa knew something was amiss, what would she do? Stupid Henry.

Chapter 41
Rewards and Rumblings

As Ibrahim drove home, he was perplexed. Watching Eliza and Henry in theatre was not what he had expected. They seemed almost relaxed together, and it was as though the drama of the last few weeks had never happened. Jemimah would think they had all gone mad if she had seen them. Well, he guessed that it would take a degree of extreme complacency or madness to have an affair with a junior doctor, if that was what had happened, and Eliza must have been somewhat in awe of Henry to let him visit her home. Perhaps this was indeed just one of those private things that he was unashamedly oblivious too, in his own world. Nonetheless, there were rules to abide by, and Henry had been terrible to him in the past. Should he just sit back and enjoy what was coming to his old bully?

He felt guilty that he was thinking like that on one hand, but on the other, he was secretly looking intrigued to observe what was about to unfold. He trusted Andrew to not let Henry get away with it all, even though they were old friends. It would be a big test of whether there really was any justice in the white boys' club. Was Henry going to get his comeuppance for all his years of seemingly invincible arrogance? How the mighty can fall! He would have to wait, and he was very glad that Jemimah was back. The next few days will be interesting as Andrew goes about his investigations.

    The next morning, Eliza met with Jemimah, and they spoke about stress and getting away. Nothing specific, but enough to ensure that Jemimah can establish herself as a trustworthy support for Eliza over the next few weeks and her dreaded meeting with the CD. Jemimah did not want to push Eliza to speak about too much. That was Andrew's domain, and her role was purely pastoral. The team was working well and at last seemed to be gelling together as Jemimah had wanted it to. Perhaps this unfortunate episode will be a team-enhancing period for them all.

Monday arrived rather quicker than anticipated, and Andrew had shuffled all of his meetings in the morning to allow for no disturbances at all when Eliza came to see him. 9.30 am arrived, and a gentle knock sounded on his door. It was a scared Eliza who stood behind it. He stood up and opened the door. He put on his kindest smile and welcomed her into his office. Jemimah was with her, and they all sat down.

"Would either of you like a cup of tea or coffee? I just put the kettle on."

"No thank you" was the synchronised reply from both women.

"Then I shall hold off on mine too. Thank you for coming here to see me, Eliza. Please don't worry. This is a friendly conversation about something that has been concerning us all. We want you to know that we all support you and want to help if you need us."

These kind words had little effect on Eliza's posture, which remained uncomfortably erect as she waited to hear what he wanted to say. She had never spoken to Dr McNair before, but as clinical director, he was a formidable figure in the trust, and she was nervous.

"Thank you, Jemimah, for coming with Eliza today. I'm so pleased you are here to support Eliza," he was easing gently into the subject of the conversation and trying to reinforce the support element of the moment.

"Now, Eliza, it has come to my attention that something rather unusual has been happening in the department between yourself and one of the consultants. Are you happy to confirm this and tell me some more about it, please, as we have all been concerned about the effect it seems to have had on you?"

Eliza's eyes filled with tears, and she cleared her throat.

"Y-yes you are right. Something did occur between me and Henry Blythe-Soames, but that is all over now. I got a bit upset, that is all, but we have spoken, and it is all ok." Her abridged version of the truth was clearly not the whole story, and Andrew was frustrated that she was trying to hide what had happened.

"Now, Eliza, you do know that we have a duty to protect you as a trainee, and Mr Blythe-Soames also knows this. Is there anything untoward that happened to explain the effect that it has had on you? What you discuss with us is entirely confidential, but we do need to know if you are willing to tell us."

"I'm not sure what you mean. What happened (her voice shaking as she said the words) is over; it won't happen again." Her partial truth did not stand well on her face, as a look of almost pleading was written in her eyes.

Andrew adjusted his position in his chair and gently cleared his throat.

"I know this is not an easy thing to discuss, Eliza, but our reasons for calling you here are related to a few things. This first has been about concerns about your behaviour at work and that you have been visibly upset for some time. This is potentially a governance issue, and I am obliged to bring it up not only to protect you but also the patients," he paused before going on to see if she would say anything.

She swallowed and said nothing for a few seconds before mustering the courage to speak.

"Yes, I was not doing well and spoke with Mr Baba, who convinced me to go home. That was the right decision, as I had not been sleeping well. I'm feeling much better now that I am back, and I also had the good news that I passed my exam." Her latter comment was thrown in to try to distract the conversation away from the topic.

"Well, I am pleased that you are feeling better and well done with your exam. Is there anything else, Eliza, about what happened between you and Mr Blythe-Soames that you wish to tell us about?" The letter to Vanessa was folded in front of him. He was not going to show it to Eliza, but it was becoming clear that it needed to be mentioned.

"I'm not sure what you mean. Whatever happened between me and Henry is over. Is that not enough?"

"Sadly, not Eliza. The reason this matter came to our attention was a very alarming letter that was received by Henry's wife. It mentions that something bad happened between you and Henry but also suggests that something else happened. Did you know about this letter, Eliza?"

Eliza was horrified. The blood ran out of her face, and tears welled up.

"No! No, I know nothing about it. What does it say? Who wrote it?"

"I am afraid the letter is not mine to show to you. It mentions that Henry has done something very serious, and that is what we need to try to understand, Eliza. Are you going to try to tell us and help us to reassure Henry's wife?"

Eliza was breathing heavily, and she looked to Jemimah and then back to Andrew. Jemimah intervened and put her hand on Eliza's shoulder. "Eliza, would you like a short break and some water? I know this is very stressful for you. If you want a pause, do tell us."

"Er…yes please. Can I have some water, please?" Eliza's voice was quiet and strained. Jemimah got up and fetched a glass of water. God, this was horrible. Poor Eliza.

"There you go," she handed a bottle of water to Eliza and opened one for herself. There was a moment of silence in the room, and Eliza's head spun. Who would have written that letter? Was it her mum? Why would she do such a thing? She said she wanted to, but had promised her she would not.

"Dr Mc Nair and Miss Withenshawe I am very sorry that Henry's wife received such a letter. I have no idea who wrote it. Did the postage not indicate where it was from?"

"Sadly, not, and that is why we are asking for your help. What did the letter mean when it said that Henry had done something bad?"

"I know you want the answers right now, but may I make a few phone calls first and then meet with you again tomorrow, please?" She needed answers.

"Yes, yes, we can do that. Jemimah, are you able to come along too?"

Jemimah checked her diary and nodded. She turned to Eliza, "Is there anything I can do to help you, Eliza? Who do you have to support you at home?"

"Oh, tonight my ex-boyfriend is coming over for a few days, so I will be OK. Thank you for asking."

Andrew realised that this was not going to be as easy as he thought. Thankfully, Eliza was not alone, and tomorrow was only a day away.

"Alright Eliza. I can see that you did not know about the letter, and I completely understand that you might need to speak to a few people, but I am hoping that by tomorrow you may have a few more answers," he had a kind expression on his face, and this helped Eliza. She did not feel so exposed now and stood up to leave, "I am so sorry that Henry's wife had to go through this. You have no idea how sorry. It is such a mess for everyone," she turned to walk out and left in tears.

Andrew and Jemimah looked at each other in a moment's silence.

"God, that was difficult, but she is hiding something, and we need to try to glean what happened before I meet with Henry tomorrow afternoon," Andrew looked at Jemimah with a pained expression. At that moment, he half wished that Henry was not a friend. It would have been so much easier.

"Well, at least she has a friend with her tonight. I am thinking this will have been a big lesson about trust governance for her, but a horrible one nonetheless". Jemimah stood up to leave. "Andrew, we need to be careful that in our pursuit to expose the truth, we do not unravel a vulnerable young doctor instead. Let us be mindful of that, OK?"

"Yes, I quite agree. It is one of the reasons I am trying to keep this whole thing quiet whilst at the same time teach Henry a lesson. I promised Vanessa I would do that for her. What a nightmare she is having with this and her sister going through chemo. I won't let it rest."

"Oh, I didn't realise her sister was unwell as well. How horrible," Vanessa shook her head as she headed to the door. "Well, I'll see you tomorrow morning. Call me if you need to offload Andrew."

"Thank you, Jemimah. I think you will make a much better clinical lead than Henry ever did."

Jemimah raised her eyes upward and laughed.

In the carpark Eliza dialled the number for her mum; she was angry and upset.

"Hello?" Justine Graham answered without having noticed it was Eliza calling.

"Did you send it? DID YOU?" Eliza's voice was angry and pressured.

"Eliza, it's you. What is the matter? Where are you?" The line of unrelated comments irritated Eliza even more.

"Stop asking stupid questions, mum, and just tell me the truth. Did you send a letter to Henry's wife?"

"What? Sent a letter to Henry's wife? …. Of course, I didn't. You saw the drafts I wrote, and you didn't want me to send them, so I didn't. Why are you asking? What has happened?"

"Well, someone sent a letter to Henry's wife telling her terrible things happened, and I have been called to the clinical director to give answers. I need to know who wrote that letter, mum. Who would have done such a thing without telling me? WHY would they do such a thing? Promise me you didn't send it, mum. PROMISE ME!" She was crying now, and her whole body was shaking. She was scared and embarrassed in equal measure, and her distress was expressed in every word.

"Darling, I promise you, I did not send anything to anyone. Why on earth would I? Don't you trust me? Did you see the letter? Was it not signed by someone?"

"No. No signatures, no postmarks. It was such a shock for Henry's wife. Who would have done such a thing? WHY would they do such a thing?"

"I don't know, but before you get on your high horse about it, you need to remember that whoever did this would not have done so if they were not deeply concerned for you. It sounds like someone wanted to help you, punish Henry, or both. Any idea who else knew about it, Eliza? Who loved you enough to be angry enough to do what I wanted to do all along? Can you think of anyone?" Justine knew it must have been Simon, and she wanted Eliza not to be a fool and throw her guilt and anger at him.

"Simon. It must have been Simon," Eliza's voice went quiet. She felt sick. Of all the people in the world, the last person that she imagined would do this was Simon. "I'm going to kill him! How could he?"

Justine sighed audibly down the phone.

"Now, Eliza, you need to calm down. You have been acting very erratically, and if Simon saw even half of what I saw, he would have felt obliged to do something. Did he know more than me? If he did, then I suspect, he would have acted with the very best intentions at heart, knowing that you would not have done anything and been left vulnerable and helpless. If Simon did do this, Eliza, it was because he loves you, so don't shout at him. Talk to him. Be a doctor, not an Eastender character. Act like my daughter. I beg you," she kept her voice calm and hoped that Eliza was listening through her anger.

"Mum, it has caused chaos and embarrassed me. Everyone wants to know everything. How is that helping me? How?"

"By telling the truth, Eliza, it will help you and give a chance to Henry to do the right thing too. Burying the truth never solves anything. You will not look any better by lying or being evasive to people who are trying to help you, darling. This is a chance for you to demonstrate self-awareness and integrity. Show your courage to stand up to wrong and do the right thing. That is what your bosses will want to see. That is what they are asking for. You don't have to tell all the details of whatever happened, but just enough to allow people to help you. Do you understand what I am saying to you?"

"I hear what you are saying, but I don't fully understand. Henry's wife is in pieces, and I have to work with Henry to get through my exams. This was not the right time. I was trying to talk to Henry to sort things out. Sort them out without upsetting everything else. Now the whole team seems upside down, and I'm stuck in the middle of it. It is chaos. How could Simon do this without my permission? How could he?"

"Eliza, he is coming to stay with you, and instead of speculating and dramatising things, you need to sit with him. Ask him for a short explanation, and ask him to help you get through this. That is what I would do. You need to control yourself, Eliza. This drama is damaging you far worse than anything else. Nobody appreciates a drama queen in a crisis."

Eliza sighed a deep and purposeful sigh. Her mum, as always, was right. Her panic had dissipated, and she stretched her shoulders back and neck upwards as the tension eased. This was a case of calm and truth. She had got herself into this mess. She needed to get through it and stop worrying about Henry. He could manage himself. She needed to look after herself. Tomorrow she would tell a version of the truth, and Simon would have to help her now that he had got her into this mess. She started the car and drove home. Her mind circulated ideas about what she might say. Every time thoughts of Henry and her terror crept in, she silenced them. Focus Eliza. Focus!

As she drove up to her house, she saw Simon's car parked outside. He was early. Of course, he was. He was worried about her. He knew why. What a stupid, kind, impulsive fool he was. At that moment, she should have hated him, but strangely, she didn't. Not at all. Perhaps this whole nightmare had been, in some perverse way, good for her. She climbed out of the car, and Simon sprung out of his with a big smile.

"Hello. You are back early. I downloaded a load of TED talks to keep me busy, but I'm still on the first."

"Hello Simon. I confess, if I had seen you half an hour ago, you might not have been so happy to see me, as I would have bitten your head off like a prey mantis. Thankfully, I am feeling calmer, and I'm glad to see you now."

"OK. That was some welcome. I think I'll sleep in the car tonight," He teased.

The joke eased things a little, but he was treading carefully because he could see that something had happened; he had an idea what and knew Eliza's temper well enough not to add fuel to it. He popped into the back seat and pulled out a pretty viola plant in a pot that he had bought for her.

"Something to cheer you up. Your favourite flower."

"Oh, that is pretty. Thanks. Shall we go in?"

The abrupt comment slightly unnerved him, but he nodded with a smile, nonetheless. They walked into the cottage, and Simon sat down. Eliza stayed standing and looked at him with her arms folded.

She was the first to speak, "Why did you do it, Simon?"

"What?" he replied. Perhaps the most inadvisable reply to give, but he did it.

"Stop with the games, Simon. Why did you write that letter, and what exactly did you say in it? Tell me the truth, please. I at least deserve that."

Simon sighed. The cat was out of the bag.

"OK. Yes. I wrote a letter to Henry's wife. An anonymous one telling her that Henry was involved with a junior doctor and that he had done something bad. I did not mention your name or give any details, though. I just wanted to catch Henry off guard and let the lava flow."

"What did you think you were doing, Simon? The shit hit the fan today. I had no idea about the letter, so it caught me off guard. Henry's wife is in pieces, and everyone is pissed with Henry. You put me in this shit so you could help me out of it. I am meeting with the CD tomorrow morning, and I need a good version of the story to keep my own reputation intact. Start thinking and think fast." She had not raised her voice much, although her tone was menacing, and she had tried to keep as calm as she could whilst also making Simon feel the awkwardness of the situation. It worked.

"Eliza, that is why I'm here. I'm here to get you out of this crap and also see that that bastard Henry doesn't feel that he could just walk away. I'm glad I told Vanessa. She deserved to know the truth. If she is clever, she will handle this without losing face. Now that the cogs are turning, let the trust and Vanessa deal with Henry and you, and I will think of a good way to clear any damage to you. Come and sit down with me. Let's talk ideas together. I am sorry if it upset you, Eliza. I truly am, but I cannot let Henry get away with it. I just couldn't. You did not deserve what he did to you. No one does, and the Henry's of this world seem to get away with abuse too frequently. This way, you might even have him eating out of your hand."

"That's all good and well, Simon, but you still haven't said what I'm going to say. I feel sorry for Vanessa as well. Her sister is going through chemo at the moment. What a nightmare."

"Eliza, Vanessa is no fool. I suspect she has had an idea for some time, having met you in her home. I suspect she had imagined more than really happened. This is a chance for her to know the truth. Rumours and suppositions are far more dangerous. Regarding what you'll say tomorrow, the key is to say enough to support the letter whilst not saying too much to paint a bad picture of yourself. Perhaps something like, 'We worked closely together for months, and there was a chemistry between us which was only that: Chemistry. At times, Henry could be more determined than I wanted and even at times, without meaning to frighten me. That is what upset me so much. He is a very strong person. I wanted to get out without knowing how to. He is not someone who accepts refusal well.' How does that sound?"

"Yes. That doesn't sound bad, but what if they blurt out, 'Did Henry rape you, Eliza?' What do I say to that? I can't talk about it, Simon. I just can't."

"I suspect they won't use those words, but you can always temper the question by saying that Henry is a strong man and may have come on a bit stronger than you wanted."

"Oh my God, Simon. Is this going to get him into trouble?"

"Eliza, the bastard raped you. Why are you worried about what is going to happen to him? Besides, isn't that CD a friend of his? If he is, I suspect nothing will go much beyond the meeting. The injustice of that alone pisses me off, but that is how things are. At least let Henry squirm a bit. You deserve that."

"I guess so. I spoke with him this morning, so you know. He said he was very sorry. Mad as it sounds, I felt sorry for him, but I suspect part of his words came from fear of recrimination, so I agree with you, I mustn't be too gullible. You are right, Andrew McNair is Henry's best friend, but he is also a very honourable person, so I suspect he may not let Henry get away with it completely. OK, I'll say it as you said it. Might work."

Simon looked relieved that Eliza was at last seeing the way out. Her way out of this trauma. The right thing to do. She had found clarity, which he feared she might not, and at that moment, he was so proud of her.

"It will work, and in some way, you and Vanessa may both get some payback from a devious and spoiled man who has been used to getting his way for far too long. You need this, Eliza, in order to move on from it and not be plagued by horrible memories of how you felt. I hate that you had to go through it, and now I want to help you recover."

Eliza, who sat close to Simon, looked into his eyes and smiled. He really was the best, and the fact that he was there for her meant the world to her. Her mum had been right; Simon was a great catch and this time she was not going to let him go if he was still interested. He was the strength that she needed when she was too scared to do the right thing.

Chapter 42
Retribution

Andrew awoke early with a sense of disquiet. Today was Henry Day, and after forty years of close friendship, the day ahead loomed over him as a heavy weight of dread. This was not going to be an easy day, and yet he had to get through it. He had to do it for Vanessa. His promise is binding, and his determination is unyielding. One of the many 'perks' of the role of clinical director made him wonder why, on earth, he took the position at all.

The first task of the day was to speak with Eliza. Perhaps the night of thought that she had requested had cleared things, in her mind. It definitely seemed that she had no idea of the letter, so he imagined it might well have come as quite a shock to her. Gently, gently, he must go with her. The wisdom of Jemimah lingered at the forefront of his thoughts as he gathered his words before Eliza and Jemimah arrived. At exactly 9.30 am they arrived at his office and were ushered in by his PA.

"Ah good morning, both. Thank you for being so prompt. I trust you had a tolerable evening."

Both nodded, but Eliza was serious and focused. She sat down first and looked straight at him. Her posture was less tense than the day before, but she was by no means relaxed.

"So, Eliza, did your friend arrive safely yesterday? I hope you did not have a too difficult evening after our meeting," he launched straight into business, and that was also good for Eliza. She had practiced what she was going to say to him and didn't want any curveballs.

"Yes. Thank you. He arrived safely. We discussed who might have sent the letter, and they wish to remain anonymous. I do, however, have a few things that I think you should hear," she went on to say everything exactly as she had rehearsed the night before, and Andrew and Jemimah listened calmly and without expression. It was as bad as they had thought, and they were relieved that Eliza had had the courage to talk about it. She cleared her throat before delivering the prepared paragraph.

"Eliza, thank you for telling us all of that. It cannot have been easy to talk about, and I am very sorry that you have been through so much and felt unable to speak up about it. How would you like to address the concerns of Mr Blythe-Soames forcing himself on you?" The words were like acid in his mouth. Henry disgusted him at that moment, and stifling his emotions towards Henry was not easy. "These are very serious allegations and are grave enough to consider referring the matter to the police. We will support you with this if that is what you wish to do, Eliza."

"Oh no. No, I don't want the story to get anywhere or into the public domain. It has damaged me enough already without becoming widespread news. There must be another way to deal with it. Something more…discrete. Isn't there?" She looked imploringly at him and then at Jemimah.

Jemimah was the first to speak.

"Eliza, assault is a criminal offence, and Henry is no more immune to the law than any of us, and as a doctor, he had even greater responsibility to control himself. First, we are here for you. Not Henry. We will be guided by your wishes."

"Oh, Miss Withenshawe I hear what you say, but it is not what I want. I feel that I was as much to blame as Henry for inviting him into his home. I feel so bad for Vanessa. I feel terrible that taking this route will be bad for everyone—that's me, Vanessa, the children, and Henry. I am as much to blame."

Jemimah looked concerned and looked at Andrew.

"Eliza, it is very normal for victims of assault to blame themselves, but you are not to blame. Have you had any counselling? Did occupational health offer you any?"

Eliza nodded.

"Yes, they did, but I declined it as I thought it wouldn't help to talk about it. What I really want is for that whole episode to end for me and to get on with my work and finish my exams. Is there a way?"

"Well, it would be very irregular to do so, Eliza, but without your consent, we cannot force you to report the allegations. As we were not witnesses to any of it, our hands are tied. As clinical director, however, I will need to speak with Henry, hear his side of things, and act accordingly from a trust perspective.

There, I cannot make any promises to you other than that your confidentiality will, of course, be protected. I think it is fair to say that you should not work alone with Mr Blythe-Soames anymore, and that can be achieved easily without anybody really noticing it as we can rotate the trainees. If, at any time, you decide to change your stance on this, please do tell me, and I will act accordingly."

Eliza nodded and looked slightly relieved. So far, it had worked.

"Thank you, Dr McNair. That sounds acceptable. When will you be speaking with Henry? Does he know about the letter?"

"I am speaking with him later today, Eliza, and no, he does not know about the letter. Let me handle that. He will be informed of all that he needs to know. Now, more importantly, what can we do to support you? How long is your friend staying here for?"

"My ex is staying until tomorrow night, so I'm OK. I might take your advice and contact the counselling service. Might help draw a line underneath the whole episode. I need to focus on my exams, and I have been a bit distracted recently."

"That is wise. I am glad to hear that, Eliza, and you know how to contact me, so reach out anytime you need to," Jemimah said. "Perhaps we should meet every week for coffee and a chat somewhere outside of the trust so that I can know how you are getting along. Would that be alright for you, Eliza?"

"Yes, that would be nice. I think I have been quite alone here for a long time, but I didn't realise it until now. Thank you, Miss Withenshawe,"

The meeting reached a natural close, and Eliza was the first to leave. Jemimah stayed for a few minutes more, and as Eliza left, she turned to Andrew and shook her head.

"My God, Andrew, it was as bad as you dreaded it might be. What if Eliza goes to the police? We all risk getting into trouble if we don't report it. Perhaps you should speak with Mark after all. What do you think?"

"Henry has put everyone in a terrible position and seems once again to have pulled the lucky card with Eliza, who seems determined to protect him and the story. I don't think she will go to the police, but if she does, I will take the blame for not acting. I will protect you, Jemimah. Henry is my problem, not yours. He is going to regret this far more than you could ever imagine. Leave it to me," Andrew's expression was grave. He felt sick to the stomach, with what Henry had done. The reverberations of his careless actions had touched so many people, and he had strutted around like the king of the world during the whole thing. What an arrogant prig he was.

"Andrew, we are a team. We stand together. We fight together, and we solve things together. If I am to be a clinical lead, you need to understand that these are my terms. What Henry did had nothing at all to do with any of us. We are just the injured parties in the debris of the bomb. If ever there was a test of our team, it is now. We have to hold together. Learn from what we have experienced, develop our self-awareness and support networks, and learn how to protect our junior colleagues better. Ibrahim had concerns months ago, and I chose not to escalate things then. I was wrong, and in the future, I will act sooner. We are all to blame for what poor Eliza went through in the end. We therefore will all bear that culpability together and work at a solution."

Andrew smiled appreciatively at her.

"Well, one good thing out of all of this is that we will have a better clinical lead in the department as a result of it. You may not want the role Jemimah, but you are exactly what this department needs. I have no idea why you didn't apply for it before."

"Oh, perhaps the imposter syndrome within got the better of me, but now I am a new person. My last few months have been like a full resuscitation. I am revived and ready for new avenues. Perhaps you are right, it is time for me to consider leadership roles".

As Jemimah left the office, she felt a new sense of freedom coursing through her. How strange it was that the old Jemimah, who craved to be Henry, was today stepping into his roles, and feeling alright about it. She did not feel guilty about it. He had made his own problems, and this was her chance to believe in herself. She valued how Andrew had complimented her, and for the first time in her life, she was willing to hear what he said without the old niggling sense of self-doubt and accept that she was his equal. This was her test, and she was going to take it in stride without reservation. She was the new Jemimah. Miss Jemimah Tuquan-Withenshawe. The name she carried within her now in her heart. Henry had not been an easy colleague to many, so she felt that the plan for him to reshape his ego for a while would be good for everyone, not least of all Henry himself. He was, in many ways, lucky that he had colleagues who were willing to take the risk to give him a chance to be a better man. Would he accept the olive branch and show some humility, or would the old showman show his ugly head and kick off again? Time will tell.

Eliza rushed to the toilet after the meeting.

Text: I did it! It worked. They believed me and agreed to deal with it internally. I'm so relieved. SOOOOOOO relieved. Exx

Simon was sitting in the garden reading as the message arrived, and he smiled; the gamble had paid off, and he was helping Eliza.

Text: So proud of you. Things should sort themselves out now. When are they meeting Henry? Sx

Text: This afternoon. I have a feeling H might have a go at me later, but I am going to ignore him for a few days. Let the steam settle. X

Text: good plan. The ball is in the trust's court now. They know what to do. I suspect H is going to get a shock. Bloody right too. Sx

Henry looked at his phone as he sat in the waiting area outside Andrew's office. It was unusual for Andrew to ask him to wait outside, but he had a feeling the shit was about to hit the fan, so he kept his cool, pretending he was checking emails on his phone. In fact, he was stressed and was scrolling through photos restlessly. After what felt like a very long time, Andrew came out of his office.

"Hi Henry. Sorry for the wait. Was just on the phone. Come in." He was unusually serious.

"Hi Andrew. This is all very suspicious. Everything OK?" He walked with a nonchalance that irritated Andrew immensely.

"Come in, and we can talk," Andrew's voice was more curt.

Henry followed obediently and in silence. As he took a seat, Andrew sat behind his desk and looked austere.

"Henry I can't quite believe what I am having to talk about today, but I need you to keep quiet for a bit and just listen. Don't butt in, please." He took a quick breath and continued. "Now, through various channels, there have been serious concerns raised about your recent association with one of the junior doctors. The details of this have spread to unexpected corners and have caused significant alarm. I have been asked to investigate it and need you to answer me honestly. No bullshitting, Henry. I need the truth."

Henry suddenly sat forward with an expression that combined shock and concern in equal measure. He was caught. Had Eliza blown the whistle? What had she said?

"What? Who has been speaking to you, Andrew? What has been said?"

"Henry confirm to me whether or not you assaulted the junior doctor, Eliza Graham. Just reply to this first, please."

"Well, er. Assault is a serious word, Andrew. What have you heard? Yes, I have spent time with her helping her, with her revision."

"Right. Helping her. That is not the whole story, is it, Henry?"

"W-well no, not the whole story. Tell me what you have heard," Henry's voice was less strong, and his body language, more introverted.

"For God's sake, mate, did you rape a junior doctor? That is what I have heard, Henry. You raped her. Can you confirm this? Did you even think for one second about Vanessa in all this? Did you know that she knows?"

"What? What does she know? Who told you? I may have come on strongly once with Eliza, but it was once, and I have apologised. Oh shit. Did she report me? How did Vanessa find out?"

"Well, you idiot took her home with you, didn't you? Then, a few weeks ago, Vanessa received a mysterious, unsigned letter telling her you had done something bad. She put the rest together. Henry, what exactly did you do to Eliza? Tell me the truth, you bastard. What did you do to her?"

"My God she wrote to my wife. What the hell? Why? Why would she do that?"

"No, Henry, the letter was not written by Eliza. It was written by someone else. Someone else knew about something you are alleged to have done. Are you going to tell me, or am I going to have to report you to the police, who can find out?"

"God, Andrew, you wouldn't, would you?" He was squirming, and Andrew was pleased to see it. Henry continued in a desperate tone. "You're my friend. Tell me you won't report me. Please, Andrew. Please. It was all a mistake."

"Friend is a difficult word right now, Henry. Personally, I draw the line above so-called friends who assault younger women as a pastime to appease a fucking midlife crisis. Is that who you are, Henry? An abusive man? Let me know. Vanessa is my friend too, and you have put me in an impossible situation. Worse still, you have put her in an unimaginable situation."

"No. I'm not abusive. I made a mistake one day. I was in a stupid mood and went round to see Eliza. I don't know what came over me, but I lost my mind and forced myself onto her without realising it. Andrew, I was such a shit. I hate myself, but I have never done anything like that before. I have apologised to Eliza, but I know that an apology is a poor substitute for my actions. Why I even did it is impossible to explain. I was arrogant and out of control. I was angry with you over the Ibrahim thing. I wasn't thinking Andrew. It was unforgivable, I know." Words poured out of his mouth, and he seemed incoherent and desperate. "It was madness, and Eliza did not deserve what happened in the end. What is she going to do? What did Vanessa say? My God, is that why she went away with the kids? Is she going to divorce me? Mate, I have ruined everything. I'm a complete idiot. That is the whole truth. No lies. Can I see the letter, please?"

"That is terrible, Henry. You raped Eliza? Do you know what that means? I should have you locked up in prison, but I cannot do that to Vanessa. She does not deserve that. What she needs, however, is to see if you face consequences, and there I can influence things. Henry, you have choices. You have admitted to what we feared today, and I am glad that you were at least honest. Nonetheless, the options are that you hand yourself in to the police," he left a deliberate pause and then went on, "Or you accept my conditions and terms, which are non-negotiable."

"My terms are that with immediate effect, you resign as clinical lead and training programme director; tell people it is for personal reasons and that I have approved your decision. You will not be allowed to train any female trainees without a chaperone present at all times and as punishment for us both, the entire lumpsum, that you and I will receive from the completion of the Holmfield Surgical Centre deal will be donated anonymously by us both to a selection of charities of Vanessa's choosing. You will give it as payment for what you did, and I will do, it as payment for shielding the criminal friend that you are from the police. Either way, your actions have hurt a lot of people, Henry, and you have a lot of wounds to repair in the future. Do you agree to my terms unequivocally?" He looked sternly into Henry's eyes.

Henry was speechless. His ego was reduced to a small tremor in his big toe, and he sat deflated in front of his old friend. Guilt circulated through his mind and his body, and the shame he felt sat as a painful lump in his throat. What had he done? He had wrecked everything. The gamble had been lost, and the area around him lay in complete carnage. A damaged Eliza; a broken-hearted Vanessa; a betrayed Andrew, and a shattered career. All his fault.

"Andrew, there are no justifications for what I did, and I know that you are offering me more than I should expect. I don't deserve a friend like you. In some ways, I want to ask Eliza and Vanessa what they want me to do. What do you think they want?"

"Well, I have spoken to them both. Vanessa is very hurt. She is loyal to your family and marriage and deserves a true apology, your honesty and patience. It will take a very long time to regain her trust, and I have decided not to tell her that you raped Eliza. She would not be able to cope with that, so I will tell her you had a short affair that ended badly. Henry, if you ever hurt Vanessa, I will see you hang. Is that clear? DO YOU UNDERSTAND ME, HENRY?"

Henry nodded. "Yes, I understand and promise you that I would never, I have never, and never will hurt Vanessa. I promise, Andrew. I really do."

Andrew went on, "Henry, I hated you so much when she chose you over me, and today, I hate you so much for hurting her. She was the best of all of us, Henry, and you simply couldn't see it. You arrogant, selfish man. Nothing is ever enough for you, is it?" He shook his head. His eyes widened and he became angry as he vented not only the immediate anger he felt but also the years of pent-up regrets.

"As far as Eliza is concerned, she wants to avoid damaging publicity and has asked me to deal with things internally. She needs to pass her exams and move away; she needs to live her life away from this terrible episode. Who knows if she will recover from what you did, but I will tell you this, Henry, she is a brave young woman and does not want to hurt you. Remember that, Henry. Both women are far better people than you and deserve your respect and humility. Never forget that. Do you hear me?"

"Yes, I do hear you, and I am truly ashamed. I accept all of your terms and hope that one day you will forgive me. I value you very much as a friend. You are right; you are all better people than me. I sometimes wonder whether I am more like my father than I want to believe. I am truly ashamed. May I ask who will take over as clinical lead? Have you asked Jemimah? I think she would be the perfect person for the role."

Andrew sighed a long sigh. It was partly heavy with sadness and partly with relief that Henry had accepted his lot with contrition. Perhaps it would all be OK. He had done what he had promised Vanessa and hoped that, with time, she might be able to rebuild her marriage with Henry for the children's sake.

"Now, Henry, I want you to sign this agreement. This confirms all that I delineated today. We should be getting the money from the surgical centre next week. Please transfer all the money to my account, and I will distribute it as per Vanessa's direction. That money is no longer ours, and we will just have to prepare ourselves to work longer. Sign here." He thrust the page at Henry. Henry signed it. Vanessa's letter would remain in his desk. The job was done. Henry was duly punished, but the punishment stretched to them all. As Henry walked out there was a look in his eye that left the impression that the hunter was not yet appeased....

Andrew texted Vanessa.

Text: Hi Van. It is done. Ax.

A month later, Ibrahim received confirmation that his CESR application was successful, and as he stood before his father's photo, he smiled. Nobody could have ever predicted that moment, and he wondered what was going to change now that he was a consultant. It was audit and governance day, so he could share the good news with the team. With Jemima now a clinical lead, things were much more relaxed, and whatever Andrew had done, Henry was outwardly a much more normal person. Despite the occasional reminder that he was nonetheless still Henry. How mysterious the powers at the top could be! Was being a consultant such a big thing after all the years of desiring it? It certainly had not been easily attained.

In the audit meeting, he looked at his colleagues; he knew well that their reputations were impressive, if in reality, embellished by a staged external aura around them that hid their secrets—all those many secrets shared or not. He was part of that story, which was a closed book from the outside. The part of the surgeon that nobody sees a club united by the long marathon of their careers in a culture where it matters more who you know and please than who you really are.

The words of Ibn Arabi (1165-1240):

My heart can take on any form,
A meadow for gazelles, a cloister for monks.
Sacred ground for idols, the Kaa'ba for the circling pilgrim,
The tables of the Torah, the scrolls of the Koran.
My creed is love, and wherever its caravan turns along the way,
That is my belief, my faith.

A surgeon's snapshot of the surgical world and the mystery of the surgeon's life. In these fictional vignettes, there are some truths that exceed all presumptions: We often do not know ourselves but feel confident that we comprehend others. Do others understand us? Do they need to? Instinct dictates to us amongst our tribe to choose and judge instead of always knowing the actual truth what we need. Prejudice is a by-product. But as a surgeon, when time is short and pressure is high, bravado and ego subsume everything else. Outwardly brave surgeons, who are moulded to fit into a stereotype, are carefully trained to give the appearance that everything is under control. The assumed power is inevitable; adrenaline is undeniable; and the consequences, potentially irreversible. Yet amidst all this, as skilled masters of the body who are drawn together in pursuit of this all-consuming toil, much remains incompatible with the human self as tides turn.